Milk and Honey on the Other Side

By Elizabeth Guider

Foundations, LLC.

Brandon, MS 39047
www.foundationsbooks.com

Milk and Honey on the Other Side
by Elizabeth Guider

ISBN: **978-1535575140**

Artwork by: Dawné Dominique

Published in the United States of America
Worldwide Electronic & Digital Rights
Worldwide English Language Print Rights

Acknowledgements

I have many people to thank for their insights, reading suggestions, encouragement or criticism in the research, writing, editing or enhancement of this novel. Among those who read all or parts of the manuscript or offered their advice about the process: Kenith Trodd, Wendy Oberman, Judi Dickerson, John Ranelagh, Pat Quinn, Liza Foreman, Gordon Steel, Danella Compton Weatherly, Virginia Steen Miller and Tom Silvestri.

For their help in referring me to or accessing relevant books, newspaper files, microfilm, photos, exhibits or archival material, the staff at the Vicksburg-Warren County Public Library, the guides at the Lower Mississippi Museum, and the staff of the Old Court House Museum (particularly for usage of vintage photos from the J. Mack Moore Collection). Among the books which grounded me in the era or pointed me in useful directions: John Keegan's *The First World War*, Gina Kolata's *Flu: The Story of the Great Influenza Epidemic of 1918 and the Search for the Virus that Caused It*, Isabel Wilkerson's *The Warmth of Other Suns,* John Barry's *The Rising Tide*, Bill Bryson's *One Summer, America 1927*, Neil McMillen's *Dark Journey*, Frederick Lewis Allen's *Only Yesterday* and William Percy's *Lanterns on the Levee* as well as numerous short stories and novels about the period and/or the people.

Special thanks too to the publishers at Foundations Press, Steve Soderquist and Laura Ranger, editor Mica Rossi and cover designer Dawné Dominique. And to my husband Walter for persevering with me during the entire period.

Professional reviews given so far

Guider's story of interracial love finds a place on my shelf along with Lillian
Smith's Strange Fruit and Flannery O'Connor's The Violent Bear it Away. The riveting central characters, Aurelia Ackermann and Curtis Jefferson, fall in love, are painfully separated and eventually find each other again during the cataclysmic flood of 1927.

Dr. E Culpepper Clark -- professor emeritus, former university dean, and historian of Reconstruction and the New South

A powerful tale that tracks an interracial love affair during the Jim Crow era.
Guider's beautiful work touches the heart in deepest, most memorable ways.

Dr. William Ferris - professor of history at UNC and senior associate director of the Center for Study of the American South

Guider has a great understanding of the characters and nuances of this particular time and place, the passions and the perils-and richly conveys them to the reader.

Peter Bart - author, editor and film producer

The story is fiction but the setting is real-and Guider weaves an intriguing romance, crossing racial lines, that makes the improbable quite plausible.

Gordon Cotton - author, historian and journalist

In Memoriam

Dedicated to my parents

Benjamin Alfred Guider and Mary Shaw Guider

PART ONE

And I looked, and behold a pale horse, and his name that sat on him was Death and Hell followed with him.

Revelations 6:8

Chapter One

Aurelia rummaged for her gloves, one eye on the clock atop the mantle. Unless she found them soon she'd be unpardonably late for Henrietta's party. Her childhood friend was entertaining, the first such affair since her marriage six months earlier to Earl Hancock. Was it cards or just sherry? Aurelia wasn't sure—a war was on, Earl was overseas, and it wasn't likely to be festive—but still, one had to dress for the occasion. Confound it, she did need those gloves, the pale kid ones, to set off her dark silk suit.

In Vicksburg appearances mattered.

Yanking open the bottom drawer of her dresser, she spotted their limp fingers coiled around a silver-mounted comb. She pulled them out, straightened up and stuffed them into her handbag. One last check in the mirror before bounding down the staircase and past the half-open door of her father's study.

He barely looked up from his chessboard.

"Cleveland is waiting and will fetch you later," Aristide Ackermann called out as he maneuvered his rook in position to attack his opponent's queen.

"Around seven should be fine. I won't overstay," Aurelia replied as she headed out to her father's conveyance. She climbed in and settled her skirts.

"War," she sighed. Even so, she was eager to observe how her friend was faring in her new wifely role, husband-less though it was. She called out the Drummond Street address to the family's long-suffering manservant.

"Yessum, Miss Aurelia. We be there in a jiffy." Clucking to the Ackermanns' equally long-serving mare, Cleveland jiggled the reins and Bessie set off.

No point peering out the carriage window to spot friends. Like Aurelia's older brother, all the young men in her circle had long since shipped off to France. In Alfred's case, fourteen months and counting since his uncertain salute in that scratchy uniform. Only the most occasional and deliberately oblique communications ever reached home. From his over-stuffed armchair, Aristide, himself a veteran of the Spanish-American conflict (about which Aurelia could never figure which side had prevailed and to what end), would adopt his most stentorian tone to read from among the blacked-out passages: *Despite their initial skepticism, the French have become less begrudging and more appreciative of the efforts—and dare I add expertise—of us doughboys, and I have little doubt that as we dig in deeper we will uproot and extirpate the Krauts.*

Such bravado from his son swelled Aristide's chest, though never, as Aurelia observed, did her mother appear anything but worried. Were Sophie knitting across from her husband, she'd lay her yarn aside, clasp and unclasp her hands.

"Go on, dear. What else does he say?"

"Not much. Heavily redacted."

In the latest one, Aurelia recalled, Alfred had mentioned running into Henrietta's husband, Earl. Sewanee-educated as well as seasoned shots, both were now officers; both had seen action (if her father had correctly read between the censored lines) in a place called the Argonne Forest. Bloody on both sides, the papers had said. Operations thereafter seemed to have halted, illness having ravaged camps in and around where the two friends were bivouacked.

Perhaps Henrietta would know more.

As the carriage click-clacked over recently bricked Cherry Street, Aurelia glanced out to admire the dogwood that dotted the lawns. In several yards gardeners tugged at unruly crab grass or clipped anything that dangled. One workman, trowel in hand, rose from a crouch, turned and stared at the passing carriage. Black as coal he stood against the hibiscus blossoms, his forehead shiny in the September sun.

"Miss Aurelia. We be at number forty-seven," Cleveland called out. "I be helping you out—you being dressed up so fine."

Aurelia flipped the latch on the carriage door and slid out, careful not to catch her hem with her heel. "Not necessary, Cleveland. But do return by seven."

Mounting the elegant, curved steps of her friend's house, Aurelia straightened her back the way her father regularly reminded her to do and ran her tongue over her lips, moistening the pale shade she had applied from her mother's small but strategic arsenal of cosmetics. She pressed the gold-plated doorbell.

A servant in starched whites ushered her through the marble foyer toward the tinkle of glasses and delicate laughter.

"Why, Aurelia, you look lovely." Henrietta beamed, taking her by the hand. "It's been so long. What with our men gone, and so much to do with the house, and...well, do come in. I think you know most everyone."

Actually, Aurelia had of late seen quite a lot of the other young women—Caroline, Marianne, Isabel among them—as they had all volunteered to wrap bandages for the Red Cross. Henrietta, however, she had not glimpsed for months. Barely twenty, she was pregnant. And barely a year ago, she had been clutching that trophy for the best essay on *Ivanhoe*, always filling the boys in on the plots to this or that novel on book report days. Alfred in particular she catered to, though to Aurelia's eye, her older brother seemed to fancy the blond curls of other girls.

Perhaps that was why Henrietta had, in the summer after graduation, shifted her affections to Earl. His people, it was said, hailed from old money, indeterminate in origin but substantial in amount. Which explained the fancy house with Doric columns but didn't account for her husband's precipitous departure after their autumn nuptials. The *Lusitania* saw to that. Like Alfred, Earl deemed it dishonorable not to take up arms against the enemy, however distant, however haphazard its assaults upon American sovereignty.

"What, Aurelia, have you been up to? And what, pray tell, have you heard from your brother?"

This overture from Caroline, who was seated on a divan near the drawing room doors, sipping tea and nibbling on a cream cake, her gloves neatly arrayed across the armrest. Already twenty-one and having spent two years at finishing school somewhere in Georgia, as Aurelia remembered it, Caroline was one of the blonds that Alfred had gravitated toward. Dances at the local B.B. Club, excursions on the river, a jaunt to New Orleans for the opera a year or so ago. *En groupe*, as Aurelia's mother had insisted it be.

Aurelia positioned herself on a nearby chair. A black maid in an outfit even whiter than that of Henrietta's doorman was at her side and proffered a glass of sherry almost before Aurelia had settled. She took the glass and ignored the first part of Caroline's question.

"Horribly censured Alfred's last letter, but from what we could tell things are improving. They've routed the Germans in places I've never heard of."

Caroline nodded, her approval apparent.

"Only that ...."

"Go on. What?"

"Illness in the camps," Aurelia added.

"Well, don't worry, the end is in sight. So boring here without them, wouldn't you say?" Caroline looked around as if to solicit agreement from the others. "And poor Henrietta. About to have a baby before her husband makes it back. Damn those Krauts, I say."

No one dissented from that patriotic sentiment but after such serious talk, the young ladies reverted to more immediate matters: the fall fashions on display at the Valley, the latest Norma Talmadge picture at the Alamo Theater, parties and picnics (such as they were without their favorite young men). Aurelia was relieved when the starched doorman appeared to say her carriage had arrived.

"Though I know you must be busy," Henrietta whispered as Aurelia fumbled with her handbag, and her goodbyes. "I do hope we can see more of you after the baby is born. Earl is quite fond of Alfred, and there will be so much for us to do for our men. Once things return to normal."

"Oh, by all means," Aurelia sputtered in reply.

To her surprise, James was seated atop the buggy as she made her way down the stone steps. She regarded her younger brother, one eyebrow raised.

"Cleveland looked t-t-tired, and I wanted the fresh air. You c-c-can ride up here if you like."

"With this dress? Not a chance. But drive slowly. Bessie looks bedraggled, and she spooks easily if a motorcar honks."

The old mare tugged at the bit, as if to indicate she had one last trip in her for the day.

Once she had settled her skirts, Aurelia leaned back to enjoy a welcome rush of cool air. Whenever the horse slowed, she could hear James humming to himself.

Thank God he, at least, was too young to go to war.

Chapter Two

As the summer of 1918 waned, the headlines became more emphatic. Unless delayed by work at the bank, Aristide would each afternoon snap the pages of the papers, wife and daughter seated across from him in the parlor, James either outside playing or in his room, presumably studying. For long minutes the patriarch concentrated. A tap of his pipe would eventually signal his readiness. As if on cue, Sophie and Aurelia raised their eyes. Aurelia knew it was the way he liked it: a captive audience, not apt to lose interest nor brazen enough to criticize.

"Listen to this," he began one afternoon in mid-September.

"'Cambria almost in grasp; Balkan and Turkish theatres show Allied gains.'" His eyes combed the columns for further references to American victories. To Aurelia's ears, it all sounded preposterously far away.

"I wish we had a more precise idea where Alfred is. It would make things tolerable, don't you think, dear?" Aurelia's mother ventured.

A flash of exasperation crossed her husband's face. "That's on purpose, Sophie. So no pertinent information falls into the hands of the enemy."

Aurelia's lips thinned. She found it hard to imagine that knowing whether Alfred was stationed in northern France or southern Belgium—or for that matter somewhere in Bulgaria, which she wasn't even sure where on the map it was—hardly could be construed as of much help to the Germans. At least not now that the Teutonic troops were in disarray. She wished the whole thing over.

"Here's something you two can do. The *Post* says cast-off garments can be taken to the train depot. Fruit pits, too."

Sophie raised an eyebrow. She reached for a handkerchief and stifled a sneeze.

As if sensing her perplexity, Aristide went on, "They're for gas masks." He didn't elaborate.

To Aurelia it seemed an opportune moment to busy herself making elderberry tea for the three. Sugar in short supply, she had picked up some honey at the nearby Piggly Wiggly.

When she returned tray in hand her father was deep into the middle of the paper. His face was bewildered.

"What is it, Father?"

"Some local fellows. I know their people."

"Did they die in battle? Does it say where?" Sophie asked.

"That's the puzzle of it. One's a sailor from out in the county died near Boston—of pneumonia; the other, from right here in town, succumbed to something in New York before he could embark."

"A shame," Sophie said, alternately sipping the hot tea and wiping her nose.

They lapsed again into familial silence. The fancy German wall clock that Aristide had acquired years ago in the French Quarter tick-tocked away in the corner. Aurelia would have offered to make dinner herself but it was not the custom for her to break the calm that settled over the parlor. That role was exclusively her father's. She watched while his large hands, still calloused from years of clearing cane-brush in the Delta, fiddled with the last few pages of the *Post*. Breathing deeply as he did after digesting the affairs of state, he soon folded the paper and deposited it on the adjacent table. He cleared his throat. Aurelia tensed.

"Your mother and I have been thinking, Aurelia Anne (he often used both her given names for added import) about what should be next for your education." Sophie raised her gaze, as taken unawares by this shift in subject as her daughter.

"Of course there is no particular hurry," Aristide went on less ominously. "The war has seen to that. We have much else to occupy ourselves with, Alfred first and foremost—and naturally, with helping your younger brother get through his studies." After a pause he muttered under his breath, "And not be short-changed."

The aside, Aurelia quickly deduced, had to do with that officious teacher, Miss Camden, who had button-holed the senior Ackermann to suggest that James was "faltering" at his elocution lessons, not to mention at several other subjects. When Aristide had glared back without deigning to respond, she, undaunted, had plunged in further.

"We at Main Street School, Mr. Ackermann, are dedicated to bestowing the best possible education on your offspring, indeed on all the children, and when we sense a problem, we are duty-bound to point it out." All this was delivered in something of a stage whisper on the sidelines of the annual school bazaar a year or so ago, an event Aurelia remembered Aristide dismissing as a women's affair, but, given his positions around town, had felt obligated to attend.

It had been Aurelia's mother who spoke up on behalf of her son. "We appreciate the concern, Miss, Miss Camden, is it? But you will have noticed that James' condition is improving. Hence, we have every reason to believe that with the private tutor we have arranged, he will make further strides." Speechless, the self-important Miss Camden had retreated to the other side of the assembly hall to take charge of the punch bowl. At the time no private tutor was in place to work on James' stutter, but that lacuna was soon remedied. Sophie engaged a retired professor of English the very next day.

"As your mother and I were saying, Aurelia, your grades have been commendable. We'd like to see you keep on with the piano, and, since you show propensity, with the languages. Hard to imagine your French as refined as your mother's," he pointed out as Sophie wriggled her nose at the compliment, "but it behooves us to have you persevere. The German as well, whatever the present sentiment in the country."

Aurelia nodded respectfully, happy enough at the idea of more piano lessons and with the notion that private sessions in both French and German would be arranged. Both Caroline and Marianne had supplemented their course work at school with such tutoring, but to Aurelia's secret pleasure, her performance in language classes already outshone them both.

"I would like that, Father, and will, with your blessing, apply myself."

Aristide flicked his hand. "We have no doubt of that, my dear. It is what comes afterward that preoccupies us."

Aurelia's fingers curled around the arms of her chair as though it were about to be pulled out from under her.

"We're considering colleges, finishing schools. Of what makes sense in that regard," Sophie interjected.

Aurelia knew it had been that way in her mother's case. Sophie's parents had steered her to and through such an establishment in Maryland before returning her properly equipped to take up her place in New Orleans society. Back home Sophie Beauchamps had waltzed through cotillions, chatted charmingly in French, plucked at the harp, played cards and poured tea, all in a largely unspoken effort to land a suitable husband. That she had ended up with—detractors said "settled for"—a dirt farmer from the Delta was something of a surprise to everyone.

Aurelia could still hear Sophie admitting to what had attracted her to Aristide at the time: not his gauche attire nor his haphazard dance steps but rather the steely gray eyes and the steady gaze. Aristide Ackermann seemed a man unashamed of whence he came and eager to get where he was going.

"I was longing for a little adventure," Sophie had confided, "so I undertook to go along."

"The times are changing," Aristide proclaimed, taking one last draw on his meerschaum before making a small ceremony of placing it on its stand. "Young people want more freedom. More opportunities. And your mother and I want them for you as well, Aurelia. Not solely for Alfred and James."

Aurelia studied her hands, not knowing what to brace for. To leave Vicksburg was not something she longed for. So much she loved about the town. The parties, the picnics, the park. The wild magenta sunsets that followed in the wake of summer rain. The whistles of steamboats, the boisterous roustabouts as they loaded their cotton bales. How was it the boats did not sink under that weight...?

"Wherever is your head, Aurelia?" her father asked, his voice peeved as always whenever he thought her mind wandered. "As I was explaining, for young ladies, it's—how shall I phrase it—delicate. Things have to be orchestrated. When the war is over, when Alfred and his friends, when things return to normal ..."

Aurelia gave a cautious nod at this stab at paternal counsel; Aristide looked over at his wife.

"What your father is alluding to, Aurelia," Sophie soldiered on, "is that we're confident there'll be a number of nice young men, who would be happy to, that might make a possible—" She left off abruptly. James had barged into the room.

"I won-won-wondered if Aurelia could help me with this book report?" he stuttered. Aristide bristled. Sophie blew her nose and turned back to her daughter.

"Do help your brother with his homework, Aurelia. I trust you understand what your father and I are in agreement about," Sophie said with a note of finality. Then, to her son, "And I would love for you to recite to me before the report is due, James. Tomorrow perhaps, since it's the weekend."

"Yes, Mother. In the afternoon, if Aurelia thinks I'm r-r-ready."

"For heaven's sake, stop twitching and stand up straight," Aristide barked. He snatched up the *Herald* and shook it into position in front of his face, a sign that his offspring should now disperse. He was irked, not only by the intrusion into what he had decided was, however elliptical, a heart-to-heart with his daughter but also by the inability of his son to utter a single sentence without stumbling through it. Despite all those private sessions.

For a while he read in silence while Sophie thumbed through the *Ladies Home Journal*. He paid scant attention to her earmarking the pages.

"Un rhume, un gros rhume," she murmured in her best French accent.

"What my dear? Did you say something?" Aristide looked up into the still luminous, if unusually pallid, face of the woman across from him. "Are you really not well?" he added, reverting to that solicitous tone he used whenever newly struck by her beauty, or her fragility. Like that first time they had gone out together, to the opera where, as he recalled, Sophie had stifled a cough throughout the performance yet during intermission dragged him to this or that box to meet her New Orleans friends. Exquisite she was, making presentations with such poise and a hint of excitement. Never had he been so gratified by a woman's social graces. But there was more. She gamely strolled with him through the rain, all the way down Canal Street to the French Market where they lingered over coffee and beignets, she laughing at the snowy landscape the powdered sugar made of their dress clothes. For an entire week thereafter, Sophie had been confined to bed and could not receive her new beau.

"This thing is going round, Sophie. So the papers say, people at the bank too. Why don't you go up and I'll have Susanna fix a tray."

Later, after poring over some loan documents, Aristide turned down the oil lamps at each end of the sideboard and slowly mounted the staircase to the bedroom. His wife was asleep on her side with a blanket pulled up to her throat, her left cheek bathed in dim light from an alabaster lamp. Deferential in public, but God willing, lively in bed, he remembered hoping as his nuptials with the elder daughter of Major Buford Beauchamps, (he of the finest clubs in the Crescent City though, if truth be told, his fortune was no longer what it had been before some bubble or other), approached. He had not been disappointed.

Rain thrummed the roof. Aristide glanced at the high window overlooking Adams Street. A little rill snaked down the glass pane; it hesitated, then resumed its inexorable course. He determined to call upon the doctor were Sophie not soon improved.

Chapter Three

Early the next day, Aurelia tip-toed out of the house to the shed where she knew Cleveland would be tending to her father's two mares or tinkering with the unpredictable motorcar. The old servant strained to rise from his haunches, then quickly wiped the dust and seed from his hands.

"Why, Miss Aurelia, you be up mighty bright."

The warm smell of oats rose to Aurelia's nostrils. She stood outside, waiting for Cleveland to join her.

"If you could hitch up the buggy, I would welcome a ride over to the Red Cross."

Before long she had joined a row of other wimpled young

women cutting and rolling bandages while several others, older and seated around a beat-up circular table, knit wool sweaters to be dispatched to base hospitals. Her florid, oft erratic handwriting notwithstanding, Aurelia was often called upon to address the cartons, some as far away as a Camp Devens outside Boston. She tried to imagine how well these hand-wrapped cloths might stanch the blood of some hapless soldier, bayoneted by some equally hapless young man on the other side. If the boxes arrived at all. She bent her head to concentrate on printing the labels as neatly as she could.

"A convoy train is passing through around 3 o'clock; the more boxes we can fill, the better," one of the organizers explained as he urged the girls to work as fast as they could. None demurred. However unclear to Aurelia the rationale for the war, she did want victory to come, and soon, if for no other reason than that Alfred would come home. Other young men too, even if no single one preoccupied her. More than once at night she had thrown covers back, scrambled out of bed and critiqued her form in the glass. Not as strikingly beautiful as her mother must have been at eighteen, but the same dark blue eyes, her face nearly as flawless, except for a few short-lived splotches. Still, no blemish to obsess over.

As the morning at the Red Cross wore on, Aurelia scanned the faces of the dozen young women martialed along the workbench. Surely, if men looked beyond mere appearances. But likely they didn't. And likely war would change nothing in that regard. And what exactly were her parents trying to get at last night? That I am unattractive, or unformed—or too willful?

"Whatever is on your pretty mind, Aurelia? So intent." The voice from down and across the bench was Caroline's, who had, without fanfare, infiltrated the phalanx of volunteers in the last half-hour. "Surely by now you know how to put this gauze together."

Aurelia collected her wits, Caroline's inquiries being famously pointed. Like rapiers. "Nothing really. I didn't sleep well and my mother's poorly. A nasty cold."

"At least there's good news from the front." Caroline's avowed acolyte, Marianne, piped up. When several of the volunteers looked her way, she expanded on what the papers had reported. "Seems the Krauts are scampering home with their tails between their legs," she expounded, "and not a day too soon for my taste."

"And, it's our boys who have turned the tables. From what Earl writes," Henrietta added in her soft voice. Despite her pregnancy, she had made a rare appearance. "His letters—they're so vivid, even with passages blacked out. The best writer in his class, remember?"

Aurelia did, but the thought only depressed her. Likely this eloquent young man was holed up in a muddy trench tossing out the occasional grenade, or worse, scrambling to locate his gas mask every time the enemy charged.

"He writes practically every day," Henrietta went on. "Especially of late. They're playing a lot of cards, those that are up to it."

"Up to it?" Isabel from the end of the row inquired.

"Those that haven't come down with something. It's already cold over there," Henrietta explained as she snipped the cloth in front of her into identical squares.

For the first time, Aurelia felt a draft. The black staffers were banging the door open and closed as they raced to load the last of the boxes onto wagons.

"All right, ladies. That will do for today. Those who can return next week, please do so. We may even manage some sweets. But thank you. And God bless our troops," the Red Cross director said.

"Amen," muttered a few of the young women as they removed their wimples and headed out either to waiting conveyances or to walk home in twos or threes.

As Aurelia marched off on her own, she heard footsteps behind and turned to see Caroline hurrying to catch up.

"That nigger not coming to fetch you?" Caroline called out. "Walk with us. Too many loiterers with nothing to do but accost us."

"I really don't think—" Aurelia started out, offended on behalf of Cleveland, discomforted by the implied disapproval of her own behavior. Before she could formulate a proper response, however, her friend cut her off.

"In fact, you must come with us. Tea at the Carroll. They've redone the place. Quite stylish they say. And we all deserve a treat."

There was little to do but acquiesce to Caroline's invitation. And to the surprise of the four young women, the dining room of the hotel was packed, the wait for a table a good ten minutes. Aurelia spotted several older people she knew by sight and others who, by their dress or demeanor, were likely out-of-towners. Half a dozen black waiters dashed about, swerving around one another with trays poised on their raised and upturned palms. Finally, one pulled up to their table and produced a writing tablet out of his red uniform.

"Why, hello, Miss Aurelia. I almost wouldn't be recognizing."

Startled, she looked up into coal-black eyes, sensing a familiar voice.

He helped her out. "I'm Grover. Cleveland's nephew, who helped with that engine that night your pappy's car done stalled."

"Oh yes. Of course. How are you, Grover?"

Before he could respond Caroline interjected.

"You can take our order and move along," she said, her tone brusque. "And while you're at it, bring sugar for the table."

If flustered, Grover quickly recovered, scribbled the orders and hurried off. Silence fell over the table, each woman feigning enormous interest in the hustle-and-bustle of the room. When their tea and pastries arrived, Marianne broke the ice.

"I don't know about you, but I'd say this has become just about the liveliest place in town," she ventured. "Easily as nice as the National Park Hotel. Wouldn't you agree, Caroline?"

"If nothing else, the prices should keep the rift-raft at arm's length," Caroline said drily.

During the rest of their hour at the Carroll, the young women chatted about their newly improvised or rediscovered entertainments. Since dances had been curtailed, bridge parties, excursions and art classes had been arranged.

"Why don't you come along to Madame André's, Aurelia? Wednesdays at ten. She has the most charming manner, even if she is improper," Isabel suggested.

Aurelia looked mystified.

"What she means," Caroline clarified, "is that the French Quarter's full of such women, willing to take their clothes off for whomever. Painters included."

"The point, Aurelia," Isabel persisted, turning her back toward Caroline, "is that Madame's very adept at technique. You do know where she lives, not far from McRaven, skirting the park?"

Aurelia nodded, unable to put her finger on the reason she associated that area with some recent notoriety. While the others chattered on, it came to her. Among the statues in the park, that's where it had happened. A Mr. Gottschalk, Gregory by name but everyone, all the young women whom he had escorted, addressed him by his surname. Always immaculately groomed—even perfumed, (which made the girls titter in the powder room of the B.B. Club). His ivory-handled revolver, "an ornate *GG* inscribed thereupon," the papers said, had been found by his side. Distraught, it was supposed, over being rejected for enlistment.

"The park is perfectly safe. Gawkers have gotten their fill, and Madame André is careful not to bring Mr. Gottschalk's name up. Doesn't want to discourage enrollment," Caroline added, as if peering inside Aurelia's mind.

The three young women finished their pastries in silence while Caroline's gaze raked the room for a waiter.

"Yessum. Will that be all, miss?" a different black waiter, more deferential than Cleveland's nephew, inquired of Caroline.

"Yes, and we'll take separate checks."

"That will be $.44 each. You can settle at the cashier's stand," the waiter explained, gesturing toward a podium near the entrance where an imperious-looking clerk stood behind a shiny black cash register, the kind many of the nicer establishments downtown had recently installed. The waiter scribbled out the bill and let it flutter to the tablecloth in front of Caroline. She glared at her plate.

"Why don't I pay at the counter—I have a five-dollar bill—and you three can reimburse me?" Aurelia offered, hoping to squelch any additional impolite remark from Caroline. The others unsnapped their purses, handing a collection of change over to Aurelia.

Out of nowhere, a gentleman materialized at their table, straw hat in one hand, a walking stick balanced beneath the other.

"I noticed you from our table against the wall—ladies," he

began, glancing in the direction of Aurelia's companions and inclining his head, "and thus, I thought if you didn't have conveyance home, Miss Ackermann, I'd be glad to accompany you. With my car. Your residence is on the way toward my own, as you may know."

Several guests seated nearby turned to observe the courtly gesticulations of the odd fellow with the cane. He fumbled with his monocle before following up. "And any of the others of you, presuming you all live here and aren't guests of the hotel."

"Oh, no. We're all local," Aurelia said. "It is Mr. Gauge, isn't it?"

"I'm sorry, Miss Aurelia. I should have re-introduced myself. Gauge, Henry, from the First National. I work with, or rather for, your father," he snuffled. Aurelia remembered him from months ago when she had co-signed with a flourish the documents that opened her father's savings account for her. It was, she confided to Mr. Gauge gaily, her eighteenth birthday as well as the eve of graduation from Main Street School. He had shuffled the papers and rose to file them away in a cabinet. When he returned, he had pulled open a desk drawer and brought out a pamphlet with Accounts Protocol blazoned on the front.

"I do need to inform you, Miss Ackermann," he had explained in a fusty, bordering on officious, manner, "that the funds become available to you only upon the signature of a male relative." She had nodded, impatient to get through with the formalities and away from this comical person—not that old really, she intuited—with a pince-nez that kept slipping off his pointy nose. Perhaps banks did that to people.

"You do understand the procedure, may I be reassured, Miss Ackermann?"

The constant repetition of her surname had annoyed her at the time. "Yes, yes, I understand," she replied, her right leg jiggling on top of her left, exposing her shiny patent leather shoe and a bare ankle.

Mr. Gauge had stared at that ankle for several long moments before elaborating: "You also should know that interest on such an account is compounded—:you have taken math, I assume, so you'll know what that means—and a statement regarding the quarterly accruals will be mailed summarily to the address you have indicated." All this palaver seemed superfluous to Aurelia at the time, since it was obvious she still lived at home with her parents, and Mr. Gauge surely knew where his boss resided. He had given the bank president lifts before in the same open-sided Edsel with which Aurelia had seen him chauffeur his aged mother around town.

In the present circumstances, and with the whole of the Carroll dining room staring, Aurelia concluded it would be prudent to accept Mr. Gauge's offer of a ride home, no matter that he irritated her. Caroline had been ill-mannered, the others too spineless or disinterested to object to her rudeness—and why should she spend any more time being (implicitly) chastised for being more civil than they were? Plus, as incongruous and pedantic as he was, Mr. Gauge had bestowed courtesies upon her father. The least she could do would be to acquiesce to such kindness.

"Why don't you, Aurelia? Our carriage takes us the other way down Cherry Street, so if Mr. Gauge is willing to escort you, it would work out splendidly. As we were saying, it's not a good idea to walk alone," Marianne said, effectively putting an end to the dilemma.

As they made their out of the hotel and said their goodbyes at the edge of Clay Street, Aurelia noticed Mr. Gauge had no real need of the cane. A mere affectation.

As long as he can drive the Edsel properly, she told herself.

Chapter Four

Mounting victories at the front aside, a pall settled over Vicksburg during the latter half of September. The bustling businesses along Washington Street, including Aurelia's favorite dress shop, the jewelry store catty-cornered from the bank, and the usually crowded Gem Café, had overnight shuttered their doors. *Closed due to the flu* read the hand-written sign affixed to the display case of the dress shop, the expression on the mannequins one of stunned disbelief. Aurelia had set out to buy a couple of wool sweaters, one for herself and one for her mother, as already autumn air had moved in. That task thwarted, and so as not to dwell on her worries, she decided to catch the Wednesday matinee of *Hearts of the World* at the Alamo Theater. The darkened auditorium would sooth her spirits, and the Gish sisters rarely disappointed. But the movie house, too, had gone dark. She wandered back up the hill and turned toward Adams Street, stopping to fork over fifteen cents to old Mrs. McCabe for a bouquet of hydrangea blossoms. They would brighten her mother's room.

At the corner, a streetcar clanged to a stop. An elderly couple dismounted, gauze masks obscuring their noses and mouths.

After tentative signs of improvement, even getting out of bed at one point to join her husband for afternoon tea, Sophie newly succumbed, her fever shooting up in ragged spurts.

Aristide could make out her rasping from the next room as he buttoned his waistcoat, tucked his gold pocket watch in the requisite slit and, irritated by his own helplessness, bunched a white embroidered handkerchief with the initials *AA* into his breast pocket. It was 7:30 a.m., and he determined to detour over to the Infirmary to button-hole Dr. Knox before his morning rounds. A family friend as well as the best medical professional in town, the doctor would simply have to break off early that day to look in on Sophie. Ackermann was not a man to whom people often said no, and, in this case, he had every intention of being as persuasive as the situation called for.

Dark circles stared back at Aristide from the mirror as he finished his morning ritual. All that was left to do was to impart instructions to Susanna to prepare a beef broth, and, whatever the patient's protestations, spoon it into Sophie around lunch time. Not that the maid would need coaxing. Like Cleveland, her cousin or some such—blood relations were never clear with blacks—she was efficient, and reliable. The good ones are worth their weight in gold, Aristide reflected, just as with us...

A soft knock on the door disrupted his train of thought.

"Sir, you be wanting some coffee and biscuits 'fore you set off?"

"No, no, Susanna. I'm in a hurry. Tend to Mrs. Ackermann. The doctor will be around later in the day."

"Never you mind, we be doing what we can."

Aristide sucked in his breath and his barely protruding paunch, and headed out. Cleveland was already waiting with the buggy.

"Over to the Infirmary if you would. I'll only be a few minutes."

"Bessie be feeling her oats this morning. We get you there lickety-split, no doubt about it."

Aristide relaxed back into the seat, content to let Cleveland handle the feisty mare. The driver's efficiency only reinforced what he'd been thinking earlier. Susanna had had the foresight to prepare the guest bedroom, scrubbing the oak floor until it gleamed and putting the best linens on the bed for Sophie's comfort.

"I seen what happens when folks be crammed into a dirty room. Long's theys breath in my body, Miz Sophie gone be clean and comf'able," the woman had said to him, without ever looking up from her pail of soapy water.

As the carriage approached the white-washed front of the hospital, Bessie baulked, pawing at the pavement. Aristide peered out the window, surprised to see every hitching post occupied. He clambered out.

"Take the horse around to the far side, Cleveland."

Once inside the hospital, Aristide scanned the reception area for someone in charge but everyone was scurrying about, carrying clipboards or bed pans. Blessed with good health himself, he had seldom had occasion to frequent the hospital, other than when Sophie was admitted to give birth. Even her periods of confinement were brief—except for the third, James having been premature, and his mother having bled profusely. Then, as now, Sophie's lips had turned a ghastly shade. Dr. Knox had steadfastly labored to bring both mother and child back from the brink. Surely, he could do so again. So many advances had been made, though for the moment Aristide couldn't cite anything specific. He vowed to read up on the latest scientific discoveries.

A middle-aged woman clad in gray and white, the unmistakable cap of medical authority perched high on her head, swept briskly past him.

"I say, excuse me, nurse. I'm looking for Dr. Joseph Knox. Might you direct me to his office?"

A purposeful face turned to take him in. "You'll have to wait your turn for admission. We're at the absolute limit."

"You misunderstand. I'm an old friend. I mean, Dr. Knox is our family physician. I need him to make a house call. On my wife, that is." Aristide heard his normally firm voice falter.

"Never mind. I'll take him up, Radigan," a younger nurse, standing against the wall to catch her breath and scan her charts, volunteered. She motioned for Aristide to follow her in the opposite direction, rolling her eyes as if to suggest she too found the older woman unnecessarily unhelpful. Nurse Radigan pivoted, muttered under her breath and vanished through swinging doors. A whiff of antiseptic reached Aristide's nostrils. Quickly then, he and the younger woman traversed a long passageway and took the back stairs. A sign on the third door on the right read Dr. J. Knox, General Practitioner.

Cleveland would have gotten his employer from the hospital to the bank by the stroke of nine had it not been for a slow-winding procession snaking its way toward the cemetery. Bessie stomped her hooves at the sight of the two black quarter-horses pulling the hearse. Aristide shuddered, leaned out and directed Cleveland to hurry on.

Chapter Five

Her father having arisen early and taken the carriage, Aurelia decided to disobey his orders and check on her mother. She tip-toed down the hall and put her ear to the half-cracked door. The rise and fall of breathing, however labored, reassured her. Peering in, she could make out her mother's form under the goose-feather quilt, the one that graced her parents' canopied bed in the depths of winter. For what seemed a perfect age, Aurelia stood frozen in her helplessness. She wiped away the teardrop that trickled down her cheek and closed the door behind her.

"How is Mother?" James asked as Aurelia pulled up a chair and poured a glass of freshly squeezed orange juice.

"Still...sleeping. I didn't disturb her."

"I'm making you toast and jam," Susanna said as she set a bowl in front of Aurelia, "unless you want to be good like your brother and eat some of this here oatmeal. No sugar in the house, but it be plenty good like it is."

"I'm not hungry, Susanna. But when you go up, take my mother some juice."

"Don't you fret, Miss Aurelia. That's what I be fixin' to do. You go about your business, and Mr. James, you get yourself on to that school."

Unsure what her actual business was now that she had graduated, parties were few, and she could only wrap so many bandages for the wounded, Aurelia tried her best to keep occupied. What had her mother recommended?

"Read in French or German every day. Otherwise you'll get rusty," Sophie had advised her daughter shortly after the ceremony at Main Street School.

Once Susanna had gone up to tend to the patient, Aurelia arrayed herself in the parlor, Chateaubriand open on her lap. The woes of his abandoned heroine Attala, however, did not seem terribly relevant. She longed for company. Racking her brain, the only thing she came up with was that watercolor class. As little dexterity as she had with a paintbrush (and as irritated as she had been with Caroline), a class would likely take her mind off things she had little control of. She put on a pair of sensible shoes, grabbed up a handbag and set off on foot.

"Why how nice that you decided to join us, Miss Ackermann," a visibly pleased Madame André said when Aurelia showed up some time later. She ushered Aurelia back to the detached shed behind her house. Five young women were already attacking their canvasses, including Caroline, Marianne and Isabel. Four other easels languished to one side.

"I do apologize for not calling ahead," Aurelia said. "I hope it's not inconvenient."

"You're in luck, Aurelia. Several sent messages to say they could not come today," Caroline informed her. Aurelia nodded, detecting yet again a note of censure in her friend's voice. She decided to remain an observer.

For an hour Madame André weaved among her pupils, offering tips or demonstrating a stroke: "I'd make my lines less severe," she advised Marianne, who was trying to convey the bend in the river south of town, and "I'd apply a dark green to bring out the leaves," she suggested to Caroline, who was rendering the Court House with its leafy oaks on the front lawn. Eventually, she returned to her kitchen to oversee lunch.

"Well, what do you think, ladies?" Marianne asked, turning her easel so that others could get a look at her river scene, complete with sandbar and wispy willows in the background.

"It's quite detailed. You can tell it's our river," Isabel said. Though she too nodded approvingly, Aurelia thought the wide brown streaks representing the Mississippi were too static to convey the swiftness of the current. But how such a concept could be transferred to canvas she had no inkling.

Later, over a lunch of Madame André's gumbo, thick with okra, sausage and unidentifiable spices, the topic du jour resurfaced. Marianne brought it up. Aurelia knew that Marianne's father, who owned the only jewelry store downtown that had remained open, kept track of all his customers.

"How is your mother, Aurelia? We understand she has taken to her bed."

"Better, I think. The doctor may come to see her this evening. We'll know more then."

Crossing her feet to keep from squirming, Aurelia studied the stray oyster floating in her soup.

"You do realize that this is a plague sent over by the Germans," Caroline declared, as if stating the obvious. Several heads swiveled. "They've infected our troops with it. Naturally, they're pleased as punch it has spread beyond the camps, and back to us."

Madame André's forehead puckered with evident irritation. "But, Miss Hilliard, I believe the Axis have come down with the grippe as well. I hardly think—"

Aurelia silently prayed that her friend would desist and eat her gumbo, but Caroline cut Madame André off. "The logic is unassailable. The enemy hasn't been able to break us, even with poison gas, so they're using disease to hamper us. Those in the know, well, they know."

Marianne and Isabel sipped their unsweetened tea in silence, their eyes upon Aurelia. She methodically spooned soup into her mouth, scrolling through Alfred's last letter in her mind. Had they missed anything between the censured lines?

As soon as the cheese and pears had been consumed, Aurelia took her leave. Madame André accompanied her to the front door.

"Now that you have seen what we're up to, I hope you'll join us. Watercolors are so cheerful—especially in the present circumstances—and it's not that hard to become proficient enough to have fun." Madame André flashed Aurelia a smile, the dark ovals of her eyes disturbingly deep.

"You're very kind. I will give it some thought. But, well, you understand. It all depends..."

"But of course, Miss Ackermann. *Ça ne fait rien*." She unbolted the heavy front door and allowed Aurelia to pass out onto the porch and down the stone walkway.

An alluring presence, Aurelia thought, as she proceeded up Harrison Street toward Cherry. From New Orleans—she wondered if her mother had ever come across her. But probably not, Madame André being so exotic, or whatever she was, and her own mother so proper, or whatever she was. And now, so ill.

No longer enthused about walking, Aurelia hailed an approaching streetcar. It was empty except for a couple of older women with shopping bags in their ample laps and a businessman with a briefcase. He was wearing a mask. She jumped off right as the car turned east on Clay Street.

For the rest of the afternoon Aurelia helped Susanna with chores, polishing silver until her arms ached and refolding every last stitch of clothing in her mother's dresser drawers. At one point she peeked into the camphored bedroom. Her mother lay on her side, arms outstretched as though beseeching help. Before Aurelia could advance further, Susanna, balancing a tray with tea and biscuits, shooed her out, went inside and closed the door.

"Your mother done ate a little. Now all we can do is call on the Lawd, and wait for the doctor," Susanna said when she returned downstairs. "Why don't you help your brother? Bent over those books he is."

The inevitable *Silas Marner*, Aurelia noticed from the open door of the bedroom, and hearing only an impatient "What?" from her sibling, approached his desk. The book was splayed open; a tablet with a few scribbles languished next to it. James was staring out the window, intent on a couple of strays fighting over a bone in the street.

"S-s-so little traffic, looks like the dogs are taking over," he said glumly. He released the edge of the curtain and turned to face his sister.

"I could help you if you like. When's it due?"

"In theory next Monday, but didn't you hear? They might close the schools. A lot of pupils have been pulled out, or maybe they're sick, too." His head gave a worried nod to the upstairs guest room.

"Father's cranking up the Victrola so she can hear the opera. And the doctor is supposed to come by. Can't hurt to get your assignment out of the way."

James shrugged, clearly uninterested in the old miser and his fardels.

And yet to dwell on their mother's condition was an even heavier burden.

"Why did she do that, do you think? Write under a male name," he asked his sister.

"Because it wasn't lady-like to be a novelist in the nineteenth century, and because people were more likely to read things by a man rather than a nervy female."

"Well, I hate to disappoint you but the book isn't all that good. Still, it's short, so I can make the report short too."

Aurelia laughed, remembering she hadn't felt that much different at James' age and that she never would have picked up another George Eliot if her mother hadn't pulled *Middlemarch* out of the Globe-Wernicke one evening. "You may not believe this but she got much better with her later novels. Perhaps someday you'll appreciate..."

James shushed his sister. Three short raps at the front door, each more insistent than the last. They raced to the hall.

"Come in, come in," Aurelia said, instantly recognizing Dr. Knox, though he appeared more stooped over than she remembered.

He held onto his black bag but hooked his walking stick on the hat rack next to three umbrellas. "You're looking well, Aurelia. And you, you must be...?"

"J-J-James. C-c-can we get you anything, doctor?"

"No, no. I'll be dining later." He pulled his pocket watch out and made a show of looking at it. "Is your father about?"

"Ah, right on time. Do come up, Dr. Knox. We can confer up here." Aristide's voice floated down to Aurelia from the top of the stairs over the strains of *La Traviata*.

With a look of unspoken agreement, the two children seated themselves on the bottom rungs of the staircase. Leaning against the bannister, Aurelia fiddled with the barrettes in her hair; James went desultorily through his pockets.

From the snatches of conversation Aurelia could make out above the arias, it was apparent the two men remained briefly in the hallway between the Ackermanns' bedroom and the sick bay.

"No one should go in or out without one on," she heard the doctor admonish, his tone brooking no dissent, not even from someone as obstinate as their father. Other injunctions were imparted in more of a mumble but something about liquids, and leaving the window cracked.

Suddenly, the scratchy sound of a needle dragged across a record. Aurelia stiffened her back against the wooden slats. In a few seconds the uneven oak floor above sister and brother creaked under the weight of the men's shoes. A door opened and closed. Unable to bear the tension, Aurelia retired to the sofa in the parlor, picking up the evening paper even though her father had not yet had his turn.

"Yank airmen in the thick of things," a front-page headline trumpeted. She didn't have the wherewithal to read on; she closed her eyes, the *Herald* limp in her lap.

Twenty minutes later the two men came downstairs, Mr. Ackermann ashen, Dr. Knox inscrutable. The visitor gave the two young people a faint smile as he shook Aristide's hand and retrieved his cane. "Godspeed, and remember, for their sakes, do what I recommend."

For the rest of the evening the family exchanged not a word about the doctor's visit. Ackermann *père* carved the roast in the thinnest of slices. Aurelia, in the absence of her mother, ladled the gravy onto the potatoes. James doled out the peas and carrots with a newly polished silver serving spoon. Only Susanna, as she served custard made with the last of the sugar in the cupboard, attempted to dispel the gloom.

"I be glad you left a little meat, Miss Aurelia. Them are two hungry dogs outside in the street, and I be feared to go home if they turn mean. Feed'em and make friends is what I plans to do."

"Take mine too," James instructed, sliding his half-full plate across the tablecloth.

"When you're done with that, Susanna, take a dish of custard up to Mrs. Ackermann. The sweetness..." Aristide wavered, his eyes bright. Before long, he clambered to his feet, nodded absently to his children and mounted the stairs. It was the only time Aurelia could recall her father had failed to perform his daily reading ritual.

After a fretful day at the bank and several attempts to ring up his sister in Louisiana, Aristide told his son and daughter of his decision.

"Given how easily this thing can spread, I've spoken to your Aunt Margaret across the river. Things have been uneventful there. Everyone's healthy. You can't be helpful here, but you can be to her—it's harvest time, and she doesn't have Uncle Samuel any longer. No point remaining here right now."

Dumbstruck, Aurelia felt as though the wind had been knocked out of her. Not helpful here? With her mother laid out upstairs, wheezing through the night. "But Father—"

"And what about school, and ev-ev-everything?" James chimed in.

"Don't contradict me. This is for the best, and your mother agrees. I told her of the plan and she managed to squeeze my hand. More than anything, she wants the two of you, and Alfred of course, to be safe. It is her fondest wish, as well as my own."

With the sun having already moved into the steady weight of the day, Cleveland labored that Saturday to load a duffel bag full of James' clothes as well as a cardboard box of school books, *Silas Marner* among them. For her part, Susanna struggled with a leather case of Aurelia's things, including a novel on the inside flap of which Sophie had penciled "my favorite Dickens." Aurelia had packed it at the last minute, thinking its title, *Bleak House*, painfully apt.

Throughout the preparations, Aristide fixed on the logistics, imparting needless instructions to his servant as to the best ferryboat schedule and what to do if they missed the 10 a.m. embarkation.

"Yessir, yessir, boss. I knows them times by heart. Back and forth, Back and forth. Don't you worry. They be fine. Beautiful day for a crossing."

Bessie stomped her hoof as the two siblings scrambled into the back seat of the open buggy. Cleveland gave the reins a decisive shake.

"Wait, wait. I forgot something!"

Before Cleveland could halt the startled horse, Aurelia jumped down, barely managing not to turn her foot. She dashed past her father, into the house and up the stairs into her mother's darkened room. Unable at first to make out the shape on the bed, she detoured to the window to raise the shade. A sliver of light cut across her mother's face. Aurelia placed a soft kiss on the burning forehead. Sophie's eyes opened. Barely. Her own brimmed over. "I love you, Mother. Get better, get better."

Within another minute she was back in the buggy. James squeezed her arm.

"Gitty-up, Bessie. Your load ain't that heavy. Not like ours," Cleveland clucked. They were off.

Chapter Six

Despite only a light breeze, the swift current forced the pilot of the Vicksburg & Delta Ferry to tack in order to stay on course. Aurelia and James held onto the railing, neither in the mood to speak. Only a couple of other passengers, both in overalls and muddy boots, were making their return to the Louisiana side, burlap bags full of animal feed on the wet planks next to them. They tipped their battered hats at the young woman and the younger man standing at her side.

"Over there, that's where Alfred dove in," Aurelia said, pointing toward a clump of cottonwoods not far from the landing on the Louisiana side. "I wanted to come along, but he would have none of it."

She had told James the story before, how on a dare, no one knew from whom, four boys had paddled over to the far side back in the summer of '16, jumped in and swum back across, minding neither the width of the river nor the treachery of the undertows. Their re-emergence on the Vicksburg side, exhausted but unabashed in their prowess, was met with howls of delight from their friends, switches from their parents.

Eventually, the engine putt-putted as the pilot skirted a newly emerged sandbar 150 yards out from the weather-beaten dock. What looked like tiny stick figures stood on the planks as the boat plied its way to shore.

"I had never seen Father so irate with Alfred," Aurelia added, shaking her head, still in disbelief (and envious) that her own brother had done something so foolhardy, and survived.

"Not a year later—remember, Aurelia? —that scrawny kid from down the street, the one with the d-d-dog. Always throwing rocks. They both drowned. The Irish setter washed ashore w-w-way downstream. They never found the boy. Just a year ahead of me."

"But not as sensible as you."

Though meant as a compliment, Aurelia knew James would have preferred to have the courage of Tommy Ferris and his faithful dog—or of their older brother. She had stood in the corridor with James one evening after he had been entangled by accident in a schoolyard scuffle. They both overheard their father grouse to their mother.

"Let it be, Sophie. He's destined to stammer through life. Only so much can we do." James' crestfallen expression at the time said it all: their father's appraisal had hurt more than the cuts and scrapes he'd endured.

"Hold tight," Aurelia said, as the boat sidled up to the waiting dock and James inched closer to her.

A few bounces off the metal sidings and the ferry bobbled into place. One of the erstwhile stick figures came to life and looped the heavy hemp rope around a thick post. Another dock hand, leather-skinned and wiry, scooted a wet plank onto the deck and grasped the upper arms of passengers as they disembarked. Then he jumped aboard and together with the pilot unloaded several crates as well as James' and Aurelia's bags.

"Damn motor. Sputtering again," the pilot growled, lighting a Camel. The slight wind carried the smoke into Aurelia's face. "We may be here a while," he added, this time addressing the handful of travelers bound for the return crossing. In response, one of the passengers spat noisily into the nearby reeds and lit up his own cigarette.

Getting her bearings and recalling what her father had instructed, Aurelia spotted a building across from the pier and elbowed James. A faded sign above the entrance read MacGregor's Grocery & Feed Supply. The siblings picked up their bags and headed to the store, in front of which they were to be met and conveyed to their aunt's farm. On the wooden steps, a black man, his close-cropped head spackled with silver, was polishing expensive-looking boots, most likely not his own. He mouthed a salutation as the two passed by.

Once inside the cramped interior, they were enveloped by the odor of freshly ground coffee. A woman with a bird-like face eyed them from behind the counter. "Git you folks something? Coffee, Orange Crush?"

For the first time Aurelia focused on her shoulder-strapped traveling case and the clip of bills her father had slipped inside along with a sealed letter to his sister. She had no idea how much he had given her, what he expected her to spend the money on, or how long he envisioned their sojourn to last. She unsnapped the gold-plated clasp, but not wanting the storekeeper to observe the wad of cash, reached in with her hand to feel the thickness of the bills.

"A cup of coffee would be perfect. What about you, James?"

"An Orange Crush is fine."

The surprisingly spry old woman flitted to a back room from which she soon re-emerged, cup of coffee in hand. With a tilt of her neck, she indicated a sugar bowl.

"Milkman don't come around until afternoon, but we still got sugar. Besides, you'd lose the chicory flavor." Aurelia bent her head in a polite nod and spooned a teaspoon into the piping hot liquid.

"Them Crushes is out there in the icebox, alongside the Cokes. That'll be ten cents altogether," the storekeeper said, looking at her two unfamiliar customers as though daring them to abscond without settling.

Before Aurelia could slide her bag off her shoulder, James stepped to the counter and handed the woman a dime. The screen door creaked as they retreated to the porch. James fished out a soda. Not knowing what else to do, the two sat on a dilapidated bench, leaving two sturdier-looking rocking chairs unoccupied.

"Do you know what time we're to be picked up?" James asked, swatting away flies on the rim of his bottle. "Or by whom?"

"Father said by lunch time. It depends on work in the fields or something. In any case, I have Aunt Margaret's phone number if it were to come to that."

For a while, they sipped their drinks and watched the ferry pull away from the dock, its capricious motor now emitting a determined chugging sound. A smattering of customers came and went while they sat there, two on foot and one on horseback. This last lugged a sack of potatoes and a bag of purple onions out of the store, hoisted them behind his saddle and headed off.

"Where exactly would you say we are? And how far from Aunt Margaret's?"

"Not far from Tallulah, so I imagine it's a few miles to her place. Not a walkable distance though, at least not with all our things."

With more flies enticed by the soda, James took a final swig and got up to place the empty bottle in a rack by the icebox. "I'll take your cup inside if you're done," he said.

Aurelia handed over her empty mug. In James' brief absence, she closed her eyes, wishing herself back home, her mother in her armchair reading Dickens aloud, pausing now and again to laugh conspiratorially at this or that comical name.

When James returned he held out his hand and offered his sister a portion of beef jerky, a food she didn't normally enjoy. But, little being normal about the day or the place, she bit off a piece. For the moment her hunger subsided.

"Tastes right good, Miz MacGregor's meat," a voice suggested. It was the old man, now dangling the burnished boots in one hand. Without waiting for a reply, he ambled off the porch and down the dirt road out of sight. The two siblings retired to the rocking chairs, wondering how long it would be before the beak-nosed proprietor ordered them off her premises.

Eventually, horse's hooves and the clickity-clack of well-greased wooden wheels roused them from sleep. From out the far side of the store, a Lindsay wagon pulled up in front. Within seconds, the driver alighted, in one fluid movement looping the reins over the single hitching post. He gave an appreciative pat to the stallion's right flank and then took in the two tired-looking people on the porch. Instinctively, Aurelia stopped rocking.

"You must be Miss Aurelia and Mr. James?" the young man, lithe but muscular, asked, pausing just long enough for the query to register. "I'm Curtis and Mrs. Taylor—your aunt—sent me to fetch the two of you."

Stunned as much by his assured use of English as by his good looks, Aurelia remained tongue-tied, trying to fathom who this unlikely person must be. Clearly not kin.

"Are you, do you…?"

Curtis laughed. "I'm a neighbor. Do some work around the Taylor place when I can. I suspect the missus, and Sarah-Lynn too, are looking forward to company. It can get downright lonely out this way."

For an instant, Aurelia detected a familiar note in his voice, but the overlaid lilt of Louisiana was an added pleasure. She jumped up and turned her eyes to Curtis' open face. He had an air of easy assurance as if little that people said or did threw him off-balance. Despite his color.

"We're ready to go," she said.

"Hold on. Might as well pick up a few things while I'm here. You—James—why don't you load the bags and I'll be out in a jiffy."

Aurelia and her brother exchanged a glance as if to say never had they met a Negro with more self-confidence—had he just ordered them around? —and never had they been so drawn to such a person. Without hesitating, James pitched the baggage and his box of books into the back of the wagon. Embarrassed, brother and sister then stood around not knowing what to say to each other until Curtis reappeared, a couple of sacks in his arms. He deposited them alongside the travel cases.

"If you're ready, so is Silver."

"Who...?" Aurelia began, but Curtis continued, "Sarah-Lynn's horse. He thinks drawing a wagon is beneath him but he's well-bred enough not to complain openly." Aurelia smiled at such an explanation. Curtis held out his right hand, palm up, to help her to the wooden bench atop the wagon.

"Could be bumpy back there," Curtis said to his other passenger, indicating the scuffed tool box in the rear of the conveyance. "Road needs patching."

James climbed in and took up a position facing backwards. From the corner of her eye, Aurelia saw him nearly fall out when Silver jerked into gear and set off with a jolt. Curtis had extended his arm in front of Aurelia, right below her breastbone, keeping her from pitching forward.

"Sorry about that," he said. "That horse is feeling his oats this morning." Aurelia let out a long breath but couldn't think what to reply. "You OK back there, James?" She noticed Curtis had already dropped the mister.

As they traveled the pitted, haphazardly graveled road to the Taylor place, fields of just picked cotton alternated with parched pastures. Cows grazed in greener patches in the distance. Round a sharp bend, cranes swooped above a small pond. The dappled sunshine was so sleep-inducing, the only things keeping Aurelia alert and upright were the occasional jolts—and the casual closeness of the body next to her. At one rutted stretch she inadvertently clutched Curtis' arm. He tensed, then jumped down to coax Silver over the worst spots until the road smoothed out. A couple of mule-driven wagons passed them in the other direction. Each time Curtis doffed his cap; only James was in a position to notice how the drivers glanced back, pondering, he suspected, who might be these citified white folks aboard a black man's buggy.

During the last phase of the hour-long journey, Silver slowed as they crossed a rickety set of wooden slats which functioned, precariously it seemed to Aurelia, as a bridge. The boards clattered; the creek below gurgled.

"Upstream, beyond that stand of pines," Curtis gestured with a tilt of his head, "is our place. My grandfather cleared it. Except when it floods, it's been real good to us."

Aurelia nodded, unsure if to inquire further.

"One need not pry into the affairs of black people," the Ackermanns had often admonished their children. "They are separate, and must go their own way."

Such a view had seemed reasonable to Aurelia given other less savory comments she grew up hearing: petulant, lazy, conniving—such descriptions not fitting the coloreds with whom she came into contact.

"They're different—Susanna, Cleveland and their kind—but that's why, or rather that's because, they're our servants," her mother had clarified. "They're dependable and capable. Your father and I wouldn't have it any other way."

Aurelia had toyed with this explanation. "So why can't I play with Susanna's children, Mother? Edie is my age, Rose not much younger and they can hopscotch so much better—"

"It's not the same," Sophie had rejoined, exasperation in her voice. "You're twelve and you need to play with your own friends—Caroline, Henrietta, and the others—from school or church. They're from good families and I'm sure they're about as accomplished as you."

That put an end to the conversation. Sophie had returned to her knitting; Aurelia had retreated to her room. Out the window, she had watched the two little black girls jump through squares in the fading sunlight.

Curtis' voice intruded on her thoughts. "You seem preoccupied or something. Is everything all right?"

"Oh, no. Yes, I mean. I was wondering about your family. Who does the farming?" Aurelia was startled to hear her own voice asking such an impertinent question.

"My mother Wilena runs the place. Women be the ones in

charge in this neck of the woods." Curtis stated this without a trace of irony.

Aurelia nodded, noticing how Curtis had unconsciously reverted to—what should she call it if not Negro speak? —when talking about his family. Complicated. She decided not to ask how old he was.

In a few minutes, Curtis reined in the horse, that, sensing the home stretch, had picked up the pace. Then barking. Two collies bounded out of nowhere, pink tongues protruding. Silver stopped in his tracks, unperturbed but jerking his head as if to say let's get this over with.

"Hey, James. Better make room back there. They won't hurt you. They're the Taylors' and they're hankering for a lift up to the house."

"Wh-wh-what are their names?" James stuttered as the two dogs leapt in, their barks turned to whimpers of delight.

"Rebel and Rover, but Sarah-Lynn's the only one who can tell them two apart."

On a slight rise which in Louisiana counted as a hill, Aurelia could make out the line of a long white fence and beyond it, a slate roof above a clapboard two-story, a chimney on each outer side as if to hold the structure together. The tops of several pin oaks poked out above the house from the back. It looked exactly as it did in her memory, some five or six years earlier, when her Uncle Samuel had died of yellow fever and the Vicksburg Ackermanns had ferried over for the funeral. Rough-hewn farmers, dusty hats in hand, had mumbled their awkward condolences as a black woman bustled about with platters of venison and ham. Could that have been Curtis' mother? She had no recollection of a small boy lurking about, and only a hazy image of the pig-tailed child with the sad face named Sarah-Lynn.

As they approached the horseshoe-shaped drive leading up to the porch, Curtis gave Silver his head.

"As you can see, he's happy to be home. We'll get you two situated and then I'll take him round to the barn and see what's making that back wheel squeak."

A tall, big-boned woman clad in a red apron soon came out onto the porch, and once Rebel and Rover started yelping, a girl of eleven or twelve bounded out.

"Safe and sound they are, Miss Margaret. None the worse for Silver's antics." The woman nodded her appreciation as Curtis lifted Aurelia down from her perch and together with James, unloaded the wagon.

"What a sight you two are. All grown up, and you so pretty, Aurelia." Beaming, their aunt extended her arms to enclose them both. She had a homey smell, Aurelia noticed, and a dependably corporeal presence not unlike that of her father. "Do come in for some sweet tea. We'll get you settled in and then dinner. You must be famished."

As Aurelia turned to shout her thanks to Curtis, a catch in his gait caught her eye. "Thank you for fetching us. We, well, we enjoyed the ride."

"Me too," he called out, tapping his hat. He continued to maneuver horse and buggy around the side of the house to the barn.

Aurelia blushed and then turned her head away from James' gaze.

"Why don't you show our guests to their rooms, Sarah-Lynn, and then give them the tour," Margaret suggested, as she ushered them into a parlor filled with a well-worn sofa and several carved oak chairs and side tables. Floor-to-ceiling bookcases covered the back wall. Hunting scenes hung between the windows. Several clocks ticked away here and there, but each said something different.

"We'll be ringing the bell in a couple of hours," Margaret informed them, Aurelia noting the authority in her voice. Like her father's, only softer.

Somewhere between the mashed potatoes and the watermelon, it hit Margaret Taylor how adrift in the world the two young people seated across from her must be. Like her brother, she was of the belief that putting order into people's days, however disoriented by circumstances, was the best way to get on with the business of living. So she had been forced to do after the untimely death of her husband, and so she had managed to do for their only child, who though now only twelve, could milk a cow, mend a hem and play the upright. The list went on.

James and Aurelia appeared to be another breed, something tentative about him, something unmoored about her. Deep down she had been pleased when Aristide had rung up and asked if he could impose on her until—

Until that phone call, Margaret had been well-nigh oblivious to the contagion going around, barely registering the gossip overheard at MacGregor's or the dress shop in Tallulah. In her experience, a bug was just a bug.

I must try to anchor these two in a more coherent world, she vowed to herself. That would be as Aristide would want it. Their own hardscrabble childhood in the Delta had turned them both into doers, determined to take charge.

True to form, Sarah-Lynn barely stopped chattering during that first meal with her cousins, except when Wilena brought a freshly-baked peach cobbler to the table.

"You folks gwine be bowled right over by this here sweetness," Wilena exclaimed as she served up outsized portions to the guests. "And tomorrow, another treat in store, ain't that so, Miss Sarah-Lynn? I reckon you be a-showin' off them creatures in the barn. As gussied up they be as this here pie."

As though given a new cue, the youngster seized upon a plan. "You'll love the horses. You can each have your own to ride. And we can swim in the lake and stuff."

James and Aurelia exchanged a glance.

"Th-th-that sounds like fun," James responded uncertainly.

Sipping her coffee as the young people excused themselves to unpack, Margaret wondered how much her brother cowed his children, and how much Sophie, with her wispy manners and doe eyes, coddled them. Somewhere in between, I should aim, she mused as Wilena clattered about in the kitchen, humming. Always humming.

Chapter Seven

The early days of October passed as in a strangely elastic dream in which time was slowly drawn taut, then jarringly snapped. As disoriented as they were upon arrival, Aurelia and James hastened to make themselves as useful as they could. Each felt obligated to be polite and unobtrusive; each also wanted, consciously or not, to push their mother's illness to the back of their minds. As Aristide had intuited, the farm was the perfect place not only to escape what was now being termed an epidemic, but also to distract their minds and tire their bodies. Through the next few weeks they awoke at dawn, donned trousers and old shirts once worn by their uncle Samuel, and tagged along with the farm hands on tractors and harvesters. On the weekends, Sarah-Lynn taught them to ride decently enough, designating Silver as Aurelia's mount and Flame as James'. In the evenings, especially when it rained, the four of them gathered around the table to shell peas or snap beans, telling stories or listening to Caruso on the Victrola.

On occasion Hiram, the foreman, would slap open the screen door and insinuate himself into the chair at the foot of the table. As Margaret too quickly explained the first time, he had come over to help with the shelling. Sarah-Lynn would flinch whenever he reached his thick fingers to retrieve a handful of beans to snap or ears of corn to shuck. More than once, he looked up from the leavings in front of him and eyed the girl. Aurelia too for that matter. Mostly, though, he limited his conversation to the crops.

"Likely be a decent harvest this next, provided the creek don't rise."

To these comments, Sarah-Lynn would roll her eyes or suddenly remember she needed to tend to the horses. It was left to James and Aurelia to fill in the gap.

"H-h-how do you d-d-do that, Mr. Hiram? Keep the creek from overflowing, I mean?" James asked.

"Ain't easy, I warrant. Depends on what happens upstream."

"Still, Curtis read up on what's been done elsewhere and the men did some reinforcing a couple of seasons back," Margaret added. Hiram snickered as he tossed a handful of ears into the basket at his feet.

It was the first time Aurelia had heard mention of the young man for days, he having not been over to the Taylors since she had spotted him on the roof replacing a shingle.

"Morning," he had called out as he came down the stepladder to pick up some brackets. "You two look like you're settling right in." Aurelia had smiled back.

"We're headed to the fields to help with the cotton," James had rejoined, stammer-free.

Curtis had nodded, his smile signaling his approval, but he added nothing.

"And later, we're picking blackberries down near the creek.

Sarah-Lynn too," Aurelia had hastened to add. "If you're still around, and want to come along." She ignored James' quizzical look.

Again, Curtis inclined his head but remained silent. He gathered up his tools and headed back up the ladder.

That afternoon when their buckets were near full and the sun had moved beyond the sycamores to the west, the three heard rustling from the bushes behind them. With two empty pails in hand Curtis appeared.

"Thought I'd join the fun," he said, smiling at all three and handing James one of the buckets.

"Why don't we have a contest?" Sarah-Lynn piped up. "You two take one bucket and cross over there to the other side, James and I will stay here, and when I shout 'ready, go,' we'll see who fills their pail first. OK?"

Curtis laughed. "You're the boss, Sarah-Lynn." Turning toward Aurelia, he motioned for her to follow him down an incline to the water's edge. A giant oak log stretched almost the entire twelve feet across the stream. Stepping stones had been arranged at the far end.

"You go first, just in case," Curtis instructed. "I'll be right behind you." When Aurelia got to the end of the log, she paused, unsure if she could jump cleanly from there to the stepping stone. She could feel a warm breath on her neck. Curtis flung the metal pail up on the bank and inched gingerly around her. He leapt to the stone some three feet away.

"See, it's not hard. And the stones are not wet. You won't slip. If you do, I'll catch you," he said, hopping to a further stone so as to give her room to make the shortest leap. She looked into his olive-green eyes, blinked and propelled herself. Though her feet hit the stone at an awkward angle, her outstretched arms managed to keep her from toppling.

"Are you two ready yet?" Sarah-Lynn called out from the other side, behind brush thick enough not to be seen through.

"In a minute."

Without further ado, Curtis held out his arms and practically lifted Aurelia to the bank. For an instant their bodies were sealed, one of his legs staked between hers to steady her. Suddenly dizzy, she clasped both his arms.

"OK, we can't wait any more. Ready, go," Sarah-Lynn shouted.

Curtis grabbed the pail and together he and Aurelia picked in silence, furiously, their hands pricked now and again by thorns, but neither complaining about the pain. When the pail was full, they didn't call out. Rather, Curtis took a few of the berries in his hand. Peering into her eyes, he said, "Take, eat. They're better this way."

She guided his hand to her mouth, using her lips to take in three or four of the berries. The rest he let fall to the ground.

"Luscious," Aurelia whispered.

"Yes, perfectly ripe," Curtis replied, his voice husky.

"We won, we won. Didn't we, James?" Sarah-Lynn's delighted squeal sounded from across the creek. "Are you slow-pokes OK? Have you finished?"

"Almost done. We'll be right there," Curtis yelled back.

Once the buckets were delivered up and Margaret had taken charge of separating the berries, the ripest to be eaten that evening, the others to be turned into jam, Curtis took his leave.

"Stay for dinner or at least take home some berries," Margaret insisted. But he was adamant, and made himself scarce for the next week.

Still, Curtis' name came up now and again in the normal course of conversation from Margaret or her daughter or even the hired hands—and when their remarks were incomplete, James often pressed for more detail. Aurelia betrayed little overt interest in the subject, and yet she quietly assembled salient bits of his family's past—: including the unusually strong bond between her Uncle Samuel and Curtis' grandfather, who had sharecropped down a dusty road not far from the Taylor place, (and lived with a white concubine no one ever saw). It was old man Jefferson who, spotting flames one night in Samuel's barn, high-tailed it over to save the panicked horses and all but two of the cows. Apparently, Curtis' father was a different story, a carouser of sorts, but about whom Margaret declined to elaborate. "Out of respect for Wilena," she said. But Curtis, their aunt did emphasize, took after his grandpa.

"October's bright blue sky," Mrs. Taylor called out as she came down the porch steps, letters in hand, to make the quarter-mile walk to the mailbox and back. Delivery and pick-up was every Wednesday and she never liked to forego her one leisurely exercise.

"Yessum," Wilena replied as she unpinned the bedsheets from her employer's clothes line. "And I suspect them young people be up to something. Ain't seen them all morning."

"Hiram took them out at dawn to help harvest the rest of the corn. We'll see how long that lasts. You know how young people are," Margaret said, laughing.

Actually, she was pleased with how well Aurelia and James had fit in despite their city ways, and how much Sarah-Lynn had contrived to keep them busy and entertained.

Even Curtis had chipped in, and why not? He was young, and responsible, and he was male. What with the war, there were not that many men around. Including their own older brother Alfred.

"Somewhere in France," Aristide had told her tersely during one of their brief phone calls. "That's all we can be told."

After only a few weeks on the Taylor farm and a lot of exercise, James' stutter had subsided and Aurelia had a quickness in her step. It was never good, Margaret mused as she walked along the dusty path, for young people to be constantly anxious or grief-stricken. As when little Sarah-Lynn retreated to her bedroom, unwilling to eat anything for weeks after Samuel died. Not knowing what to do for her daughter, she had floundered in her own right. It was left to Hiram to thrust some bill under her nose or hold out some new seed for her to sniff and approve. One day the foreman lost his patience and had dragged little Sarah-Lynn out to the barn to help milk the cows. "Not much time for moping on a farm," he had groused when asked for an explanation.

Opening the mailbox, Margaret retrieved a Sears Roebuck catalogue, a few bills—and a letter. She placed her own packet deep inside to protect it from the elements. Once back in the house she sat in the quiet of what had been her husband's study, opened the antique desk and pulled out the brass letter opener. The catalogue and the bills could wait.

Dear Sister,

This will be brief as the business at the bank never lets up, even less in wartime. And now with this scourge, the few that do come to work are doubly burdened. But that is nothing as compared to others' sacrifice, our soldiers and my Alfred among them.

I did want to reiterate my thanks for taking in the children, and I trust they have not been an undue burden. I will naturally recompense your efforts on their behalf once all this is over. (So like her brother to be punctilious; he never seemed to realize how off-putting it was.)

On the issue at hand it pains me to specify so let me just say that despite all that's being done for her, Sophie shows scant sign of recovery. The doctors do their best but they too are overwhelmed, and without any real remedy. Whatever the rumors, no effective vaccine has been concocted, and no cure found. However and from wherever (Spain, it is said) this flu originated, it is stubborn, lethal for some and lingering for others...

In the interim, I do hope you and Sarah-Lynn are WELL and that this thing has not wormed its way into your bend of the river. Likewise, I trust that Aurelia and James have bucked up.

May God protect and succor all of us,

Aristide

Chapter Eight

In the silence that followed Margaret's mention of her brother's letter at dinner, Aurelia could sense her heart pounding. Until then she had managed to keep the image of her frail mother tucked away in the back of her mind. Whenever it started to obtrude, generally at night, she would busy herself, vigorously brushing her hair or burying herself in *Bleak House*. Now she felt newly stricken.

For a long minute only the sound of hens clucking in the back yard could be heard around the table. Unease on his face, James slowly put down his fork.

"What does Father say about our m-m-mother, Aunt Margaret?

Is she better?"

Margaret stopped serving the apple crumb pie that Wilena had set in front of her.

"It's not an easy case, he was letting me know. Your father's only solace—and your mother's too—is the knowledge that the two of you are safe and sound on this side." Margaret recited her lines in what Aurelia assumed was an attempt to be reassuring, but she felt her aunt was holding something back.

"When do you think we can go back? Did he say?" James persisted.

"He didn't spell that out. I suspect this will drag on for a while."

"Do you mean the war, Aunt, or this, this"—Aurelia couldn't bring herself to utter the word epidemic— "this pneumonia thing?"

Hiram butted in. "Mercifully, the war's about over. Our soldiers—all the young men who went over—will be home soon." He put the emphasis on "young men," and in doing so, he looked straight across at Aurelia. She glared back, thinking Sarah-Lynn was right—: the foreman was fatuous and tiresome.

"This affliction will pass too," he assured them. "Meanwhile, it's important to eat well and stay out of harm's way. Isn't that so, Margaret?"

"Amen," she said.

Aurelia noted the foreman's familiar use of her aunt's name, but for once Sarah-Lynn didn't get her dander up. She had something else on her mind.

"The Bianchettis, Mama. They're having a shucking party, on Saturday. Can we go—can we all go? They'll have music and everything."

Margaret had started to shake her head when Wilena spoke up. "Why that sounds like a real fun time, Miz Taylor," the housekeeper interposed. "These youngins' been all cooped up, what with so many bad things going on. And those Bianchetti folks be Italian. They got music in the blood. Ain't I right, Miss Sarah-Lynn?" She continued to clear the table, humming some unidentifiable but unmistakable Neapolitan song as she did so.

Sarah-Lynn turned to Aurelia and James. "They play accordions and things; other folks bring banjos. It's so lively. Especially the dancing."

"Sounds like fun," Aurelia said, smiling at her cousin's enthusiasm. "James?"

"Yes, it does. But I have no idea how to dance."

"Why, Mr. James. Everybody dance when they got the rhythm," Wilena chuckled, sliding a heaping plate of pie practically under his nose. "Don't you worry none. Curtis bound to teach you the basics."

"How come he's lying so low, Wilena?"

"Working into the night at Willy Mayfield's mechanical shop, Miss Sarah-Lynn. And on the farm when he can. Reading them engineering books when he's done with everything else. Ain't nothing that can keep him down," Wilena said, though her voice wobbled at the end, as if, of a sudden, she wondered if something might be bothering her son.

Aurelia wondered too.

In the end, Margaret had agreed they could all attend the party. That Saturday evening, Sarah-Lynn squeezed Aurelia's hand in uncontained excitement as the Taylor buggy pulled up in front of the ramshackle Bianchetti home. A couple of older women scurried about the sagging porch carrying food and drink. Field hands unloaded a half-dozen wagons stacked with bushels of corn or beans, and a couple of dogs cavorted at their feet in anticipation of their own meal. A dark-haired woman clad all in black made her way down the steps and out to the arriving carriage with the aid of a walking stick. Aurelia reckoned she must be the elder Mrs. Bianchetti, known throughout those parts, Sarah-Lynn had confided, as *Signora*, her first name unknown to outsiders.

Inclining her head ever so slightly, the elderly woman held out her free arm to Margaret and encircled her.

"Benvenuti, benvenuti," she blurted several times, patting Sarah-Lynn on the head and bobbing her own head at Aurelia and James.

"Thank you, *Signora*. You already know my Sarah-Lynn, and these two young people are my niece and nephew, from Vicksburg," Margaret explained, her words purposefully slow and deliberate.

"She never managed to get on with English despite thirty years in the Delta," Margaret whispered to Aurelia. One of the *Signora*'s grandsons came to the rescue.

"*Bene, bene*, Grandma. I'll take them round to the barn," he said, smiling at the newcomers. He put his arm round the old woman and helped her back to a waiting rocker on the porch. "Rest here, Grandma. I'll be back in a minute."

By that time several other buggies had pulled up to deposit an assortment of worn-looking men, tidily attired but coarse-skinned women and freshly scrubbed children. Mostly other sharecroppers, Aurelia assumed, since the older ones addressed Margaret politely as Mrs. Taylor and inclined their heads in deference to her companion, Mr. Hiram. A little further away, two wagons of black families unloaded their passengers, but these folks lingered near their conveyances as though at any moment they might be asked to depart.

Eventually, the effusive Bianchetti grandson, Paolo by name, made his way over to this latter cluster and with an expansive Italianate flourish invited them to join the others in the barn. "Shucking is about to begin and as soon as that's out of the way, we're to be eating." His infectious smile drew Aurelia in as much as it did the families. "Venison, quail, collard greens, black-eyed peas, yams. You won't be sorry."

"No sir, no sir. We be mighty glad," one of the men, his face heavily lined, replied, and with a wide toothless grin thrust a couple of jugs of moonshine at the Bianchetti boy. The latter nodded politely and tilted his head to signal the womenfolk to lead the way, children in tow.

After Margaret had gone into the house to assure herself there was no help needed and come back outside to report there was no room anyway—the Bianchetti women were elbow to elbow in the kitchen while a dozen youngsters ran about the parlor, slamming doors and screeching in some incomprehensible patois—her group too decamped to the barn.

A smell of cider greeted them as they entered the outsized building, rimmed by long cedar benches along the sides and festooned with red, green and blue balloons tied to the rafters. At the far end were five or six upturned barrels; seated upon the middle one was an old man in a black waistcoat. The elder Mr. Bianchetti, Aurelia surmised, having heard her aunt describe him as, like his wife, "obstinately old world" despite decades in the Delta.

"We must pay our respects," Margaret whispered to Aurelia and James, ushering them up the center of the room toward their host.

Sharecropper though he was, Mr. Bianchetti persevered in the social rites of his Tuscan upbringing. If unable to rise easily from his settled position, especially with an accordion in his lap, he still managed to straighten his spine, brushed his lips along Margaret's extended hand, gave a stern nod of manly recognition to James, and, according her the obligatory once-over, declared Aurelia *bellissima*.

Formalities over, it was time to roll up sleeves. Paolo and his younger brother Eduardo showed Aurelia and James how to strip the husks and where to toss the ears: in one barrel the full-kernelled, ripened ears; in another, the spotted, diseased or immature cobs.

"It's been a good harvest, so these containers will fill up and be replaced quickly," Eduardo explained. "And once the corn is done, snap beans and lady peas. Watch Sarah-Lynn. She's good at everything."

An hour or so passed, everyone bent on the task in front of them, the whites arrayed on one side of the room, the blacks along the other. The little ones of both races scampered about, chasing the dogs or playing hide and seek. The younger men, with Paolo and Eduardo at their head, carried bushel after bushel of shucked corn to wagons hitched outside. Canvas bags bulging with peas and beans were then brought in. The women, led by Mr. Bianchetti's daughter-in-law, began snapping and sorting. A few stragglers arrived with fiddles and arranged themselves in a semi-circle around the old maestro to warm up their instruments. Men uncorked kegs of beer and women placed several cut-glass bowls filled with punch on the tables. Aurelia and James snapped, shelled and sorted along with the rest, enjoying the easy chatter and the collective effort. As the light waned, the younger Mrs. Bianchetti leaned across and down the table to address Aurelia.

"Don't know whether you cotton to such entertainments, since you're from the city, but tonight's a blue moon. After the dancing, my husband will hitch the horses for a hayride. You two are welcome to go along."

Before Aurelia could respond, a commotion broke out at the entrance. She stopped her shelling. A small group of black girls gathered round the latest arrivals; over their heads she could make out Curtis, who had his arms around a girl of about fourteen or fifteen. Both Curtis and the girl were dressed in their Sunday best, he with a felt hat in his hands, she with pink ribbons on her pigtails. Disentangling himself from the gaggle, Curtis escorted Wilena to a chair alongside several other black women and then deposited two covered dishes on the table in the corner. A smell of warm berries drifted across the room. Someone handed him a glass of the moonshine, and he turned to take in the scene.

His eyes found Aurelia's.

Curtis took a couple of swallows and set the mug on the table. He wiped his mouth and stood motionless, until a gray rat scuttled across the floor, prompting squeals from several of the girls and sending several of the boys as well as the Bianchetti cat in hot pursuit. As the hapless rodent ran hither and yon, finally eluding his would-be captors by high-tailing it through a crack at the back of the barn, Curtis made his way across the room.

"The Bianchettis put on a good party, despite a rat or two," he said, smiling at the two cousins. "I hope you're having a good time."

James nodded so vigorously his hair flopped over one eye. "W-w-we missed you over at our aunt's house, Curtis. Wilena said you've been busy at that shop."

"More and more cars to repair," Curtis said, his tone easy, but his eyes alert. (A few of the seated women had tensed; the shelling of peas stopped.) He took a deep breath. "But I was thinking. Why don't you come over to Tallulah one day, Mr. James? I bet you'd like to look inside some engines. Never hurts to have an extra hand."

James beamed, and Aurelia smiled at the thoughtfulness of the offer. (The other women tentatively recommenced their shelling.)

"Turns out that the boss is toying with the prospect of opening up shop across the water. A bigger market over your way, so many workers gone to war and so many motor cars that need fixing."

"In Vicksburg. That's great, Curtis. And, and, I'd like that. To come by. One day next week, if our aunt...Yes, I'll let W-W-Wilena know a day ahead," James replied, his stammer barely perceptible, his pleasure palpable.

"And, Miss Aurelia, what about you?" Curtis ventured, playfulness as well as politeness in his tone.

She instantly reddened but before she could put together a response, the girl with the pink ribbons was tugging at Curtis' arm. Quite fetching, Aurelia decided, if a little young...

"OK, OK, Cassie," he said with a laugh, pulling at her pigtail. "But first, I want you to say hello to Mr. James and Miss Aurelia, the two Taylor cousins Mama told you about." And to them: "My kid sister."

The youngster peaked out from behind her older brother. "I'm not a kid," she replied, poking his ribs. She ducked her head to the visitors but wouldn't look at them and couldn't seem to muster anything to say. She turned back to her brother: "You are going to do the dancing, right? We needs more boys to have a reel."

"Whatever you have in mind, Cassie. And get Mama up and out there."

At that point most folks had finished up the shelling and had wandered over to get a taste of the Bianchettis' cooking. James scrambled to his feet and offered to fill plates.

Curtis and Aurelia were left alone, she sitting with a stack of snapped green beans in front of her, he standing across from her.

"Hopefully, you will like the dancing, and afterwards, they're hitching up the horses for a hayride, down to the joiner." When Aurelia raised an eyebrow in question, he continued: "Where two creeks come together on their way to the river. The moon will be bright. Sometimes, ghosts wander into the clearing." She smiled at such a fanciful suggestion, unable quite to raise her eyes to his.

"A sight to behold..." he added, his voice throaty.

She felt his eyes fixed on her face, entreating her to look up. Instead, she clutched the rim of the bowl of beans, her eyes riveted on the scratches on the table. Not only was a young man she barely knew flirting with her smack in front of several old biddies but the young man in question was black.

"We was talking about you the other night, boy. Sarah-Lynn claims you be the only one who can keep that stallion of hers in line." It was Hiram. He had ambled over, whiskey in one hand, a heaping plate of indeterminate meat in the other. "Needs a firm hand, that's for sure—and new shoes, I reckon. If you can be bothered..."

"Been busy, at Willy's repair shop, Mr. Hiram. But I should likely get over in the next day or two."

The foreman snorted as though to indicate he wasn't entirely satisfied with Curtis' explanation, or the coolness of his tone. "You should get yourself some grub. *Signora* still knows her way around a stove, and it's free, after all."

Curtis didn't respond to the snide; Aurelia kept her eyes squarely on the beans. Before long, Hiram moseyed off to join a group of farmers outside discussing the one topic that obsessed them all—not the war but the weather.

As soon as old Mrs. Bianchetti's custards, Margaret's cakes and Wilena's pies had all been devoured, the accordions and fiddles tuned up. Almost automatically, two sets of dancers formed circles, kicking aside clumps of hay or corn husks that might trip them up. Paolo and Eduardo grabbed two unsuspecting girls as partners to anchor the first group. Cassie and a couple of her friends got up to form the latter, smaller group, cajoling several young men, including Curtis, to join them. Without anyone's having to arrange it, the first group consisted of all whites, the second all blacks.

Aurelia and James watched as the dancers dosey-doed up and down the floor. As everyone picked up what they had forgotten from years' past, the musicians played faster, with more verve. So many folks had taken to the floor, so much bumping and stomping of feet, that it made sense to coalesce into one outsized ring.

"What you two waiting for? Get on out there." Wilena had

waddled over to the table where Aurelia and James still sat, their feet tapping in rhythm but neither having made the move to join in.

"OK, let's do it, Aurelia," James said.

For an hour or more, black hands briefly clasped white ones, white shoulders grazed black ones, including every so often Aurelia and Curtis. Eventually, the caller, a grizzled sharecropper that everyone referred to as Gussy, became so hoarse he had to relinquish the role to a less accomplished hoe-downer. That's when old Mr. Bianchetti erected himself long enough to lead his ragtag band in a spirited tarantella. Several of the older folks took to the floor, including a couple of gray-haired grannies whose husbands had long since been danced into the grave.

Out of nowhere, Paolo was standing in front of Aurelia, his hand extended.

"I have no idea how to do this," she responded.

"Don't worry, I do," Paolo said. Before she could demur, Aurelia was whisked around the perimeter, the folks along the sides a whirling blur.

Only James noticed the one set of eyes which never left his sister.

When it came time for the hayride, two Clydesdales were hitched to the first wagon, a couple of complacent plow mares to the second. The white kids, including Aurelia, James and Sarah-Lynn, were directed to pile into the first, and the black children, Cassie, her three friends and some older boys, into the latter.

"You keep an eye on Cassie, Curtis. And while you be about it," here Wilena jerked her head over toward the lead wagon, "help Aurelia climb up. That dress ain't fit for no hayride."

"Why don't you ride with us?" James blurted out, as Curtis grasped Aurelia's arm and with his other around her slim waist, helped hoist her in and onto a bale at the back of the lead wagon. No one else paid any attention, what with banjos being tuned, hot chocolate handed round and blankets spread about.

"Reckon I'll need to make sure Cassie doesn't get into any mischief," Curtis said, as he rattled the back board of the wagon to make sure it was securely latched.

"Hey, Curtis, ride up here with me." It was Eduardo this time, calling from aloft the second wagon. "You know the road better than anyone. And the mares can be skittish."

From her vantage point in the back of the first wagon, Aurelia saw Curtis take the reins from Eduardo. A call-out from Paolo and the two wagons set off, clip-clopping down the gravel road toward the mysterious joiner. Aurelia pulled a blanket up over her knees. Someone strummed a banjo. When the distance between the two wagons shortened, she could make out the sound of singing. "Jordan's river is deep and wide, Alleluia..." In the star-studded night the sound was silvery.

Eventually, the Clydesdales came upon a crevasse. They pawed at the ground, snorted and refused to proceed. Curtis jumped down from his wagon and went around to the front of Paolo's.

"Hold the reins loosely but firmly and we'll entice them to move along the ridge," he called out, and without waiting for a reply, took hold of the harness. Speaking softly, he coaxed the reluctant horses to skirt the ditch. He then did the same with Eduardo's two mares, though in a sterner voice and with a slap on their flanks. Twenty minutes later the road dead-ended, at which point the Bianchetti brothers tied the wagons to the nearest alders.

"Let's build a fire down near the water. Plenty of logs around," Paolo suggested. James helped Aurelia down and they walked together to the embankment overlooking the site where the two streams merged. A few fish broke the surface.

"Come on, you two. We're going to do a sing-along, and we need every voice to frighten off the bears," Paolo called out.

"Bears, really?" James asked.

"Not likely," Eduardo said with a laugh. "They don't like fire, or singing!"

Again, the blacks assembled on one side of the fire, the whites on the other. But they did sing in harmony, Cassie, church-trained, hitting all the high notes. One of the older boys edged closer to her as the embers started to die down, but Curtis intervened to separate them. Then he walked away to check on the horses.

"I'll be back in a minute," Aurelia said under her breath, and without waiting for James to object, she scrambled off toward the wagons.

"Are they all right, the horses?" she asked softly as she approached Curtis.

Taken by surprise, he turned suddenly, assuming his sister had followed him. "Oh, it's you. I'm glad—that you decided to come along."

"It's an enchanting place."

"But you haven't seen the best part. Beyond that clump of trees. Come. We may be lucky." Automatically, he took her by the arm to avoid outcroppings in the patchy light. Aurelia could feel the strength of his body beside her.

Within a couple of minutes, they came to a meadow where the moon shone on several milky white deer. A buck with prodigious antlers grazed apart, near where the woods took over. Immobile, Curtis and Aurelia watched the creatures in silence.

"Like you said—ghostly," she whispered.

"So they are."

Eventually their scent drifted toward the animals. One by one the deer stole away. Curtis took a deep breath and turned to face Aurelia.

"You do know how things stand, don't you, Aurelia?" he asked in a voice tinged with sadness.

"I'm not sure what you mean," she said. Her hand traced the smoothness of his arm, from elbow to wrist and he shivered.

"This cannot be, Aurelia. You saw that crevasse in the road. The one that separates us is a thousand times wider, ready to swallow up anyone—" Curtis stopped, not wanting to overdramatize, or overwhelm his companion.

Aurelia shook her head in denial. "But you are so different—and other people, other white people, know it as well. So, really, I don't understand why I, we..."

Curtis half-wanted to explain how misled she was—to point out that boundaries had blurred because of the war, that as soon as things returned to normal, the walls that separated black from white would be back up. But it was midnight and they were alone in the moonlight. He took her in his arms and gently put his lips to hers. She kissed him back, inexpertly but eagerly.

A line had been crossed.

Chapter Nine

During the next several days Aurelia did her best not to dwell on the ghost deer or the stolen kisses. She took turns on the upright with Sarah-Lynn, who, self-taught, could perform from memory any number of melodies. Wilena rattled about but kept her distance, something reserved in her demeanor. As for James, he had been taciturn ever since she had re-emerged out of the shadows and sat down next to him in front of the bonfire. Despite, or perhaps because of his implicit criticism of her behavior that night, Aurelia redoubled her efforts to tutor her brother.

Toward the end of October, she glanced at the three-day-old headline in a copy of the *Post* on Margaret's writing desk: "Reports from western front increasingly good." Further down, she noticed, the local health board in Vicksburg had authorized druggists to fill night orders. All schools were to remain closed. Indefinitely. She couldn't bring herself to read further.

That evening Aurelia insisted her aunt phone over to find out how her mother was doing; finally, after a dozen rings Susanna shouted into the receiver.

"Why, Miss Aurelia, we've been a'thinkin' of you two. Your mother faring poorly, got the new-monia, they all saying. No, Mr. Ackermann holing up at the bank. Into the night. Real tired he is too. Mr. Alfred? No more letters, I don't allow. Yes, that doctor coming over when he can. But we're praying and Lawd knows we're doing all we can. I tells your father you and Mr. James doing fine, don't you worry none. Better you stay put in Lusiana."

As disjointed as Susanna's run-on commentary was, Aurelia felt relieved that their long-time servant, apparently as robust as ever, was in charge. In his helplessness, her father, she feared, had locked himself away as in a bank vault. No one but his wife would have the combination, and she too weak...

After the call, Margaret went straight to the kitchen to heat hot chocolate and to slice a cake. The foursome sat in the parlor munching in silence.

"Let's not study tomorrow. The horses need exercise and we can ride as far as the Bianchettis, or the other way, toward the Jeffersons," Sarah-Lynn chirped.

"Good idea, sweetheart. I'll make you sandwiches in the morning. Just make sure you're back before dark."

"Don't worry, Mama. We'll be fine. So, what do you think, Aurelia? Sound like fun?"

"Absolutely."

After they dealt with the dishes, all three retreated upstairs with the idea of getting an early start the next day. Except Aurelia couldn't sleep. After tossing and turning for an hour, she threw off the quilt and stole downstairs in hopes another glass of hot chocolate might soothe her nerves.

When her slippers hit the bottom steps she heard voices—

familiar ones—coming from the parlor. She had only a partial view of the room. Hiram. He must have appeared after the three went to bed.

"You need to get a handle on this, Margaret," the foreman insisted. Aurelia heard the bang of a glass put down on a hard surface. "Them two making eyes at each other as though—"

Aurelia could imagine her aunt bristling at Hiram's uncouth, and ungrammatical, language. Not to mention his none-too-subtle accusation.

"You think the war is making everybody equal, everybody with the same chance, like those northern politicians been drilling into us, but you ain't looking around." After a pause, he continued in a more menacing tone, "Don't forget, I'm from Bastrop and round there we don't tolerate tomfoolery."

Aurelia caught a glimpse of her aunt staring off into space, taking a quick gulp of whatever she indulged in late at night but not deigning (or maybe not daring) to respond.

Hiram paced back and forth, apparently more riled up with each idea that came into his unsorted mind. "Not what it used to be when you and that brother of yours with the fancy name—Aristocrat, is it? —lorded it over folks in the Delta, aping those highfalutin' Percys. But scratch the surface, and..." The foreman tapered off here, turning to see if the mistress of the house fathomed what he was driving at.

For an instant, Aurelia prepared to retreat but curiosity got the better of her. Surely her aunt would now speak up.

"In any event, Hiram, no need to get so worked up. Wilena tells me Curtis will soon be long gone, up north. Aurelia and James will return to Vicksburg, whatever the outcome with poor Sophie, and Aristide—that's my brother's name—will make sure they comport themselves all nice and proper."

Aurelia had never heard her aunt be so withering.

"To be sure," Hiram said, picking up on one of the threads Margaret had tossed out and apparently unaware of the sarcasm in her retort, "they don't stand for such things across the river. Anytime one of them Vicksburg tar babies steps out of line—dares even park his fanny upfront on that streetcar they're so proud of—there's hell to pay. Threw one of 'em clean off for sitting next to a lady."

Aurelia winced. She failed to catch Margaret's riposte, though she glimpsed her aunt's taut face in profile. She retreated a step or two. To complicate things, Rover and Rebel wandered over and wagged their tails. "Shh," Aurelia whispered, patting each on the head and praying they wouldn't start yelping.

"Obviously, we don't see eye-to-eye on this subject," her aunt wound up, "but most would concur that Curtis is exceptional. Explains why my niece is taken with him. I'm sure, even at her age, she's smart enough, as am I, to realize that such attachments can lead nowhere."

Such a convoluted remark likely left the literal-minded Hiram flummoxed. Slowly though he gathered himself up, apparently determined not to let the argument end on an ambiguous note. "Nowhere? From what I reckon it ain't nowhere those two have been, if you get my drift."

Now in full view, Margaret looked up from her drink, her narrowed eyes saying she hadn't missed the insinuation.

"As I was saying, Miss Aurelia may fashion herself some kind of Negrophile," Hiram sniveled. "But if she truly likes that boy, she'll leave him be. Don't forget how they found his juke-joint pappy: stone-cold on the floor of a flophouse."

Aurelia closed her eyes, trying not to conjure such a scene.

"For your information, Curtis takes after his grandpa, whom, by the way, Samuel greatly admired." Aurelia assumed her aunt's pointed comment would put paid to the conversation, and put Hiram back in his place.

Minutes passed. Rover had curled up on Aurelia's slippered feet; Rebel had sniffed his way up the stairs. Aurelia heard the tinkle of ice in a glass. She craned her neck to see further into the room. Hiram had his head tilted toward the brass chandelier, ruminating.

"Well, Margaret, you can stomach whatever you can stomach. But that don't alter one iota the nature of things. And them things are black and them things are white." Margaret grimaced, but either not noticing or pretending not to, Hiram quaffed the last of his whiskey and delivered his final thrust. "In the end, Curtis—as bright-skinned and biggity as you and your niece would like him to be—ain't nothin' but a nigger."

He stomped out the door, sending Aurelia and the dog scurrying up the stairs. A half-hour later Aurelia was still uncertain as to how she ended up back in bed, shaking under the covers, both dogs on the hemp rug, their heads cocked to one side as they watched her. She willed sleep to come.

The next morning the three youngsters saddled up early, the sun peeking over the barn, a soft breeze blowing the first yellowed, crinkled elm leaves to the ground. Sarah-Lynn ran back to the house as James and Aurelia finished buckling up and grabbed the wicker basket her mother had assembled late the night before. On the top of the basket she left a scribbled note: *Have a good time, honey, but look after your cousins. They're not as accustomed to the horses as are you. See you back here before sunset. Mother.* Sarah-Lynn crumpled the note, eased the back door onto its latch, and with little effort mounted Thunder, the friskiest of the three Taylor stallions.

They rode cautiously at first, Sarah-Lynn patiently demonstrating all the gaits the horses could be put through. Her cousins caught on quickly, though Silver occasionally balked at Aurelia's too vigorous or too ambiguous commands.

"You have to show him who's boss," her cousin called out, "but if you're too demanding, he's going to resist." Aurelia bit her lip in determination and let the horse lope along largely at his own pace.

Eventually they came upon an open meadow where a few black cows grazed. Under a leafy poplar they spread the checkered tablecloth Margaret had folded on the top of the basket. They took their time eating while the sun prowled in and out of puffed-up clouds. As they handed round a thermos of water and finished off their meal with ripe bananas, Sarah-Lynn eyed the changing sky.

"We might want to head back soon."

"Not until I climb that tree," James said, gesturing toward a nearby oak whose thick branches arched low. The two girls shrugged as if to say boys will be boys, Aurelia secretly pleased to see how self-confident her brother had become in little over a month in the country.

"I'll be right behind," Sarah-Lynn answered, hitching up her trousers and clambering up behind her cousin. Aurelia busied herself gathering up the remnants of their picnic and placing the leftovers back in the basket. Still tired from the night before, she stretched out on the tablecloth and closed her eyes.

Twenty minutes later she was jolted awake.

"You would not believe what we could see from up there," James exclaimed. "To the east, the river. Barges and steamers going up and down. We could make out the smoke."

Sarah-Lynn nodded, holding out her hand to help Aurelia up. Together they folded the tablecloth. "Not to mention a bank of rain clouds, huge purple ones. Coming our way."

Within minutes, the weather curdled. After soothing the nervous steeds enough so they could mount, Sarah-Lynn nudged Thunder in the ribs. Aurelia and James did the same to theirs, but as they picked their way through uneven terrain, thunder cracked overhead. Aurelia tensed, pulling the reins back so hard as to spook the unsuspecting horse. Her balance lost, she tumbled off, her left foot torqueing as it caught in the stirrup. She dangled precariously before hitting the ground. Silver ambled on several more paces and then turned to look back at his hapless rider.

The first thing Aurelia felt were greasy leaves stuck to her face, the next a sharp pain in her ankle. She brushed off the foliage and tried to right herself. In a flash, Sarah-Lynn dismounted and yelled for James to hold the reins of both horses.

"Are you all right? You've scraped your head," Sarah-Lynn said. She gestured toward her cousin's left temple.

"That doesn't hurt," Aurelia said, touching the sticky hair around the cut. "It's my foot. I may have sprained it—or worse." She fumbled to pull up her trouser leg. The ankle was visibly swollen.

It took barely a minute for Sarah-Lynn to issue orders. "James, go tie Flame and poor Silver to that elm over there—hurry—and then let's get Aurelia under that oak. I'll take Thunder to the Jeffersons' place. It's not far. Be back with help as soon as I can."

Aurelia would have objected to this plan but she knew getting back on her mount was out of the question.

The two siblings huddled under the tree, James having poured the remainder of the canteen on Aurelia's head injury, dabbing at it with a wet cloth. He wrapped another around her ankle and propped her leg up on the picnic basket. When she shivered, he took off his corduroy jacket and draped it over her shoulders. The two horses, the drizzle notwithstanding, seemed unperturbed by the misadventure.

"I wish they'd hurry," James said. The sound of wheels creaking eventually brought him to his feet. Despite a now steady downpour, he ran toward two fast-approaching mares hitched to a wagon, Curtis and Sarah-Lynn atop. Without delay, they lifted Aurelia, who winced but did not cry out, into the back of the vehicle, then insisted she stretch out, her head cradled in James' lap.

"Hold this canvas over your heads the best you can, James. Sarah-Lynn and I are already soaked." Turning to Aurelia, Curtis added in a less commanding voice, "If we go too fast and it hurts too much, call out." She smiled, grateful for his concern.

Once the wagon pulled up in front of the Jefferson house, Cassie bounded out with an umbrella, holding it mostly over Aurelia's head as James and Curtis carried her inside. Wilena had already spread blankets on the sofa in the parlor and filled a couple of kettles with hot soapy water. Curtis' mother took charge of Aurelia while he went back outside in the rain to coax the four drenched horses into the barn along with Thunder.

Once Aurelia's scalp wound was washed, the bleeding stanched, and alcohol applied, Wilena eased Aurelia's trouser leg up to her knee and positioned her foot on a pile of cushions. As gentle as the older woman was, Aurelia grimaced with the pain. Curtis stuck his head around the doorway and then hurried away with a muttered, "I'll help Cassie with the tea and biscuits."

"Done swelled right proper," Wilena mumbled. "Not as bad as

Curtis', the main thing being as you gotta get it fixed sooner rather than later, chile." Aurelia nodded in agreement though not understanding the older woman's reference.

"Don't you think we should get her home to Aunt Margaret's?" James ventured. "Maybe we should call her." (He looked around but saw no phone.) Making matters worse, the deluge was now accompanied by horizontal streaks of lightning and thunder claps.

Without answering James, Wilena called out to her son. "Get yourself in here, Curtis. I needs your help."

He appeared at the door, an unopened tin of biscuits in his hand.

"What do you think, a sprain or a fracture? Or, don't you remember what it look like when that buggy done run over your foot? You a-hollerin' like I never heard." Wilena shook her head at the memory of it. "And those white folks kept right on driving. Nobody stop or done nothin'."

Embarrassed by this recitation and having made it a point of pride never to refer to, or use as an excuse, his gimp leg, Curtis set the tin aside and squatted on his haunches. Ever so carefully he lifted Aurelia's foot by placing his open palm under her heel, his other hand under her calf for support. She flinched despite the care he took, and he wondered if it was from the pain or from his touch. James stood behind the sofa dancing from one foot to the other.

"From what I can see, it's only twisted, but she's not likely to be able to put any weight on it." Aurelia inclined her head without speaking. Curtis didn't have the courage to look her in the eye, not with both his mother and her brother standing there.

"Still, if I'd known of some doctor," Wilena said, "you'd have been fixed up proper, right there in Tallulah, not waiting a whole week for Dr. Davis to come over. 'Too late for fixing,' he said. And you limpin' round, big smile on your face."

Getting up from his crouch, Curtis glared at his mother, letting out a sigh of displeasure. It didn't stop her.

"Why you'd be in the Army now, in one of those outfits with shiny buttons, looking so handsome, if that recruiting station hadn't turned you down. And they took that Billy Madison boy, who can hardly count to ten. All because—"

"That's enough, Mama. No one wants to hear this," he snapped, his tone sharp enough to put an end to her lament.

So chastised, Wilena resumed her position on a stool next to the patient and re-wrapped the foot in a cool towel. Cassie handed Aurelia and James glasses of sweet tea with a sprig of mint.

"Thank you, Cassie. Tastes real good, doesn't it, Aurelia?" James said.

"Refreshing. I already feel a little better."

"I knows what Miss Margaret would want," Wilena went on, glancing up at her son. "We needs to get a doctor over here—and ain't no white physician in these parts on a Sunday. So, I'm thinking, Curtis, you'd best be knocking on Dr. Davis's door."

For an instant Curtis thought how unprecedented, not to say unseemly, that a Negro doctor would be tending a white patient, and a young female at that. But circumstances were what they were—and no one else needed to know the particulars.

"Take Thunder. He's fast," Sarah-Lynn said.

And that was that.

Dr. Davis, although vocal in his displeasure about being disturbed on his one day of rest, hitched his buggy and drove the two miles to the Jeffersons. Like Curtis, he took one look and determined that Aurelia had nothing more than a badly sprained ankle. He applied a tight bandage, dispensed several Bayer aspirins and admonished the patient to stay off the foot as long as possible. Meanwhile, Sarah-Lynn and James put bridles back on Silver and Flame and galloped back to the Taylors.

However anxious about what her ordeal meant to all concerned—she couldn't shake Hiram's ugly words—Aurelia was too much in discomfort to object to Wilena's ministrations. One night in that house, on the downstairs sofa smothered in blankets, should not destroy her reputation in perpetuity. A cup of restorative tea, and her mind was clear enough to wonder what her friend Caroline would have made of it all.

Curtis absented himself shortly after the doctor's visit, mumbling about chores in the barn.

The next morning Aurelia heard Wilena clattering around in the kitchen as she prepared breakfast.

"Jinx be here with the carriage, but coffee first," she called out to the patient in the other room, and then she muttered just loud enough for Aurelia to hear: "She be doing the right thing, Miz Taylor, getting her niece out of here. Lickety-split too."

Before either Curtis or Cassie awoke, she and the field hand assisted Aurelia in hobbling out and into the buggy.

Toward the end of that day, Aurelia revived. The pain, if not the swelling, had subsided and her aunt, albeit more subdued than usual, had not castigated any of the three for the mishap or for their decision to seek out the Jeffersons. Sarah-Lynn rattled off the war headlines from Sunday's paper but skipped over references to the epidemic. Instead, she scoured the inside pages in search of things light-hearted. "A woman named Margaret Owen has set a typing record, 170 words in one minute. Do you know how to type, Aurelia?"

"Not at all. But Father says the bank now has a machine on every desk. It's likely a good thing to learn."

Tiring eventually of the small talk, Sarah-Lynn and James set up a card table next to the couch and coaxed Margaret into playing gin rummy. While the game was in full swing, they heard a knock at the door. Sarah-Lynn answered it, returning shortly with a pair of rudimentary crutches.

"They're from Curtis. He carved them last night, from pine wood he had in the barn. He wouldn't come in but said to tell you he hoped you were feeling better, Aurelia."

"That was kind of him," Aurelia responded.

Shortly, all four lost interest in the game.

On her new crutches, Aurelia hopped her way to bed in a makeshift guest room downstairs, drained.

Chapter Ten

After a see-saw month in which Sophie showed intermittent improvement but then relapsed, Aristide figured the contagion had left him unscathed. He refused to don a face mask or remain sequestered on Adams Street despite the quarantine imposed by Mayor Hayes. Like all men with a little power, he took pleasure in flaunting a few of the rules which should have applied to him, as they did to his inferiors.

Susanna remained at her post, fixing up a storage room as a servant's quarter. Aristide hardly saw her, but he knew she lay on a creaky cot whenever she could snatch a few hours away from the sick bay. Aside from Sophie, who regularly and increasingly drifted off, she had no duties other than his own breakfast grits and coffee to attend to. She stayed out of his way when, after glancing at the headlines, Aristide would pad down the lonely corridor and crack open the door of Sophie's room, listening for any sound that might suggest his wife's breathing was calm, normal. As before.

Occasionally, he was overcome by the memory of slights he had inflicted on her—visits to brothels included, though those lapses were rare. Sorry too that he was constitutionally incapable of apologizing to the wraith-like figure in her fevered state. As undemonstrative as he had been toward Sophie in the last few years, the more he had come to depend on her, especially as regarded their three children. That such burdens might now fall principally to him was more than he could bear to contemplate. But, at his age, to take a new wife to share his bed seemed sacrilege; to put another woman in charge of his offspring unimaginable.

Not that he had to angst over-much about Alfred. Provided nothing untoward happened to his son during what he surmised were the last fitful, albeit brutal, weeks of war, Alfred would come home more disciplined and focused than when he boarded that convoy seventeen months ago. That's what the Army did, as it had for him back in '98. He had emerged with his medals ramrod-straight, eager to assert himself in the larger world. Vicksburg was large enough, yet circumscribed enough, to allow him to do so. Like father, like son, Aristide believed. Once decommissioned, Alfred would practice at the bar—bless Sophie for insisting her elder son acquire a law degree—and that would be that. He would become a model citizen, marry well, father children, and make Aristide ever prouder.

Their other progeny was a different matter, however much Sophie claimed there was little to worry over.

"Not everyone need be as accomplished in society as you are, Aristide," she would point out, such an indirect compliment preventing him from being overly critical of either Aurelia's waywardness or James' timidity. "They each have talents, laudable qualities," she would hasten to add, though she never spelled these gifts out.

About two things Aristide was certain, Vicksburg having made him acutely aware of how crucial the perception of one's conduct might be. Aurelia was, at eighteen, appealingly high-spirited, but reckless. She needed "finishing," be it from an institution dedicated to applying such touches or be it under the firm hand of a husband. Or both. He had never articulated it to Sophie but he suspected something untethered about his daughter. Having high tea at the Carroll Hotel with other young ladies or trying her hand at watercolors was not sufficient to alter his opinion in that regard. She reminded him of a horse he owned years ago in the Delta. For no reason the mare had bolted, breaking free from its harness, causing the carriage she was pulling to overturn into a ditch. Her own leg shattered, she had to be put down.

As for his youngest child, Aristide was equally at a loss. It wasn't solely the occasional seizures or the persistent stammer, he tried to get across to Sophie, though those impediments would likely exclude his son from a number of respectable occupations. It was James' morbid attachment to his sister.

"He thinks Aurelia hung the moon. It's not natural, and it will make people leery."

Distressed by this characterization, Sophie had come up with an alternate description which put her younger son in a much fairer light.

"Empathy," she told her husband, "is what James radiates. It's a gift."

Bristling, Aristide had loudly snapped open his newspaper, buried his head therein, and muttered under his breath "for a girl." Sophie had returned to her knitting making no rejoinder to his last utterance. Without telling his wife, Aristide determined that upon James' sixteenth birthday, he would be dispatched to a military academy in Tennessee. Empathy be damned.

If these ruminations kept Aristide from sleeping as well as he might, he banished them once he crossed the marble threshold of the First National Bank. Too much to attend to work-wise what with so many men called up, so many shortages of food and fuel, so many projects put on hold or gone south. As the head of the board—the sole one routinely referred to in the local papers as "the prominent banker and city council member"—he was regularly called upon to express his views, whether to pave a street or extend a sewer line, hire more policemen or sponsor a fundraiser. He prided himself on holding—and "most ably expressing," as the papers often couched it—progressive positions, on everything from the latest farming methods to the benefits of a bridge across the Mississippi. By and large, elected officials and assorted bigwigs lent their ears and regularly were swayed by whatever he had proposed.

Only on one topic did Aristide find himself out of step. If it seemed reasonable to argue that white men of all happenstance, inasmuch as superior to blacks, should be responsible for encouraging the inferior race to rise to their full capabilities, to espouse such went against the grain.

Despite its cultural pretensions, Vicksburg had a vicious streak.

His first inkling of that undercurrent came about inadvertently a few years before the war broke out. Fellow banker and board member Horace Hilliard invited the Ackermanns to join a committee of which he and his wife were instigators. Turned out to be an anti-miscegenation league, Hilliard's harangue to his assembled guests putting Aristide's teeth on edge. The Ackermanns left the cabal early.

"Beyond the pale," Aristide had said as they settled into the carriage.

"I agree, my dear," his wife responded. "Yet we don't need to make a federal case of it, especially since it would likely do no good. And, do remember, their daughter Caroline is Aurelia's close friend. It would be a pity to ruin that."

Sensible, his Sophie. She knew instinctively when to turn a blind eye. Starting with their marriage vows, which he began to break soon after Alfred's birth, perhaps even before, he couldn't recall precisely. Aristide had only ever focused on that particular Levee Street property because a new owner had come up from New Orleans and swivel-hipped her way into the bank for a loan. He had handled the paperwork, but poorly, as he was distracted by the octoroon's glances. She had wanted to turn the place into a proper gentlemen's club, like the ones up Greenville way, she had explained. Emerald eyes and scented skin she had, not unlike, he soon discovered, those of the girls she oversaw, and whose charms he, every now and again, paid for. Year after year he had indulged himself, mostly with the owner Miss Belle herself. Until a murder on the premises. The victim was a Negro—somebody Jefferson, from across the river—but nonetheless the scandal made the papers, and the police were involved, at least lackadaisically. Aristide had his reputation to protect, and he was getting older.

Slights to his wife weighed on him; injustices in the community ate at him. Like the growing, and to him galling, list of strictures which were being put into place by the city fathers. Yet, to speak out might jeopardize his standing—especially at the moment in 1914 when he had vied to become president of the bank. Thus, when it came to an ordinance to keep Negroes from driving motorcars on main streets, Aristide had reluctantly raised his hand along with everyone else on the council. An exception, which he urged on the assembled, was for those blacks chauffeuring the white owners of said vehicles. Aristide made sure Cleveland learned to drive the Ackermanns' Hudson as expeditiously as he did. Still, he was disappointed in himself.

Things got worse. About the time the flu epidemic flared, vigilantes tarred and feathered a local black doctor. Cleveland had whispered the news to Aristide on the way to work one morning, lamenting that the unsuspecting physician was the only one who knew what to do for his lumbago as well as for the flu sufferers.

"What's to do, Mr. Aristide? A lot of sick folk, and some be real scared for being roughed up themselves and Doc Miller, what ain't done nobody no harm."

That wasn't the end of it. Several other prominent blacks—a dentist, a pharmacist and an attorney—were similarly badgered. Aristide scoured the paper for reports, but found only scant mention.

"Been searching for an explanation as to why this Dr. Miller was banished from the city limits. Anybody know precisely his misdeed?" Aristide tossed out as the next town council wound down, careful to keep his indignation in check.

Several of the attendees, heretofore itching to get to their own offices, stopped dead in their tracks and sat back down. The mayor took a couple of deliberate puffs on his pipe.

"He was uppity, the doctor. The others too. We can't tolerate these jigaboos acting out of line." A few heads bobbed up and down. Hilliard muttered "Amen to that"; Big Ed Barrett, the beefy police chief, guffawed in agreement.

Aristide still looked unconvinced. His moustache twitched. "But what did these men do?"

Several seated across from Aristide glared.

"The mayor done told you," Big Ed, who was still standing and whose paunch jiggled when he spoke, barked. "Have you forgotten there's still a war on? With so many of our boys over there our job here—to keep order and respect for those in charge—has got to be carried out. Vigorously. Wouldn't you say so, J.J.?"

Mayor Hayes had started to stuff papers in his city-issued leather briefcase with the gold-embossed clasp. Others followed his lead, stubbing out their cigarettes or taking a last swallow of lukewarm coffee, which the A&P duly biked over to City Hall every Wednesday morning 8 a.m. sharp. At no charge. For an instant Aristide thought it would be pertinent to remind that many local coloreds had also volunteered their services on behalf of the country, but remembering how several such conscripts had been beaten (showing off to some white girl coming out of Walgreens, the papers said), he let the opportunity pass.

As they shuffled out of the conference room, the mayor assumed a more collegial stance. After all, whatever the views of the bank president, and they did seem more extreme of late, he had served long and faithfully as a councilman. "I say, Ackermann, how is your wife? Coming round, I trust."

Wanting to get away from all these people who would now judge him differently, Aristide couldn't muster the courage to say that all that could be done was being done for his wife—by none other than a black servant who refused any defense against the contagion herself and whose attentions were arguably the only thing keeping the patient alive.

"As well as can be in the circumstances," he said.

Back at the bank Aristide took charge of the property disputes that arose out of these banishments. Seems the doctor and the others had done well enough financially to own houses in the better parts of town, houses that white folks might as well occupy.

"Outrageous," Aristide fumed as the weeks went by and low-ball bids to buy the properties off the owners *in absentia* were placed. He dilly-dallied as best he could, postponing a board meeting to consider the offers (one of which, he noticed, had been lodged by none other than Big Ed) and otherwise claiming he needed more time for assessments of each lot. In the interim he pumped Cleveland for more news.

"I only hears what I hear, but no sir, Mr. Aristide, they ain't setting foot in this town again. They gone for good. And here we be with all this sickness, and no medicine-filling."

Aristide leaned forward in the open buggy and instructed Cleveland to detour by the Infirmary before going to the bank. The least he could do was cajole Dr. Knox into giving him an extra bottle of aspirin and whatever else he was treating Sophie with.

"I'll try to stop by this evening, Ackermann. Though to be safe, you shouldn't be out and about either. How is she doing?" Dr. Knox asked, his expression telling Aristide he already knew the answer.

"Not well. But whatever you can do."

"Stay by her side. That's the main thing, at this point..."

Ruefully, Aristide told himself, the flu does not discriminate. Before heading into the bank—the clock outside said 9:10—he handed Cleveland a small paper bag with the pills the wearied doctor had taken out of the dispensary.

Chapter Eleven

Aristide arrived home early, having wrapped up the sales of the black houses, however reluctantly, and without wishing his bank colleagues good evening. He had walked at a brisk pace, ignoring passers-by. Though Susanna remarked on his own tired face, he ordered her to go home, heated up the broth she had prepared and took a bowl to Sophie's room. Only the lamp on the night table was lit, but Aristide could make out the gaunt outline under the goose down. As he sidled closer, he saw a stick-like arm lying limp across the pillow. He lowered himself into the chair beside the bed and put his hand gently on his wife's arm.

One, then the other of her eyes flickered and opened. They were darker in color than Aristide remembered, but at least they were open. She made a feeble attempt to lift her paper-skinned hand. Sensing her effort, he took her wrist and raised it to his lips.

"If you can, sit up a little and sip some broth," he whispered. "I'm here to help you."

However enfeebled, she pulled her body up enough to prop herself against the pillows and took in a spoonful of the sustenance he placed between her lips.

"I wanted to tell you…" Aristide began, but couldn't arrange his thoughts. For a moment her eyes searched his face. "I wanted to tell you many things, but principally, the children are well. There's a letter, downstairs. I'll read it to you when you're better. From Alfred. The war is virtually over. His impatience to be home comes through in every line." Aristide's throat tightened but he pushed more words through. "Aurelia and James are still at their Aunt Margaret's. Soon, we'll have them back too." He blinked back tears.

Her momentary show of strength gone, Sophie sank back down, only to be convulsed by rasping coughs. Aristide froze, not knowing what to say or do, half-wishing that Dr. Knox would magically appear. But as quickly as the spell began, it ended. Lying on her back, curiously straight, she now breathed evenly, her chapped lips arranged in a wan smile.

Aristide swallowed hard. "I also wanted to say, dearest, that I love you more than anything—and need you again, at my side."

As had been her wont all the years of her marriage, Sophie struggled to mouth a wifely response. Aristide put his ear to her dry lips. "Yes, my dear" was all he could make out.

By the next morning the shades were drawn on all the windows of the noiseless house on Adams Street. Sufficient the signal. A stream of sympathizers flowed into and rather quickly out from the front parlor through the afternoon. Standing stiffly in a freshly laundered waistcoat, Aristide shook each hand and left it to Susanna to arrange the gifts of food or drink on the quickly cleared sideboard. His wife, dressed In a white lace gown, was laid out between the two front windows. Tall vases of blue hydrangeas stood guard at each side. A few of Sophie's friends paraded by the open casket but none lingered. They had been through the same wearying ritual multiple times in the last six weeks. As dusk dulled to darkness and the last carriage pulled away, Aristide knew he could delay no longer. He had to break the news to his children across the river.

As luck would have it when the call came, both siblings were out in the barn helping Curtis tend to the horses. Like Aurelia, Silver had turned his ankle in the accident. No one had ridden him and Hiram had made himself scarce ever since the sharp exchange with his mistress.

For a different reason, Curtis too had kept his distance from the Taylor place, not venturing over since he delivered the crutches. He threw himself into his work at the repair shop and otherwise helped to patch a break that had been detected in the nearby levee after that torrential rain. Though he steeled himself not to inquire, Wilena occasionally updated him on Aurelia's progress—and on how diligently she and her brother, Sarah-Lynn too for that matter, were now applying themselves to their studies.

Eventually though the rains had slacked off. The outside beckoned, and, as Sarah-Lynn had related to Curtis when he got there to tend to Silver's leg, she had gone to the barn with the idea of taking Thunder out for a gallop. That's when she noticed Silver standing awry.

"I told your mother she had to ask you to come over or it was bound to get worse. Mother told me she would ask Hiram to take a gander this morning," Sarah-Lynn snorted. "But I said if he were any good with the horses, Hiram would have noticed and done something already."

Although he feigned indifference when his mother passed on the request from Sarah-Lynn, Curtis was anything but. Of late he lay awake nights amid snarled sheets searching Aurelia's beauty for some blemish that might throw cold water on his fantasies. After all, he had long-nurtured plans, practical plans, to test his mettle in the larger world whatever its color or contour. To be out in it and of it, and to succeed at it. Without interference from anything, or anyone.

"I will go, if only to see after a horse," he deluded himself into believing, nonetheless taking a fresh pair of trousers and a clean shirt to work the next day. He would change out of his overalls and go directly to the Taylors before the sun set. To see Aurelia again—pointless, foolhardy, perilous. And yet he could not shake the thought of her. He was living on the outside of his own skin. Blind to its color.

When Margaret put down the receiver, she headed straight to the barn. In the fading light, she spotted her daughter and James swabbing out Thunder's and Flame's stalls, their clothes caked with oats. She ventured further inside, toward the rear stall. Poised on one knee, Curtis was attaching a makeshift splint to Silver's injured leg. Aurelia, her face luminous, leaned against a bale of hay, watching the procedure, the crutches propped next to her.

"This ought to do the trick, and unless I'm mistaken, you'll be able to ride him again in no time," Curtis said without taking his eyes off the horse's leg. Silver snuffled against his shoulder.

In that instant, Margaret decided she could never marry Hiram.

"Aurelia, your father is on the telephone. You and James must come immediately," she said, keeping her voice as neutral as she could. Her niece grabbed up her sticks and hobbled out, calling loudly for her brother. Curtis righted himself and along with Sarah-Lynn followed the two out of the barn and into the house.

Aurelia let out a sharp cry as her father relayed the news. She propped herself against the wall and Margaret could hear her brother over the loosely held receiver in Aurelia's hand.

"Your mother loved you. She was at peace to know you were both safe and sound," Aristide was saying.

Her hands trembling, Aurelia passed the receiver over to her brother and slid down the wall, crutches askew on the floor in front of her.

Curtis rushed past the others, crouching to cushion her fall. Without hesitating, she put her arms around him and broke into tears. James let go of the phone and knelt beside the two forms huddled on the floor.

"Father s-s-said Cleveland w-w-would be waiting at the l-l-landing, around n-n-noon," he managed to force out, whereupon Curtis gathered him into the circle. Sobs echoed through the parlor.

Margaret stood nearby, unable to intervene. Inviolate, such sorrow, she reminded herself. Even so, the scene so disconcerted her she sent Sarah-Lynn to the kitchen. "Make some lemonade, or hot tea, or whatever you can find. We all must sit and consider what to do."

Then she noticed the phone, still dangling by its cord. "Aristide, are you there?" He was.

"The service will be in the afternoon of the eleventh," he told his sister, his voice without affect. "All obsequies are being held to fifteen minutes. I don't know what the world is coming to."

"I understand, Aristide. And we're so sorry. I will ferry over that morning along with Sarah-Lynn."

Later, the five sipped lemonade and patted the collies, both of which, sensing something amiss, curled up on the sofa between Aurelia and James and buried their wet noses in the two laps. Curtis sat bolt upright across the room in a straight-back chair. Margaret knew it would be therapeutic, or at least distracting, to concentrate on logistics.

"Sarah-Lynn, why don't you go on upstairs and pull out the suitcases." Turning back to her niece and nephew, she said, "I'll make us a light supper and then you two will need to pack."

Curtis scrambled to his feet. "Miz Taylor, I will be happy to drive them to the landing, as I did before...at whatever hour."

"Yes, I would like that," Aurelia rushed to say.

Although Margaret had made up her mind to accompany them to the landing herself, something definitive in her niece's voice stopped her. She acquiesced. "Round about seven, Curtis, if you can arrange it."

Nodding, he crossed to the sofa and held out his hand to James.

As he turned and headed toward the back entrance where his own horse was hitched, Aurelia struggled to her feet.

"Wait, wait. I need to—"

James handed his sister each of the crutches. She staggered to the back door. Grasping Curtis' arm, she whispered so softly that Margaret couldn't hear her words.

"I'll get our packing underway," James said and retreated upstairs. Margaret registered the resigned note in his voice and thought it was none too soon that he and Aurelia left, although she would not have wished the reason for their departure on anyone.

The trip to the landing was bumpier than usual. At the last minute Rebel and Rover had lolloped over to be petted, school books strewn about had to be boxed up, good-byes had to be said to Silver and Flame. Curtis had to compensate by urging the horse along faster. He insisted sister and brother face each other in the buggy, ostensibly so that James could monitor Aurelia's ankle but in reality because he was afraid what he might confide were she to be seated aloft beside him. In any case, none of the three felt up to making conversation.

Once their bags were loaded onto the vessel and the captain's bell rang out, Aurelia clutched Curtis' sleeve, near desperation in her swollen eyes. "Write to me, let me know, I will miss you more than—"

His eyes darted about. Several passengers looked their way. One man with a mean-looking bulldog in tow grumbled but Curtis could not make out what he was going on about.

"I will, you know I will. But go. I have to get off now."

As the ferry pulled away from the dock, Curtis narrowly avoided a fall into the muddy water. He righted himself on the wet planks and headed straight for the buggy, calculating he'd be two hours late for work. He would make it up by staying at Mayfield & Co. long into the night.

Chapter Twelve

From out of the First National Bank, Horace Hilliard charged out onto the sidewalk, the hot-off-the-presses edition of the *Herald* under his arm. The day had dawned crisp and clear, a cobalt sky displacing weeks of slate gray. He took a puff of his cigar and, spotting a few uncomprehending shoppers, brandished the headline. In all bolded caps: "**FIGHTING CEASED ON WESTERN FRONT**." After glad-handing everyone in sight—a pertinent exercise since he had his eye on the mayor's office—he zig-zagged across the street to Yoste's jewelry store, one of the few that had defiantly remained open despite the quarantine. A silver cross encrusted with diamonds would be the ideal gift for his wife, and she could wear it that very afternoon to Sophie Ackermann's funeral. He hadn't felt this ebullient in months.

The war was over.

Amid Aurelia's sobs, James' bowed head and Aristide's blank stare, Sophie was laid to rest that same day. Well-wishers filed past the grave, pausing to drop rose petals on the coffin before moving on. Several other funerals were unfolding at that very hour in other parts of the graveyard. One couple made an ostentatious show of their commiseration, the overly-dressed wife wearing a be-jeweled cross pinned to her suit and making abundant use of her silk handkerchief. Several young ladies stepped forward to embrace Aurelia, she having limped her way to the grave site without the use of crutches.

Once back on Adams Street, gloom settled back down like dust after the carpets are beaten. At dusk Margaret quietly instructed Susanna to raise the shades on the windows while she sorted through the baskets of food and flowers on the sideboard. After a repast in which she and Sarah-Lynn did most of the eating and the talking, she turned to her brother.

"We might, Aristide, think about a letter to Alfred. It's only fair he have time to absorb the news before he returns. Mercifully the war is over and such news, sad as it is—well, at least he won't be in danger on the battlefield from such a blow."

Aristide inclined his head from the other end of the table. Watching him reflect, perhaps on whether or not such a letter would ever reach his son, Margaret thought he looked worn out, lines etched on his forehead, his hair grayer than his fifty years would warrant.

"Meanwhile, it is a day, despite our poor Sophie, to be thankful for. We should let these young people partake of it." The three cousins looked up from cold roast beef and boiled potatoes. "It couldn't hurt to let them go out, not participate in but at least observe the celebrations." Her brother looked dubious; she could almost hear his thoughts. His wife had just been buried. His children gadding about?

"I would think a stop at that lovely hotel—the Carroll, isn't it? — where they might have hot chocolate and watch the comings-and-goings. Sarah-Lynn has never seen a downtown in any proper sense."

"Oh, that would be fun, Mother. Please, Uncle Aristide! We might even see the fireworks."

"Mightn't we, Father?" Aurelia seconded her cousin. "Cleveland could hitch up the hack and wait for us. We wouldn't be out that long."

"It would be something to treasure for the rest of their lives, Aristide—where they were when victory came," Margaret added. "Not just the memory of their loss but the recollection of things to rejoice at."

All eyes at the table upon him, Aristide twisted his onyx ring. "After everything that's happened, hard to deny them. If you think proper, Margaret." He gazed at his children, his expression softening as theirs instantly became less woebegone. "Go, and enjoy yourselves. But do make Cleveland wait around the back of the hotel if all the posts are taken out front."

The night of November 11 was the noisiest any of the three had ever experienced. Cleveland took them down Washington Street past revelers with whistles and drums, martial music blaring from cafes and street corners. An impromptu parade of folks beating pots and pans wound through the main streets, shouts of encouragement coming from bystanders. "We whipped them Huns!" read one placard. Another banner, this one outside the Valley dry goods store, read simply, "4 Years, 4 Months, 31 Days."

"I be telling you, this is some frolicking," Cleveland called out to his passengers as he maneuvered the buggy along North Washington where a sizeable crowd of Negroes had gathered. He waved to a couple of acquaintances in front of black-owned Crown Drugs, then swerved to avoid a couple of tipsy old men careening across the street. Aurelia reckoned she had never set foot in this part of town. At least not on her own. Cleveland did not take them down to Levee Street, though they could hear the occasional pop of firecrackers—"Oh, let's go, let's see," Sarah-Lynn had urged—and faint strains of ragtime. Instead, he turned Bessie back up toward the Carroll.

"Don't worry. You'll like this place too. It's the most beautiful building in town," Aurelia told Sarah-Lynn.

She wasn't wrong. The chandeliers of the hotel burned brighter that evening, the starched waiters moved with greater alacrity, the guests hobnobbed with more animation. A small band performed waltzes, every so often punctuating their repertoire with a Sousa march. From a corner table, the three cousins drank hot chocolate, ate cream puffs and took in the crowd. Several couples got up to dance. At one point, Aurelia spotted Caroline with her parents but her ankle twitched and she remained seated. Eventually, James pulled out the pocket watch his father had lent him.

"You don't have to tell us," Aurelia said.

Sarah-Lynn sighed, up-ending the last of the hot chocolate. "I could stay here forever."

"And what would Thunder do, or Rover and Rebel?" Aurelia said with a laugh.

"Oh, you're right. But wait until I tell Curtis. He won't believe how beautiful this is."

Neither sibling responded.

By chance the next evening, as she aimlessly turned the pages of the *Post*, Aurelia came across a minor item. "Frolickers nearly beat one Johnny Bland, a Negro, to death in alleyway behind the Carroll Hotel." She said nothing to either her brother or her father. She did think of Curtis.

Ten days later all the talk around town was of kings and kaisers who had one after another abdicated and of Army vessels which one after another were bringing the doughboys home. The Ackermanns had not heard from Alfred since early October, but like other families with sons in the service, they figured no news was good news.

Chapter Thirteen

Tired and unshaven but otherwise unscathed, Alfred stood on the deck of the Stalwart in Le Havre counting his men one by one as they boarded the transport ship. Among the thirty-odd soldiers under his command, eighteen were fit enough to make the crossing; five others had been consigned to one of the hospital ships, the *Comfort* or the *Empress*. The others had all been killed, either during that first, ferocious encounter with the enemy near the Meuse River or later during the long months of hand-to-hand combat, trench by muddy trench, mile after dreary mile.

He flung an acrid, half-smoked Gaulois overboard into the

murky water. Among those shattered in mind or body was his friend Earl Hancock, who also, given his higher education and his dexterity with guns, rose quickly in rank, ending up a first lieutenant. The last time they had run into each other—September it must have been, *Chemin des Dames*, where a combined force of British and American troops routed the Germans—Earl and he had enjoyed a late-night cognac together. Cannon fire reverberated in the distance but so inured, they barely noticed.

"Don't know what news you hear from back home, but mine is that Henrietta is pregnant. Going to have the baby any time now."

Automatically they took their sore, booted feet off the table to raise their glasses. As he slipped out of Alfred's tent to return to his own men, Earl had whirled around, still holding the damp canvas flap in his hand.

"Whatever it takes, Ackermann, let's dispatch these Huns, and get out of this hell hole."

Not a month later Earl's entire regiment had been sidelined by an outbreak of influenza. The lieutenant, someone told Alfred, was in particularly bad shape. It was the last he had heard of his friend.

Despite an incessant drizzle, Alfred moved to the rail and watched the lights of the French port flicker on one by one. Like so many of the towns he had trudged through, this one must be charming, he guessed—at least when not convulsed by war. He took a deep breath of the bracing air, hoping the crossing would not be unduly rough.

Out of the darkness a steward shouldering a thick leather pouch materialized.

"Captain Ackermann, this one's for you," he said, holding out a letter. "The last packet before we lift anchor."

Within minutes the forlorn ship's horn sounded thrice. Despite himself, Alfred fought back tears. "It's over. Done with," he said to no one in particular, though a few other soldiers had at the last minute wandered out onto the soaked deck to watch the rooftops, France, the war itself recede in the distance.

"Amen to that," one of them replied.

Back in his quarters Alfred pulled off his boots and sat at a small desk to read his letter.

My Dear Alfred,

I write this with a heavy heart but with the hope that it reaches you before you set sail. Sadly, your poor mother has, like so many others here and, as we've read, over there, been felled by this epidemic. Though all that could be done for her was, she left us on the morning of November 9, wanting more than anything else that her children be forever safe and happy. We are in deepest mourning but please know that our hearts will be lifted when, finally, we see you again. You have been through much, I am certain, and it pains me to add to that burden. Nonetheless, your mother would want us to rejoice when next we see you—and so we shall. In the meantime, we all send our love,

Father

Stunned, Alfred sat motionless, staring out the porthole as the night set in and the ship began its labored roll over the insistent Atlantic waves. He didn't know what to feel, having been purged of normal human emotions during the last eighteen months. Though not enamored of poetry, his mind wandered to the verse he was made to recite, in front of all the proud parents and teachers, that last year in high school. A smattering of the lines came back to him: "a darkling plain," if he remembered rightly, where what? — "ignorant armies clashed by night." His male friends had poked fun at his performance; Henrietta had declared it sublime. Still, he struggled then to understand what the poem meant.

Now he knew.

PART TWO

That all the world will be in love
And pay no worship to the garish sun

Romeo and Juliet

Chapter Fourteen

Soon it would be spring. Mayor Hayes had lifted the quarantine; the soldiers had been discharged and gradually found their way back home; businesses had re-opened, boats crowded the waterfront.

For the first time since her accident Aurelia would walk rather than ride downtown, if need be insisting to Cleveland that she'd manage adequately on her own. She shoved the crutches into the back of her armoire and locked it. "Use a key so as to stifle temptation," her father had advised, now that she had inherited most of her mother's jewelry, including a sapphire necklace with matching teardrop earrings. She couldn't imagine who that had access to her bedroom might be so brazen—hard to picture Susanna with gems dangling from her ears—but Aurelia did as she was bidden. Nor had she felt up to wearing anything elaborate in the bleak months following her mother's death. Until now.

Aurelia buttoned her gray wool coat and slipped on matching gloves. Outside the half-open window, the March sky was ice-blue, the wind gusty. She touched her ears to make sure the sapphires were tightly screwed on.

When she tip-toed down the stairs, the cruel emptiness of the house newly unnerved her. For her own family, recovery still seemed far off. Aurelia's father spent most of his time at the bank or in the fields of the Big Black basin where he was experimenting with a new crop, some kind of foreign bean, if she had heard correctly. On the weekends he retreated to his study to play chess with a neighbor, drinking bourbon and eating from a tin of biscuits.

As for Alfred, ever since he reappeared mid-December, he was jittery or withdrawn. An hour after his arrival, Aurelia heard the creak of the cedar chest in the upstairs hall. A glance from her doorway revealed her brother placing his neatly folded uniform in the trunk. Occasionally, she caught him staring at everyday objects—a letter opener, the sherry decanter—as though confronting them for the first time. One night Aurelia heard him arguing with their father, something about a woman in Paris, and putting a stop to such shenanigans. At the dinner table he limited himself to neutral topics—which law firms around town were prospering, what new buildings were going up—cutting James off every time he managed to ask what it was like in Europe.

And *managed* was the operative word with regards to James. His stammer had worsened since the return from Louisiana and, despite his progress while at the Taylor farm, he struggled at school. Aurelia did her best to tutor him, writing the book reports herself and making her brother practice them aloud. The two siblings spoke only rarely about their sojourn on the other side—except for the day in February a letter arrived.

"I'm s-s-sorry," James blubbered, thrusting the envelope into his sister's unsuspecting lap. "I didn't know...I thought it was from

Sarah-Lynn." James placed the rest of the correspondence on his father's table and hurried out. Aristide looked up from his paper, glanced desultorily at his daughter but went back to the headlines. Within a few minutes Aurelia rose, inclined her head, and quietly traversed the parlor, the letter discreetly tucked within the pages of the *Ladies Home Journal*. Her heart raced.

Standing by the window in her bedroom, the door closed, she scanned the single sheet of stationery, the neat cursive, the steady hand.

Dear Aurelia,

You had asked me to write to you that morning at the landing, and so, even after all these months, I am doing so. I have thought of—rather, I think of—you often and thus I took the liberty. I trust that you are better, and that other things have distracted you, and James, from your grief.

Things are improving here as no doubt they are in Vicksburg. Mr. Mayfield has proceeded with plans to open a shop there and has called upon me to survey sites along North Washington Street and talk to banks as his representative. He is convinced that motor cars will be big business, for our people as for yours. And keeping them running even bigger!

This last reference made Aurelia take a deep breath. She read on:

In short, he has set up introductions on March 15 at the Mound Bayou Bank, the Lincoln Savings and a couple of others, all of which, I believe, are on or near Washington Street. I do not dare presume, but if you were to be on that street during that morning, a glimpse of you would suffice. And if not, so be it. My mother is set upon my going north by the fall; her people are trying to secure me a place at a technical institute in Chicago. It will be cold in so many ways, but it is a chance to do something, become somebody. I trust that you understand.

Tears clouded Aurelia's eyes.

As impatient to get on with her life as Curtis was with his, she knew that each was stymied by the other. If she didn't go downtown that day, it would, if she read him rightly, be all over. She would have to become newly excited about the resumption of dances at the B.B. Club, Madame André's watercolor classes, packing crates at the Red Cross office.

But in her heart Aurelia knew she couldn't. Love had turned her inside out, into another self she barely recognized. She circled the date in her mind. And plotted.

Out of the blue an occasion presented itself.

"She's still dejected despite the baby, but it's time for her to get out and about. Not dances, mind you, but lunches, card games, the watercolor class—with us, her friends," Caroline rattled on one February day while they were stuffing blankets and sacks of flour into boxes bound for refugees abroad. She was talking about Henrietta, who ever since Western Union had delivered that tersely worded telegram, had not set foot outside the Hancock home on Drummond Street.

Up to a point, Aurelia could empathize. She had lost her mother but Henrietta had lost a husband—and the father of her baby. She would take her friend to lunch at the Carroll; and she would make the date for the Ides of March.

Despite her closely-pinned cloche, Aurelia's hair was out of place when she arrived a few minutes early at the hotel. She retired to the powder room to fix her do. When she returned to the reception, she inquired for a table at the far edge of the dining room and sat down near the entrance to await her friend. Several travelers milled about, checking in or asking directions of the concierge. If the lunch with Henrietta went as planned, she would have a few minutes thereafter to prepare herself. She would see her friend into her carriage, check again on her own appearance in the powder room and then discreetly exit via the back entrance. Niggling, though, that last detail. In her note back to Curtis she hadn't specified at which entrance she would await him. She had simply said that on March

15th she was, by coincidence, dining with a friend at the Carroll and would be leaving the premises as the clock struck two. After struggling to get the tone of the note right—breezy without being casual—she had failed at the central purpose: where to meet without attracting undue attention. Any attention at all.

At 12:45 her friend arrived.

"I'm so glad you agreed to come out. We've all wanted to see you again," Aurelia said as they studied the menus.

Henrietta raised her eyes and took in the room. "I heard they had fixed it up. It does look ever so elegant, doesn't it?"

"Oh yes. The marble and the chandeliers add the right touch."

Within a few minutes a black waiter dressed in a bright red uniform swooped by and took their order: cream of potato soup, followed by rack of lamb, with butterscotch pudding for desert.

Over the first course, Aurelia inquired after the baby, which inspired her friend to elaborate on every milestone little Emily had met. "And, by the way, we have hired Madame André to come over next week and sketch the little thing: her mouth, her eyes, so like her father's." Here Henrietta faltered, wiping at the tears that stained her cheeks, but one escaped, dripping into the soup. "I apologize, Aurelia. I have these moments."

"Yes, I understand," Aurelia said. As Caroline had advised, she tried to steer the conversation to neutral ground. "I've been thinking myself of going back to the watercolor class. Not that I was as accomplished as you but it was such an enjoyable experience. Might you resume as well?"

"So my parents have been urging. Earl's, however, disapprove. Too soon in their estimation. In fact, the Hancocks would likely frown upon my being here with you. You know how by-the-book people can be."

Aurelia did but said nothing.

It took longer than she had calculated for the lamb. Fidgeting, she tried to catch the eye of the waiter but he obstinately went about serving other customers.

"Is something wrong, Aurelia? You seem agitated."

"No, no. I just didn't want us to have to wait unduly."

"To be honest, I don't mind. I haven't been out much—the baby and things. To see people moving about, doing things, even those I don't know, is diverting. As, of course, is seeing you." For the first time Henrietta perked up, flashing a smile. "And I must say, Aurelia, you are looking marvelous. So rosy-cheeked."

"That's because I walked," Aurelia said, laughing, glad now that her friend seemed at least temporarily cheered up.

The lamb having finally arrived, they ate in silence, listening to snatches of conversation around them and a familiar waltz played on the piano by a black musician in the lobby. Over the custard Henrietta asked after Alfred.

"Oh, you know, he's settling back into things. Joining one of the law firms in town," Aurelia said.

"The war has changed things," Henrietta said in a tone both wistful and rueful. "Remember how excited they all were? Earl, Alfred, all of them. The lucky ones, the ones who did come home, are not the same. Those who didn't..." She dabbed her lips with her napkin. "And, as you can see, things are likewise different for those they left behind."

A widow at twenty-one with a newborn, Aurelia thought. Her heart went out to her friend.

"Anyway, I do hope Alfred will call on me, on us, when he is..." Here she paused, as if searching for the right phrase, "...properly situated. He and Earl, well, we were all such friends. It does seem so long ago, doesn't it?"

"Indeed," Aurelia agreed, moved by her friend's loss but determined not to let her wallow in it. She beckoned, this time successfully, for the check.

One other thing Aurelia hadn't bargained on was the delay at the cloakroom. Several guests stood in front of them chatting as the clerk lackadaisically retrieved their wraps. By the time Aurelia and Henrietta handed him their tickets, the clock in the lobby had struck two.

Outside, pressing her hat to her head in the sharp wind, Henrietta turned to face Aurelia. "Are you sure my man can't give you a lift back to Adams Street? It's getting colder. You don't want to come down with something. This thing has lingered."

"Thank you, but no. My coat is quite warm and I have a few things to do," Aurelia replied as her friend climbed into her carriage and held out her gloved hand. But Aurelia had turned to look elsewhere. Across the street, Curtis. Pacing, intermittently eyeing the front of the hotel. Better attired than most local blacks on a weekday, in a chocolate brown overcoat with matching hat, he stood out. He stepped off the curb and bounded toward the hotel entrance.

As he approached, Aurelia looked into his eyes. But she dared not move.

"You came," he said softly, removing his hat.

"Yes, I was here anyway," she replied, her words lame before they left her lips. "I am here but I can't stay."

"Of course. You are trembling. You must be cold."

"No, yes...I mean, how are you?"

"Well. At least now I am."

"Miss, do you have a carriage?" the doorman called out. He stretched himself to his full height, squared his braided shoulders and glowered at Curtis. "Is this man bothering you?"

"There is no problem, but thank you. This man asked for directions, that's all," Aurelia replied without deigning to cut her eyes at the doorman. Instead, she pulled on her gloves and walked away from the hotel entrance. Curtis trailed a step or two in her wake.

"I must leave you now," she murmured, gesturing toward Washington Street. "But I will write."

"I cannot tell you—"

"I know."

"If you could come across the river, return, as before..."

"Nothing is as before." Aurelia raised her gloved hand again, as though to check again on her hat, but on purpose brushing the sleeve of his coat. It was the closest she could come to a caress. Before he could react, she turned on her heel and headed in the opposite direction, up the Clay Street hill toward home.

Curtis willed himself not to watch her. Instead, he hurried back down to Washington Street to meet up again with Mr. Mayfield. Together they would present the application for a loan to the third bank on their list, the First National, it being the most prestigious, best-financed—and white. As his boss had explained on the ferry over, doing their presentation to the two black-owned banks first would be good practice for their appearance in front of officers of the white-owned one.

"You talk so good, I be letting you do the 'splaining. Go off and have your lunch but mind you be out front before three o'clock. No good keeping no white man waiting," Willy had cautioned.

Cold and hungry though he was, Curtis dared not do anything to call any more attention to himself. Judging by the shoppers, the establishments along that section of Washington Street catered mainly, or solely, to whites. Only a few Negroes loitered about, keeping to themselves. He didn't want to take a chance, so he walked several times around the block waiting for Willy to reappear with his newly-purchased leather briefcase. What he did notice was cars, more than he had ever seen along the streets of Tallulah. And to a man, all the drivers appeared to be white. But Aurelia is right, he told himself—: nothing is as before. Our people will have cars too; it's just a matter of time.

Once their pitch to the sallow-faced young banker was over, Curtis and Willy rose, hats in hand, to take their leave.

"Please wait here, uh, sirs." The loan officer, whose name according to the plaque on his mahogany desk was Darrell Morrison, glanced at the paperwork in his hands. "Mr. Mayfield and Mr. Jefferson. I'll need approval to proceed."

The two would-be borrowers stood awkwardly, not knowing what to do with their arms or where their eyes should alight. A couple of young women carrying folders and affecting an air of serious purpose disappeared into a corridor at the rear. An older woman with horn-rimmed glasses pecked away on a huge typewriter. Otherwise, everyone else within eyeshot was male, and white.

"I'd hazard you fit right in, son. That was one mighty fine speech you gave. My wife, she done trained you up well." Such a compliment from Willy, and at a volume that anyone close by might hear, made Curtis squirm. That his boss introduced him as the junior partner in this repair shop or the prospective manager of the branch in Vicksburg he accepted as necessary to shore up the proposal. But he was still rattled by his encounter with Aurelia. For her sake, he did not wish to be singled out.

Within a few minutes Mr. Morrison returned, an older man with a handlebar moustache close behind. To Curtis the latter looked as if the loan officer had been importuning him about some request or other.

Willy fumbled with his hat but made no sound.

Mr. Morrison cleared his throat. "Ah yes," he said, glancing once again at the papers in his hand, "Mr. Mayfield and Mr. Jefferson. I have the honor of introducing the president of the bank. He'll make the final decision."

"We appreciate the opportunity to do business through your bank," Curtis said.

Aristide noted the young man's aplomb as well as his good looks. By comparison, the junior loan officer seemed more gauche than ever. Irritated by his own employee, Aristide decided to engage.

"Morrison tells me you've narrowed your choice to two potential sites. A warehouse you're planning to build?"

"No, sir," Curtis corrected. "Mr. Mayfield and I are in the mechanical repair business—wagons, buggies, motor cars. We are considering North Washington Street, it being, from what we observe, largely undeveloped or under-developed."

An impressive distinction, Aristide thought, especially since the young man wasn't local but had apparently assessed how rundown the businesses, almost all black-owned, had become at that end of town. On the other hand, they likely didn't know about the ordinance forbidding blacks from driving on the main thoroughfares. In addition to a loan, these two supplicants could use a good local law firm—though it was not his place, nor prudent on his part, to go out of his way for two Negroes. He could only imagine what Hilliard would have to say.

"You might want to consider an adjacent street," Aristide suggested. "Several derelict properties are located up along Jackson Street or thereabouts. Eyesores that could be remedied. Already a white-owned shop you might have noticed, Christian and Burroughs, on Washington Street. Should be cheaper, the real estate on Jackson, and more of your people would have ease of access."

Curtis hesitated. "To be honest, Mr., Mr.? —I beg your pardon, I must not have heard your name properly," he said, turning toward the junior loan officer, who had failed to introduce his boss by name.

"It's Ackermann," Aristide said, giving Morrison a bored look. He caught the widening of Curtis' eyes when the young man heard his name, but the expression was quickly gone and Aristide gave it no more thought as Curtis continued.

"To be honest, sir, we're hoping to attract business of all kinds—from all different folks. Isn't that right, Willy?"

"Like we done in Tallulah. I'd bet we have most all people's vehicles we can handle there, what with Curtis being so good with them engines," Willy added.

Aristide could understand why the older man had let the younger do the talking.

"Well, ambition is a good thing. Naturally, the bank will look over your documents. May I assume you have proper references?"

"Yessir, yessir," Willy interjected. "White folk too. Some for the work we done and some for our character. Ain't that so, Curtis? Them Bianchettis and that missus on the big farm, that missus...?"

"We should let the president, and Mr. Morrison, get back to their desks, Willy," Curtis interrupted, cutting his partner off and looking anxious to take his leave.

Aristide held out his hand and Willy hesitated but then reached out and shook it. For a brief instant Curtis searched the banker's face. Then he inclined his head in a sign of thanks. Aristide could almost hear the thoughts of the other bank employees who watched this scene from their desks—unusual for a board member, let alone the president, to take an interest in a simple loan application, especially given the borrowers in question.

Later that evening Aristide was still replaying the odd encounter. Perhaps he should have suggested the idea of engaging a Mississippi law firm. Mayfield and Jefferson were Louisiana natives and whether they knew it or not, the legal system there was Napoleonic in origin, hardly useful for what they might require to run a business in Mississippi. On the other hand, this Curtis fellow was apparently at ease across the divide, as it were. He might already have thought of such a need.

"I'm curious, Alfred, about Jeffries, Greene." His son put down his sweet tea and looked up. "I know they represent plenty of well-heeled clients, and you've been there a few weeks now."

"Your point, Father?"

"On the commercial side, do they handle any work for the coloreds?"

"Don't really know. Why ever do you ask?"

"Nothing special. We had a potential client in today—mechanics from across the river. They'd like to open a shop here. It may be more complicated than they bargained for, their being from Louisiana. Not to mention being black."

A sudden clatter in the kitchen made Alfred jump. Aurelia, reddening, studied her plate. No one at the table spoke again until James piped up to ask if he could go to the pictures the next evening with friends.

Once excused from the table, Aurelia retired to her room. As she unlatched the whalebone hooks of her Gossard, she studied her form in the mirror, her flesh thin and pale. Painfully so. Why on earth did she bother with such a punitive garment? She tossed the corset on the bed and sat down to brush her hair. And to think. If ever another rendezvous were to be arranged, it could not take place in front of the Carroll Hotel—or anywhere else so public. Too dangerous for Curtis, too compromising for her. She felt hemmed in. Like that hot night, early on during the war, when to combat the feeling she slipped out at two in the morning to run barefoot in her nightgown all the way to and around the Court House. For no other reason than the thrill of it.

A knock on the door brought her back to the present. It was James, with a book tucked under his arm, his hand on the knob. He looked at her closely.

"Did you know?" he asked.

She feigned puzzlement.

"You know what I mean. That Curtis was in town today."

She continued to brush her locks, watching her brother's face in the mirror. He stepped inside and closed the door.

"I like him too, Aurelia, but he's off-limits. Against the law, against the church, against everything we learned in school." He paused to catch his breath, arrange his argument. "Father would have you locked up somewhere, c-c-committed to Whitfield, if—"

She turned around on her stool and smiled, happy that there was one person privy to her unspoken passion, even if he was standing there to plead with her to give it up.

"He could pass if he wanted to."

James looked baffled.

"Aunt Margaret said as much. His grandfather lived with a white woman. Uncle Samuel adored him, and ignored the gossip. And Wilena—you could see it—is somehow mixed. Think about it. Their eyes for one. That makes Curtis a quadroon, at the most."

Her brother shook his head. "You can do all the math you want, Aurelia. It doesn't amount to a hill of beans. He has Negro blood. Not to mention that Curtis, in case you haven't noticed, is proud of what he is. I doubt if such a ruse has ever crossed his mind—however much he might like to be with you."

But he does, he does, Aurelia repeated to herself but did not say aloud. James was upset enough; arguing would do no good.

After a pause, she stood up and changed the subject. "So, what are you reading?"

"*Tess of the d'Urbevilles*. I'm finished but I thought you might help me with the report."

Aurelia nodded, relieved to have something less fraught to focus on.

"And, by the way," he added, "the heroine—: she reminds me of you."

Chapter Fifteen

Six months after the end of the war, Madame André's classes were again full. Most all of the young women who had devoted their energies to the Red Cross or the Salvation Army during the hostilities had returned to pick up their paintbrushes. Whatever it was that nice people had whispered about the woman—that she was the mistress of some dissolute, albeit celebrated, New Orleans painter or that she solicited, for her own "artistic ends," certain young men to pose in the nude—the rumors didn't deter respectable matrons from dispatching their daughters to her atelier. Watercolors, it was agreed among the Vicksburg *illuminati*, was a perfectly ladylike pursuit that couldn't hurt to have in one's arsenal of accomplishments. Such weaponry, especially if beauty or brains were in short supply, was *de rigueur* if said young ladies wished to attract suitors.

Aurelia did not have to angst. Polite males did not automatically turn their heads when she walked by and some females might have decried her lips as too full, but most young men found them, and her dark eyes, alluring. Several had tried, and one or two clumsily succeeded, to kiss her in unsuspecting moments during high school. If flattered by such inchoate attentions, she never let on and rarely spent more than a few minutes in front of a mirror. Until recently.

Despite James' upbraiding and her own trepidation, Aurelia dressed every day as though there might be a chance encounter with Curtis. Aristide seemed pleased when he got the bills from the House of Fashion each month, probably thinking his daughter newly caught up in the town's social whirl. And she did try to enjoy the dances at the B.B. Club and the occasional movie or play with Caroline and company. More often, though, she day-dreamed as to where she might run into Curtis; she rehearsed what she would say, what he would respond. And then she would snap out of such foolishness and will herself to take up something more productive. Anything more productive. He had not contacted her since the encounter in front of the Carroll, nor had she succumbed and written herself. Still, from snatches of conversation between her father and older brother, she gleaned that plans for the wheelwright shop on Jackson Street had gone forward—with, of all things, financial and legal help from her own family! Perhaps Curtis had put two and two together—the Ackermann name hardly a secret—and become more skittish.

One morning in May, she resumed the watercolor class, pleased to see that Henrietta was seated in front of an easel and resigned to having Caroline, at one nearby, regale them with her running commentary on the resumption of dances at the B.B. Club.

"It's not about how many times a man asks you to waltz, I keep telling Marianne, but how he holds you when he does. Presuming that he knows the steps and isn't merely holding on to you for dear life." (Aurelia exchanged a look of indulgent bemusement with

Henrietta.) "Of course, I'm not speaking about Alfred or his clique. They're adept, even if...Well, it's different since the war. They're different."

For an instant Caroline grew quiet as if she tried to pinpoint how the war had changed things. Since no one volunteered to elucidate, she soon went back to her palette, making something of a mess of a still-life of flowers in a vase. Henrietta, on the other hand, was engrossed in a rendition of Trinity Church, complete with steeple.

Occasionally Madame André would wander by to demonstrate a stroke here or apply a color there. Aurelia noticed she limited her comments to the positive, or to the diplomatic. "Permit me, Miss Hilliard, if you dip into the purple to outline the blossoms—like so." Here the instructor took up a brush to accentuate a few curved edges. "See, now they look more like irises, which is what I believe you intended."

By and by Caroline returned to play variations on her theme. "Speaking of different, our Mr. Gottschalk certainly had us fooled. Despite his fancy moves on the dance floor."

Henrietta paused from her painting. "But Caroline, I thought it splendid, the way he danced with everyone, wallflowers included. Admittedly quaint but unfailingly polite."

"Quaint, my dear, is hardly the word," Caroline lobbed back. She squiggled some pink onto her blossoms. "I was told, in strictest confidence, not only did the police find the body at the foot of some Confederate general's statue..."

"But?"

This from another of the young women who had stopped what she was doing, her brush dripping in mid-air. Madame André pursed her lips in irritation.

Caroline lowered her voice and applied a darker shade, as it were. "He left a note, but, being so *quaint*, he had written it on the finest vellum. To a young man going off to France. The thrust of the letter was—how shall I put it? —unsavory." Several additional pairs of eyes turned in her direction, Caroline made a show of concentrating on her canvas without further comment.

"Unsavory" was the apposite word, Aurelia thought, but it

applied more to Caroline than to the hapless Mr. Gottschalk, whatever his sins. Discreetly, as the other students packed up, she asked Madame André if she might switch to an afternoon class.

"*Bien sûr*, my dear. I do understand."

During the next several months Aurelia grew proficient at her easel, completing several competent landscapes. One in particular—the only one that included human figures—caught the eye of Madame André. Over tea late one afternoon, she said, "I must compliment you on that latest effort, the one of the deer in that clearing, and those two figures eyeing them." She poured the hibiscus-flavored liquid into her Dresden cups. "Something—or someone—close to your heart must have inspired you."

Color rising in her cheeks, Aurelia sipped in silence. She had grown fond of Madame André, whose every movement seemed unflustered, whose every utterance arresting. So unlike the girdled matrons in her parents' circle or the oh-so-proper young ladies of her own set. Afternoons in that oasis of color and clutter were more stimulating than anything in her own prosaic existence. In madam's parlor, silk flowers languished in vases, gilt mirrors adorned the walls. A harp, albeit with a couple of strings missing, held court in the corner. To Aurelia, it was magical.

"It's a place across the river where I was very happy," Aurelia volunteered, the touch of Curtis' hand on her arm suddenly palpable, his latest, and unexpected, letter vivid in her mind. "You might want to read this in private," James had whispered when he handed over the envelope, once again postmarked Tallulah, with no return address. *On whichever side of the river, I long to see you again. But you know better than I, it cannot be in public.* Aurelia had not known how to respond.

"And the young man? Does he actually exist?" Madame André asked as she bent to proffer a tray of freshly baked lemon cookies.

"Thank you. These smell delicious," Aurelia said, placing one on the rim of her teacup. "And yes, he does exist, over there, on the other side." To her own ear, the place reference sounded as far away as heaven.

Madame André returned to her armchair, her hand to her chin, and eyed her pupil.

"I take it your father doesn't approve—or doesn't know."

"I'm afraid no one would approve," Aurelia responded, before quickly adding, "though that doesn't stop us from wanting to..."

"Well then, you should have a place to meet," Madame André declared and offered Aurelia the use of her studio for an eventual tryst with the young man of the watercolor.

Chapter Sixteen

During that summer of 1919, Curtis made a point of familiarizing himself with the stretch of Vicksburg from North Washington Street to the bluffs overlooking the river on the southern end of town. It helped that a so-called cousin, not precisely a blood relative but nonetheless an affable old codger named Josiah, had an extra room in his shack near the cemetery.

"Quiet, and the buzzards don't bother me none. You be welcome as long as need be. Your pappy was a character. Sat right there on the porch when he wasn't raising the roof," the old man said, chuckling between puffs on his corncob pipe.

Not wanting to encourage more graphic tales of his murdered father's caterwauling, Curtis busied himself on his sojourns to Vicksburg by painting the outside of his host's place, fixing leaky faucets and oiling stubborn hinges. Otherwise, he found sufficient reason to be on-site to help transform the abandoned building on Jackson Street into a functioning wheelwright shop and to accompany Mayfield to the bank and to the law firm Mr. Ackermann had recommended.

It didn't take Curtis long to realize that the young lawyer in charge of their commercial permits was Aurelia's older brother. Curtis wasn't sure if the impersonal demeanor of this Ackermann could be blamed on his experience in the trenches or his displeasure at being stuck with black clients. Often he seemed impatient with Willy's ineptitude with the language or ignorance of the legal process. In those instances, Alfred would bite his lower lip and turn his deep-set eyes—so like Aurelia's—to the younger client as though to signal the two of them would have to circumvent the principal party to get things squared away.

On one occasion when Willy was occupied with business in Tallulah, Alfred invited Curtis to share a smoke outside the office building. With Camels in hand and only an old woman to bother them with flowers for sale, the two hammered out the final disposition of Mayfield's Vicksburg venture. Ownership would reside exclusively with Willy, the younger partner designated a paid employee. Curtis insisted the name of the company include the word *motor*—"so as to be forward-looking, fixing car engines not just wagons"—a view that seemed to impress the lawyer, although he said he doubted there'd ever be many blacks who could afford cars, even broken-down ones.

"How is it going with your first clients, the mechanics from Tallulah?" Aristide had inquired over the claret one evening as Aurelia helped Susanna clear the table and serve, as a special treat, chocolate cream cakes from Koestler's Bakery.

"Impressive, the younger one. Name's Curtis. Not presumptuous, rather..."—Alfred dabbed his mouth with his napkin as he tried to come up with an apt description—"self-possessed. Without being disrespectful."

"Don't dither, Aurelia. Sit down and eat your dessert," Aristide detoured, irritation in his voice. When she had brought her plate to the table, he continued to his son: "Well, you must be relieved one of them is so competent. If more were like that fellow, we'd have fewer troubles."

Sampling his own sweet, Alfred toyed with his father's observation, in tacit agreement that Curtis belonged to a rare breed but not convinced that he wasn't "trouble" in some other sense. He was still puzzled over the young black man's reluctance to be drawn out about his family relations with Aristide's sister across the river. All he had allowed—shifting his weight from one foot to the other, puffing on a cigarette he clearly didn't enjoy—was that his mother worked for the missus Taylor, as did he "from time to time." And his reluctance to be made a partner in the mechanics shop when Willy kept crowing that "nobody done ever fix a brougham like my Curtis" and the protégé insisting it wouldn't be fair given he was heading north to college as soon as, well, as soon as he could manage it. "He already be knowing more than most folks these parts, Curtis does, so my teacher of a wife done yammered to me over and over."

As their lawyer, Alfred declined to intervene in such exchanges between the two black clients. If he marveled at Curtis' equanimity under this badgering, as good-natured as it was, he suspected old man Mayfield had a point. Smarts in a colored man could be as much a liability as an asset.

It all depended.

After dinner Alfred put aside these reflections and prepared to go out with friends. Cards it would be, bridge rather than poker, ladies being present. If he remembered rightly, Caroline, even for the first time Henrietta, among them. Fastening his cufflinks, he wondered why Aurelia rarely seemed to socialize. Not like her before the war, or before their mother's death. But seven or eight months had passed since the end of hostilities, and things had changed yet again. Communists were seizing control in Russia and elsewhere; America could be next. Of course, this was the Deep South and, luckily, far from those anarchists in Boston and New York.

Looking in the full-length cheval mirror, Alfred straightened his spine. The Ackermann family could count on money and goods in kind—:he rattled the ebony box of tie pins and assorted rings to hear the reassuring sound of solidity—status, however, was another thing. To his generation it was no longer automatic; it had to be achieved. Newcomers—or as the good citizens of Vicksburg dismissively put it, "interlopers from who knows where"—were as likely as not to scramble for position, at the hospital, the bank, the cotton exchange, the law firms.

"*Carpe diem*," Alfred mouthed, giving his figure one last appreciative glance in the glass. His waistcoat buttoned and pocket watch secured, he headed downstairs and out the front door. The August heat still oppressive, he hurried around back to crank up his father's motor car.

Back upstairs, Aurelia heard footfalls approaching. It couldn't be Alfred as his car had just sputtered into action; her father had retreated to his study with a tin of crackers in one hand and a decanter in the other. She ran her fingers over the curves of a cut-glass container on her dresser, one of the last remnants of her mother's daily ritual. Whenever Sophie had been in a playful mood, she would dab her face powder on Aurelia's nose, declaring, with puff aloft in her manicured hand, her young daughter "a white princess," ready to be bestowed upon a worthy prince. A last sniff of the powder box, and knowing it could only be James who was now knocking at her door—so tentative in his every action—she called out, "Come in."

"You do know Father is s-s-sending me away? To Branham & Hughes, don't you?"

Hollow-chested and peach-fuzzed, James looked paler than ever, despite daily walks to and from summer school and whatever else he did outside in those long blistering afternoons. She studied his form closely, thinking he looked more and more like a starved poet.

"But only for a year, right?" (Despite her tone, Aurelia couldn't help but think strengthening of body and mind might stand him in good stead.)

"Even a month would be too long," James uttered in a voice both plaintive and resigned. "I don't want—" His lip fleering, he averted his eyes from Aurelia's face and settled them on the vials on her dresser. "Leda...elixirs of the gods," he murmured, his voice next to inaudible. "Potions that could work magic." Aurelia was about to question his meaning when he made an abrupt shift of topic.

"The other day, I bumped into our friend—Curtis—on the street. After school, not far from here. He was with an old man who smoked one of those corncob pipes." Aurelia sat up straighter. She was glad James had closed the door. "He asked after you, said we were missed back, you know, across the river."

"And what did you tell him?" Aurelia asked in a low voice, her eyes rising to meet her brother's in the mirror, beseeching him to elaborate.

"Nothing much. He didn't want to linger, the other man either. You know how it is with them, in public." Feeling light-headed, Aurelia saw her reflection nod.

"Anyway, now that I'm going away, and he's here on that wheelwright business, you need—" He glanced at the door and then said in a firm voice, "You need to tread carefully, for both your sakes. Father, Alfred...You know what they'd say, what they'd do."

Twisting on her stool, Aurelia leaned down to buckle the clasps on her shoes, and to consider a response to her brother's admonition. More than anything, she wanted to remove herself from his steady gaze, knowing he was right, knowing that she would ignore his warning, that she would take Madame André up on her offer.

"Malgré tout," she muttered to herself, remembering the desperation of the George Sand character she was reading about.

"What was that you said? Something in French?"

"Nothing, James. I appreciate what you're telling me." She was bent on changing the subject. "More to the point, I will miss you while you're away."

"Well, don't fool yourself on that score. From what I heard him and Alfred saying the other night, Father is set on your going away to college." Aurelia's mouth and eyes went round. "You're surprised? Isn't that what you wanted before, you know, before all this?"

The *before* hung in the air like a bird with a broken wing, quivering, unable to rise to a safe perch. Aurelia thought of her mother—so unerringly educated, so properly finished. What was the name of that place, somewhere in Maryland, of which Sophie rarely spoke? Aurelia closed her eyes, trying to call up the framed diploma she had only months before placed in the cedar chest along with other of her parent's effects.

"Hood College. Is that where they were talking about sending me?"

"I don't think so. I heard them mention other places. In any case, it w-w-would be far away from e-e-everything."

Aurelia stood up, unnerved by the helpless expression on her brother's face, it occurring to her that he could have benefitted more from their mother's attention than she. At seventeen, to be so fragile—and shunted off to a military academy where, what? They paraded around with heavy rifles and slept on thin mattresses, as if that could compensate for the ravages of a war in which so many had died. Alfred may have filled out his uniform as though he were born to it, but James? The physique of a poet indeed, a hungry, penniless one.

Shaking off such digressions, she righted herself as though to indicate the conversation was over. "You'll be fine there in Tennessee, James. You may enjoy getting away from everything. A new place, new people."

"Precisely what I wish for you, Aurelia. Let things go, let him go. We both like Curtis too much to get him into trouble." As she assented, he turned the doorknob and stole out of the room.

All enthusiasm for going out evaporated—friends of her father had invited her to sit in their pew at a Trinity Church concert—she read in bed for a couple of hours, the unhappily married heroine of Sand's novel *Indiana* eventually ending up—well, it wasn't clear yet. At midnight she dozed off, James' cautionary words a niggling thread running through fitful dreams of Zeus curved over Leda, feathers flying.

Chapter Seventeen

Wilena could hardly contain herself. The long-expected letter postmarked Chicago and addressed to Mr. Curtis Jefferson arrived on a Saturday in late August 1919. She dared not unseal it but she couldn't resist holding it up to the light from the window. Several pages, she judged from the weight of it, which might change the course of her son's life. A second letter, this one in a pale blue envelope with no return address, had also arrived for her son that morning. She left them both on the kitchen table, propped up against the salt shaker. Curtis wouldn't be back for hours, having ridden off with some men to check on the levees. Seems black bear or wild boar had been rooting along the berm, undermining the thickly matted rye grass. A rat-a-tat-tat on the wooden door at the crack of dawn, three whites in coarse denim and a couple of blacks hanging back, shovels and picks strapped to their mules. All business-like the whites, declining her strong coffee but telling her to rouse her son. "He knows them spots, and we got to get them critters off the top or—You mind waking him?"

As proud as she was of Curtis—why, whites as soon call upon his services as anybody, be it buggy break-downs or river banks that needed shoring up. Ain't nobody like my Curtis for figuring. Even Miz Taylor's foreman, and whatever else he was to her (none of her business but yet a shame, so inferior to her poor dead husband, Mr. Samuel) would, when not reeling from his liquor or otherwise in a foul mood, collar Curtis. Pumping him for advice on any and everything that needed a-fixin'. Never a thank you for any help, she had noticed, graciousness clearly beyond that peckerwood's ken.

That's why Wilena had set her heart on that technical college. Too many Hirams in the world. If my Curtis could go up north, get hisself an education. She scrubbed the washboard, shirts caked with axle grease, calculating how much she had saved up for this eventuality, and how much Curtis had put aside from his job at the shop. With pride, too, he had handed over the dollar bills each month, until recently.

"All that will change when he reads he's been accepted," she declared aloud, hanging the shirts and trousers and a couple of Cassie's dresses on the clothes line back of the house. In the August heat they'd be dry in an hour. It being her day off from the Taylor house, Wilena spent the afternoon sweeping and mopping her own floors, determined to stay calm as well as busy.

When Curtis did return, the full moon had climbed high in the heavens, throwing a sliver of light into the kitchen. Wilena gestured toward the two letters, making an elaborate show of polishing the copper pots and pans which ordinarily hung undisturbed over her counter top.

"For you," she said, stealing only a furtive glance at her son's streaked face and dirt-stained overalls before turning back to her task as though of the utmost importance that the utensils be burnished to a high gloss that very evening.

Without speaking, Curtis rinsed his hands and face in the sink and pulled up a chair to eat the thick sandwich his mother had placed on a chipped salad plate, one of a set Mrs. Taylor had parted with during her annual spring cleaning ritual. He munched with a deliberateness that told Wilena he was reluctant to unseal either envelope, interspersing bites of ham with gulps of milk straight from the bottle. The pale blue one he stuck straight into his shirt pocket, again without a word. The other he picked up, turning it over and over until, her elbows aching and her impatience mounting, Wilena could no longer hold back.

"Aren't you going to see what they say?" she asked, putting down her dish rag and taking a chair across the table from him.

Her tone jolted him. If he had often imagined this moment as full of excitement, he now felt disembodied, as though at the bottom of a well, no one at the top to hoist him up, reconciled to whatever fate awaited him in the depths. He rose and jerked open a stubborn drawer for a knife to rip the sealed envelope in the proper fashion. He read through the three paragraphs, his breath shallow.

Wilena held her tongue while he read. The ceaseless *kree-kree* of crickets outside the screen door was deafening.

Finally, Curtis looked up, ashamed at his own lack of enthusiasm but determined to make amends to his mother. "It's good news, Mama. I've been accepted, and they've waived the tuition fees. I'd still have to pay for the books, and the lodging, and the travel."

"That's wonderful, Son," she said, a film of tears making her eyes shine. "And don't fret about the cost. I've saved enough. And my people up there will help. You can put what you've earned away, in the bank."

He would have remonstrated over this last point, but his stomach was churning. He handed the admissions letter over to his mother and rose unsteadily from the table. "I'm tired now, Mama. We'll talk about it in the morning."

"Of course. I'll be writing your aunt in Chicago, your cousins too. They'll be delighted to know you'll be headed their way. Go, go." She waved him away.

Once in his own room, work shoes kicked off, Curtis sat on the side of his bed, his head in his hands, trying to make his queasiness pass. He could hear his mother still moving about the kitchen, pots and pans clanging, the wrench of a faucet tap, footsteps on linoleum. Within a few minutes he had regained enough composure to flick on the brass lamp next to his bed and retrieve the letter from his pocket. He read with relish, lingering over the graceful lines of her cursive, a faint odor off the delicate paper making him newly light-headed.

The contents were as he hoped, and dreaded: a time and a place to meet, alone together, unobserved. The studio behind the home of a Madame André, whoever that was, whatever that name might imply. Not far from an old Vicksburg landmark called McRaven—anyone he might ask would point him in the right direction. He thought of his father, ensnared, fatally as it turned out, in some other madam's lair. "So tawdry, a cathouse," he had overheard a cousin or other hiss in the aftermath of the elder Jefferson's stabbing. And he only twelve, clad in a hand-me-down suit, barely comprehending what his father had been up to. Bitter the memory of it all, bile seeping into his chest. He swallowed hard and drank in the words again.

Need I say that I have missed your presence and hope that once again we can be together, if only briefly. Thus, I can be no more forward than this: if you are inclined, come around 7:30 and tap on the windowpane; if not, I still pray all will be forever well with you. Aurelia.

Curtis knew every interaction with a white woman was fraught with peril; like every Negro male, he instinctively grasped that inordinate care around them had to be taken.

And yet.

He folded the single sheet of stationery, replaced it in its envelope and lay it on the night table next to his bed. He slept deep and long and hard.

Chapter Eighteen

No excuses had to be concocted to be in Vicksburg the following week. In fact, Willy had prevailed upon Curtis to ferry over daily to install windows and affix the locks to his new building. Within weeks, the two hoisted and nailed the open-for-business sign above the entrance. Mayfield & Sons MOTORWORKS it read, in bold red letters. It was Curtis who had argued that the name aptly suggested modernity. About the "Sons," Curtis was at first perplexed, since the Mayfields had no offspring.

"You, my friend, are like a son to me, and sooner or later..." his boss had said as they stood on Jackson Street surveying their handiwork.

Later in the day, having tidied up and changed into their Sunday best in the back room of the shop, they headed to the bank to pay a courtesy call on Mr. Ackermann. Rarely had Curtis so demurred but Mayfield insisted.

"He respects you. Wants you to do the talking about a story for the papers. Wouldn't work otherwise," the older man had persisted.

A couple of the secretaries eyed them yet again as they were ushered, hats in hand, into Aristide's office by a brisk assistant. Ten minutes later they were back out on Washington Street, only Curtis having noticed that Mr. Ackermann, albeit courteous, seemed anxious to wrap up the encounter. Whether the bank president was unusually busy or embarrassed by having two black workmen as clients, Curtis wasn't sure. Either way, he stepped out onto Washington Street more afraid than ever to imagine what the white man would think if he knew about his—what would it be called? —his friendship with his only daughter.

"Damn, Curtis, we be in business and that Mister Ackermann—more upright than most of them peckerwoods—be on our side. Calls for likker."

Although reluctant, Curtis accompanied Willy up North Washington to a hole-in-the-wall from which tinny music and the smell of cheap whiskey emanated. Once their eyes had adjusted to the dim interior, they propped themselves up at the bar and ordered two shots, straight up. Several regulars, slouched over their mugs and chatting with the bored bartender, eyed the strangers with lackadaisical interest. Otherwise, the place was deserted, it being not yet six o'clock on a weeknight. The alcohol burned Curtis' throat but steadied his nerves. He needed to take his leave in order to get where he had to go and not get lost in the process. Plopping a sawbuck on the counter, he turned to his boss.

"Got somewhere to be, Willy. You stay. Have another drink and remember, the dock is walking distance."

Mayfield grinned. "Already making friends here, I take it. Them ladies, city ladies, mighty fine. Can't say as I blame you." Rather than object, Curtis nodded and headed out.

Trying his best not to appear up to no good by hurrying, or

loitering, he made his way up the hill away from the main commercial streets and past an imposing church whose steeple bells began to chime as he skirted the façade. The half-hour, he figured. He was already late, the distances around the residential part of town greater than he had estimated. Nonetheless, he forced himself not to pick up the pace. Don't run, don't look suspicious, don't eye anyone—don't, don't, don't.

As he crossed Cherry Street, an open car came out of nowhere, going thirty-five and honking.

"Outta the way, nigger," a young man on the passenger side squawked as the occupants whisked by. Squeals of laughter from the girls in the back seat. Curtis lowered his head and kept moving, turning down the descending slope of Harrison Street. A couple of horse-drawn buggies went by but otherwise the street was deserted, just two old women tending their flower gardens. He stared at the stretch ahead, not daring to rest his gaze on anything other than the numbers on the houses. Within minutes, he was in front of 107, and, afraid to pause, darted down the side path edged by a luxuriant fig vine. As instructed, he rapped on a dilapidated door half off its hinges. From the inside, he heard rapid steps.

"You came," Aurelia whispered, looking up into his olive eyes. He swept past her as she shut the door and turned toward him. Neither spoke as he took in the helter-skelter of canvases and easels, empty stools, and smocks hung against the far wall on wooden pegs. She took Curtis' hand and led him past a work table piled with half-empty jars of paint toward a chaise lounge wedged in the corner, an overstuffed chair to its side. A faint odor of turpentine rose to his nostrils. As she positioned herself on the low-slung chaise, the last rays of the sun lit her porcelain face. She looked up.

"Please," she murmured, motioning for him to take the chair next to her. They say in awkward silence until Curtis broke it.

"How is your brother now?" he ventured, trying his best to keep them both from being overwhelmed by the occasion. Aurelia looked startled, like a deer suddenly aware of human presence. "We met, by chance, on the street. He said he was being sent away, to a military academy. Didn't seem altogether happy about it."

"You're right. Father thought it would be best for him, though...well, we shall see," Aurelia managed, her words disjointed. She clasped her hands tightly in her lap and re-crossed her feet.

Curtis nodded, feeling he should offer something to cheer her. "Perhaps the experience will give him more confidence. Not likely a whim on your father's part. He seems quite a—quite a considered man."

"Indeed," she replied. She looked as if she wanted to say something further, but didn't. For his part, Curtis wanted but did not dare ask to whom this unlikely place belonged nor what Aurelia had to do with it. For a few minutes, awkward silence descended once more while Aurelia's eyes looked everywhere but into his.

"I need to tell you something else," Curtis eventually resumed. "Something that I may have mentioned to James." For the first time she looked straight at him. "I too am going away. Chicago. Remember how my mother went on about my becoming an engineer? That teacher, Mrs. Mayfield, too. You met her at the Bianchettis."

Aurelia's breaths came fast and she nodded. He pretended not to notice how a few tears beaded in her long lashes.

"If I don't apply myself now—a new decade, a chance for me to make something of myself, up north, where..."

...we wouldn't have to meet in secret.

He saw understanding in her eyes, but all she said was, "An excellent plan," and ran the back of her hand against her nose as the tears stained her cheeks. "It's just that you'll be far away, and for such a long time. I won't—"

Curtis dug in the pocket of his trousers and pulled out a folded handkerchief. "Please don't cry, Aurelia," he whispered, and hearing himself utter her name, he succumbed, taking her wrist and putting it to his lips. She turned her hand over and felt his cheeks, his forehead, his eyelids. The gesture, more electric than anything he had ever let himself imagine she might do to him, left him taut with desire and drained of energy.

For the life of me, we cannot let this happen. Instead, he pressed his own strong fingers into her temples. "However forbidden, this is not wrong. And I won't be gone forever."

"I know. Or, I will find you, there," Aurelia returned, resolve if not outright defiance in her voice.

Knowing that if he kissed her, he wouldn't have the will to leave, Curtis dropped his hands from her face. He forced himself to stand. "Don't move from here for three or four minutes. If you pass me in your carriage, do not call out. I will know you are there. And you will know I am thinking of you."

Darkness fell.

Aurelia sat counting the seconds after Curtis stole out of the studio. Were it not that her father and brothers would wonder what had become of her, she would have curled up on the chaise and slept through the night, to be awakened by the smell of Madame André's hot coffee and whatever sweet she might have conjured for the two of them to share. What confidences too each would then divulge and what sympathies would be extended one to the other. But then came the hollow beat of hooves and a familiar voice: Cleveland's. She gathered up her handbag and a leather satchel with her recent sketches.

Outside, rain pelted the stone walkway. She hurried to the street and into the cushioned safety of the carriage. With a giddy-up from Cleveland, the drenched horse set out at a clip. Aurelia shook out her wet skirts and peered through the window at the foggy corona of street lights along Cherry. Other hooves swished past them. A car horn honked in the distance. No sign of Curtis. Perhaps he had veered into a back alley or taken cover under an unsuspecting ledge. If only she could catch sight of him—so much she hadn't said while they had the chance and now there might not be another, for however long she dared not think.

"I knows what I knows, Miss Aurelia," Cleveland clucked as he handed her out of the carriage on Adams Street and walked her, umbrella overhead, to the front door. "Lawd help us." She feigned surprise at this exhortation but that only seemed to embolden him to persevere. "I seen him, and I be certain as the day is long that no good gwine come of this here business."

Instead of responding, she turned the key in the latch and bid the old man goodnight. Giving off an audible grunt as if to signal he knew his admonition fell on deaf ears, Cleveland shambled down the stone steps to stable the bedraggled horse.

"We didn't wait dinner. Susanna, however, left a plate for you in the kitchen."

Reproving, Alfred's voice confronted her, as though to convey that he himself would not have been as accommodating as their servant. In the brightly-lit vestibule, his eyes had a peculiar glint as they scrolled from Aurelia's dripping curls to her mud-caked shoes. She fumbled for an explanation but her brother side-stepped her, selected an ivory-handled umbrella from off the hat rack and turned the brass knob of the front door. What had moments before been a squall had morphed into a soft mizzle.

"Oh, and once you've supped," Alfred added as if an afterthought, "Father would like to see you in his study." The door slammed. Aurelia stood shivering, her feet squishy in her high-tops, her gray silk blouse and black skirt streaked with water.

Ruined, she thought.

Chapter Nineteen

A few minutes later Aurelia stood on the threshold of her father's study, having downed a glass of sweet tea and taken a few bites of cold chicken and sliced carrots. The remainder on the plate she scraped into the garbage and then tidied herself in the downstairs bathroom. Her hair had dried but the curls had tightened, giving her the visage of some distraught medieval virgin, Flemish or northern Italian—she couldn't recall which—from one of the picture books Madame André kept on what she referred to as her Louis Philippe table. She shook her head to loosen the tangled ringlets and pinched her cheeks to encourage color.

As she stole down the hall, every floorboard heralded her

approach.

Her father was hunched over his roll-top, which was piled higher than usual with ledgers, papers, books. He was writing, occasionally dipping his pen into the inkwell to his right.

"You wanted to see me, Father?" she ventured, clasping her hands in front of her but not daring to invade his sanctuary. She knew her father hated to be disturbed, even by his wife, who had only after long practice determined when an occasion to do so was propitious, and to her advantage. Her children had never become so adept, or perhaps Aristide had never countenanced their interruptions with the same patience or pleasure.

He was so concentrated, he barely sensed a presence in the open doorway. But tonight he did have something to get off his mind, or rather, as *paterfamilias*, he did have a decision to inform his daughter of—though she should have been at the dinner table to be so instructed and not poking her head in now at such an hour. She was becoming erratic.

That's why he was newly glad to have taken the steps so long contemplated, but like so much else in the last few years, postponed or abandoned or forgotten. The war, Sophie's death, and machinations at the bank had all done their part to scuttle his best-laid plans. Placing his pen on the inkwell, Aristide turned in the high-backed swivel chair and pushed his eye-glasses up on his forehead. For an instant he was taken aback. Poised as she was on one foot, her hands locked together, hair glistening, she, his only daughter, could have been his wife. Rarely had he remarked the striking resemblance, though the light in the hallway likely reinforced the *chiaroscuro* effect. Yet again it hit him how much he missed his Sophie, how much he had relied on her counsel and basked in her approval.

It was not that the children were disappointments—definitely not Alfred (however tightly wound and sealed-off from others), who had become more single-minded in his ambitions than he himself had ever been—but his younger son was another matter: soft like Sophie on the outside but without her backbone. As for Aurelia, she was too independent-minded for a young lady of her breeding. What was it she had had the audacity to argue at the table the other night? That those suffragettes were courageous, and right, irking her older brother no end. Whatever controversial opinion his dear wife would have harbored, she would have never deemed it proper to disagree openly with the men of the house, most assuredly not at the dinner table. What other so-called advanced positions his daughter entertained he dared not imagine. And yet, Aristide did not find her views or her behavior entirely unattractive or unjustifiable. After all, he had always prided himself on his own liberal ideas. Wasn't that what elevated him above many of his peers, that he too espoused, occasionally acted upon, the progressive opinions of the day?

Though not of late. He had overheard the gossip at the bank—that he, the board's president by God, had started to cater to blacks, loaning sums at rates hitherto reserved for white clients, and for that matter attracting too many of the former and not enough of the latter while other board members were forced to take up the slack with disproportionate energy. Nor was he unaware of the general consternation whenever those two Negroes from Tallulah—"Ackermann's motor mechanics," the snooty designation from Hilliard—shuffled in, hats in hand. For those two in particular, he had gone out of his way, lining up a law firm (the one in which his own son was a junior associate) to handle their venture in Vicksburg, even making a visit to the building site during office hours to check on "the bank's investment."

To cap it off, he had happened by the doorway of a seldom-used back office on his way to return some deeds to the vault one afternoon. When cigar smoke reached his nostrils, he discovered the impromptu gathering of his colleagues and heard a peremptory voice he recognized as that of Caroline's father.

"Out of line, but not likely to get out of hand. We'll see to that," Hilliard was promising in what had become his increasingly authoritative, and to Aristide, insufferable tone. How dare his colleague so overstep his bounds, and yet, what defense could he mount? He had, consciously or not, favored the few blacks who had had the wherewithal to approach the First National. They too, he believed, had a right to get on in life, even if on a different, lower plane. Not every customer could be that white fellow who came up with the idea of bottling Coca Cola, and whose business Aristide had singlehandedly landed for the bank and seen flourish. (To his dismay, he had of late been obliged to remind colleagues of his so-called "coke coup" when called on the rug for his more questionable loan prospects.)

His daughter cleared her throat. Aristide dragged his thoughts back from the insurrection he had stumbled upon at the bank.

"Should I come back later? I must be disturbing you." Aurelia stood stiffly, her head bowed as if braced for a blow, the way she used to as a child when she had been sent to him in punishment for some transgression.

Aristide allowed himself a brief smile of satisfaction at her meek demeanor. His eyes, however, had come to rest on the mud-spattered hem of his daughter's silk skirt.

"Quite a storm from the looks of you," he said, beckoning her to take a seat on the couch across from his desk.

"No harm done. Cleveland fetched me," she replied while crossing the carpet. Once seated, she spread out her skirts and crossed her feet at the ankles, glancing at the clock on the end table—the one with the globe that revolved with the hours. "Amazing how your clock keeps ticking after so many years," she observed.

Sensing that he was being humored or purposely distracted, Aristide twirled his moustache, toying with the pros and cons of investigating his daughter's unexplained whereabouts. He was entitled to know. On the other hand, Aurelia had been brought up properly—bless Sophie for attending to that—and she was no longer a child. Almost twenty, and presumably with a head on her shoulders, an Ackermann head. Moreover, things had changed since the war. Progress—he extoled it, suffered the sneers of the small-minded for it—was being made on many fronts: cars for the middle class, soda in bottles and, for heaven's sake, shorter skirts for women. (He approved of this last too!) Assessing the stubble on his chin, he decided to drop any inquiry into his daughter's comings and goings and proceed to the matter at hand.

"I invited you in here for a reason, Aurelia Anne," he commenced, dropping his voice a register. His eyes searched hers. She was sitting as upright on the sofa as Alfred did at the dinner table, perhaps too rigidly for a young woman. Still, he'd not criticize her posture—he had this business to get off his chest, and then back to his own pressing affairs.

"You do remember how we spoke, your mother and I, about furthering your education, do you not? That college might be the appropriate next step for you, and that you would be pleased for us to look into the matter?"

Silence.

More closely now, Aristide scrutinized his daughter's flushed face and disarranged hair, wondering if he should revisit the idea of demanding her whereabouts after all.

"You look discombobulated, Aurelia."

"Oh no, Father, or rather, yes, I am surprised, in that it's disconcerting, that is," she went on, brushing an aberrant curl off her temple, "I hadn't entertained such a prospect for some time, but, well, I have kept up with my French, and my music, though not as proficiently as mother...Be that as it may—"

Unable to abide the jagged cadences and random gibberish that came out of the mouths of young women these days, his daughter, alas, included, Aristide cut her off.

"Enough, Aurelia," he snipped, glancing away at the far window. "Your preparation is sufficient for what we have in mind. To be clear, I've not done this entirely on my own. At one point your mother enthused about Hood—the institution she attended in Maryland—but not long before she...Anyway, I distinctly recall her harboring second thoughts."

For a moment Aristide was distracted, trying to pinpoint what it was that had made his wife reluctant to recommend her alma mater for her daughter. Something to do with her own vaguely described experience there. Confound it, he groused to himself. Women! Either spewing nonsense with utter conviction or jealously guarding secrets they have no right to hoard.

"So, do I understand you would rather see me go elsewhere?" Aurelia asked.

"Precisely. I've discussed it with your Aunt Margaret, whose years at Stephens—not far from St. Louis—stood her in excellent stead. I dare say my sister could never have run the farm so expertly, especially after Samuel died, had it not been for her studies there."

"Whatever you decide is best," Aurelia replied, though she couldn't immediately imagine what her aunt might have learned in college that helped her to put up fruit preserves or wrangle the hired help. After a pause: "We became very fond of Aunt Margaret, James and I, last autumn. If going to Stephens might help me emulate her, then that would be a positive."

One fewer problem to deal with, Aristide thought, delighted to hear his daughter accede to his wishes.

"That settles it. I'll write to the college administration and we'll aim for you to matriculate spring term."

Her expression blank, Aurelia nodded in response. When she turned to leave the room, Aristide glanced at her water-spotted outfit. He added a footnote.

"The weather will be colder up that way. A shopping trip to New Orleans will be arranged. Alfred will accompany you there, you two can stay with your aunt and uncle, and then he'll escort you by steamer on to St. Louis."

His daughter closed the door in her wake, and Aristide returned his attention to the arguments he was marshalling against his so-called friends at the bank. So what if his lending practices involved catering to a few Negroes with gumption. How could it be improper or unprofitable to encourage a new business enterprise? Automobiles—engines—tires. That certainly was a line of reasoning to be presented at the next board meeting. Investing in people with vision, skills, ambition. Especially in someone like—what was his name? Curtis, the mechanic from across the river who was more impressive than many white clients he dealt with. Or, (and this he wouldn't utter aloud), as clever as many of his own colleagues, including that conniving son-of-a-bitch, the would-be-mayor, Hilliard.

PART THREE

L'Homme ne peut découvrir de nouveaux océans tant qu'il n'a pas le courage de perdre de vue la côte.

(Man cannot discover new oceans unless he has the courage to lose sight of the shore.)

André Gide

Chapter Twenty

"You look so much like your mother, Miss Ackermann," the clerk in the dress department of D.H. Holmes remarked as she studied Aurelia's profile in the three-way mirror. "Such style she had. Sad what happened. I read about it in the *Picayune*." Miss Markham picked up her box of pins and set about to hem the skirt her young customer had tried on. "You'd be surprised how short they're worn down here in New Orleans. I'll pin this one up and, if you and Mrs. Durrell approve, do the same for the others, except the two wool suits. More practical to leave them ankle-length."

A short time later, Aurelia's Aunt Sybil barged into the dressing room, laden with sweaters. "You can never have too many of these up north, my dear." She fairly beamed, pleased to, finally, be doing something useful for her niece, who did remind of her poor sister Sophie, arguably even prettier, less put together than her mother but beguiling in an unadorned fashion. Forlorn, perhaps, but then why wouldn't she be?

"When you two are done with the alterations, Miss Markham, do bring her along to cosmetics," Sybil said. The clerk, several pins between her teeth, nodded. "And Aurelia. I want to treat you to powder and lipsticks. Needless to say, there'll be a number of nice young men at the Comus Ball."

Her aunt had not exaggerated. To Aurelia it seemed that every young male who had made it back in one piece from the war converged on a certain St. Charles Avenue mansion to celebrate at that Mardi Gras ball. Never in Vicksburg had she seen so many together at once except at the military parade down Washington Street, the one in which Alfred had so proudly marched, the one where thereafter he and several friends had gotten roaring drunk before piling into those Army vehicles. She and Henrietta, Caroline too, had waved long good-byes to Alfred, Earl and the others as the trucks lumbered uphill and away to war.

"You look enchanting, my dear," her uncle Philip had exclaimed as they climbed into the Durrells' fanciest carriage and headed the several blocks to the party. A bright splay of winter stars lit their way.

Aurelia clutched her brother's arm as they ascended the ivy-bordered steps, glad he was her date, glad too to be wearing the pale pink rouge and lipstick her aunt had insisted upon. The rose-colored gown as well. Aurelia could feel eyes upon her, a few from behind glittering masks.

"Don't fret. I'll introduce you to a few of the fellows I know. Aunt Sybil will do the rest," Alfred whispered as they stood in line to enter the foyer. "Just smile and look pretty," he added in his annoying but brotherly way. As they made their way down the receiving line, the strains of a Strauss waltz rose above the chatter.

Mostly, the young men were polite and most knew how to dance as well as, if not better than, their peers upriver in Vicksburg. One led Aurelia in an energetic foxtrot around the crowded floor. By the time it was over, she was breathing hard, not having had ever to concentrate so strenuously at the B.B. Club.

"You dance nicely, Miss Ackermann. Very light on your feet." Such compliments, uttered with every nuance from bland formality to outright flirtation, were bestowed by all her partners, except by one. Unlike the others, this one regarded her with a bemused air. He corrected her footwork. "This is where you could pause on the beat and pivot on your heels," he explained during a Viennese waltz. Aurelia paused as instructed but did not hazard the pivot.

"Where exactly did you meet my brother?" she asked, more out of nervousness than interest.

"During the war," he said, distracted, having returned his gaze from the far end of the ballroom. "I was stationed in Paris. Your brother was on leave from, well, wherever." He stared off at the other dancers. She declined to pursue the topic, it being tacitly understood that few men wished to dwell on their experience overseas. Rather than escort her back to her place next to the Durrells, the young man held on to her arm as the band segued into an upbeat number.

"We'll assay the two-step," he commanded, edging her back into line of dance, which by that time, given the free-flowing drink, had largely dissolved. Aurelia struggled to follow his lead, intent upon her feet, unsure what, if anything, she should say.

"Alfred said you're headed up north to college. I forget where."

"Missouri, though I'm not sure one would refer to it as the North." For the first time, she looked up at her partner's face, his thin lips fixed in what appeared to her a self-satisfied smirk. "Well, with respect to New Orleans, or your Vicksburg, I suspect that you will find it very much the North."

"Not that I'd be bothered. The whole idea of college is to enlarge the mind, wouldn't you agree?" (She couldn't summon the name of the tune they were playing, but she did recall that her brother had introduced his friend as Charles something or other.)

He appeared to turn her retort over. "As long as it is not so enlarged, dare I suggest, as to no longer be able to fit within the confines of the circles in which you belong, Miss Ackermann—Aurelia, isn't it?"

"Oh, I don't know—Charles. Perhaps the idea should be to extend the confines of one's society rather than squeeze oneself back into some sort of straitjacket," Aurelia heard herself assert. She blushed, thinking suddenly of Curtis and embarrassed that her words came out as pretentious or too antagonistic for the circumstance.

"An ambitious notion, Miss Ackermann," Charles returned, in a tone to put an end to the matter, all the while maneuvering her through the chatterers and back to her table.

Caught up in conversation with other guests, the Durrells failed to acknowledge the young man. Aurelia thanked him and sat back down, glad to have a moment to recuperate. She only learned his last name later that night.

"Oh, that Truard boy you danced with. What did you make of him, Aurelia?" It was her aunt who broke the silence as the carriage made its way down the nearly deserted avenue around two in the morning. Aurelia had been staring out the window at what few lights were still on inside the stately mansions they passed, and what few revelers were at that hour still carousing. Alfred looked toward his sister.

"Oh, I don't know. I danced with so many. All very nice. If anything, he seemed cocky."

"That's the family money talking," Philip interjected. "Though I'm guessing a goodly portion has already been squandered."

In the moonlight Aurelia could see a flash of impatience cross her aunt's face. She was going to add that she detected something dissonant about the young man, but thought better of implying that she had been intrigued enough to notice.

"Let it be, Philip," Sybil said. "Charles Truard is still his father's son, and, like Alfred, a lawyer. He may very well buckle down and make something of himself." Her husband shrugged, too sleepy or disinterested to remonstrate. "In due course," she added.

Turning to her brother and a subject she would not have broached were it not for the last flute of champagne she had imbibed, Aurelia inquired about the encounter in Paris.

Alfred shifted his weight and frowned.

"Nothing really. Charles—C.T. we fellows called him—did me a favor, that's all. Extended my leave." He fixed his stare out the other side of the carriage. "*Ça suffit*," he muttered under his breath.

Chapter Twenty-One

"Ça suffit, ma petite amie," Claudette commanded as she peered over Aurelia's shoulder at the book her roommate was poring over. "*Il y a* dancing, and men and boo-sing," she went on, twirling now in front of her companion and unaware of or unconcerned about her colorful mispronunciation. Or her linguistic mélanges.

Aurelia smiled, placed her pencil inside the page she was focused on and lay *The Decline and Fall of the Roman Empire* atop a pile on her desk. She knew to remonstrate with or to ignore Claudette was well-nigh futile. Besides, she needed to take a break before exams, and despite their differences in temperament, she thoroughly enjoyed her exotic roommate's company.

For three years they had roomed together, at first on the small leafy campus where hall monitors, as in older ladies with the sole purpose of protecting the virtue of their charges, policed their comings-and-goings. For the past year, they had ensconced themselves in a well-appointed private boarding house not far from St. Stephens.

That Aristide had allowed his only daughter to live off-campus with another young woman—from Chicago, that den of iniquity however wealthy her parents—was a minor miracle. But Aurelia saw that he had been charmed by such an unexpected personage the summer break Claudette had accompanied Aurelia home for a visit.

"How droll your moustache—so *distingué*," the guest had flirted when first introduced to her host. Aristide had stroked the graying bristles above his lip as though for the first time, and that very evening made out a check to the owner of the boarding house to cover the entire upcoming year of Aurelia's schooling.

Still, Aurelia spent their visit home to Vicksburg hoping Claudette would make no mention of the many letters she received postmarked Chicago. She had done her best to keep her sporadic correspondence with, and her feelings for, Curtis to herself, though Claudette was, despite her incessant chatter, keenly observant.

"My dear Aurelia, it's the 1920's," the girl had said when Aurelia broached the subject that first afternoon of their summer visit. "The war is over, the rulers have fled, the world belongs to us. All those sonnets you love, what do they invite readers to do? *Carpe diem, carpe diem*." This Claudette declaimed with arms outstretched, palms up as if the very gesture would summons the shade of some long interred metaphysical poet. To cap it off, she lit a Lucky Strike and blew smoke toward the ceiling of the Ackermanns' parlor. "But I will say nothing to your papa."

Aurelia had smiled ruefully, knowing then that she still hadn't the courage to divulge, even to someone as uninhibited and unprejudiced as Claudette, that the distant object of her affections was off-limits in the most immutable of ways.

Alone that evening back in the boarding house and exhausted

by her attempts at deconstructing the Catiline Conspiracy for the third-year final the next day, Aurelia pulled out the packet of letters she had cached in the back of her desk drawer. Two, starchily worded but affectionate, were from her father. Several others were from James, who, from what she could fathom, had resigned himself to the rigors of Branham & Hughes. Those from Curtis were wedged in the middle, in case prying eyes alighted on her trove. She singled out the latest, dated April 6, 1923, and poured over the contents for whatever previously missed signs she could extract.

Dear Aurelia,

Though I have commented on it before, you'd be amazed at how frozen things still are here, the weather keeping me indoors and fixed on my textbooks enough to satisfy most all my professors. So much so that I am happily on track to—as they say here— "ice my exams," which will be a relief, and, as you can imagine, make my mother proud. Speaking of whom, she is still working for your aunt, and says both Mrs. Taylor and Sarah-Lynn (so tall, so grown up, I'm told) are well. My little sister, too. You'll remember her, Cassie, from that night in the barn...Turns out she's engaged now to a doctor from Monroe.

Need I repeat how much I think of you—and how much a visit here would mean to me? Chicago is immense and anonymous. City folk, I have found, are, if not better than they are down South, at least more distracted, caught up in their own affairs. Is not your friend Claudette from here? If she could not accommodate you, perhaps I could arrange something with a few young women I am acquainted with.

My plans after graduation are up in the air but a few offers of employment have already been dangled. Still, I think of home and people I love, so it is hard to settle on anything that would keep me so distant. Despite the dangers.

As ever, I await word from you.

Curtis

Aurelia sat listlessly, hearing only the melancholic strains of "All

Alone" from the boarder's room down the hall. When the phonograph stopped, she re-folded the two sheets of stationery and slipped the letter back into the pack. A month had passed but she had been at a loss to respond. If her perspective had been enlarged by three years "up north," the experience had not made her notably braver about defying her upbringing or dashing her father's expectations. And yet every fiber of her being called out to unite, however briefly, with the man she loved.

"Curtis," she whispered, to the uncaring walls, the blank windows.

To her astonishment, Claudette the very next day made the whole thing plausible. "Come home with me, after exams of course. My parents won't be a problem and we can celebrate. You like?"

The unexpected invitation came as the two rushed across campus, Claudette toward the physics building and her most difficult exam—the sciences were not her forte though the basic principles of the universe were being required of all the young ladies—and Aurelia toward the humanities department where she'd be interrogated on 2,000 years of world history.

"I'd love to. I must ask Father but he was so charmed by you I'm sure he'll consent," Aurelia hastened to respond.

"Don't get excited. I know there's someone you want to see there—and don't worry. I can keep a secret though I can't imagine...Well, *quel que soit*, you are the most exasperating person. What I'm trying to say is, he should be more excited than you are. That's how you have to deal with men."

Aurelia shook her head, fighting back the desire to hug her roommate. "I'll ring my father this evening and that way—"

"Dass ist genug," Claudette chuckled, peppering her speech with foreign expressions, something she did whenever highly amused or embarrassed. "I am glad to make you so happy. I should have done it sooner." She gave her friend's arm a squeeze. "But now, it's time to concentrate. Let's do well and no one will be able to deny us—anything!"

Chapter Twenty-Two

Hats. In their thousands, Aurelia calculated, as men materialized from off the platform of the El, striding purposefully toward offices in the Loop. Soberly suited women too, also wearing hats, some tilted, some with veils—all apparently pinned expertly to keep from blowing off in the blustery wind off Lake Michigan. Aurelia watched the parade of bobbing heads from the window of the Nowitskis' high-rise apartment building.

"You must make Aurelia another blintz. And more coffee to pour for everyone," Claudette's father called out to his daughter as he rattled the pages of his Polish newspaper and lit his first cigar of the morning.

"You mind not?" he asked in his heavily accented, and only rarely attempted, English. Without awaiting a response, he struck a match and puffed away. Claudette had told her that Mr. Nowitski, a prosperous European arms dealer turned Midwestern junkyard boss, was not accustomed to being disobeyed, certainly not by women and never in his own home. Still, he seemed affable enough, with expressive hands and a twinkle in his eye. He addressed his wife with the expression *kochanie*, which Aurelia intuited as a Polish endearment.

"*Ça arrive soudainment*," Claudette shouted back from the kitchen, having reverted mostly to the French her mother spoke, only rarely, in deference to Aurelia, addressing her father in his native language.

By contrast, Mr. Nowitski's wife was more demur in her manner, sensual in her movements. To Aurelia's eye, Claudette had inherited the allure, without, as yet, the weight her mother concealed beneath expensive clothing.

With a gracious smile, trying to formulate something neutral to say to her hosts, Aurelia returned to the table and downed the last few drops of the strongest coffee she had ever tasted.

"*La domestique*. Her day off," Claudette's mother announced in explanation as to why Claudette had been tasked with putting together the breakfast.

"Not a problem, Madame Nowitski. The coffee, *c'est delicieux*."

Rarely had Aurelia felt so inadequate in making small talk, but sensing that such was a burden, as well as a novelty, for both the Nowitskis made her efforts that much more labored. Damn the blintz, she thought. She couldn't wait for Claudette to reappear.

Putting his paper down, Mr. Nowitski tried his guttural best to be sociable. "Your first time Chicago?" he managed, eyeing their guest with the kind of interest one might bestow on a cat that just happened to wander in. "You like?"

"*Oui, si,* I mean yes, it is. Fine, that is," Aurelia stammered, not knowing what to add, having seen so far only the half-deserted train station at midnight and the inside of a speeding taxicab. She wished herself back at the picture window.

"*Bien*," Mrs. Nowitski interposed. "*Pas Paris, ni Warsavie, n'est-ce pas, mon cher?*" she said. He inclined his head. "*Mais*, still, many things to do here. Claudette and you—to have fun. Young."

However telegraphic her discourse, Mrs. Nowitski's views were, to Aurelia's mind, sensible enough.

"Yes. I am looking forward to sightseeing—and I appreciate your hospitality," she replied, exaggerating every syllable.

Both Notwitskis seemed to register the compliment as having put a welcome close to the conversation, such as it was. When Claudette re-entered bearing blintzes and the newly filled coffee pot, her father rose, muttered something in Polish, and took his leave. Aurelia accepted another pastry and a second cup. Claudette and her mother conversed briefly in German, something, Aurelia intuited, about places to go, what the weather might do, and how not to expect them home early. What was clear to Aurelia from the exchange was that the daughter had the upper hand in this arrangement, having grasped the mores of their adopted country more adroitly than her parents. To all intents and purposes, she was American, her parents still alien, if not alienated.

After whiling away the morning to recuperate from the train trip, the two young women set about to take in the sights downtown, first on their list the city's famed Art Institute. Then, around nine p.m. they were to meet Curtis—a rendezvous pre-arranged by phone—at what he had suggested was a nightclub where the jazz was hot and, though he didn't spell it out, where their being together would not be looked upon askance. She might want to take a cab rather than the El, and yes, bringing her friend along would be an excellent idea.

It had been almost a year since Aurelia had glimpsed Curtis, his face shiny with grease in the doorway of Mr. Mayfield's auto repair shop on a scorching August afternoon. The night before, Aurelia had insisted at the family dinner table that something was wrong with her father's Hudson—a strange catch in the engine, she suspected.

Before either Aristide or Alfred could voice their doubt she knew what she was talking about, she had rushed ahead.

"I'll have Cleveland take it around to the shop tomorrow. Better not to let things worsen," she advised, putting her dessert fork down and leaving the table before they could object.

At the last minute she had jumped in the back seat of the car behind Cleveland, whose mumbled objections she ignored. "I knows where you want me to take this flivver, Miss Aurelia, and you knows what I think about it. Besides, ain't a thing wrong with Mr. Aristide's car. I be taking extra care of it, just like I done with ole Bessie."

"Well, we'll make sure about that, won't we, Cleveland. No harm in that, is there?"

"No harm as yet, Miss Aurelia, but I ain't betting on the future."

While Curtis had poked around among the Hudson's pistons and pinions, Aurelia sat on the wooden bench reserved for customers in front of the shop. She kept her gaze fixed on her white sandals except when she couldn't resist a glance at her lover's back as he bent over in search of some loose screw. A couple of other mechanics eyed Aurelia askance. Cleveland paced up and down the uneven planks that served as a sidewalk along Jackson Street, alternately wiping the sweat from his brow and calling on the Almighty.

Within a few minutes Curtis had straightened up, banged the hood, put down his wrench and ran the back of his hand across his glistening forehead.

"Tightened a couple of bolts but everything else is in good order. There'll be no charge for bringing her in," he said, addressing his assessment to the chauffeur and at the same time opening the back door to allow Aurelia to climb in.

"At eight tomorrow?" he whispered as she brushed past him.

"Thank you for taking the time," Aurelia murmured in assent, her eyes meeting his.

During their brief tryst the next evening in Madame André's atelier, the two vowed that somehow they would manage to meet up north.

"Chicago isn't paradise but safer than here. For us too, if it were to be," Curtis had promised her between caresses.

When they prepared to part, Aurelia retrieved something from an easel in the far corner. It was a pen and ink sketch of the shop, Curtis standing beside an automobile, wrench in hand, and a young woman seated primly near the door, white sandals crossed at the ankles. The likenesses were stark. "The idea came to me as I waited for you today."

He took her in his arms, and, as he had done times before, quickly relinquished his grasp. He was gone. In a trance, Aurelia went into the washroom to splash water on her face. Against the small window high above the basin she could hear the faint sound of raindrops, the first sign that the summer heat would soon abate.

As she made her way along the slippery paving stones between the house proper and the hedge, the rattle of a window sash startled her.

"Aurelia, would you mind? Please. Come in the side entrance if you would."

It was Madame André and her tone bordered on severe. Aurelia took a deep breath and obliged. Once inside the parlor and her eyes adjusted to the candle light—Madame André was nothing if not theatrical—the first thing she took in was the glassy green ovals of Matisse. The Cheshire was perched on the arm of the divan next to his mistress. With one hand Madame André stroked the feline's back. With the other she imbibed from a crystal glass half full of sherry. Aurelia took a seat in an adjacent armchair. No refreshment was offered.

"My dear Miss Ackermann, I will be succinct, as clearly you are in a hurry." Aurelia turned her countenance, as neutrally as she could arrange it, to her hostess's face. "*Bref*, I can no longer accommodate"—here her arm left the cat and circled the air as she struggled to corral the most all-encompassing descriptive—"encounters that you are engaging in in my studio."

Though she kept hoping Matisse might bolt and upend a candle, setting all three of them on fire, reducing the house to ashes and bringing an end to what was shaping up as an excruciating exchange, Aurelia was not to be so fortunate. The cat remained immobile, imperturbable, superior to the petty problems that ensnared human creatures.

"Can I be confident you follow what I'm alluding to, Aurelia?"

"*Bien sûr*, Madame."

"Not that I wish to be misconstrued but I have a reputation to uphold. Despite the masterpieces in this room, and my own evolving *oeuvre*, you can appreciate that I too must make a living."

Aurelia nodded, not fully absorbing the point but grateful that the reference was vague enough to spare her from further shame.

"New Orleans, as you may conjecture, is a colorful place, and one can lead a vivid life there, if one is clever and creative." She paused and then continued, "However, we do not reside in the Crescent City. Vicksburg is cramped, its citizens are upright—need I spell it out? —often close-minded. Anonymity is hard to come by, and the color divide, well, *c'est immense*."

"Of course. I do know what you mean," Aurelia babbled in response, pondering what exactly Madame André had seen, or heard, or intuited. She stared at the decanter on the table, feeling that at any moment she might in her humiliation involuntarily reach for it and down the entirety.

"As for *moi*, I would have no problem—he, your *petit ami*, is very handsome—but neighbors are nosy. They sniff things out. Clearly, he is not the gardener, and if not my lover, then presumably he is someone else's that I am abetting."

A few aberrant tears trickling down her burning cheeks, Aurelia turned her head enough to take in the oil of Madame André in the nude on the wall.

"You see the dilemma I face, do you not?" the older woman asked in a more sympathetic voice.

"It will never happen again. It was presumptuous of me, and inconsiderate." Aurelia reiterated her contrition, blew her nose several times in quick succession, and willed herself not to break down. Madame André remained seated, shaking her own head as though to lament the injustice of the world around them. Once the human sobs were stifled, Matisse rousted himself, stretched his full length and jumped into his mistress's lap. Stroking his neck, Madame

André heaved an audible sigh and with her other hand indicated to her guest the front door.

"It's not exactly the Louvre or the Kunst—ah, Vienna—but it does contain some respectable Renaissance paintings. Titians and Tintorettos, that sort of thing. Even a smattering of the French Impressionists. And didn't you tell me you did watercolors back in Vicksburg?"

Aurelia could feel Claudette's inquiring glance as they crossed Michigan Avenue on their way to the Art Institute. Her hostess-cum-tour guide had been chattering non-stop, pointing out this and that landmark along the street, but Aurelia had been so engrossed in reliving that dreadful scene at Madame Andre's that she had paid scant attention.

"Is everything OK, Aurelia? You seem preoccupied. Don't worry, you will get to see your mystery beau before long, and I promise not to interfere."

"I'm sorry, Claudette. And yes, I'd love to see the Impressionists, and whatever else appeals to you. It's the city. Everything's a little overwhelming," Aurelia responded, not wanting to appear rude to her roommate, and not wanting her to pry too closely into her personal affairs. Her friend would find out the particulars soon enough.

Chapter Twenty-Three

"Menses."

Aurelia's eyes widened as Claudette blurted out the Latin, and a blush stained her cheeks when the cabbie's knowing eyes caught hers. She shrank into the corner of the back seat.

Claudette lowered her voice. "You've got to be careful. Time things right."

Aurelia squirmed, fiddling with the thin straps on the tight-fighting gown Claudette had pulled out of the closet earlier that evening. She prayed that her friend would desist in her advice. Especially with a man in earshot. She wasn't sure what Claudette meant by "timing things right," but she had no intention of asking. Besides, who said anything was likely to happen? The Cat's Meow was a club for dancing and, however much now against the law, for drinking. She hadn't permitted herself to dwell on the other possibility. What had her mother said, the year before she died, that evening Aurelia was arranging her hair-do with the silver-plated brush and comb? Something about the importance of waiting to bestow herself until the marriage bed, and being clean and scented and never acquiescing during her indisposed time. She had avoided the maternal gaze in the dresser mirror, concentrating on securing the French twist high and tight on her mother's head. For a party she and her father were attending to celebrate the departure of Alfred, and other of Vicksburg's finest, to the war. It all seemed impossibly long ago.

"Hopefully, he'll know what to do—Curtis, right?" Claudette took a jeweled compact out of her handbag, squinted at the tiny mirror and dusted her nose. She pulled out a lipstick but put it back after the cab hit a hole, evidently deciding the ride was too bumpy to re-apply it.

Ignoring Claudette's question, Aurelia turned to look out the window at the changing streetscape. The prosperous thoroughfares crisscrossing the Loop had given way to rutted streets with derelict tenements or vacant lots separated by chain-link fences. A few people milled about, especially under the street lamps, but none seemed as purposeful as those she had marveled at during their promenade up and down Michigan Avenue. They drove on and on, past warehouses with peeling paint, the cabbie swerving now and again to avoid the larger potholes. Eventually, the driver pulled up in front of a flashing neon sign and clicked off his meter.

"Whatever else, Aurelia, don't fret. We're here to have fun—and if your 'friend' does bring someone else along, I'll be happy to let you two catch up on your own. He has nearby lodgings, *oui*? You can always—*enfin*, don't worry."

Aurelia was too busy scanning the cluster of nattily dressed young men and ruby-lipped women outside the club to formulate an adequate response to Claudette's nonstop nattering. As they clambered out and stood poised on the pavement, she saw Curtis. Off to the side, next to another young man. He seemed taller, more erect. When he spotted her, he grabbed his friend's arm and hurried over.

If Claudette was stunned by Curtis, she didn't let on. Rather, once the introductions had been made, she flashed one of her alluring smiles at both the men, and without missing a beat, took the arm of Rufus, a move which encouraged Aurelia to do the same with her escort. The sound of a lone trumpet blared from inside.

"Let's go in, shall we? Can't wait to hear some jazz," Claudette said. A bored bouncer paid them no heed, waving them in with a flick of his head. This is Chicago, Aurelia thought. No one cares who you are or where you're going—or with whom.

Curtis clasped her bare arm as they weaved among tables toward an empty one in the corner. Her blood stirred.

The first thing—drinks, just in case the police decided to raid the place, though boozing was, Rufus was quick to reassure, still going on across the country, not just in Chicago. The men recommended gin fizzes—"what the ladies seem to prefer"—Aurelia quaffing hers in one go, so nervous she was.

Over the music they chatted, Curtis inquiring how Aurelia was enjoying her first taste of the big city.

"Immensely," she said, smiling at Claudette. Feeling encouraged, she elaborated. "It's like a kaleidoscope, dazzling, the patterns ever-changing, an assault on the senses." (The drink inspired her.) "Not to mention everything we saw at the Art Institute."

Curtis' face lit up. "Ah, Cézanne, the rigor of perspective." Here he threw up his arms as though sketching in mid-air. "That still-life. It's not the vase nor the apples in and of themselves that draw you in but the abstract logic behind them," he enthused. (Aurelia thought maybe his drink helped too.)

The two women smiled at each other. Rufus gawked from across the table, clearly out of his depth.

"Studying art, are you? Americans are not usually so well-versed in the Impressionists," Claudette inquired.

Curtis lowered his gaze. "Not at all. Engineering, hydraulics, things like that. It's just that beautiful lines are inspiring."

"I'll say, especially those right in front of us!" Rufus quipped, bringing the conversation back down to earth.

The ice was broken.

During the first set, and thanks to some red-hot horns, dancers took to the floor, slithering up and down each other in time with the syncopation. Later, when the music slowed, they too took to the floor. Aurelia soon found her body pressed close against Curtis. She didn't mind. Out of the corner of her eye, she glimpsed Claudette prop her half-exposed breast against Rufus's seersucker jacket. He seemed not to mind either.

"*Mon Dieu,* Aurelia. Your Curtis is *bien dans sa peau,*" Claudette observed when the two men got up between sets to order more drinks from the bar. A grateful smile crossed Aurelia's lips as Claudette added, "Whatever the color of his *peau*." When the two men reappeared, glasses in hand, Aurelia downed a second gin fizz. She felt exuberant.

In the powder room Claudette commented—loudly—that Aurelia never ceased to amaze her. She ignored the other women primping in front of the gilt-edged mirrors: a statuesque black wearing vertiginous heels and two white women with florid faces and wine-stained lips. "Nor can I blame you one bit. As the song says: 'There's Yes, Yes, Yes in your eyes.' " Nothing could deter Claudette once she got started; either she was shameless or oblivious or both.

In any case, Aurelia had made up her mind at the first sight of Curtis that she would defer to whatever he proposed, he having mentioned in that phone call to the Nowitski residence something about a friend's apartment nearby the nightclub. Weaving their way back to the table, where Curtis and Rufus were puffing away on Camels, Claudette modified her tone, adopting the one she used with her cowed parents.

"I'll tell my parents you're temporarily staying with other friends. But by Tuesday at the latest you must reappear. Promise?" Aurelia nodded her head.

By the time the musicians cased their instruments and the

speakeasy emptied out, it must have been two in the morning. Aurelia was uncertain how the two couples parted, or exactly where Claudette ended up.

"Don't worry. Your friend is in good hands. Rufus wouldn't take advantage," Curtis had assured her during the short walk from the club to a nondescript building several blocks away. "Nor will I," he added. "It will be all up to you."

The cool air cleared her head enough that she registered the significance of the moment.

Once inside, they could not resist. For hours they fastened upon each other, he slipping inside her, over her, under her, coaxing her into this position or that. She brushed her nipples against his chest, gripped his hips, clawed his spine. On and on until exhaustion. Until they could not separate their two bodies, hers milk-white in the dim light, his unburnished gold.

They got up, made toast and took a bite or two, lay back down. Countless times. They found a few red apples in a bowl, peeled and ate them. Drank what they could find, mostly water, only one bottle of milk unspoilt.

On the second night they slept off and on. Aurelia dreamed, finding herself amidst deer. The creatures slacked their thirst one after another from a lake. She stood motionless and watched. Other times, half awake, she whispered in Curtis' ear, or he in hers.

And they talked. And talked. What each liked about Chicago, what each missed, and what dreaded, about home. What people or books or music inspired them, what dreams each nurtured.

Never had Aurelia been so queried—not by her mother, nor her father, nor her brothers, none of whom expected her to do anything but conform, and keep her opinions to herself. But this man, not because (or despite the fact) he was black, but because he was who he was—a complete person, who thought of her as such.

On the third night, Aurelia pleaded that she must leave when morning came. Curtis held her one last time, toward dawn coming inside her, along with her.

Stripped of its inhibitions, her body had become a new thing.

Later, out on the street, she insisted he not accompany her in the taxi, the daylight a reminder of how exposed the two of them were, however anonymous the city, however uninterested the few passersby. After handing her into the back seat and instructing the driver, Curtis slapped his palm against the cab's fender.

"My mother sent a letter," he said. "Cassie. The wedding will be in early September. Your aunt has insisted upon helping with festivities. You—and James—must come." The cab drowned his last words. But she nodded, her slender hand pressed against the pane.

Afterwards, three days later it would have been judging from the wall calendar in the Nowitski kitchen, Aurelia savored the cup of coffee Claudette had handed her without a word, both women unusually diffident after their separate adventures over the weekend.

That was the expression Claudette had used when she opened the door to let her friend in that Tuesday morning around ten.

"*Quelle aventure, n'est-ce pas?* Very bad girls, we." Without waiting for a response, Claudette had gestured toward the kitchen and retreated to her own bedroom, shutting the door behind her.

Relieved to be left alone, Aurelia looked out the picture window at the slate-colored lake below. By squinting, she could make out several sailboats bobbing in the shimmering shallows of Lake Michigan. From up high in the Nowitski home, they looked like the tiny vessels in that painting of the harbor at Honfleur. Was it by Monet or Manet? She couldn't remember. But she did recall Curtis' exuberance in the nightclub, conversing about Cézanne, of all things. Somewhat fuzzier in her mind was how they got to that room with the threadbare carpet, though she did remember a long key inserted expertly into a lock, the eagerness with which he turned the knob.

Moving back into the parlor, Aurelia made an effort to focus on the here and now, thankful that her friend's father had already left for work and her mother had slinked back to her bedroom. Small talk in broken English would have been beyond her today.

But Claudette? So taciturn. Was it that after so much

encouragement she disapproved in the end of Aurelia's behavior? Or, was it that such intimacies as each had indulged in made for awkwardness? Aurelia downed the last of her coffee and tapped on Claudette's bedroom door.

"*Alors*...?" Claudette inquired as she stroked her raven locks and eyed her friend in the mirror of her dresser. "Don't just stand there. Come sit and tell me all about it."

However little she wanted to be interrogated, Aurelia could see no way around it. Claudette had supported her, risked her own parents' displeasure. Besides, who else in the world could she confide in? Only she had no idea where to begin.

As if sensing her dismay, Claudette rose and crossed the room, reaching out to take Aurelia's hands in hers. "You don't have to say anything, *ma chère*. I can see it in your face. As I saw it in his."

Aurelia nodded in the affirmative, relieved that her friend did not judge her ill. "I could not help myself, we could not *not* do...You understand, don't you? I love him, I did before, and I do now more completely," she confessed amidst tears that she could no longer stifle.

Claudette pulled open the tiny drawer of her night table and retrieved a lace-bordered handkerchief. "Here. Use this." With a faint "thanks," Aurelia took the square of fabric and wiped her eyes.

"Aurelia..." Claudette hesitated and Aurelia glanced at her. "Did you, did your Curtis?..."

"What do you mean, Claudette?" Aurelia asked, lowering the handkerchief and folding her hands in her lap.

"When I was sixteen, there was a soldier, during the war. An English infantryman. He was...so young, so eager. We were—I was so besotted. There were...consequences. I waited for every word, read every redacted missive. Until the Somme." Tears misted her eyes, and Aurelia handed the handkerchief back to her. "No more word from him came. And I was left...As I said, there were consequences. Do you understand?"

Her face flaming, Aurelia nodded and cast about for something, anything to change the subject. She blurted the first thing that came to mind.

"If it's still something you'd like to do, I'd be delighted to go to the symphony."

Claudette's mouth twitched, but she said only, "Splendid. The music will do us both good."

Aurelia rose, thinking enough had been said between them, but Claudette's next words halted her.

"One more thing, Aurelia. I do understand but mustn't be foolish, you—not get carried away. I would say this even if Curtis weren't black, but he is, to intents and purposes—isn't that the expression? —and *ergo*, things are more complicated."

Her hand already on the doorknob, Aurelia's body tensed for the inevitable *coup de grâce*.

"In Vicksburg, at your family's home. I saw how things stand. Chicago is one thing, the South another, *n'est-ce pas*? Dangerous for you, worse for Curtis. Don't be idiot. Get this out of your system now, over the summer." When Aurelia didn't budge or respond, she continued, "When we're back at Stephens in the fall there'll be other men. You'll have your pick."

"My pick? I have already picked, and been picked," Aurelia mumbled under her breath. Without looking around, she turned the knob and tiptoed to her room.

The two friends skirted any mention of Curtis or Rufus for the rest of Aurelia's visit, filling their last day together with sightseeing and their evening with the concert. Majestic, Beethoven's Emperor Concerto, Aurelia thought, her own heart beating faster in response to the pianist's performance.

"Bungled here and there," Claudette observed afterwards. "The orchestra covered up what they could, but, enjoyable enough for you, I hope?"

"Oh, absolutely." Despite her musical training, Aurelia had not registered the missed notes. She suspected why. Small towns, like her own, were arguably less demanding, even at the piano stool. Chicago, she now saw, was a city of strivers: they strode rather than strolled to a more ambitious place. Whatever that might mean for her, Curtis belonged in such a place. Not only might he survive, he might even thrive.

Chapter Twenty-Four

Wilena had the jitters. That Mrs. Taylor had offered to host a party after the exchange of vows—an informal outdoor reception her employer had described it—was more of a worry than a relief. Though it would cut down on expenses, the inevitable intermingling of the races could be looked upon askance, even by her own kinsmen. Not to mention by the likes of Hiram. If only the missus would see the light and throw that good-for-nothin' out.

"Ouch," she winced, as a trickle of blood oozed from her finger onto the potatoes she was peeling. She stuck her hand under the tap and glanced out the window. Cassie and Curtis had driven up in the second-hand Chevrolet he had bought weeks before off of old Mr. Mayfield.

"You need an auto, Mother. Can't always depend on buggies, or other people," he had insisted, vowing to show her how to drive. Cassie too.

True to his word, every July morning before the heat wilted them, Curtis took his younger sister out on the dirt road and made her take the wheel. "Reverse, brake, use the clutch, watch the ruts" until ten days on she had mastered the thing, at least well enough to get herself to Tallulah and back. "Don't forget, Sis," he warned her during their last lesson, "never honk at white folks, and never pass a white driver. Go where you have to go and be done. No foolin' around." She rolled her eyes. Just what he expected. In his estimation Cassie was flighty and sassy—attributes that could get her pegged as a hussy. Even worse, as a black hussy driving a car. Curtis raised his voice. "It's not a joke, Cassie. Do as I tell you or I'll take the car away. It's really for Mother."

"Don't you worry none," Cassie responded, her voice serious for once. "I be sticking to the back roads, except with Lawrence."

The siblings had motored to Monroe to pick up Cassie's wedding gown and to introduce Curtis to Lawrence. The two men hit it off, Curtis struck by the composure of the doctor and his effortless ability to calm those around him, Cassie included. The doctor had, in turn, seemed impressed by the slow-burn ambition in his future brother-in-law.

"I understand you're getting a job up north—something involving hydraulics?"

"An outfit outside Chicago, working on dredging equipment. They've got business all along the Mississippi. I'll be headed back there after the wedding. Looking forward to that, though."

"We are too," Lawrence said with a chuckle, turning toward Cassie. "And having my wife here with me in Monroe. I'm sure she told you I'm in practice with my cousin. No shortage of sick folks." He patted Cassie's arm as he said this, and tugged at her hair ribbons. Curtis felt relieved at Lawrence's words. One fewer thing for his overburdened mother to worry over.

As her son and daughter pulled up in front of the house after their trip, Wilena shambled out on the stoop, a dish towel in one hand and the other pressed against her aching back. She gave Curtis a sharp look, but he avoided her gaze.

Shaking her head, she said, "We'll be eating at 7:30, so wash up. After dinner you can show me the dress."

Though Curtis was oblivious, having plunged into non-stop work either in the fields or at the repair shop since arriving home in late June, Wilena fretted. She had expected her son to seem different. How so, she couldn't articulate, but she had not expected withdrawn. All that he had accomplished up north, a degree, a decent job waiting, presumably new friends, (though she had only heard the name Rufus ever mentioned), he downplayed, always returning to what needed to be done around the house or at the shop. Mostly he brooded, breaking his silence only to be civil, or in odd manic bursts. As when he showed up that muggy afternoon with the car.

"You must learn, Mother. It's the only thing which will ever help us," he had half-cajoled, half-commanded. Not wanting to disappoint, Wilena did her best but, despite Curtis' demonstrations day after day, his hands atop hers, on the throttle, the shift stick, the wheel, she couldn't coordinate the movements. Her back ached, her head hurt, and it was no use.

"Why don't you concentrate on Cassie? She's young, picks up quick," she had, as off-handedly as she could, suggested.

The one time that summer Wilena brought up Aurelia's name—over slices of watermelon from the garden, Cassie chattering away about the guest list for the reception at the Taylor place, Curtis flipping through *Popular Mechanics*—she could see her son tense.

"Miss Margaret done told me all the Ackermanns, not just Aurelia and James but her father and the older son, be invited. 'An opportunity to see them all together in happier circumstance,' Miz Taylor done explained." Neither of her children spoke. "You needs to be specially noticing them, Cassie. You hear me?"

"I knows what to do, Mama," she replied as she pressed a slippery seed between her thumb and forefinger and flicked it across the table at her brother. Curtis brushed it off his cheek but didn't return the salvo.

"Leave your brother alone, Cassie. He's studying. And you heed what I say."

"Never you mind, Mama. We gonna do the bowing and scraping. Plus, James and Aurelia, they be good people, not stuck-up. Ain't that so, Curtis?"

Her brother drank his sweet tea and retired to his room to figure how he might avoid awkwardness, or worse, with the Ackermanns. If only people like Hiram weren't always begging for a fight. Ordinarily, Curtis could deal with slurs made by the foreman but in front of Aristide or Alfred Ackermann? He tried to sleep, having volunteered to show up the next morning to help with a barge run aground on a sandbar. Instead, he tossed and turned most of the night, waking up in pools of sweat every couple of hours.

Margaret Taylor too had agonized for several weeks over her spontaneous offer to host Cassie and Lawrence's wedding reception on her own front lawn, although she felt she owed it to Wilena for the housekeeper's loyalty. She was not worried all that much about the neighbors—the Bianchetti clan had often hosted mixed affairs and no one seemed to think ill of that—nor about her own workmen, as black and white had labored shoulder to shoulder for years in her fields, chewed tobacco on the porch once the cows were milked, supped side by side at her table. As for Hiram, he kept an aloof distance but only because he fancied his position as the foreman, she told herself. No, all that mingling would scarcely raise an eyebrow with the country folk. Her own family, especially her brother, was the greater problem.

"But they have to come, they have to come, Mother," Sarah-Lynn had kept insisting.

"Naturally they're all welcome." Margaret didn't tell her daughter that she hadn't actually mailed the fussily engraved invitation that Lawrence's parents had supplied. However progressive she remembered her brother's views, he was the head of a bank, his older son an up-and-coming lawyer. Being invited to an essentially black wedding reception was unusual enough; attending might be controversial if anyone in Vicksburg cared to notice. She would take her chances that Aristide and Alfred would decline by ringing up, casually, as it were, to invite them.

"I'm thinking Aunt Margaret needs to get out more, give up that rinky-dink farm, travel, take up something."

Alfred, smoking a Camel, tossed that idea out to no one in particular as the Ackermanns sat in the parlor awaiting their evening meal. Re-crossing his legs, Aristide slowly lowered the *Herald*, aware that if any of his children spoke during his perusal of the news, they dared do so only for an important reason and to elicit his reaction. Alfred blew a smoke ring into the air and waited for his father to react. Without speaking, Aristide eyed his son as if to say the ball was still in his court.

"She rang up late yesterday. Seems she's holding a reception, on the 3rd of September at her place—but for, of all people, her hired help."

From across the room, Aurelia dropped the copy of *National Geographic* on the floor, drawing the stares of all but James as she bent to pick it up. Aristide glowered at her, wondering what there was in Alfred's words to rattle the girl.

"Anyway, she called to invite us all to attend," Alfred resumed, stubbing his cigarette in the ashtray next to his armchair. "James and Aurelia, if I understood her correctly—Aunt Margaret does yap a mile a minute—presumably being acquainted with the bride. Cassie somebody, a president's name I think, but then, what does that matter? She's a ninny."

"We do know them: Cassie, her mother Wilena, the, the whole

family—and we'd get to see Sarah-Lynn and the farm, a-a-and all," James burst out.

Again, Aristide scowled, irked as much by his son's persistent stutter as by the social miscues of his widowed sister. He refilled his meerschaum and took a couple of studied puffs, the usual prelude to remarks that would settle whatever matter his children had raised.

"We should invite your Aunt Margaret, Sarah-Lynn too, here for the holidays. The girl, she must be going on fifteen or sixteen, needs to start socializing. With proper folks," Aristide said. Turning toward Alfred, he added, "As for my sister floundering on that farm in the middle of nowhere, she needs a husband. It's been long enough..." His adamant tone suggested (wrongly) that he had been swishing the problem around day and night and had finally come to a decision.

Anyone but Hiram would be acceptable, Aurelia instantly thought but said nothing.

"Dinner is served, Mr. Ackermann." Susanna stood in the doorway, ladle in hand, chest out, back straight, and announced the meal in what was obviously a well-rehearsed accent, one she had probably picked up from the caterer who had organized formal dinners for Aristide and Sophie before the war. But it was equally as obvious she couldn't sustain the pose or perform with the proper grammar for long. "Made your special chicken and dumplings, Miss Aurelia. You be a little peaked. Must be the heat now you be 'customed to those northern winters."

Aristide inclined his head, rose from his chair and stood next to Susanna while his children filed past him to their assigned places. Aurelia ate largely in silence, mulling whether it would be propitious to directly ask her father if she and James could in fact go across the first weekend of September, and trying to figure what else he might object to or query her or her brother about. As long as Curtis' name doesn't come up, or how it happens we know him so well, Aurelia kept telling herself, hoping too that James would not let slip anything compromising.

As long as I can glimpse him...

Like that time with Henrietta, delivering pots of stew to the poor. Screen doors barely on their hinges, dark eyes from within variously curious, furtive, grateful. Amid shacks near the cemetery they came across a freshly painted one with new shingles, a trimmed hedge. In profile, talking to an old man on the stoop, a mongrel curled at his feet, was Curtis. He held clippers, gesturing toward tomato vines along the side.

As they walked back toward their car, Henrietta said, "Do you think, Aurelia, they'll ever progress, or that God will intercede to change their lot for the better?"

Aurelia had hesitated, unsure how to unravel her knotted feelings. Not until the Ford turned onto Clay Street, its prosperous homes a visual reminder of the distance they had traversed in a matter of minutes, did she try.

"I don't know, but so many things, including things white people do, keep them down."

"I say, Aurelia, are you listening?" Alfred put his knife and fork down on his china plate, the decisive gesture precipitating Aurelia's abrupt return to the present. "There's an end-of-summer party in the Garden District, friends of Aunt Sybil and Uncle Philip," he went on. "And, by the way, last time I was there, C. T. asked after you."

Aurelia snapped to attention. "If we do anything that last weekend before we both head off to school"—here she glanced at James to rally his support—"I think it should be to Aunt Margaret's. From what you and Father were saying, having us—family—there is a positive thing for her, and for Sarah-Lynn."

Alfred took this objection in and did not press her.

"Who, pray tell, is C.T.?" James asked his brother. Aristide looked over at his older son.

"One Charles Tarleton Truard," Alfred intoned in what Aurelia thought was a very good nasal imitation of his friend's accent. "Took something of a shine to Aurelia a few years ago. At the Comus Ball."

Annoyed, Aurelia declined to add anything, not having a very positive memory of the young man on the dance floor and not wanting Alfred to exaggerate their acquaintance.

But Alfred turned to his father. "C.T.'s the scion of a very proper family, friends of the Durrells, as well as someone I bumped into during the war. Considered a catch. He just joined a firm down there, or a second firm, I'm not sure." A pleased expression on his face, Alfred wiped his lips and laid his gravy-stained napkin next to his plate.

"It never hurts to know the right people," Aristide intoned, "as many of them as possible, as they don't all end up being as right as one might like."

Alfred dangled a dumpling in mid-air.

Aristide stared at his half-empty plate, he too as disoriented as Alfred obviously was by his sphinxlike pronouncement. However much he prided himself on keeping his professional headaches to himself, or at least away from the family dinner table, the thought of Horace Hilliard had a way of obtruding. How underhanded Hilliard had become, sabotaging Aristide's authority as head of the bank—belittling him in front of the secretaries—and angling not only to replace him as board president but also to run for mayor against their mutual friend, Hayes. And that gaudy wife of his, egging him on. Sophie had had that woman's number. If only his wife were still...

I must get a grip, Aristide told himself.

Over the lemon custard, he announced his decision about the wedding reception across the river.

"Very well, you two," he said, turning his gaze from one to the other of his younger children. "You can accept your Aunt Margaret's invitation. But remember, both of you need to be back right after to get off to school. And Alfred, give my best to Sybil and Philip. Perhaps we'll have them up for New Year's as well. We should have a little fun around here. That's what your mother would want."

Chapter Twenty-Five

The first indication that they'd been spotted heading toward the Taylor place came in the forms of Rebel and Rover. Despite their advanced years, they still guarded the expanse of corn field and cow pasture that had been their territory since they were pups.

The driver slowed to a halt. "They could use a ride. Open your door, Mr. James, and they'll jump right in." He shook his head as the dogs quit barking and climbed into the back seat. "You'd think they'd be used to this here car by now."

Mr. Pickens, whose real name was Henry but given his rail-thin frame was universally known as Slim, was an accommodating sort, as fond of the dogs as anyone on the farm. Aurelia relaxed as soon as she recognized him at the end of the dock, a big gap-tooth smile overwhelming his face. "Lookin' mighty fine, Mr. James. You too, Miss Aurelia. Awful pretty."

That was about the extent of Slim's volubility, such effusiveness causing blood to plump his hollow cheeks. He picked up the leather bags the siblings had brought and led the two straight to the waiting car.

"Big doings tomorrow. Got to pick up a few cases of that Coca-Cola they bottle over in your neck of the woods," Slim said, shutting the door behind Aurelia and retrieving a piece of paper from the back pocket of his overalls. "You two need anything from MacGregor's? Going to be right hot today."

"We're fine, Slim. Can we be of help?" Aurelia asked.

"Don't you worry none. The widow's got that kid to load up."

During the wait for their driver, Aurelia grew anxious, her leg twitching beneath her cotton skirt. James put his hand on her bare arm. "It's going to be OK. I know you want to see him. I do too. And I'm sure you managed to do so up north, where"—her brother halted, as if not wanting to contemplate what most likely happened between the two— "where you could be much more relaxed."

Soothed by these sympathetic words, Aurelia had taken James' hand in hers. It felt as soft as her own, despite his three years of military school.

"I am so lost, James. I do know how Father would suffer, Alfred too. Not to mention what might befall Curtis." Beseeching him to counter that she was exaggerating, Aurelia paused, but James kept his gaze straight ahead. "You know better than anyone I didn't set out to do anything wrong. Nor did he."

She fixed on their clasped hands in her lap, unable to continue her defense, hoping her brother would say he understood the force of her feelings, that he forgave her such a trespass, and that somehow things would work out.

Sighing, James withdrew his hand from hers. "Well, we're on his territory now, and, knowing Curtis, he'll be as mindful as things call for. Glad to see us but focused on his family."

As I so egregiously am not, Aurelia thought to herself.

"So, don't do anything others can make something of. Let's just have fun. Aunt Margaret and Sarah-Lynn deserve at least that from us."

Aurelia shook her head. James was right. Surely for two days...Then late on Sunday afternoon, as the reception wound down, perhaps Curtis rather than Slim could drive her back to the landing (he behind the wheel, she ensconced in the back seat), though the trip might take longer than the miles would suggest. No one the wiser for what moments they had snatched, she would ferry across to be met by Cleveland, pack up her things the next day, and be on the train for St. Louis at noon on Tuesday. She took a deep breath and gave her brother a peck on the cheek.

In a couple of minutes Slim reappeared lugging a case of Cokes, a scrawny youngster of about sixteen with the same avian appearance as Mrs. MacGregor carrying a second load in his wake. After several more trips in and out the store, Slim slipped the kid a quarter and climbed in behind the wheel. Mrs. MacGregor stood on the porch leaning against a stack of cattle feed. Watching. As they pulled away, Aurelia saw the youngster hand over his coin to her outstretched claw.

Other than the dogs, the first friendly face James and Aurelia saw as they came up the Taylor drive was an unfamiliar one waving energetically from the front porch. They gestured back uncertainly. With her short bob and taller, fuller frame, neither had recognized Sarah-Lynn. Not in fact until they opened the car doors and Rebel and Rover bounded up the front steps, barking up a storm. Soon both Margaret and Wilena joined the commotion, everybody exclaiming over either how grown-up Sarah-Lynn was or how beautiful a young woman Aurelia had become.

"I declare, Miss Margaret, the pulchritude this weekend gwine be downright overpowering," a beaming Wilena exuded.

"Absolutely. Your Cassie too," Margaret added, ushering her guests inside and motioning to Slim to take the bags upstairs. "Only problem until then, I need alert you two, will be all the hammering. The men are putting up a tent and a makeshift dance floor. Didn't think of it earlier, so tomorrow's a good day to take the horses out or go fishing."

Which is what the three did, Aurelia atop Silver, James astride Thunder and Sarah-Lynn on her frisky new filly Cassandra, so named, she informed them, after a summer immersed in a book on Greek myths. They picnicked aside the lake, Sarah-Lynn recounting over the roast beef sandwiches all the courses she would soon be taking in her senior year, in the hopes, she told them, of leaving the farm to attend Sophie Newcomb in New Orleans.

"Won't your horse be lonely?" James teased as he swilled sweet tea from one of the canteens Margaret had filled.

"Yeah, unfortunately. No way I can take her," Sarah-Lynn responded. "Actually, though, it's Mother I'd hate to desert."

"But she has Hiram, right?"

Aurelia, who had been peeling the fruit and re-wrapping leftovers, happy to let the other two carry on the conversation, realized she had not laid eyes on the foreman.

"They're on the outs. Fine by me, but Mother seems at sixes and sevens. Could be the thing for Cassie, her being black and all—and Hiram being..." Sarah-Lynn shrugged her disapproval. James nodded.

For the next hour the three lazed around in the grass under a giant elm, took a dip in their undergarments, skipped stones, and led the horses to the water's edge before heading back by a different route, Sarah-Lynn in the lead. Before long they came upon a clearing, a rushing stream to one side, a stand of pines in the background.

"I remember this place. There were deer," Aurelia said, the memory so vivid it was as though the years between had been erased.

"It's Curtis' favorite spot. He told me so barely a month ago, riding alongside to help break In Cassandra. She got spooked here," Sarah-Lynn added, patting her horse. The three squinted in the sunshine but could see no sign of movement in the trees. "He said ghost deer live in the woods yonder." Sarah-Lynn gestured toward the far pines.

"Ghost deer?" James asked.

"White as ghosts, seldom venturing into the open—if they exist at all," Sarah-Lynn explained.

"Unearthly," Aurelia said. They lingered in their saddles, scouring the far side of the stream despite tugs on the reins from all three horses.

"Looks like we're out of luck spotting any deer, real or imagined," James concluded, swatting at the flies that had begun to alight on Thunder's withers. "We should think about heading back."

"At a gallop if you're up to it. Ye-haw," Sarah-Lynn called out, giving Cassandra a sharp nudge with her stirrups.

That night, after helping set up saw-horse tables outside and arranging chairs on the lawn, Aurelia went to bed bone-weary. For a few minutes she tried to distinguish the voices of the workmen down below putting the final touches on the dance floor and stringing Japanese lanterns. Her mind wandered to the clearing. She wondered what Curtis had done with the watercolor she'd painted for him so long ago.

The guests began arriving early, around 2:30 in the afternoon, and as three cars pulled in within minutes of one another, it was as Margaret suspected. Not as many white folks as she had invited. The phone had rung twice Sunday morning while she was taking biscuits out of the oven.

The Callaways called to say they couldn't make it—a sick cow, weeks before market. Then the Sanfords, who owned the main dry goods store in Tallulah and whose son had spent an entire summer at Samuel's knee learning how to farm. (He then went off to war and got himself killed.) "Something's come up. Business with out-of-towners. Perhaps another time," Charlotte Sanford had clipped in a most unconvincing tone.

Never mind. The Bianchettis were sure to show up, accordions and banjos in tow, as were the Morgans, with their twins Amy and Alma, a little younger than Sarah-Lynn, homely but good-natured. Maybe even the Fullers, with any number of their offspring. To offset the imbalance, Margaret decided to corral her own workmen—Slim, Jinx, Scotty, a couple of others, to join in and partake of refreshments.

With more enthusiasm than usual, Margaret leapt off the front porch steps to welcome the Morgans and the Fullers. "My, don't you two look adorable," to Amy and Alma, in their identical pink frocks and black patent leather pumps. Giggling, the two girls ran inside to find Sarah-Lynn. Margaret herded the others, including the Bianchetti clan, over to the tent where two punch bowls sat on each end of a long oak table. "Help yourself, folks. There's bottled Cokes and cider. Sandwiches on the way," Margaret said, as she helped old Mr. Bianchetti to a chair near the wooden dance platform.

"Where's the bride, where's the bride?" he kept mumbling, unaware of what was happening around him.

A stilted half hour passed. The young people milled about, not knowing what to do, while their elders made sporadic small talk, the women looking starched, the men peeved. When Aurelia brought the last tray of Margaret's ham and tomato sandwiches to the tent, she could feel the tension.

"Music might help," Sarah-Lynn whispered as their paths crossed. They beckoned to Paulo to start uncasing the fiddles.

By the time the wedding party arrived, a further hush fell over the assembled. Sarah-Lynn scurried out with her mother to greet the bride and groom. Aurelia remained inside the tent, forcing herself to chat with the twins, her back to the arrivals. James joined in, handing his sister a glass of punch. As Cassie and Lawrence made their way forward arm-in-arm, the musicians struck up Mendelsohn, masking the silence among the guests. Several of the couple's young friends followed behind, their own faces suddenly wary. Mrs. Morgan murmured something to Mrs. Fuller, but Aurelia wasn't close enough to catch it.

"Lookin' real pretty, Miss Cassie," Slim called out from the sideline. Instinctively, Aurelia turned to see the bride. In a store-bought gown, Cassie shyly took in the compliment and waved her hand at no one in particular. Lawrence, erect and smiling, patted her arm in support of the consensus, such as it was. A smattering of polite applause followed. Then Aurelia saw him. Curtis. Shepherding his mother and another elderly woman, possibly the groom's mother, to a bench across from where the white folks were congregated. He was wearing a shiny black tuxedo, likely rented. When he straightened up, he scoured the room. Their eyes locked, fleetingly, because Aurelia lowered hers and grasped James' arm. Once the music took hold, Aurelia did what she could to help her aunt, carrying trays of food or replenishing drinks.

Curtis did the same, delivering lemonade and soda to the older folks and allowing himself to be dragged onto the raised platform to dance with one or another of Cassie's bridesmaids. Even a quick turn with Sarah-Lynn he submitted to. As he led her back to her seat between Amy and Alma, they heard snickers from the sidelines.

"Would never happen if I had my way," Hiram snarled as an aside to Jinx, who spat on the ground in tacit agreement. The two men were leaning against one of the sawhorse tables swilling beer. Curtis knew better than to let himself be baited; Sarah-Lynn had no such qualms.

"You're despicable," she hissed, color rising in her face. The twins froze, not looking in the direction of the men. But Curtis was sure they could hear the sniggers and smell the alcohol.

"Takes after her mother, two peas in a goddamn pod," Hiram retorted, his voice venomous.

"You three OK?" Curtis queried the girls.

Sara-Lynn nodded, but the color in her cheeks made it clear she was boiling.

Curtis headed back to the buffet table to get out of Hiram's earshot. He filled several cups with lemonade. A cool arm brushed his. He had to think fast.

"Meet me in the tack room, where the harnesses are," he whispered, his voice barely audible. Disembodied.

"Now?"

"In fifteen minutes." Trembling, Curtis replaced the ladle in the bowl and carried the glasses across the tent.

"You all right, Curtis? Lawd of mercy, you work yourself too hard. Sit down and rest your bones," Wilena lamented, accepting one of the cups and patting the bench next to her. Obliging, he downed the liquid and feigned interest in the reel being performed in the middle of the floor. Other than Paolo and Eduardo, the twins and James, all the dancers were colored. What white guests were still present, he noticed raking the room, had coalesced into a jealous knot, as though compressing themselves into an ever tighter space might protect them from whatever contagion was in the air. Before Cassie or one of her friends could grab him up for the next number, Curtis mumbled something about Thunder.

The horse whinnied as Curtis lifted the stallion's back left hoof, deciding that the shoe had deteriorated. No time now. He would tend to it in the morning, after chauffeuring guests back to Tallulah, detouring to the ferry landing for a last glimpse of Aurelia, heading home to get some sleep, doubling back to the Taylors the next day—a fishing expedition with James, fixing a few things for Sarah-Lynn, taking his mother home once her duties for Mrs. Taylor were complete.

While at college he had gotten in the habit of making lists. "Write them down," one of his professors had advised, but Curtis preferred to keep them compartmentalized in his head. He rarely had the fortitude to bring the long-term goals to the fore, not wanting to dwell on them and too beset with getting through the tasks at hand to worry over them. Except alone, in the dark, except when he had to face the fact that his heart ruled his head more than he knew was good for him.

"You understand, don't you Thunder?" he sighed, patting the horse's flank. The animal snorted and pricked his ears, not at Curtis' touch but at the click of a woman's heels on the sawdust floor. Not to frighten her, Curtis waited until Aurelia made it to the back of the barn. Within seconds, he re-closed the stall and followed the sound.

They embraced, Curtis stunned once again by the force of the heart beating against his. He up-tilted her head and kissed her on the forehead, the cheeks, the lips. On her tiptoes, Aurelia pressed her breasts to his chest, and for balance, Curtis backed into the wall hung with bridles. The smell of leather and turpentine mingled with the scent of their bodies.

They had little time. Better to talk than to allow themselves caresses. "I've been thinking. Now that I'll be working, I can take the train to St. Louis. I can rent a place, or if your friend Claudette...My darling, tell me you want this. I will have money, not a lot, but enough. We can—"

A noise brought them bolt upright. Men's voices, joshing with each other. Heading their way. Curtis put his finger to Aurelia's lips and flattened his palm against her spine to keep her still. They froze in effigy. He recognized the approaching voices as those of Hiram and Jinx.

"You grab one, I'll handle the other, the bigger. Waited long enough for the hard stuff, don't give a shit what she'll say."

"Damn right, Hi, especially when we're told to dance to the tune of a socialist nigger-lover like that dago Bianchetti. Don't know which end is up, the whole lot of 'em."

Curtis motioned with his eyes for Aurelia to fix on the rickety door against the far wall. It would surely give their whereabouts away were he to jerk it open but at least she could high-tail it to the big house. He would snatch up something heavy from the table, a chisel, an anvil, the first thing he could get his hands on, and defend himself.

But the footsteps directed themselves to the other side of the barn, the room where the feed was stored. And all those jugs. Moonshine. Within a minute they heard louder expletives and the sound of jugs being slid across the wood floor.

"Damn rodents. Let's get out of here." Their footsteps faded toward the front of the barn.

For an eternity the two lovers did not dare move. Curtis strained to detect any sound other than their own shallow breaths and nickering from one or another of the horses. Weak-kneed though he felt, he forced himself to issue orders.

"Go out this back hatch, through the house, and back to the tent as though nothing were amiss. Slim, I reckon, can take you to the dock. I have to take some of Cassie's guests home but I'll detour to the landing. A last glimpse we'll have of each other until, listen to me"—: he gently shook her trembling shoulders—"before the leaves are off the trees, we'll be together again. Now go."

"But Curtis, I don't think I can—"

"You must. I'll help you."

Prying open the rarely used door, he handed Aurelia outside and crouched to see her cross the garden onto the back porch of the house. Curtis checked on all the horses, as much to give himself time to calm down as to nurture to them. Thunder studied him with his big blurry eyes, wondering why he was being hand-fed a bunch of oats at such an hour. "You're right, fella. You don't care what color your rider long as he can control the reins," Curtis muttered, stroking the horse's withers.

By the time Curtis got back to the tent, the bride and groom were waving their good-byes from the back of a rented Cadillac, a chauffeur taking them back to Monroe for the night. He called out to Cassie but the car was too far down the driveway for her to hear.

"My baby girl. I can't believe it," Wilena was whimpering, a handkerchief daubing her eyes. One of Cassie's friends, Coral, had caught the bride's corsage and was being teased by other of the young women. With all the commotion, it took Curtis a half hour to arrange the transport home for the bride's friends. In the end he would be chauffeuring four of the young women, with Coral living the furthest distance, on the far side of Tallulah. From there, he could, if he stepped on the gas, double back, hopefully in time...

Before departing, he looked around for James.

"Did your sister get off all right?"

"I suppose so. Slim is—you can see him slouched over there in the corner—so Aunt Margaret yelled at the other workmen. Something about the heavy stuff being off-limits. Anyway, Hiram spoke up. Took his own car, I think."

Curtis opened his mouth to say something but thought the better of it. Instead, he wiped the sweat from his brow and forced a smile. "Your last day tomorrow, right? We'll go fishing as soon as I tend to Sarah-Lynn's horses. Round about ten."

Barking to the girls to figure out who would sit where and to get themselves settled in his Chevy, he escorted his mother into the house and took his leave.

Chapter Twenty-Six

Hiram's car sped through the dappled sunshine, bouncing gold flecks off Aurelia's hair. She had taken up post in the back seat of the hatch-back, instinctively recoiling from sitting next to her driver. He might be her aunt's special friend—whatever that now might mean, since it didn't seem they exchanged a single civil word—but he still was hired help, and so she felt perfectly justified in putting a row between them. Unease rose in her stomach nonetheless; nor did the foreman's pumping of the pedal, bumps in the road be damned, help soothe her. Still, the party could be described a success, at least for the bride and groom, oblivious to the begrudged best wishes from the white guests, oblivious to almost everything going on around them.

Rightly so, she thought. Aurelia fixed on the back of Hiram's bull neck, wondering if he had any suspicion of what happened in the barn, and not daring to contemplate what such an ill-tempered bigot would do had he come upon them, *en flagrant*, as her friend

Claudette would have dramatically put it, her arm extended in full Gallic flair.

Aurelia smiled, suddenly realizing how much she looked forward to the return to Stephens and her final year together with her irrepressible roommate. Claudette's only letter that summer had posed the crucial question. *So,* ma chère, *nothing unwarranted to report since your tryst with Mr. C., I trust?* Très bien. *Presuming then you have tackled* La Chartreuse de Parme*—Stendhal does not disappoint—while I wallow in Proust, which is what I believe he intended for readers to do*... And so on, through amusing bits about Goethe and Manzoni—her roommate read those languages too—and on to an obscure reference to Rufus, and how even in Chicago one had to be careful. *You Americans, everything so black and white.*

Hiram surveyed his distracted passenger in the rearview mirror. Her porcelain face, like fine china, but her expression, haughty, distant. Women. They all need to be chipped or broken, he muttered. How infuriating of Margaret to so peremptorily, in front of Jinx and the other hands, order him to drive to the ferry. Yet he alone had the constitution, and the wherewithal, to hold his liquor. Gotta be at the ready: goings-on behind his back, fellas who would rat on him if they could and conniving coloreds playing an angle. And that Curtis... He looked again in the rearview, his eyes narrowed to slits.

"Watch out, watch out, there's a deer," Aurelia screamed before being thrown to the floor as Hiram swerved to avoid the animal, the right front bumper catching the buck's flank. The creature bounced off.

"Goddamn deer. Fucking menace," Hiram growled as he slowed the car to get back onto the right side of the road.

"Aren't you going to stop, see how he is?"

"For a fucking deer? Not a chance."

Aurelia righted herself and kneaded her whiplashed neck. Before long Hiram diverted from the main road to a dirt cutoff parallel to the river and which, when not underwater, saved time on the trip to the ferry. Aurelia stiffened but said nothing. She reckoned it couldn't be more than a few miles, ten or fifteen minutes, to their destination. The bumps would be worth it. She looked east out over the tall rye and, if her eyes didn't deceive her, the protective berm beyond.

Of a sudden the car lurched, and then sputtered, a ribbon of hot vapor rising from under the hood.

When it came to a complete stop, Hiram jerked open his door, cursing under his breathe. For a couple of minutes, he disappeared into the tall brush. Aurelia scanned the horizon for any sign of life but there was not a soul to be seen, not a house nor a car, nothing but a flock of wild geese hectic in the sky. The sun was huge and purple to the west.

Wadding a dirty handkerchief from his rear pocket, Hiram pried open the hood and allowed the rest of the steam to escape. Then he moved from one side to the other of the auto, tinkering with this or that valve, twisting this or that gasket. If only they had taken Aunt Margaret's sedan, Aurelia thought, this might not have happened. Still, the accident wasn't of Hiram's making. Perhaps she should get out and offer to help, or hold something, or suggest something.

As she approached the front of the car, a streak of blood along the fender caught her eye. That too wasn't anyone's fault. For an instant, she wavered, watching Hiram awkwardly balanced on one foot. Then she cleared her throat.

"I'm sorry, Hiram, for this, but if we are so close to the landing, perhaps we could walk the rest of the way."

Shoulders tensed, he cocked his head enough that his rabbit-pink eyes met hers. Disconcerted, she couldn't stop herself. "Aunt Margaret could dispatch Curtis first thing tomorrow. He'll have it up and running—"

Before she could complete her sentence, he had her by the neck. She gasped, and he loosened his grip, but his nostrils flared as if he'd caught scent of his prey. His grease-stained hands found the contours of her body under her flimsy cotton dress.

Hiram shoved her into the ditch, one arm pinning hers behind her back, the other fumbling under her skirt and up her unsuspecting thigh. She turned her head only to have it scraped by a sharp-edged rock.

"You nigger-loving whore. Don't think I don't know what's up with you," he hissed.

Aurelia thrashed to get loose, kicking him in the shin with her shoe, calling out, pleading, tensing her limbs. To no avail. Twenty-five years in the fields had toughened her assailant. He forced himself inside her—pump, thrust, pump, thrust. Ceaselessly. The odor of alcohol on his breath and motor oil on his hands made Aurelia pass out. Cicadas in the nearby grass hummed and thrummed, indifferent.

Eventually, Hiram yanked himself out of her, righted himself and buttoned up his britches. He spat on the ground and stared off toward the river. Aurelia lay still, moaning, not daring to move. She could feel the hard earth beneath her, dirt in her nostrils, a trickle of blood running down her cheek. And an ache deep inside.

The car started up with the first crank. Letting it idle, Hiram slammed the hood and gathered up his near lifeless victim, bundling her into the front passenger seat.

"Here, wipe your face off with this. You don't want to attract attention."

Too numb to resist, Aurelia took the filthy handkerchief and blotted her cheeks, smearing the blood. Hiram accelerated, his eyes fixed on the road. Within five minutes, they had made it to the back of MacGregor's, pulling up next to sacks of chicken feed.

"You need to go inside, fix yourself up, then get yourself to the dock. The ferry will be pulling away within five minutes," Hiram said matter-of-factly, as though nothing were more amiss with his passenger than a wind-blown hair-do. Aurelia sat stock-still, vacant-eyed. Incensed, Hiram came round to the other side of the car, yanked the door open and pulled her out. She flinched at his touch, her lip fleering, but he shook her arm, the force of his grip sure to leave bruises.

"And don't forget, bitch. You say one word, I'll finger that nigger of yours in a heartbeat."

To her ears, the threat was the deepest thrust of all.

The brakes squealed on the old Chevy as Curtis pulled up in a cloud of dust. He was still irked that it took Coral, his last passenger, so long to get her things together and actually get out of the car in Tallulah. She'd flirted with him, waved the bride's bouquet under his nose, dared him to come in to meet her family; he all the while had been calculating the time it would take to swing by the ferry landing.

Curtis jumped out of the car, unsure whether to run down to the dock or stop in the country store first, just in case...

"You looking for that girl, the one from Vicksburg?" a voice called out.

Taken aback, Curtis scoured the porch for the source. It was the skinny kid that helped load groceries. Old Mrs. MacGregor's grandson. Perhaps he had seen her.

"Wanted to check she made the ferry in time, on behalf of Mrs. Taylor," he explained. Rarely did Curtis lie, but in the circumstances.

The kid put down the knife he was using to chisel away at some indeterminate musical instrument. "Had to help her. Said she had fallen. But, yeah. Only one other passenger so they held it for her."

Fallen? Whatever did that mean, Curtis wondered, but as Mrs. MacGregor had lumbered out onto the porch, he didn't prolong the exchange. Instead, he walked down to the dock and scanned the wide muddy water before him. The faintest of lights flickered from the far side. He took a deep breath in the windless dusk. Tomorrow he'd figure out what had happened. From James, or Hiram himself.

"Flick the wrist, flick the wrist," Curtis called out from his end of the boat, demonstrating with his own arm as James cast his rod in a wide arc in the air, a hapless grub dangling from the end. Barely missing an overhanging willow branch, the hook landed in the water feet away from a rotten log. Not bad, Curtis thought, though the real test would come when the line got a nibble.

Five or six bright bream later, James had acquired the knack. After an hour or so, they paddled to a cove on the far side edged by cottonwoods. Several turtles sunned themselves on the muddy bank. In silence, they cast their rods and waited, Curtis all the while trying to figure how to broach the subject that had troubled him through the night. He had gotten to the Taylors early that morning half hoping to run into Hiram before the foreman headed off on his rounds. Mightn't he even, without being prodded, volunteer that Aurelia had slipped in her fancy shoes when she got out of the car? A banged elbow, a scraped knee. He could nod noncommittally and there'd be nothing more to it. But Hiram had been nowhere to be seen, even though Curtis took his time tending to Thunder's hoof and repairing a couple of bridles that Sarah-Lynn had put aside. "Morning," was all he got—from Slim, who, having slept off his drunken stupor, came around the house early to make himself useful. "Seeing as you are tending to things in the barn, I'll take down that fixture in the yard," the workman had said, grabbing up a toolbox and heading out to disassemble the makeshift dance floor. Curtis nodded but said nothing.

Here on the lake might be his last chance. Curtis looked across at James' delicate profile as he jiggled his line. So uncannily like Aurelia's...

"Did you know she fell? On the way to the dock."

James looked up, uncomprehending.

"I swung by, after taking the girls home. That skinny kid from the feed store told me. Shaken up, he said, but managed to get on the last ferry. I thought perhaps she might have telephoned later to say she had arrived safely."

"You mean Aurelia? I haven't heard anything. Hiram took her to the landing but he didn't mention anything—or rather, I didn't see him this morning."

"Nor did I."

"I suspect it's nothing."

Curtis nodded in tentative agreement.

A flock of cranes swooped overhead. To Curtis, the air felt heavy.

"You do know, don't you, James, how much I care for you—and for your sister. If anything were ever to happen—"

"I know, Curtis," James broke in, his voice a pitch higher than usual. "And she does too. Care for you, I mean. It's just that..."

"You don't have to explain. It's what I tell myself every waking hour." Curtis turned his head away toward the bobbing cork twenty feet away.

"It's the world, Curtis. They have it wrong. But you and she, it's dangerous. More so for you than for her."

A bass took the bait, pulling it under in a swift tug. Easily a six-pounder, and not one that wished to be caught. Curtis had to help James land the fish. With their haul flopping in the bottom of the boat, they paddled back to shore. Nothing more was said on the subject of Aurelia, and no Hiram appeared that evening, though Curtis had more readily than usual accepted Mrs. Taylor's invitation to stay for fried fish and turnip greens. A knock at the back door turned out to be Slim, who, hat in hand and contrite of voice, announced that the yard had been cleaned up and the cows milked. If nothing more were needed he'd be heading home.

Back at the table, Margaret sighed. "Moonshine aside, he's the only one around here I can rely on. He'll take you to the landing in the morning, James."

"And I'm coming along for the ride," Sarah-Lynn piped up. "If only you didn't have to go back to Chicago, Curtis, we could all still be together. Wouldn't that be wonderful?"

Curtis smiled but soon took his leave.

Chapter Twenty-Seven

Doctor Knox was flummoxed. The third house call he had made to the Ackermann home that fall and yet he was no closer to knowing what ailed his patient. She had the same vacant stare as her mother had those years ago in the throes of the flu, but no obvious symptoms of illness. He latched his phaeton to the hitching post at the corner of Adams and China and mounted the steps, black bag in hand. Her condition was of another order, something mental, or spiritual. If only Aristide or her brother Alfred didn't hover at the foot of the bed, as though guarding Aurelia's virtue against, of all people, the family doctor. All he had been allowed to observe when first summoned were scratches and bruises, and those odd indentations on her back as if acorns had been ground into her. As he suspected, those outward signs had cleared up by the second visit in late October, and yet—and this he did not foresee—she still flinched at the touch of a hand. Grooves of distress still outlined her mouth. A banal fall, she had insisted—but to miss her last year of college, the joys of being young, and pretty, and living in such an age?

For the better part of the autumn, though, Aurelia had kept to her bed, creeping downstairs only at midday when no one save Susanna was about. Often she would open and close the lace curtain on the front window, repeatedly, without any idea as to why she did it. Once in a while she would intercept the mail, leaving the post addressed to her father or brothers on the table in the hall and mounting the stairs with any correspondence addressed to her. She had only ever opened the first couple of letters from Claudette, which had come within a few weeks of Aurelia's "accident."

The contents were now muddled in her mind. *Whatever has happened, Aurelia? How is it you are not coming back for our last hurrah? Write me you must. Rufus has spoken to Curtis. He is beside himself.* She had, in her dull delirium, dashed off a brief response. *Too ill, please forgive me, Claudette. And so that he knows, with Curtis all is over. The dangers were, and would be, insuperable, as you surmised, and I have not the strength.*

What she didn't say but thoroughly believed was that she was now so sullied she no longer deserved such a friend as Claudette, nor such a lover as Curtis. And, even if part of her knew the assault was not her fault, any attempt to take down the perpetrator could backfire. What had Hiram said? Something about how they do it in Bastrop? Lynching...

Too good for some niggers. His precise words.

Claudette's missives, the ones she had opened and the subsequent ones she had not the will to read, she tied up with string and placed in an empty hat box in her chifferobe. The three postmarked that fall variously from Chicago, Cincinnati and St. Louis with no return address, she dared not allow herself to open. These she placed alongside Claudette's. Not wanting, or believing she deserved, to bask in the light from Curtis' eyes, relish the words on his lips, thrill to the tautness in his loins. Even in memory. If she prayed that the dreams he had confided to her in that tiny room in Chicago might come true for him; hers, she believed, had been dashed on a dusty road along the Mississippi River bank.

She locked the chifferobe door on that part of her life.

Once again it was Aristide who responded to the doctor's knock at the front door.

"So, Ackermann, how is our patient today?"

Aristide shrugged, exasperated as well as anxious by a condition in his daughter that defied diagnosis or treatment. "Hard to say. Helps with the meals, organizes the household accounts, things like that. Hasn't ventured out. Only talks at any length to my son James. Whenever he makes it home."

Dr. Knox construed these developments as positive signs, tentative but positive. "Well, I've brought the latest tonic on the market. Nu-Vim. Might give her energy, encourage her to get back into things..."

Aristide assented, not necessarily convinced but glad the doctor had come with something, anything that might accelerate his daughter's recovery.

"Couldn't hurt you either, Ackermann. You look haggard. All the politics, I reckon. Not a polite game from what I read in the papers."

About the politics, the doctor wasn't wrong. The mayoral election in early November had been neck-and-neck, and Aristide had done his best, not so much to campaign for his own spot on the city council but to support the re-election of the incumbent. Hilliard alienated a fair number of voters in the home stretch with a barrage of scurrilous insinuations about his opponent. Not to mention the public appearances of that wife of his with the jangling bracelets. As a result, J.J. Hayes squeaked back in and Aristide retained his council seat. Vindictive sonofabitch that he was, Hilliard lashed out by redoubling his efforts to oust his erstwhile friend as bank president.

"Time to make the bank more responsive to upright citizens rather than to riff-raff," he had argued at one meeting.

Cynical chicanery, Aristide had thought. His one plea to the board before the definitive vote: the First National needed to respect its own moniker. "National" implied a broad field of operation, facilitating opportunity for any and all that had the gumption to apply themselves. And that meant enlightened lending practices, of which he for one was proud. Hilliard and a couple of his cronies on the board scoffed at the lecture. No one else spoke, except Fried, the electragist who sold wireless sets, and Paxton, who owned the town's leading foundry. They both supported Aristide's assessment. Cigar smoke filled the room. The vote in favor of Hilliard as new board president went seven to six.

"I probably could use an extra bottle, Doc."

That evening Aurelia made an effort to come downstairs for dinner. The tonic that Dr. Knox had insisted she take tasted awful but had the desired effect. She felt energized or at least shamed by the doctor, who had, once Ackermann left the room to attend to business, insisted that whatever mishap had befallen Aurelia, nothing was her fault. It was time to rejoin the circle of life. It would be what her poor mother would have wanted. Dr. Knox had taken Aurelia's hand in his as he dispensed this advice, and for the first time she did not recoil. In fact, she squeezed it.

"It is good, my dear, that you are up to reading (Stendhal lay open on the quilt) but you must mix with people. I'm sure you have many admirers here in town. *Tempus fugit*, Aurelia. The holidays are upon us and you should try to be with family and friends."

Once the doctor had left, Aurelia determined to take his advice and "rejoin the circle of life" by making the effort to be with her family for the evening meal.

"My, my, Miss Aurelia, you be looking ever so much better," Susanna exclaimed when she joined her father and brother at the dinner table, their first course already in progress. A wan smile plastered on her face, she determined to eat a respectable portion of the roast chicken and boiled potatoes the servant rushed to put on her plate.

"Glad you've come down, Aurelia. I was telling Father about all the people who've asked after you, not only the usual crowd from the B.B. Club—Henrietta, Caroline, Isabel—but the New Orleans clique as well." Aurelia looked blank, not aware of anyone in the latter city who would be thinking of her other than her aunt and uncle. "Fellows from that carnival dance, years ago, still remember you. Especially C.T."

Aurelia spooned sugar into her ice tea. She couldn't recall what the *C* or the *T* stood for.

"A lawyer, isn't he?" Aristide inquired, looking up from his oversized serving of potatoes, which despite his protests Susanna continued to apportion him.

"If he'd apply himself. Changes firms as often as he changes shoes. Says he needs a change of pace. Even hinted," Alfred added, with a sly glance toward Aurelia, "that he wouldn't mind giving Vicksburg a chance." He waved away another helping of gravy, and instead, reached for a second biscuit. When no one took him up on this revelation, Alfred changed the subject. "What were you about to say earlier, Father, about Aunt Margaret?"

Aurelia took several quick gulps of her tea.

"As I mentioned months ago, I invited them to spend the holidays with us. A change of scenery, people to meet, things to do..."

"And so, are they coming?"

"Margaret is. Seems Sarah-Lynn has examinations to study for and parties to attend over there around Christmas. She'll ferry over for New Year's."

Aurelia took a deep breath, thankful not to have heard the name of the man who was her undoing. How could her aunt not know what dastardly things he was capable of, and yet, how could she alert her without arousing other suspicions, which Hiram would be the first to foment?

"So that it's clear," Aristide began, putting down his knife and fork and fixing on each of his children in turn, "it's incumbent on each of you to pitch in to make your aunt's, and Sarah-Lynn's, visit memorable. Alfred, tickets to the opera—I believe *Otello* is on the boards for the holidays—you should procure. And of course the law firm's party at the B.B. Club. Aurelia, you will see to Trinity's festivities—caroling, midnight mass, anything else uplifting."

"Fair enough, Father," Alfred said, checking his pocket watch and warding off Susanna's cheese and fruit plate. "Cards and drinks, over at the Hilliards." Aurelia noticed a cloud pass over her father's face.

"What about it, Aurelia? Would you like to come along? Nothing fancy. Caroline, Henrietta, all of them keep asking after you."

"Not this evening. But send them my best," she managed. Grateful for the distraction, she ate a ripe apricot in silence, forcing down every bite and steeling herself to remain downstairs until her father retired for the evening.

She did so by flipping through the latest *Ladies Home Journal* while Aristide scoured his invoices from the recent auction of cotton and corn.

"You must make an effort, Aurelia. I'm expecting that of you," Aristide said out of the blue as he rose to go to bed.

"I will, Father. I promise."

It was ten o'clock and the first time she had remained downstairs in company since before her "accident." But as soon as her father ascended, she turned down the lights and crept back to the sanctuary of her own room.

Chapter Twenty-Eight

Even before she spotted the black man waving from atop the only carriage at the dock—what was his name? Some city. Boston, Toledo. She couldn't dredge it up—Margaret heard bells peeling the noon hour. How reassuring, she thought, to have the day clocked by church chimes so that all and sundry could be alerted that they were in a city, together, and, whether they liked it or not, in God's care. Her hat adjusted, Margaret picked up her leather bag. Cleveland was his name. She waved in return.

"Looking mighty fine, Miz Taylor, though it be way too long we ain't seen you here," Cleveland said as he took charge of the bag and handed the visitor into the carriage. "A tonic for Miss Aurelia. She don't get out much, not since she come back from the other side."

The carriage door latched, Bessie set off lickety-split before Margaret could think what to respond. As they approached Washington Street, Cleveland slowed to allow shoppers to scurry out of the way. The two-days-before-Christmas frenzy had set in. Hitching posts were bedecked with tinsel and a string of lights overhung the intersection with Clay Street. Two young women, dressed like elves, stood at opposite corners, energetically ringing bells to solicit donations. Bracing, Margaret thought, to be in a city at such a time, away from the farm and her soured relations with Hiram. She had so jumped at the idea of a visit that her brother had no need to press his case.

It being midday, neither Aristide nor Alfred was at home to welcome their guest, but Susanna greeted her with a wide grin and led her immediately upstairs to her room.

"Miss Aurelia done made the arrangements, pulled out Miz Sophie's finest bed linens, picked the hydrangeas for your night table. Done her a world of good. When you're settled in, just knock on her door."

In due course Margaret did, stifling her shock at seeing her niece so pale, startled like a deer when she looked up from her book.

"I am so glad to be here, on your side of the river, my dear. I hope not to be too much trouble. The flowers are beautiful. You needn't have."

"After all you and Sarah-Lynn have done for us, the times we've been at your place. It's the least…." Aurelia's voice sounded fraught with emotion.

"As I told your father, Sarah-Lynn so wanted to come over with me but promises to be here on the 31st. So many exams to prepare for—I did tell you she's planning to go to Sophie Newcomb in the spring, didn't I?"

Aurelia smiled, relieved that she had but one guest to tend to for a few days.

Not that entertaining her aunt was taxing. Margaret geared right in, in full throat among the Trinity Church carolers as they wended their way Christmas Eve up and down the hills, accepting hot chocolate from the prosperous houses at the top, bestowing candy canes and makeshift crosses on the poorer folks relegated to the bottoms. Aurelia had begged off, afraid the walking would be too strenuous.

Later, at midnight mass Margaret sat to the left of Aristide, Aurelia to his right, James and Alfred flanking the two women. As longtime members of the congregation noticed, it was the fullest Ackermann contingent on show since before Sophie had died. Afterwards, Henrietta and Caroline made a beeline to meet the newcomer—and to get a close-up view of their recuperating friend.

"We will see you all at the B.B. Club on New Year's Eve, won't we? You too Margaret," Caroline said, clutching Alfred's arm. Aurelia saw Aristide stiffen and then relax when his gaze landed on Horace Hilliard, who was holding forth along the aisle opposite. She wondered what that was about, but forgot it in the general exodus.

"My dear, I can't tell you how good it is to see you up and about," Henrietta confided to Aurelia as they stepped out into the star-lit night. "When you are ready, do come over. So much to catch up with." Too overcome to respond, Aurelia squeezed her friend's hand.

Alfred pulled out his pocket watch. It was 6:30 and he was the last lawyer in the office, wrapping up a proposal related to the bridge construction and filling out several last-minute court orders. Jeffries and the others had all taken their leave, thanking him in their off-handed way for tying up the loose ends. Even old man Greene had paused in the doorway to commend him.

"Doing well, my boy. Doing well. Trust we'll see you Saturday night in full regalia."

"Indeed, sir."

When the most senior partner's uneven footsteps had faded, Alfred put his feet up on his desk to await the last client of the day. He had already seen eight supplicants, including two that Jeffries had reneged on due to his overly long lunch. One more to go. Even so, he'd never make it home in time to dress for the opera. He phoned to insist James accompany Aurelia and Aunt Margaret in his stead. Besides, *Otello* he had attended not two months before, in New Orleans, and as much as he enjoyed being surrounded by the bare bosoms and clinging gowns of pretty young women, he was usually antsy by the third act. (Except he had been intrigued that time when he spotted C.T., with binoculars focused throughout the performance on a single group of young men in the loge section, never, that he noticed, on the goings-on on stage. Such an odd fellow.)

At precisely seven, the firm's long-time receptionist, a spinster named Miss Buchanan, appeared at Alfred's door. "Sir, your last client for the day—actually for the year—is here. Shall I show him in?"

"Yes, yes, and you may leave as soon as you're done. We hope to see you on Saturday night." Alfred made a mental note to have a corsage sent round to Miss Buchanan's rooms at the Aeolian Apartments. After all, she arguably worked the longest hours, for inarguably the least salary of anyone at Jeffries, Greene. If he were to vie for partner within a year or two, such gestures toward this fixture of the firm could only work in his favor. He turned to the last folder on his desk.

A man in the doorway cleared his throat.

"Ah, I wasn't expecting—it's you, Jefferson. Curtis, rather. Is your partner not with you?" Struck by how arresting a figure the black man cut, standing on the threshold hat in hand yet in such command of himself, Alfred rose unthinkingly to his own feet. "Do come in and we'll go over this application. Seems straightforward enough."

Curtis quickly obliged and looked straight at the lawyer across the desk. Something about Alfred's mouth reminded him of Aurelia but otherwise he seemed cut from the same cloth as his father—squared shoulders, prominent chin, confident in his privileges.

Within fifteen minutes the paperwork had been filled out,

attesting that Mayfield & Sons MOTORWORKS had repaid its original loan in its entirety and was forthwith applying for a second line of credit. While Alfred tinkered with the legalese, Curtis sat with his hands in his lap, eyeing as inconspicuously as possible the photographs on the desk. In one a young girl, clearly Aurelia, sat astride a white pony, a boy on each side. They were all squinting into the sun. At the bottom he could make out *At Cooper's Well, 1909*.

"If you make it to the bank tomorrow, my father can shepherd the loan. Should be no problem. You are—Mr. Mayfield, rather—is in good standing and I see no reason why an expansion of the business, selling new as well as used cars, isn't a good investment."

"I appreciate your efforts, Mr. Ackermann," Curtis said as he slipped the papers into the inside of his suit pocket and rose to leave. "We'll stop by the First National around eleven tomorrow."

Alfred came round to shake his client's hand. "I never asked. Have you returned for good? To work with Mayfield?"

"Not at present. I did a degree—engineering—in Chicago. I'll be working with a hydraulics firm, up and down the river."

"Very impressive," Alfred said.

Curtis felt he should say something on behalf of his benefactor. "It's not, I hope you understand, that I don't appreciate everything Mr. Mayfield, his wife too—she was formerly my teacher—have done for me. I enjoy engines but I love the river more."

Alfred paused, then picked up on the poetic note. "Yes, the Mississippi. Like a woman, right? Wayward but enticing."

So unexpected was this remark from the lawyer that Curtis blushed. "Indeed," was all he could think to rejoin as he backtracked into the hallway.

Taking the cue, Alfred passed in front of his client to escort him to the steps outside. As they shook hands, Curtis felt the firmness of the other's grasp.

"I almost forgot. I wanted not only to thank you on Mr. Mayfield's behalf, but to wish you—all of your family"—: he dared not mention any of them by name—"a prosperous new year."

"Why, thank you. And remember, ask my father about the going rate," Alfred called out. "No more than 5%. Insist upon it."

Curtis turned up his collar against the crisp air and tipped his hat. Unlike the night before, he decided against circling past the house on Adams Street, turning instead toward the repair shop where Willy had converted a back shed into sleeping quarters. An Army cot, a rudimentary hand basin and shaving mirror and, (somewhat incongruously) on the opposite wall, the sketch Aurelia had done in front of the shop.

Chapter Twenty-Nine

Only in the dimmest of lace-curtained light had Aurelia bathed during the last three months, never daring to glance in the mirror at her naked body. Though the cuts from Hiram's assault had long healed, her mind did so only by fits and starts. Whenever her thoughts strayed to that awful episode, she would reach for the silver-handled brush and stroke her hair hard and fast, as though bristles to the scalp could dislodge the demons inside her head. Her gold-flecked locks grew long, but despite the bobs that were now all the rage, she could not gather herself to make an appointment for a trim.

Rarely did she set foot outdoors, unless to cut flowers or pick up something from the Piggly Wiggly. But now with Margaret as their guest, Aurelia willed herself away from the edge of things. She had gotten through midnight mass on Christmas Eve and the opera a few nights later. She had exchanged pleasantries with a few acquaintances, not registering much of what was said other than the surprised greeting from Madame André at the performance of *Otello*: "*Quel plaisir de vous voir, mademoiselle, après trop longtemps.*" Her own response was uninflected, "*Le plaisir est tout à moi,*" which effectively ended the dialogue. With Sarah-Lynn's arrival set for the morning of the 31st, she agreed to accompany her aunt to shop for something suitable for her cousin to wear to the B.B. Club.

"Hopefully, we can find something festive that will fit her—you can imagine how limited the dress shops are in Tallulah," Margaret said once in the carriage. "Oh, and, if you don't mind, we'll stop by the bank thereafter. Your father has advised me to open an account there, and not rely solely on the Hibernia."

Aurelia directed Cleveland to drop them off in front of the Valley. If not the fanciest of stores, its selection was the widest in town, and the clerks busy enough with customers not to be overly insistent.

After browsing the ground floor, they took the elevator past the mezzanine to the second floor where evening wear was arrayed. It was only 9:30, but numerous customers were about. Eventually, the two settled on three possibilities from off the rack, the best-looking a green taffeta affair with an empire waist and puffy sleeves. In the three-sided mirror, Aurelia's reflection stared back, her face all angles, her body swallowed up by the dress she had agreed to model.

Despite how it hung on her niece, Margaret stifled any comment. "It's perfect. Sarah-Lynn will love it."

On their way out, she bought herself a jar of Anna Lynne face cream and two boxes of Elizabeth Arden face powder, one a shade lighter than the other.

"This one's for you, Aurelia. Albeit you don't need it, it might heighten your complexion." The hint, though hardly more diplomatic could it have been couched, made a little color rise in her niece's face.

"Let's window-shop our way to the bank," Aurelia then suggested. "So many new stores have opened. You might see something you'd like for the house. And it doesn't cost anything to look."

Margaret laughed, glad to see this spurt of enthusiasm on the part of her niece, and glad to have a chance to be in town without any obligations to speak of.

"I don't know whether your father mentioned it," she ventured as they studied the rings in the casement outside Yoste's jewelry store. "But I'm thinking of moving to New Orleans, where Samuel and I had a few friends, where Sarah-Lynn will be studying."

Aurelia felt her heart sink like a stone. "What about the farm, the horses—everything?" She braced herself against the glass display, her ungloved hand leaving a smudge.

"Oh, don't worry. We'll keep the house, a few acres too. The farming, though, it's become a headache. So few workmen of any worth, so many problems."

Aurelia tensed for the sound of Hiram's name but it did not come.

"Truth be told, and as these concoctions can attest," Margaret added brightly, holding up the meticulously-wrapped package of cosmetics, "I'm not getting any younger. That's why I'm opening this account, so that your father can advise on the sale of the land."

"I think it sounds exciting. Something new," Aurelia forced herself to say.

A uniformed guard held wide the heavy bronze door of the bank when they reached it. The place was busier than usual, it being year's end, taxes and bills looming. Aurelia scanned the room for any sign of her father.

"Why, Mrs. Taylor. What a surprise. And—"

The two women both jerked their heads in the direction of the familiar voice. Curtis' eyes had locked onto Aurelia's startled face but he seemed unable to utter her name. Willy mauled his hat and bobbled his head as he tended to do in front of any white woman.

"Why Curtis, Willy, how nice to see you both," Margaret responded in a voice Aurelia thought too loud. The older woman extended her gloved hand. "Whatever brings you here, to Vicksburg, to the bank, I mean?" she asked, as if not fully grasping how unorthodox their encounter appeared.

"Bizness, Miz Taylor. We be expanding the shop," Willy mumbled. "Mr. Ackermann, with Curtis' help, done 'bliged us with financing."

To Aurelia's relief, Mr. Gauge made his way over, effectively forestalling any further comments from Margaret.

"Miss Aurelia, as ever, and I presume Mrs. Taylor. If you'd be so kind, we can get you all set up," he said in his most bankable voice. He ignored the two men and gestured for the ladies to follow him.

For an instant Aurelia raised her eyes to meet Curtis' animal-sad gaze.

"I trust you are well," he said.

"Better, thank you," she mouthed before she numbly followed her aunt across the marble floor to Mr. Gauge's desk.

Outside on the pavement, Curtis took a deep breath. He started to walk at a faster pace than usual, Willy having to make an effort to keep up.

"Now I remember," the older man exclaimed as they started up Jackson Street. "The girl on the wall." Curtis had no intention of giving his companion any satisfaction. "I seen it, in her eyes too. You'd best not be fooling with folks like that."

A pinch in his brow, Curtis stared straight ahead. "I am nothing to her, nothing," he muttered.

However unorthodox Mr. Gauge found the quartet blocking the entrance, he prided himself on a banker's number one asset, discretion. Thus, without any allusion to the two men now referred to routinely by colleagues as "Ackermann's motor mechanics," spread out the requisite paperwork.

After initialing the required boxes, Margaret rummaged in her handbag for what she told the loan officer would be her opening deposit. If impressed by the amount she handed him, he remained impassive.

Aurelia sat mum throughout the transaction, ignoring Mr. Gauge's pleasantries. To compensate, Margaret admired his efficiency and shook his hand vigorously.

Once out on the street, Aurelia set off at a clip. Margaret kept up and, as agreed that morning, they entered the crowded lobby of the Carroll Hotel for their one o'clock lunch reservation.

"What a charming place. If I lived here, I'd probably come for lunch every day."

"Actually, I think some people do," Aurelia replied. "I too used to enjoy it so..."

"You will again, my dear. Time is all it takes," Margaret avowed. What precisely could have precipitated, she still wondered, such an altered state in her once-lively niece? For months. Only recently had she taken tentative steps to re-engage with the rest of the world.

For twenty minutes they sat toying with their tea, feigning enormous interest in the other customers before any of the officious waiters paid any attention to their order. When the cream of mushroom soup finally arrived, Margaret had rolled all her thoughts into a little ball and was ready to toss it out. Especially since, with Sophie dead and the New Orleans aunt, Sybil, unaware of anything awry up in Vicksburg, it arguably fell to her to act as Aurelia's sounding board. Unsentimental advice needed to be dispensed—even if she herself had not always made the wisest of choices, especially when it came to matters of the heart, or, dare she admit it, the loins. She looked across at the younger, and, powder or not, beautiful woman across from her, whose whole life lay before her.

She cleared her throat. Her niece took a first spoonful of the hot soup and looked up.

"I do not want to be intrusive, Aurelia, but, as I'm sure you know, it is incumbent upon you to continue to make efforts to, to—"

"To what, Aunt? Eat lunch at the Carroll? Go shopping? Accept invitations to the B.B. Club?"

"Well, yes," Margaret sputtered, flabbergasted by her niece's vehemence. "Going through the motions can help get us back on track, even if we don't know why we got off in the first place."

Margaret turned to her soup, playing for time to steer the conversation back to what she had previously determined to say about the incident at the bank.

"In my case, Aunt Margaret, I do know."

"Well, that brings me to this morning, since clear to me, if hopefully not to others, Curtis is at the heart of this."

"About that, you do not have to fret. What happened has nothing to do with him. There is—there can be—nothing between the two of us. Let us please, if you will, put the subject to rest."

As unsatisfactory as this exchange was, Margaret acquiesced. She could feel that her niece had drawn a curtain and defied anyone to ruffle it. She looked around the room for something neutral to alight upon, settling on a lady's hat, the boa so long it practically brushed the woman's salad bowl.

Alfred rose several times that evening to adjust the knob on the wireless, the crackling pronounced whenever he tuned to Cincinnati. But, as he explained, that station played the best music with which to digest a hearty meal. He and Aristide read the papers while James marked passages in one of his law school textbooks. Margaret leafed through a magazine, pointing out a hair-do, which, holding aloft the page, she suggested would be ever so becoming on Aurelia.

The girl smiled, continuing to take up the hem of the skirt she said she planned to wear on New Year's Eve. "Everything's shorter, my dresses included, but I'm not yet ready for the beauty parlor."

Aristide eyed the two women from across the room, pleased that he had the good sense to invite his sister to town, and pleased that Aurelia had made an effort to remain in the family circle, way past the dinner hour. Susanna had already cleared and washed up the good china, surprising them all with steins of hot chocolate before taking her leave around 9:30.

Toward the end of *Eine kleine Nachtmusik* the phone rang. Again, Alfred rose and went into the hallway.

"It's for you, Aunt Margaret. Sarah-Lynn."

When she reappeared, Margaret's face was all acute angles.

"I do apologize, as does she, but Sarah-Lynn shan't be coming tomorrow. I'm not sure—we'll see. Strange though; she so rarely succumbs to anything..."

"Anything we can do?" Aristide asked, folding the newspaper and removing his spectacles. He considered the idea of rising to embrace or otherwise sustain his sister in her distress.

"No, no," she remonstrated, waving him off, her face modulating into a more relaxed expression. "I doubt it's serious. She'll call again if things worsen. So," she added, a feeble smile on her lips, "the B.B. Club is still on. I'll simply take the ferry the next morning—on New Year's Day—and that will be that."

"Too bad," James chimed in. "You have no idea, Father, h-h-how much fun we have together w-w-with Sarah-Lynn."

"We'll just have to try to make up for it, won't we?" Aristide replied curtly, more irritated with his son's stutter than disappointed over Sarah-Lynn's absence.

Chapter Thirty

Had Margaret known the real reason her daughter was in no condition to travel, she would never have stayed over for the celebration at the B.B. Club. Not that the evening wasn't interesting in its own right. Her brother, seemingly pleased to have her on his arm, introduced her to the good and great of the county. A Dr. Knox, the mayor (J.J. something or other), the parents of Henrietta, a couple of young men who described themselves as friends of Alfred or Aurelia, and who made quite a fuss over her— "Surely, your cousin and not your aunt, right, Aurelia?"

Another—tall, blond, having come up for the purpose from New Orleans—insisted Margaret do him the honor of a waltz. The firm's senior partner, Mr. Greene, most of whose remarks to her were drowned out by the chattering, did make a point, gesturing with his cane, of singling Alfred out in the crowd as their up-and-coming star.

At the midnight hour the guest from New Orleans magically reappeared with champagne for both her and her niece. “To your health, to a prosperous 1925, and to your crossing over more often,” he toasted, raising his own flute. Margaret couldn’t decide if this C.T. was charming or off-kilter, or perhaps charming because he was off-kilter.

But the music and laughter of New Year’s Eve seemed far removed once Margaret ferried to the other side. A glance at her daughter’s bruised jaw dispelled any notion of illness.

“What in the world?”

Then, in crashing waves, a torrent from Sarah-Lynn, Wilena all the while murmuring like a Greek chorus. She had been at the piano, fingering a Scott Joplin rag when the screen door in the kitchen banged open.

“I thought someone was coming in for ice tea or something”—but suddenly an arm grasped her wrist, pulling her from her stool. Hands fumbled over her breasts for buttons. A mouth reeking of whiskey searched out her own. She fought to free herself but got slapped across the face and pinned against the upright.

“He kept cursing, Mother. ‘You bitch,’ he said. ‘I’ll ride you like that damn horse of yours. Like I did your whoring cousin.’ Horrible things like that.”

She paused, gasping, and then rushed on. “I got my arm free, grabbed the bookend. Shoved it in his chest. He kept cursing and cursing but I heard Jinx. He was standing in the doorway to the parlor. ‘Let her be, you fool,’ he said, and I thought he was going to help me, but he didn’t, Mother.”

Sarah-Lynn was sobbing by now, and Margaret gathered her up in her arms. Her daughter’s words were muffled against the front of her dress, but she heard them as clearly as if Sarah-Lynn had shouted them.

“He snickered, Jinx did, and told Hiram, ‘You’re in no shape for this. Not now anyhow,’ and then he laughed. That’s when I ran upstairs to my room. Locked the door. Came back down to phone you after they left."

Margaret smoothed her daughter's hair back, holding her tight.

"I'm so sorry, Mother. Missing the trip and everything..."

"Not your fault, Sarah-Lynn," she said, dropping several kisses and not a few tears on the girl's head. "And it'll never happen again."

"That Hiram be a devil, Miz Taylor. Ain't no two ways 'bout it," Wilena added, winding up her chorus.

Without another word, Margaret marched straight to the gun case in the front hall and took out her dead husband's loaded shotgun. For the next hour she waited in the barn for the men to return from the fields. Rarely had her resolve been so unshakeable. Involving the law in this mess? Not a chance. The whole thing would be dismissed as kidding around. And Aurelia? Now she knew the reason for so much...and why her niece had never spoken up.

"It's up to me—as it should be," she told herself.

Chapter Thirty-One

On New Year's Day Aurelia settled on a resolution, feeling that the very act of writing it down would compel her to put it into motion.

"The more specific, the more likely you will be able to accomplish your goal," Henrietta had suggested the night before. She had just finished waltzing with Alfred—for the second time—and seemed flush with excitement. "I am single-minded about mine, I can tell you, and as you can imagine, it involves your brother." Aurelia had nodded in polite encouragement, although noticing her brother in huddled conversation with Caroline over at a far window.

Her own resolution, Aurelia decided, would not revolve around sentimental attachments but on acts of usefulness to others. Acts that might supplant thoughts of Curtis, which, to her dismay, had resurfaced after that excruciating encounter at the bank. She had thought about the inscriptions on her father's onyx ring—the one she had been entrusted to polish every few months. *Probity* was not an attribute she could claim for herself but *Purpose*, engraved on the other side of the band, she could adopt. Thus, she would devote herself to her father. For three years away at Stephens, she had become oblivious to the creeping predictability of his routines. On too many evenings he retreated to his study, often with crusty Mr. Kreisler (he of vocal pro-German sentiments) to play chess, drink bourbon or both. This is not the way a bank director should behave, she told herself, and not what my poor mother would want. To start, she would shower him with tickets to this or that entertainment, and insist on accompanying him to the occasional party or official get-together.

Knowing her father's aversion to being bossed around, Aurelia proceeded with studied casualness, often playing on the fact that it was she who needed to get out more. By the late spring, father and daughter had become a fixture around town, inviting a few guests into their box at the opera, showing up for church socials, or taking in the latest D.W. Griffith or Charlie Chaplin picture.

"You doin' him good, Miss Aurelia. Your father be spry as a chicken. You too be looking like your old self," Susanna let out one rainy April afternoon as together they polished Sophie's prized silver coffee urn. "I can finish this. You needs go draw a bath if you 'spectin' to go with the menfolk to Miss Henrietta's."

For the first time in ages Aurelia took extra time to prepare, trying on several outfits before settling on a powder-blue shirtwaist and her mother's sapphire earrings. In the mirror, she admired the bob she had finally submitted to. It set off her face and made her jewelry more conspicuous. Not that the invitation to the Cartwrights' *soirée* was billed as anything other than a typical Vicksburg party given by a prominent couple with extended business and social contacts. But, from what Henrietta had confided during one of their recent missions to the poor, her father's insurance business was booming, what with all the companies vying for contracts related to the bridge construction.

"My parents want to host a party—to thank their clients and

friends—but they also want to signal that I am still alive, well, more than that, that I am an active—dare I use the word? —available member of the community. Hence they plan to do it *chez moi* on Drummond Street. You and your brothers, your father too of course, absolutely must come."

Whatever had been the expectations of the Cartwrights or their daughter that evening were dashed when the Ackermanns pressed the doorbell. To Henrietta's consternation, father and daughter presented themselves *sans* Alfred.

"I'm so sorry," Aurelia babbled. "A last-minute business trip. And James is still up at Ole Miss."

Deflated though she was, Henrietta ushered them in and busied herself with other guests. Around nine her daughter Emily, a pretty child with the same black curls and violet eyes as her mother, toddled into the parlor to be ooh'd and aah'd over before being taken up to bed by the nanny. Several of the men, including Aristide and Hilliard, then congregated in the library where a huge map of possible construction sites for the bridge was spread out on a table.

"I took the liberty, gentlemen, so you could see, graphically see, what a communal effort it'll take to get this done, and done right," Jasper Cartwright said, scanning the room. "Thought Major John Lee might want to say a word."

"Jasper's right, sirs," rejoined the purposeful-looking head of the Mississippi River Commission. "This span will put Vicksburg, indeed the entire region, on the map, as it were. But, mind you, it's going to take civic leaders—you bankers, lawyers, merchants—as well as us engineers to get this done on time and on budget. A dedicated labor force as well. I trust that we're all on the same page?"

Several guests muttered their general assent. Major Lee's gaze scoured the room, his sights settling on Aristide.

"You're a banker and a councilman, Ackermann. You think we can get this done—provide the necessary loans at competitive rates?"

Taken aback, Aristide paused to put his drink down and to shape a cogent response. “As far as the bank’s concerned—”

“With all due respect, Major, I should be the one to address that issue,” Hilliard butted in, jerking his face first in Aristide’s and then back in Lee’s dumbfounded direction. “The bank is prepared to back all the stages of the project, the terms and conditions of the bond issue already fleshed out, ready to go.”

Several in the room exchanged glances, Hilliard’s effrontery apparently as off-key to them as to Aristide in what was supposed to be an informal conversation among like-minded gentlemen. Over Cartwright’s best bourbon, to boot. The major, however, shrugged as if to acquiesce to an importunate, if legitimate, intruder. All Aristide could do was submit to the insufferable tone of his nemesis. What was it Sophie used to say about the Hilliards? Boring and boorish. She could be withering...

Aristide did catch the tail end of the remarks, something about keeping the costs of construction under the projected $8 million by relying on cheap labor.

“We can get niggers for next to nothing around these parts. As long as we have guns to keep them in line,” Hilliard concluded, looking ever so proud of himself for having usurped the role of the absent Mayor Hayes as well as representing the bank. A couple of guests gave hesitant nods, but Aristide could not let the last comment go unchallenged.

“We might, I submit, do better to pay people a decent wage,” Aristide said, scanning the room for moral support. “Including whatever laborers will be risking life and limb below and above the water. If we corral a competent work force, guns can be left at home.”

“Here he goes again,” Hilliard snorted, throwing up his arms as though to suggest he’d heard such drivel from his colleague many times over. “Always taking their side, always standing up—”

“That will do, gentlemen,” Cartwright broke in. “Let’s not get testy. Plenty of time for argument at City Hall, when J.J. is up and about again.”

Their host maneuvered around the table and involved the major in a closer critique of potential sites for the bridge, effectively dispelling the tension. Since Aristide had already seen the blueprints, and since he hardly wished to squabble in public, he turned on his heel and harumphed out of the room.

"Why don't you sit with me here, away from the madding crowd, and bring me up to date on Ackermann affairs?" Henrietta suggested when he reappeared, obviously rattled and without a drink in hand. She took his arm, gestured to a servant for two bourbons, and led him to an empty couch.

If her motive was to discover what kept Alfred away so much, Henrietta soon found herself pleasantly surprised by the older man. Less starched than she had assumed, and, for whatever reason, in the mood to open up.

"You grew up with Alfred, my dear, so you can appreciate the ambition he harbors," Aristide volunteered. The war—: sidetracked him for a while. Hard to get past such things but he's ever more bent now on moving ahead, laying the groundwork for expansion, that sort of thing."

Henrietta took all this in, not allowing herself to ask anything more personal about that particular Ackermann son. "And James? Such a sensitive young man. Devoted to Aurelia. What are his plans after university?"

"Those too have been scuttled. During his spring break he confessed he had abandoned the law course. The stuttering, I guess," Aristide confided, surprised at himself for sharing this piece of news, not because it wasn't apparent to anyone acquainted with his son that he suffered an impediment but because he typically muzzled his own disappointment in his son's handicap. "It appears he'll devote himself to, of all things, accounting while still up at Oxford," he added, his face falling.

"Well, I think that's splendid. Better to do something one feels comfortable with or that is attainable. And, mind you, accounting has its own merits, and challenges. But I needn't tell you that, Mr. Ackermann, you being a banker and such."

This Henrietta said batting her violet eyes, and patting him on the arm. Almost flirtatiously, Aristide imagined, and not at all unwelcome. They glided smoothly over other subjects—little Emily's education, the growing hustle-and-bustle downtown, and Henrietta's own desire to travel.

For once on the ride home, Aristide did not quiz his daughter as to whether she had enjoyed herself, it being now clear to him that she had overcome her debilitating "condition," however unknowable its cause. Besides, during their *tête-à-tête* Henrietta had inadvertently mentioned that her best friend was searching out colleges closer to home than St. Louis, where she might complete her degree—another indication that his daughter was knitting her life back together. As they approached the intersection of Cherry with Chambers Street, Aristide suddenly let off the pedal to allow a skittish buggy horse to make the turn.

The liquor having loosed his tongue, he mused aloud, "I wonder why your friend—so charming, I was pleased to find—hasn't considered re-marrying. Despite the child, she's still attractive, the Cartwright family well-established, no reason..." Aristide shifted the gear stick and the car lurched forward.

That night, Aurelia lay awake, listening to the rain lash the windows and thinking about the various states of loneliness in which her father, Henrietta, and she, too, found themselves. Only in the milky light of early morning did she allow herself to picture Curtis—he conceivably as lonely somewhere in the cold North.

Widowed, all.

Chapter Thirty-Two

Of all the books Aurelia tackled that summer, the one that most unsettled her was *Madame Bovary*. She found too much of herself reflected in Flaubert's heroine, including her flaunting of propriety. She vowed to write to Claudette, who had by sheer propinquity fine-tuned Aurelia's ear to the sound of French, German and even Italian. Sufficient enough that she could now accede to the most advanced courses in comparative literature at Belhaven, a small Christian college in Jackson.

She wouldn't even have to domicile in the capital city. James, his own degree in accounting now in hand, volunteered to drive her once a week for the seminars that required her presence. Four months of perseverance and she would be awarded a liberal arts degree.

It was on one of the drives in late November that James let slip the latest news from what they both referred to as "across the river." Up until then they had avoided all discussion of the Taylor household, especially its hired help, but James had the month before ferried over to help with the auction of furniture and livestock now that Sarah-Lynn was enrolled at Newcomb and Margaret had disposed of the bulk of the land. Only Slim and his family were kept on to manage the remaining acreage, see to the upkeep of the house and tend to the horses that neither of the women could bear to part with.

"Did you know about Hiram? Banished to Bastrop, right after New Year's. Seems that—and I'm only telling you because of what h-h-happened to you, which I would have k-k-killed him for had I known at the time—he tried to assault Sarah-Lynn. During the holidays while Aunt Margaret was with us in Vicksburg."

Blood drained from Aurelia's face.

"Nothing happened. Sarah-Lynn fended him off. Aunt Margaret waved a shotgun at him—told him to vamoose or else."

"H-how did you know I...he..." Aurelia couldn't utter the words.

"Sarah-Lynn, quite matter-of-factly, told me all this when we met up in New Orleans, the weekend she registered for courses. Evidently Hiram bragged about it when he attacked her."

"Maybe if I had said something..." Breathing spasmodically, Aurelia closed her eyes to fix and then disassemble the image of Hiram in her head. "He's gone for good—is that what you're saying?"

"Back to his cousin's dirt farm. Jinx got fired too."

"So, they'll all be leaving. Nothing left..." she murmured.

"Not entirely. Aunt Margaret is holding on to the house, the gardens and such." He paused before the next revelation. "Wilena is following her to New Orleans—too old now to manage her own place—but Curtis insisted they keep that cabin that belonged to his grandfather. And that pond where we fished, the woods nearby..."

The home of the ghost deer. Aurelia smiled but said nothing.

Back in her room that evening, she penned that note to Claudette. She didn't have the fortitude to read the still boxed-up letters received from her friend during the past year, but starting the correspondence anew in the hope that her friend would pick up where they had left off, she could now do. It took reams of her pale blue stationery to compose something she considered heart-felt without being overwrought or apologetic. Among other things, she asked Claudette's opinion of Emma Bovary (not to flatter her former roommate but to pay homage to their many hours arguing about tragic heroines). She asked after the elder Nowitskis but made no inquiries after Rufus.

As for the other letters languishing unopened in the second box—five altogether postmarked from up and down the Mississippi—she pressed them to her lips but could not imagine writing in response. At three in the morning she carefully re-positioned both boxes at the back of her wardrobe.

Two weeks later Susanna limped laden with mail into the parlor, her knees acting up in the unseasonably cold December. She placed several business envelopes and gold-embossed invitations on Aristide's pipe stand, dropped a couple of letters on Alfred's armchair, another on James'—both young men apparently working late—and a personal letter in a dark rose envelope post-marked Chicago she handed to Aurelia.

"Smells like flowers, Miss Aurelia," Susanna whispered as she straightened her back and headed off to the kitchen.

As sacrosanct as personal correspondence was in the Ackermann clan, the reading thereof was customarily done in the bosom of the family circle. If Aurelia preferred to retire to her room to peruse her own, she resisted the urge. She put Balzac to one side and unsealed the envelope.

Ma chère,

Overwhelmed I was. What? A year has passed—and yet you are still alive, and remember our friendship. Should I be angry? Mais non. *I am only too happy to hear from you. And to know that you are better. And finishing your degree.*

The last year at Stephens sans toi *was miserable. My new roommate, Hortense, from what is considered in your country august lineage, from Saratoga or some such place, was unbearable. Such a prig. But that is over now. Believe it or not, I graduated with honors—the* summa cum *being taken quite seriously here—my parents befuddled but proud.* Mais ça suffit. *All the rest is much more interesting, complicated but interesting. You did not ask, but Rufus continues to be hard to throw over, despite—well, you know what I'm referring to. Once, in the late spring, he came down on the train with Curtis, and, dare I surmise that you still care? He–Curtis, that is–drove me to distraction with his questions. What could I tell the poor man...even more handsome by daylight he is! Like him, I was totally in the dark.*

Nevertheless, it is probably for the best the thing be ended between you two. Or discreetly prosecuted. So think my parents as to my predilections in that regard and in response they have introduced me to—yes, of all prospects—a Pole, from the Old Country as they eagerly put it. Not that Stanislav Kazinski acts like the count from Krakow that he is, or was before the war; rather, he is changing his name to Stan Katz to facilitate his business affairs. Anything can be done in America, right? That accomplished, he says he hopes to change my name as well...

Meanwhile, I believe we should continue to seize the day. Now that we are again in contact, I hope to travel down to New Orleans before too long. If I remember, you have family in the Crescent City so perhaps we can rendezvous in the Vieux Carré. Such would be merveilleux, n'est-ce pas*?*

Claudette

p.s. Emma Bovary would fare better nowadays. She could, and we can, make our own way in the world if need be. We simply have to have—a new word for me—gumption!

Every contact with Claudette, even epistolary ones, made Aurelia's mind race. Hadn't the Ackermanns just been invited to spend the holidays with Aunt Sybil and Uncle Philip? And wasn't

Aunt Margaret, who had already bought a place Uptown, planning on her own house-warming there? Surely, Claudette would make for a lively addition to the guest list. Aurelia glanced at her father, who looked to be nearing the last inside page of the paper. She waited until he completed the ritual, lit his pipe and began to sift through his own pile of letters.

"I have an idea, Father." Aristide arched his eyebrows as he inserted a silver letter opener into an envelope. "I've received a letter from my former roommate—you remember Claudette—and it occurs to me that inviting her down to New Orleans for the holidays might be in order. If, that is, Aunt Sybil, and Aunt Margaret too, wouldn't be overly inconvenienced."

Aristide slipped the document out of its envelope and pushed his spectacles up his nose. He grunted noncommittally.

No matter how hard she tried, Aurelia couldn't stifle the tentativeness in her voice whenever she addressed her father. Even her syntax oft undercut her purpose. Annoyed with herself, she took a deep breath.

"In short, it would be amusing for me, and so, if you have no objection, I will ring up Aunt Sybil, and then Claudette, this very evening."

"Fine, fine, my dear. The more the merrier as far as I'm concerned," her father responded, waving his daughter off and ripping open another envelope.

Aurelia took the hint, relieved that her father had found nothing immediate to object to. Before he could though, she slipped outside to clip rose blossoms for the dinner table.

For his part Aristide was more confounded than he let on. He had gone to great lengths to court—if that at his age were the right word—his daughter's widowed friend, proposing (and then putting up with) a recent weekend jaunt to Cooper's Well with the Cartwrights as well as with little Emily. He judged it a propitious moment to invite Henrietta, on behalf of his entire family naturally, to join them in New Orleans for New Year's. She had seemed eager as he counted off the other attendees: their hosts, the Durrells, naturally, his sister Margaret who had relocated there and her daughter Sarah-Lynn, Aurelia and James, and Alfred, who would be bringing Caroline. For no reason he could fathom, she abruptly stopped in her tracks (they had been walking alone in the woodsy expanse, admiring the autumn leaves), and declined, something about her own family having obligations over the holidays. It had ruined the rest of the outing.

Women, he sighed, as he relit his pipe. Especially this younger generation. They demand more than Sophie ever did. More freedom to change their minds, for one thing...Still, he supposed all the changes could be construed as progress: the vote, for example, higher education, jobs in the business world. His mind alighted on the pert young things behind the tellers' grates at the bank, definitely an improvement. And closer to home, Aurelia. She was coming out of her shell, and that Claudette would no doubt goose the effort. A veritable firecracker—not quite acceptable (she was both foreign and northern) but intriguing. For the moment, Henrietta be damned.

Aristide slit open the final component of his correspondence, gratified to see the personal note the mayor had scribbled at the bottom of the document from City Hall: *A: heard about the incivility at the Cartwrights. Be assured your viewpoint is valued in this office. Much to discuss next week, the bond issue not the least thereof. Hayes*

Now that he thought about it, Hilliard be damned as well.

Chapter Thirty-Three

About Claudette, Aristide was not wrong. She had a mischievous streak, which meant as soon as she had accepted Aurelia's invitation for the holidays in New Orleans, she hatched her own provocative plan. If seeing Rufus in Chicago had become tricky, given the full-court press Stan (abetted by her own parents) was subjecting her to, she would arrange a tryst elsewhere. Especially since he had adroitly insinuated himself into the nightclub business, his razzle-dazzle swagger being considered a plus by his bosses, and was now routinely dispatched (to procure dancers or booze, she was never quite clear) not only down river to St. Louis but as far south as

Memphis. Why not New Orleans, and why not, since Curtis had connections there too, make sure he was apprised of their movements?

Albeit English was her fourth or fifth language, Claudette had read between the lines of the invitation from the Ackermanns. Aurelia's erstwhile lover still ruled her heart, and he, Claudette had observed with her own eyes, still longed for her. As surreptitiously as it might have to be arranged (though she figured the Crescent City was more insouciant of *liaisons dangereuses* than that vigilant Vicksburg), a rendezvous, however brief, with Rufus and Curtis would be that much more delicious.

As proposed, she arrived by train in the Crescent City on Dec. 27, met by a thinner, paler Aurelia and her ever stiffer brother, Alfred. For the first several days sight-seeing took up most of the afternoons for the young women and, as Claudette had suspected, formal dinners hosted by the Durrells or their friends in the Garden District dominated the evenings. Not that they didn't have a good time traipsing through the Quarter. Claudette picked out an ivory brooch for Aurelia on the Rue Royal; and, not to be outdone, Caroline overpaid for a topaz necklace for herself, which Aurelia confided to her in whispers, was like most things pertinent to the Hilliards, ostentatious. Feeding the swans in City Park, where one of the more aggressive bit Caroline's hand, was rollicking good fun, she shrieking, the others stifling their laughter.

More taxing for Claudette were the dinners, as clearly hostesses expected her to behave properly, which meant deferring to the men whenever they expressed their views and thanking the lady of the house at every interval between courses. Not that the food wasn't excellent, the wines, especially the Loire vintages from the Durrells' cellar, superb, but the young men invited to sup—to her they seemed feckless. Except for one. Introduced to her as C.T., he exuded a whiff of the dissolute, though punctilious in his attentions to the Ackermanns. He talked politics to Aristide, insurance fraud to James and art to Aurelia. Anything that Alfred opined, he seconded; anything that Caroline offered her two cents on, he tolerated. It was hard to figure his game.

Harder too than Claudette had anticipated was finagling to get Aurelia away long enough to meet Rufus and Curtis. No mention of the latter had been made, except when they all congregated at Margaret's new home on Pine Street, a dignified dwelling near enough to Newcomb for Sarah-Lynn to walk and spacious enough to entertain a discrete circle of friends. They had come over from the Durrells the morning of the 31st to help arrange things for the evening meal and midnight champagne toast, Wilena already bustling about in a too frilly white-lace apron.

"Why, Miss Aurelia. The Lawd did his work bringing you back to health. And Miss Claudette, is it? You too, most welcome."

Wilena's olive-green eyes—identical to *his*—allowed Claudette to put two and two together, but a sharp glance from Aurelia stopped her from saying anything about it.

"What I need you two to do is test them biscuits in the oven. Then we can count and arrange the chairs. Miss Margaret and Sarah-Lynn out shopping for the morning and be resting the afternoon. 'Spect you two be doing the same."

Aurelia did not move. She could hear the swish of a pendulum. A grandfather clock, the most imposing one from the Taylor farm, hung on the far wall between two French windows.

"How is he, Wilena?" she asked, hoping the older woman didn't register the plaintiveness in her voice.

"He be fine, my Curtis. Moving right up, from what I knows. Going after a job with the Army." Aurelia was flummoxed until Wilena went on. "Army Corps of Engineers. High falutin.' Not sure they take him..."

Aurelia willed herself to desist asking any further questions. "Let's try those biscuits," she said, leading Claudette toward the kitchen.

After doing what they could to help Wilena arrange the place settings and submitting to a lunch of cold cuts, Claudette made her move, telling Aurelia she had a surprise in store. A cab came almost instantly, what with the streets deserted, only a few random firecrackers popping in the distance. The driver sped along St. Charles Avenue toward Canal Street and the Quarter. Handed a slip of paper, he took a right onto Rampart Street, then a left, pulling up in front of an unprepossessing boarding house, a couple of scraggly cats hanging about.

"It's the last day of the year. Only a few minutes. You can't *not*," Claudette said, thrusting a ten-dollar bill into the hands of the cabbie and shooing the vehicle off.

From his window on the top floor Curtis saw the two women step out onto the pavement, Aurelia turning her head this way and that. Warily. Across the street an old man in a shaggy sweater sat on a stoop polishing a trumpet; further along two pig-tailed girls played at hopscotch. Otherwise no one was about. Curtis surveyed the neat if unassuming room he had inhabited for the last week. He pulled down the oilcloth shade against the low winter sun and walked out to the landing. As arranged, Rufus had awaited the two women at the front door. Soft voices. The stairs creaked as first he led Claudette to his own room on the first floor and then escorted Aurelia up to the third.

Anxious, Aurelia did not unpin her hat. Rather, she stood in the middle of the room, uncertain, until Curtis scrambled to pull up the lone armchair.

"Thank you," she murmured, "though I shouldn't have come. It's too—"

"It's all right, Aurelia. We don't have to..."

"No, you deserve to know why." The echo of Hiram's insult bounced off the walls, though only Aurelia could hear it. She glanced around at the neatly-made bed, the desk piled with charts and maps, the lone window. Curtis took her hand. The sound of Hiram's words grew fainter.

"They are tied up with string, in a box. I couldn't bear—" He looked confused. "The letters you sent me. Unopened, still."

"You were unwell."

"No, no. Someday I will be able to tell you, that is, though, as of today, it no longer—"

Matters. At that moment she knew only love, their love, mattered, however impossible, however imperiling.

A tap at the door disrupted her jagged thoughts.

"For the years to come," Curtis whispered in her ear as his fingers released her hand. "Now go, and embrace your life."

Plaintive notes of "Amazing Grace" rose from the sidewalk below.

The only guest at Margaret's New Year's Eve housewarming who thought anything of Aurelia and Claudette's late arrival was James. He and Sarah-Lynn had gone walking through the Garden District in the late afternoon, and, as was her wont, she had prattled on about not only her new friends at college but her old ones as well. Including Curtis. He was in town, lodging in the Quarter along with a friend from up North—the friend was handsome too, a nightclub operator or such. They had gone to look at houses for Wilena, everyone over the moon that Curtis might be spending more time down this way.

"And you two? Whatever were you up to this afternoon?" Margaret asked Aurelia, as Wilena ladled turtle soup to the dozen guests, including a late-addition school chum of Sarah-Lynn and the aloof C.T.

"Browsing through the Quarter again. Such an amusing place," Claudette responded.

Aurelia fixed her gaze on the lobster bisque in front of her.

Eventually, Alfred broke through the chatter about this or that, firmly tapping a fork against his goblet.

"It's early yet but before we all become high and happy on the champagne that Uncle Philip has supplied us, I have an announcement to make." There were titters from Sarah-Lynn and her friend, and a sly smile on Caroline's face. He paused until all eyes rotated in his direction. "I'm sure you'll all want to congratulate our friend C.T. here. In the next month he'll be joining our law firm and relocating to Vicksburg. I propose a toast."

Aristide volunteered a "hear, hear" and all save Caroline, whose expression was noticeably dazed, politely raised their glasses.

C.T. inclined his head in acceptance, looking as if he had graciously acquiesced despite considerable sacrifice to the general clamoring after his person. In actuality, he had finessed his final card with Alfred only days before over whisky sours at his father's club. "Belleau Woods, awful mess. But we both made it out, comrades-in-arms forever. Remember Paris? Unearthing lodgings for you and that wench, vouching for you with the brass..."

As little as Alfred liked to be reminded of the war, or of Paris, he subscribed to the theory that one favor between officers deserved another. "To be clear, C.T. No more horsing around, no more—whatever it is you're up to. It'll be my reputation on the line as well."

At the train station two days later, Aurelia and Claudette embraced. Neither had spoken again of the rendezvous off Rampart, only focused on things they might do, books to be read.

"You must tackle *Anna Karenina*, even in translation, Aurelia."

"And you, in English though, *Middlemarch*."

But from her compartment, steam rising from the exertions of the engine, Claudette dispensed a final admonition.

"It's now clear to me, Aurelia. Seeing Curtis may be dangerous but he is true. That C.T. fellow? Tread carefully."

From the platform, Aurelia couldn't help but laugh. "Is that from Tolstoy?" she asked, loping alongside the slowly chugging train.

Claudette shook her head. "No, no. From my heart."

Chapter Thirty-Four

Well-finished young ladies of Vicksburg—of which the town had a superfluity after the war—could be counted on to attend this or that afternoon lecture at the B.B. Club. Though most all were by definition properly educated, meaning they believed Lord Tennyson the epitome of a poet and Sir Walter Scott the most inspired of novelists, few had ventured on to college or spent time further afield than Jackson. In this regard, Aurelia figured as something of an exception, and not altogether a positive one. Caroline had made sure of that, regaling the others with her account of the holiday in New Orleans, and what an execrable example this creature Claudette—a northerner, foreign to boot, and she smoked in public—set for their mutual friend Aurelia. Such gossip made Henrietta bristle. How could Alfred even contemplate...

That particular Wednesday in May a professor of English literature—all the way from the British Isles, the papers had reported—would be lecturing on Jane Austen. Henrietta had no trouble rounding up friends to come along even if they had only a hazy recollection of *Pride and Prejudice*. To their surprise, Dr. Barineau was a horsy-faced woman, who Henrietta thought looked as though she could have figured as a minor character, a sensible cousin or some such to the Bennett daughters. The tweed-suited professor argued that Miss Austen was way ahead of her time.

"It is reciprocal esteem that underpins the best of marriages, that which we are assured Elizabeth Bennett and Mr. Darcy will have, and which stands out as the relationship *par excellence* in the novel," she concluded, looking out at the faces before her. "Remember too," she later added over tea and what passed in Vicksburg for crumpets (biscuits with muscadine jelly), "that nothing is didactic in Austen. That's the beauty of it: the wit." Henrietta, Aurelia and Isabel had lingered after the lecture. "Starting with the opening sentence...Do any of you happen to recall it?"

Henrietta exchanged a glance with Aurelia before responding. "Unless I err, 'It is a truth universally acknowledged that a single man in possession of a good fortune must be in want of a wife.'"

"Precisely, my dear. From the outset, it's all in her tone—sardonic, ironic by turns," Dr. Barineau exuded. Mrs. Millstein, one of the Jewish dowagers in charge of the gatherings, materialized. Eyeing her watch, the professor put down her teacup, brushed the jellied crumbs from her sleeve, and stood to take her leave. She had the look of one who never had enough time to deliver the last, best insight in her teeming brain.

On their way up the hill to Adams Street, Henrietta picked up a loose thread from the lecture. "Do you think, Aurelia, that our emotions—our romantic notions and such—lead us to make wrong choices in love?" A quizzical look from her companion. "I mean, wasn't the professor, indeed Austen herself, arguing that intelligence would lead us in a more propitious direction?"

Aurelia didn't answer right away, and Henrietta wondered, and not for the first time, just what had caused her friend's strange introversion over the past year.

"I wouldn't rightly know," she began, but then thought better of hazarding much more than a simple, if cogent enough, answer. "But I do suspect that getting the heart and the head in concert is not an easy feat, and not just in novels."

As soon as they had refreshed themselves, Henrietta phoned home to make sure the nanny had little Emily under control and to say she wouldn't be back until late. In the Ackermann kitchen, a pot roast had been expanded with carrots, butter beans, squash, okra and extra potatoes, hourly it would appear from the pots and pans since piled in the sink.

"Every vegetable in the house done been peeled and tossed in, Miss Aurelia," Susanna said, "every time I hears someone else be coming."

By the time the three Ackermann males arrived, the two young women had set the dining room table with Sophie's better china and unfolded two card tables in what the family now called the living room. Aristide told the women since his Hudson was in the repair shop, he had walked from the mayor's office where yet another heated discussion about how the city would fund the bridge construction had flared. Soon after, James came in with a young woman who, thanks to her coif and cosmetics, Henrietta thought bore a passing resemblance to the actress Mae Busch. He introduced her as Evelyn, a clerk at the Valley. In the perfume department, the girl was quick to specify. She smelled of several scents, though not sufficiently to overpower the odors from the kitchen.

While Henrietta had mentally steeled herself for Alfred's entrance with Caroline on his arm—she had observed their friend slip out before the lecture had ended—he arrived with a fellow lawyer who went by his initials.

It was not the first time C.T. had supped on Adams Street, at each successive encounter paying greater attention to Aurelia. If Alfred noticed, he made no comment either to his new colleague or to his sister. She minded less and less, convincing herself the young man's conversation was more stimulating than his manner off-putting.

Pleasantries quickly dispensed with, the parties ate—and drank one of Aristide's better Bordeaux—with gusto, the conversation so spirited that Susanna tapped guests on the shoulder to get their assents for seconds.

"Jane Austen? De *gustibus non est disputandum*, but for my part too many petticoats and *pettegolezzi*," C.T. proclaimed at one point.

"What on earth is that word?" Evelyn broke in.

"It's Italian for idle gossip, which Austen revels in, but which, despite her wit, can be wearying."

"It would have been amusing had you been there today, as no one made any objection to Dr. Barineau's praise of her," Henrietta rejoined.

"Don't misinterpret. There's much to admire in her novels, though for my money George Eliot has more depth. Would you not agree, Aurelia?"

"Indeed," Aurelia responded, gratified that C.T.'s tastes seemed to dovetail with her own.

"Are we talking about the same Eliot?" James intervened. "The one who sad-sad-saddled us all with *Silas Marner*?"

They all laughed, except for Evelyn, who was clearly out of her depth and had no idea why this Eliot was referred to as a *she*.

Alfred then steered the conversation in a different direction. "Don't know what you think, C.T., but we here in Vicksburg seem stuck in the last century, literarily at least. You heard Caroline the other day at lunch: 'What about more modern authors?'"

"Amusing, her sudden interest in books, since Caroline has never succeeded in getting through a single volume of Dickens," Henrietta blurted out. Aristide gave her a startled look; Alfred lowered his eyes and made a show of cutting his meat. Aurelia hid a smile, silently agreeing with Henrietta.

"Well, Henry James has been claimed by both sides of the Atlantic. He's arguably modern," C.T. responded.

When no one took him up on this, Aristide stepped in. "Have

you actually plowed through any of Mr. James' tomes? I hear they can be tedious."

"Dense they are, sir, but also deep. For example, he describes the treachery that underlies relationships better than anyone."

Aurelia knit her brow, remembering the odd warning Claudette had called out that day from the moving train.

For an hour after dinner they played bridge, Evelyn surprising the others with her aggressive bidding and winning hands, at least when partnered with C.T.

"Too bad we're not doing this for money," she said when the tallies were counted. The others indulged her with smiles.

It was midnight before the guests departed, James accompanying Evelyn home to her mother on Belmont Street and C.T. preferring to walk to his suite at the Carroll. Alfred insisted—vehemently—that he motor Henrietta home in his Nash.

In silence the two old friends drove through the deserted streets, Henrietta looking out the passenger window at the few lights still burning in homes along their route, Alfred gluing his eyes to the road, despite no traffic to trouble with. When he pulled up to the curb in front of the Hancock house, he turned to face his companion. By the streetlamp she could see the contrition in his face.

"I waited until now as I wanted you, my dearest friend, to know first. I haven't even told Aurelia. This afternoon—must have been after that lecture at the B.B. Club—I asked Caroline to marry me." Henrietta's face fell and she bit her tongue to keep from protesting. "She would have come along to dinner but you know Caroline. She raced home to tell her parents."

Rubbing the knuckles of one hand against the other, Henrietta struggled to formulate a reply, but she couldn't get those beads Caroline wore out of her mind. Eventually she got hold of herself.

"I shall be happy for you both, Alfred." He started to elaborate but she cut him off. "If you don't mind, I should like to walk to the front door alone. Thank you for bringing me home, and"—her voice faltering— "for letting me know your intentions."

As if moved by her distress to some action, Alfred seized her hand and put it to his lips, but she pulled away, scrambled out of the car and marched up the stone steps and into her widow's sanctuary.

Chapter Thirty-Five

It took C.T. only four months to propose. It wasn't so much that he considered Alfred's engagement an inspiration—since, if anything, he found Caroline obnoxious, barging in at the firm to discuss houses for sale, derailing dinner conversation to go over wedding invitations—but, despite his salary, he was running low on funds. As stipulated in the trust set up by his father, he would come into half of his inheritance upon marriage. Besides, he sensed that people were beginning to notice his comings and goings from the Carroll. If any hint of gallivanting—as Alfred had euphemistically put it—got back to the firm of Jeffries, Greene, his job would be at risk. That he could ill-afford, given his previous scrapes in New Orleans. A wife, in short, was just the ticket to respectability.

Jane Austen had not touched on all the angles, C.T. considered over the roast beef sandwich one of the waiters had delivered to his door on a sweltering Sunday evening in August. He had opened the corner windows to circulate air through the top-floor suite. By all accounts, his was the nicest and the best ventilated of the rooms in the establishment. Even so, sweat had dampened the back of his pale gray silk robe.

"Compliments of the house, sir," the young man had said upon knocking, holding out the silver tray for inspection.

C.T. hesitated, eyeing the peachy down on the cheeks of the waiter. He quickly recovered. "Thank you—Jason, isn't it?" he inquired, depositing a dollar bill into the outstretched palm.

Amenities aside, it was time to move on from such a conspicuous address. But how? Over lunch, in the hotel dining room. All he had to do was be charming.

The actual words came over the butterscotch pudding, which, it being the hotel's specialty, he and Aurelia both ordered. He had meant to get it out of the way over the salad but he had gotten into an argument with the waiter over the lettuce, declaring it unconscionably wilted. Aurelia had already eaten most of hers without complaint, which the waiter made a point of noticing. Silence fell over the table; the entire room emptied out by the time the desserts arrived.

"So that we may continue to debate—with civility, I trust—the finer points of books, or indeed of food, and otherwise that I may continue to enjoy your company, I suggest that we marry. I'd be honored if you would consider the idea."

Had this contorted proposal come months earlier, Aurelia would have dismissed it out of hand. But Charles had grown on her, thanks to the bridge tourneys, the dances at the B.B. Club, and dinners at home, where he was an antidote to Caroline. (For an indeterminate period awaiting their own house to be built, Alfred and his bride had commandeered an entire wing upstairs on Adams Street as their own.)

But the too-close quarters at home were not the only reason that marriage seemed to Aurelia an appropriate option. An off-handed remark from Sarah-Lynn had tipped the scales in favor of matrimony.

"Can you imagine, Aurelia? We ran into Curtis in Tallulah. With a woman called Loretta. A secretary in some shipping company. Showing her where he grew up, he said."

Aurelia, Sarah-Lynn and James had been walking in the Military Park, about to climb the observation tower at Fort Nogales.

"You two go on up. I'd like to look around down here," Aurelia replied, her breath labored.

"Are you sure?" Sarah-Lynn asked. "I hope I didn't—"

"Come on, Sarah-Lynn. I'll race you up," James said, grabbing his cousin's arm and pulling her toward the circular stairwell.

Alone atop the hill once claimed by Spanish explorers, Aurelia had gazed out at the river beyond. In the afternoon sun the bend resembled a wide ribbon wrapping the wooded landscape. Of course Curtis was right, she told herself, remembering his parting words that afternoon in New Orleans.

"I must do what it now behooves me to do. What Mother would want. What Father expects of me," she vowed.

Before she gave Charles a final answer, Aurelia had hoped to confer with Henrietta, but her friend had, with no fanfare, some months ago sailed to Europe for an extended trip, leaving little Emily with her grandparents. A cursory note addressed "to the Ackermann family," expressed her regret at not being in town for Alfred and Caroline's nuptials.

Chapter Thirty-Six

Knocked off-balance by Henrietta's abrupt departure, Aristide reverted to his old routines by, among other things, entreating Kreisler to return to the chessboard. It wasn't enough. A month on, he found himself newly upended when, out of the blue, C.T. asked for his daughter's hand in marriage. The three were standing in the living room, Alfred and Caroline having retired upstairs, Susanna having washed the dishes and departed.

Aurelia quickly poured the two men some cognac.

"How well are you fixed, sir," (what kind of a name was C.T. anyway?) "...to set up house and take care of my daughter?"

"I shall come into a substantial sum soon enough, Mr.

Ackermann, so no worries on that score," C.T. responded. "Besides which, I am doing well at the firm. I'm sure Alfred will attest..." His voice trailed off.

Well-heeled enough, yet something about the young man disturbed Aristide. As for Aurelia, she too was an enigma. Questionable acquaintances. Why even that mechanic—Willy Mayfield—had asked after her, that time he took the Hudson in because there was too long a wait for repairs at Christian and Burroughs. A Negro inquiring after his daughter. Then backtracking to say it was that Jefferson fellow, "friend" of the Taylors, who actually knew her. Very well. For many years. Confound it. How was it he had so little idea what went on with his own children? And now this.

"Charles and I would like something simple, Father. Elegant but simple. Here in the house. With just family and a few friends. The Durrells and Truards, of course, and Aunt Margaret, Sarah-Lynn."

Aristide took a swig of the tangy liqueur. At least she had the sense to call her fiancé Charles. And mercifully, not another lavish affair at Trinity Church, or the forced camaraderie with Hilliard. "Well, you two appear to have figured things out already if I'm not mistaken," he responded, his tone less gruff.

"Not without your blessing, Father," Aurelia persisted, taking his hand in both hers.

"So, my dear, most importantly, do you love this man?" Aristide asked, looking his daughter up and down, deliberately excluding C.T., who had turned away and downed his snifter of cognac in one gulp.

"Of course, Father. We plan to be very happy together, but that can only start with your blessing."

Aristide gave his consent, albeit something in his daughter's eyes filled him with misgivings.

The arguments started before the actual vows were exchanged. Without her mother, and with Henrietta still abroad, Aurelia found herself without a female to confide in. She wrote to the only friend who knew her heart in the hope that she might visit and advise, even stand in as the maid of honor.

"Claudette—that frightful person? Utterly inappropriate."

"But Charles. She's my closest friend. I owe it—"

"Then you must rethink your attachments," he retorted with ice in his voice. Aurelia did not dare confess that she had already mailed the letter. "If it's so important to you," he veered in a more conciliatory direction, "sound out your cousin. Countrified but adequate for the occasion."

During that and subsequent nights Aurelia wrestled with her fiancé's remarks, not so much the aspersions cast on her friends, dismaying as they were, but throw-away lines like "adequate for the occasion." Perhaps she was placing too much emphasis on the wedding ceremony. It was the afterwards that matters. Marriage (as Dr. Barineau had stressed) was supposed to be founded on affinity. Surely they had that, though beyond the foxtrot and bridge, she was too weary to pinpoint what they shared. Or, perhaps for Charles, he being a man, it would be principally about the sex, an idea in principle which did not altogether dishearten her. Aurelia strained though to picture the two of them in the throes of lovemaking. How would those exertions ever obscure the memory of —she would not speak his name—the one man she did love? She pulled the pillow over her head, trying to bury the recollection of that tiny room in Chicago.

James, too, had reservations about the step his sister was about to take, especially after he heard the gossip from Evelyn, who lived not far from the rowdy waterfront. Young men carrying on in the middle of the night "like tomcats in heat," she put it. One inebriated gent she heard make a fuss with the cops, claiming he was a lawyer and would report them for false arrest. Despite his qualms, James didn't want to break whatever spell Aurelia was under. She deserves happiness, he told himself, especially after what she suffered at the hands of Hiram. If this C.T. is the man who can provide it (and supplant Curtis in her affections), so be it.

Nor did he object when the prospective groom let out one evening that he had leased a dignified enough two-story home on Baum Street.

"I trust that you will find it suitable enough for the interim," Charles said in an aside to Aurelia, and then to Aristide: "Belongs to a Mrs. Wilkerson, doubtless you all know her. Client of the firm, but on her last legs. Not likely to come out of the Sanitarium." He returned to his roast pork, as if daring any of the Ackermanns to question his unilateral decision.

"Eleanor Wilkerson was quite a beauty in her day," Aristide eventually declared, wiping his chin with his napkin and shooing Susanna and her tray of seconds away. "She and Robert used to entertain regularly. Bösendorfer in the parlor; both of them played, if I remember rightly."

"Now that you mention it, the place does need some work," C.T. went on. "Perhaps, Aristide, your man Cleveland could tend to the window sashes, replace a few floor boards, patch a leak in the carriage house."

If Aurelia was mortified by her exclusion from such a crucial decision or the casual request for Cleveland's services, she kept it to herself, relieved at least that Caroline and Alfred were out for the evening so that she wouldn't have to endure her sister-in-law's sneer. Whatever her concerns about the rental agreement, she would wait to be told. In matters of marriage, she had gleaned from the pages of *Ladies Home Journal*, to acquiesce to the wishes of one's mate was the preferred *modus operandi*.

All those years her mother had managed to nudge her father this way or that, how had she never observed the technique? Rarely had she missed her mother so acutely. Claudette too, who arguably would ask why they even needed nowadays to resort to such ploys.

Her friend had telegraphed her regrets: *Timing alas all wrong, Mother not so well, the "count" ever more insistent. Best of luck, C.*

Aurelia was relieved that she would not have to either rescind her invitation or argue with Charles about Claudette's inclusion in the wedding party, but as the actual day drew closer, she felt a keener need for a confidant. In the meantime, she oversaw the repairs, which were more extensive than C.T. had let on; she held nails for Cleveland, hired Susanna's niece, Rose, to mop the oak floors, and polished the antique furniture, including the out-of-tune piano, herself. The Wilkersons' tastes were refined but eclectic, ranging from a couple of Chippendale chairs to Art Nouveau lamps, but Aurelia found the overall effect not displeasing. She brought C.T. up to speed on her progress whenever he asked but otherwise volunteered little. Especially after he reprimanded her for bringing in a high-priced piano tuner from Jackson to revive the Bösendorfer.

"Expenses, Aurelia, need to be agreed with me *a priori*, not *post*," he had carped. She felt relieved when he took a business trip to New Orleans ten days before the wedding ceremony.

In his absence, she leaned on her brother for moral support.

"You're a man, James. To what might Charles object—or still require?" Aurelia asked, as she pulled him along to show him what was essentially a renovated house. The modern and quite expensive stone fixtures in the kitchen were a gift from her father. Her brother looked around upstairs and down, side-tracking into the master suite with its canopied Mallard bed and matching dressers between the windows, catching a glimpse of the freshly painted carriage house beyond.

"Quite livable, Aurelia. Other than bottles for the liquor cabinet I can't think Charles would find anything to object to," he replied in a neutral voice. Aurelia turned away rather than betray her anxiety.

The first week of marriage did not allay her fears.

Freshly bathed and powder-dusted, her thick hair pinned up but easily let down, she awaited her husband under the mauve canopy. Like most of the older homes in Vicksburg, the Wilkersons' was draughty, especially in damp December. She pulled the linen sheets and a fleece blanket up around her, though not so snugly as to look uninviting. And she waited, eyes shut, struggling to assemble a relevant passage from her French novels. Surely, George Sand had detailed something of use, some phrase to be whispered, gesture to be made, limb to be exposed. *"L'amplesse l'amplesse,"* she murmured to herself, the memory of those acts she had performed so eagerly, so thoroughly, in perfect synchronicity with—

A floorboard on the staircase creaked. She propped herself up against the pillows, trying to strike a pose somewhere between casual and eager. But the expected knock on the door did not come. Rather, she could make out footsteps descending the staircase and shortly afterwards the click of a cabinet. Then silence, save for crackling in the grate across the room and the clock on the mantelpiece striking the midnight hour.

She fought off drowsiness as best she could but drifted off. Eventually she was roused. A hand groped under her satin negligee. A soured breath, mumbled words, though not her name. Acquiesce, accommodate drummed in her head. Arching her back, Aurelia tried to move in unison with the body astride her but she couldn't sense a rhythm. She tilted her torso so that her breasts rubbed against the exposed chest above her. To little effect. The body pulled away abruptly to the edge of the bed.

For what seemed an eternity she dared not speak.

"Come to bed, Charles. It's late," she finally said as matter-of-factly as she could. He exhaled but did not turn around to face her. Without trying to sound knowing, she added, "And remember, dear, this is but the first of all our nights together. Some things take time." She extended her arm to take his hand but C.T. brusquely rose and robed himself.

"Get some sleep, Aurelia. I will see you at breakfast," he said. Before she could demur, he had crossed the room and closed the door behind him.

A week later Aurelia took Margaret and Sarah-Lynn to lunch at the Carroll, an outing which she would have ordinarily enjoyed. Having camouflaged as best she could her puffy eyes, she chattered about the house, the tutoring she planned to do, the trips she hoped she and C.T. would take.

"Perhaps Europe. It seems to have done Henrietta a world of good," she went on over the soup. She avoided Margaret's eyes, knowing her aunt would sense something amiss, would know she was, so soon, putting a brave face on things.

"Paris and London aside, Aurelia, we want to see you two in New Orleans, or indeed you on your own. Whenever the fancy strikes you."

Doing anything because the fancy struck her seemed unlikely to Aurelia given the strictures under which she was now operating as Charles' wife. Or figuring out how to circumvent. That very morning over the poached eggs she had prepared, he detailed the provisions of her monthly allowance.

"For clothes, entertaining, incidentals, fifty dollars should be adequate. Anything over and above you should clear with me. I'd suggest we have an accounting at the end of each month. See how it goes…"

She had sipped her coffee and decided not to reveal that she had her own substantial account at the First National, under her father's management. As for how those other things in their marriage had gone so far, neither made mention. C.T. had not returned to their bed since that first abortive night.

"That's lovely of you—both of you," she said now to her aunt and cousin. "I, we, shall take you up on it. In the spring perhaps. *Belle of the Bends*, they say, is surprisingly luxurious for a steamer."

"Of course. You two need to focus on each other. With Samuel, it took well-nigh a year to smooth things out. Marriage is a wonderful institution, but I dare say it takes work."

Aurelia nodded in polite agreement, and urging her guests to finish their dessert, she rose to attend to the bill.

At the cashier's stand, she couldn't help but overhear two clerks on their break. "Checked out with nary a word. A real heartbreaker, huh?" The younger one, barely in his twenties, took a long puff on his cigarette but volunteered nothing. "Getting married of all things. Left a hefty tip though."

Later, sitting alone in the semi-darkness of the empty master bedroom, that cryptic exchange rang in her ears. Aurelia had an urge to get up and move—to find out where Charles was sleeping. But upstairs both guest rooms were neat as a pin, her mother's hand-embroidered cushions placed where she had put them days before they moved in. Downstairs, the newly upholstered couch in the living room appeared untouched. Baffling.

Ah, the carriage house. Oblivious to the cold, she mounted the wooden stairs. But the door was locked; she would have to ask Rose for the key.

Chapter Thirty-Seven

Curtis was more anxious than he was willing to admit. For weeks, he had prepared for the interview he was granted at the St. Louis office of the Army Corps of Engineers. He had amassed a dozen written recommendations, from professors at Chicago Normal College and from the various supervisors he had labored under, including his current boss at Norris & Co. He had taken great pains to rehearse, until he was able without hesitation to articulate the relative advantages of dredging the river bottom or shoring up the banks. He had even splurged on a wool suit and genuine leather dress shoes at a fancy department store Rufus had dragged him to.

"Look the part, look the part," his friend had repeated over and over as they trudged through freshly-fallen snow along Michigan Avenue on a frigid mid-January day in 1927. "Barriers don't come down, Curtis my man. You have to knock them over."

During the next few days as he traveled by train down to his interview, Curtis tried to remember what Loretta had advised, something rather different from Rufus. Warning him, he now recalled, against being perceived as uppity.

"Be smart but let them seem smarter. No way white folks gonna sit by and feel inferior," she had counseled as she carefully applied what had become her trademark red nail paint. Curtis watched her bosom rise and fall through a peignoir with each practiced dip of the brush into the bottle. It occurred to him that she was the only woman he knew, black or white, who applied color to her fingernails. Toenails too, he had had occasion to observe whenever she wore one of her many pairs of spike-heeled sandals. More to the point, he thought as he sat across from her in her untidied kitchen, she knew first-hand of what she spoke. After all, and she had not been shy about admitting it, she had slept with a succession of white men in what was, calculated or not, her irresistible rise to administrative assistant to the head of tugboat operations.

About the Corps, Curtis had suspected rightly. Despite its claims of opportunity for all, it was a tight-knit coterie that did not easily cater to outsiders let alone to Negroes, the very reason he had neglected to point out beforehand that he was colored. The few blacks who were on the payroll qualified (or ended up) as janitors or low-level clerks.

Fluke that it was, Curtis found himself in a room seated across from three uniformed Army engineers, who appeared nonplussed at the sight of him yet determined to be courteous. Curtis was sure that someone in personnel who hadn't thoroughly vetted the application would subsequently be dismissed.

As the encounter progressed and Curtis sensed he had nothing to lose—two of his interlocutors had started doodling on their notepads; only the third, a youngish officer with a Boston accent, paid any attention—he argued that the urgency to act had never been greater, what with the river at record levels, the rain relentless. The trio occasionally nodded and consulted their watches.

However impressive your application or fervent your arguments, Mr. Jefferson, unfortunately other candidates have more relevant credentials and more pertinent experience, the official rejection letter read. The Corps would keep his request on file.

Loretta simply shrugged when he told her of the rejection.

Chapter Thirty-Eight

For the next several weeks after the lunch at the Carroll, Aurelia walked on eggshells around Charles, unable to verbalize what was uppermost in her mind. Over breakfast, the couple chatted about the weather, the rising river, the ground-breaking for the bridge—topics about which disagreements were unlikely.

"They're battening down the hatches in places up north," he would say. "Going to put a crimp in business." She seconded his observations, pretending more interest than she felt.

Evenings were more challenging—so much so that Aurelia grasped at the flimsiest of invitations, finding that being in company brought out the best in Charles, or at least relieved her of having to be constantly *en garde*. During their drives home from such affairs, Charles would deride "fatuous twats" like Horace Hilliard or "windbags" like Mayor Hayes. Amusing enough *aperçus* to temporarily distract her, except when he would belittle her friends. Marianne was "an empty-headed chatterbox," Isabel "an *arriviste*," and Henrietta "a dour do-gooder." Rarely, as time passed, did she rally to the defense of any of these since whenever she did, Charles would not speak to her for days on end.

At one point, however, he surprised her, suggesting they have a few people over for dinner.

"A couple of the lawyers and their wives, your friends, too."

Aurelia went out of her way not only to accommodate but to do whatever she could to enhance her husband's standing with the firm, calling in both Susanna and Rose to prepare roast duckling and trimmings for two dozen guests. Though she didn't articulate it, she recognized that this was a last-ditch effort to save her marriage, or at least shore up the appearance of one. Hadn't that been what her fictional heroines had tried to do? Dorothea, Emma, Tess—too many to name. Too few who didn't fare badly.

She would outdo them.

For the first time Aurelia brought out her mother's gold-rimmed Dresden china. The envy on Caroline's face as she studied the pattern would be especially gratifying. From her closet she chose her most subtly revealing silk gown. The barely disguised leer on old Mr. Greene's lawyerly countenance would be worth the gambit.

Most everyone was fooled. Aristide confided to James that he thought his daughter ravishing, if draped a little too daringly, her conversation scintillating, her manner gracious. Alfred breathed a sigh of relief and told James he was thankful that his colleague, whatever his prior proclivities, had been so properly domesticated at his sister's hands. And though she had not a mean bone in her body, James had seen the jealousy on Henrietta's face upon seeing both pairs, Alfred with Caroline and Aurelia with Charles, socialize in the style that only married couples do.

James, however, found his sister close to the edge. He had

brought a less heavily perfumed but overly lipsticked Evelyn, to whom more than one of the unattached lawyers paid unusual attention. And to his chagrin, she responded in kind.

Passing Aurelia in the hallway between courses, he brushed his sister's arm.

"Is everything alright? Anything I can do?" He was alarmed at how immediate the tears were that filled her eyes.

"I shall be fine, James. But thank you, thank you," she whispered.

Later, when the women arranged themselves in the parlor, the men remained at the table to smoke Cuban cigars and drink cognac—both shipped upstream recently by Truard Transport, C.T. did not neglect to point out. The talk among the men was all of the river, what the engineers were saying, what Coolidge might do. Aristide suggested the city ready some sandbags, sections above the city being particularly vulnerable. As if on cue, Hilliard pooh-poohed the idea.

"If things don't improve come the spring, we can do what they did in '12—round up a bunch of niggers and lay them like planks atop the levees." No one laughed but no one had the wherewithal to object. Aristide turned away, his disgust evident. Eventually through the haze of smoke, James heard the tinkle of piano keys and voices singing. Irving Berlin gave way to Irish favorites as soon as they joined the ladies, Aurelia at the Bösendorfer throughout.

Any party that went on past midnight in Vicksburg was tacitly judged a success. By the grandfather clock in the hallway, Aurelia noticed that the very last guests, James and Evelyn as well as a couple of lawyers, did not leave until quarter past one. She decided against marking the achievement: not being a native, Charles might find the idea silly. As the last of the car engines cranked into gear, he closed the heavy oak door against the sharp wind. In the stillness, the only sound was of Rose rattling pots in the kitchen.

"I must say, Aurelia, you acquitted yourself admirably. At the piano too."

For an instant her eyes met his, before, in acknowledging the rare compliment, she lowered them to the level of his waistcoat.

"It's late. You must be tired," he added in a more matter-of-fact tone as he switched off the chandelier in the hallway. "I'll tend to the lights and deal with Rose. She can finish up in the morning."

Once up in their bedroom, Aurelia stoked the fire, adding a couple of logs against the January cold and the prediction that snow might dust the town overnight. She unclasped her sapphire choker and replaced it in the jewelry box on her dresser. Almost tenderly, she undid the tiny silk-covered buttons that held her gown and let it fall to the floor, along with her undergarments. For the first time since Hiram she admired her body in the glass, burnished to a sheen by the orange glow of the fire.

"If only," she murmured, before walking barefoot into the adjacent bathroom. Given the hour, superficial ablutions were all she could manage, but the water refused to warm up. She dried her hands and returned to the relative warmth of the bedroom and another presence—Charles at his own dresser, in the process of removing his diamond cufflinks and tie clasp, his waist-coated back to her. But he could—did—see her in all her bright nakedness in the mirror. She did nothing to cover herself, arms loose by her sides, desire apparent in her taut nipples. Unflinching, she gazed straight at the mirror.

"You'll catch your death, Aurelia," he said in a voice like cold metal as he watched her reflection. Her bare toes dug into the oak floor. The click shut of his jewelry case shattered the air, putting an end, Aurelia surmised, to whatever words were left unuttered. Charles must have thought so too, as he gathered up his silk robe (why ever did he bother to leave it in the master suite?) and retreated down the stairs in darkness.

For the rest of the night, Aurelia thought about cufflinks. Not the diamond ones, which, like all of Charles' personal effects, were, thanks to the tastes of his mother, elegantly understated and, thanks to his father's fortune, costly. Rather, she fixated on the ones she found in the carriage house, the day she had insisted Rose hand over the key. The silver-plated baubles on the night table. Strange that they would be there, her husband being so particular in his routines, so finicky in his tastes. She started to pick them up with the idea of returning them to his jewelry box, but something stopped her. She turned to Rose, who'd been carrying on behind her about Mr. Charles whacking her upside the head.

"You can make the bed, dust the furniture, as and when Mr. Charles requires, Rose. Otherwise, you are not to enter."

"Oh, I knows it. Only when he 'bliges me."

PART FOUR

I've known rivers ancient as the world
and older than the flow of human
blood in human veins.
My soul has grown deep like the rivers.

Langston Hughes

Chapter Thirty-Nine

Like folks up and down the river that winter of '27, the citizens of Vicksburg were jumpy. Reports from up North had it that levees along the main channel had burst, sweeping away entire swathes of field and forest in the far northern reaches. Mayor Hayes publicly downplayed such alarmist rumors; behind the scenes, though, he arranged meetings at which the top brass from the Mississippi River Commission reassured the city fathers that their bulwarks against Mother Nature were impregnable. Jabbing at charts with a government-issued yardstick, Major Lee extolled recent improvements in the earthworks—willows planted along the approach to the barrow pits, matted rye atop the berm that bordered the levees proper.

"The best scientific minds in the country have worked on these safeguards," Lee told the assembled. "We'll be able to handle the odd breach if such there be." Aristide knew Lee glossed over the many ways a levee could be compromised, everything from burrowing beavers to passing barges. But most in attendance seemed relieved or eager to get on with other business. Never one to forego a chance for further advancement, however, Hilliard rushed to escort the major out, seizing the occasion to lobby for a position on the bridge council.

As for Aristide, he reckoned that those most needing to prepare for the worst were those with property or livestock close to the water, men who frequented Planters Hall rather than City Hall. Delta-bred that he was, he got his own herd to auction early in February, not wanting cows pastured along the Big Black River basin if flooding did occur. And still, the rain rarely let up, turning the bottoms where most blacks lived into muddy flats, their junkyard dogs ever more aggressive. Even homes in the center of town had to contend with leaky roofs and sodden lawns. Whenever the downpours ceased, people ventured out, bent on getting things done before another storm drove them back indoors.

The Valley did a brisk business in galoshes—so much so, James told him, that Evelyn was moved out of cosmetics to shoes. When Aristide took his car to Mayfield's Motor Works for a minor repair, he found it backed up with more banged-up cars in one month than in the entire previous year. Willy, obliged to hire two more mechanics, apologized for the delay.

"Sho' wished I managed to keep Curtis, Mister Ackermann. Sho' do."

The party and its unpleasant aftermath behind her, Aurelia redoubled her efforts to make her days useful. If her marriage was a sham or a punishment for her unlawful passion, she would find other purpose in life. Nor, given his own mysterious comings-and-goings, would she directly ask permission of Charles to do so. Were he to ask about her movements, she would expound. Otherwise, her days would be her own affair, needing no justification. She would start with Mrs. Wilkerson's Packard, carefully backing it out of the garage each morning after Charles left for work and waiting for James to swing by and give her a driving lesson. The car was cranky and the hills slippery from the spitting rain, but after a couple of weeks, Aurelia had mastered the pedals well enough to take the car out on her own.

With Henrietta in the passenger seat, they delivered church-sponsored baskets to the needy two or three times a week, starting in the weed-infested byways leading off Marcus Bottom and finishing in the alleys bordering the cemetery. The old man with the floppy-eared mongrel was nowhere to be seen. Nor the tall young man with the clippers.

And then there was Bethel, the black church next to Planters Hall which had encouraged Saturday morning tutoring sessions for children who had fallen behind. Even had a write-up in the *Herald*, which Aurelia clipped and showed to Henrietta one morning as they wrapped up their deliveries.

"Why don't we volunteer to teach? You know as well as I that food baskets will never be enough to change things," Aurelia suggested.

"What will Charles have to say?" Henrietta asked.

"Likely he won't inquire."

Word did, however, get out that along with a couple of veteran teachers from Main Street School, two young white women had offered their services, going over English grammar and instituting writing exercises for the various pupils. Susanna let the cat out of the bag at the Ackermann dinner table one Sunday evening.

"Miss Aurelia done put the ABC's in the head of my grandchild. A miracle she be performing over there at Bethel," she bragged, as she poured red wine into the goblets.

Caroline made a show of putting down her knife and fork after Susanna left for the kitchen.

"As I've mentioned before to Alfred," she began, hunching her bony shoulders and fixing her eyes on her father-in-law, "Aurelia seems to have loosed herself on the town, driving through disreputable neighborhoods to deliver God knows what to the Negroes."

None of the men took her up.

"Often, I might add, with Henrietta in tow." This aside she made while glaring directly across at her husband. "And now, of all things, she's worshipping at that black church."

Alfred gave her a sideways glance but said nothing. It was James who set the family record straight.

"Act-act-actually, Aurelia drives better than most men around Vicksburg, I have observed." Aristide raised an eyebrow as his son continued. "As for Bethel, our sister volunteers there. Tutoring the underprivileged, as Susanna indicated. I, for one, think it's worthwhile. If only m-m-more people did such things..."

"Well, she's certainly qualified enough, if that's what she wants to do," Alfred added drily.

"I would have thought ministering to her husband's wants would be more of a priority," Caroline huffed. "Just as I—"

"That will do, everybody," Aristide snapped, never pleased when he himself wasn't in charge of the dinner table conversation. Nor did he appreciate hearing his own daughter maligned, and she not there to defend herself. If only Henrietta would accept one of his invitations to dine on Adams Street such carping might be avoided. He looked at the two women who were present. Caroline had grown tiresome like her father, he thought, wondering suddenly if Alfred felt the same about the woman he married. Evelyn, on the other hand, had risen in his estimation—the wrong fork in her hand notwithstanding. She was plucky. And to think someone so ambitious had fallen for his ineffectual son.

Still, he had to admit he liked the way the boy had stood up for his absent sister.

He rapped on his glass to command the attention of the foursome. "If you all would allow, I'd like to offer a toast, to Evelyn, on her promotion at the Valley." They duly raised their glasses to the young woman, who days before had been made an assistant floor manager.

"And more to come," James added, delighted that his father, for once, appeared not only to approve of his choice of a companion but of her own accomplishments, however modest her background. He admired that open-mindedness in his parent—especially since it had cost him his position at the bank. Evelyn, too, he was proud of, she having impressed her supervisor by breaking up an argument in the shoe department, all over the last-in-stock pair of high heels which two women had set their hearts on.

Whether through Caroline or Alfred, C.T. too heard about "the goings-on" at Bethel Church on Saturday mornings, about the same time that he noticed the Packard parked askew underneath the carriage house. He did not relish a confrontation with Aurelia, aware of his own glaring failure in the most intimate of marital requirements. He had lain awake multiple nights in the carriage house trying to formulate an apology.

None of this is your fault, my dear, he rehearsed, though he couldn't bring himself to utter the words and thus risk being asked what the 'this' consisted of. Nor could he come up with an excuse for his behavior that might paper over the problem, allowing them, as was as much his wish as likely hers, to establish some basis for a relationship, even if one that discounted the bedroom. On the other hand, he was reluctant to let things ride since it could be construed that Aurelia was deceiving him. With his own finances not what he had hoped, appearances were that much more crucial.

"Above reproach," he whispered to himself, thinking not only of his own behavior but of his wife's. Advancement at the law firm—indeed, holding on to his job at the law firm—depended, as Alfred had intimated more than once, on the solidity of his marriage as well as on his personal probity. That was the unusual word his brother-in-law had used. Probity. Raised eyebrows were the last thing C.T. needed to contend with.

When he did broach the subject, one evening after Rose had

served dinner and retreated to the kitchen, he made matters worse. Rather than bow her head and mumble an excuse, Aurelia stared her husband down from across the table. Before he knew it, he heard himself suggesting that her latest exploits—"consorting with Negroes in their own church" is how he described it—was not only scandalous in its own right but detrimental to his—their—standing in the community.

But Aurelia's emotional armor had hardened, her defensiveness transmuted into some more durable alloy. What audacity, she thought, curling her lip at the idea of his having presumed to appropriate the community, her community, as his own. She stirred her coffee for a long minute and then tapped the silver spoon against the cup, as though to signal that she would, against such unwarranted a rebuke, stand up for herself.

The drum of rain against the bay window steeled her resolve. She would defy him.

"Scandalous, Charles, is not how the best souls in this town would describe the activities at Bethel, and I have no intention of discontinuing what is helpful to these poor children and fulfilling for me, as it is for others, my friend Henrietta included."

"I would offer that not even your own family would agree with your actions, Aurelia," Charles shot back.

"If such be the case, they will no doubt let me know of their disapproval. Meanwhile..."

"Meanwhile, what?"

"Nothing," she tossed out, her tone now more insinuating than contemptuous. "I was wondering to whom belonged the cufflinks left in the carriage house. Do I need to have them returned to someone?"

A twitch of his nose was the only sign that Charles registered this unforeseen jab. He folded his linen napkin and placed it next to his dessert fork.

"I think we both recognize, Aurelia, that if you go too far, it will be regrettable." Before she could counter that the same applied to him, her husband left the room.

For long minutes Aurelia remained seated. A keening wind

rattled the shutters. She wondered where on the ever-rising river Curtis might be, in what port, in whose arms.

"You there, I here/With just the door ajar/That oceans are"...Sad lines from a sad poet.

Regrettable indeed, she sighed.

As for her present circumstance, she could not even seek refuge in family. Her father was caught up in the wrangles at City Hall. Alfred and Caroline expected their first child soon, and James finally enjoyed the attentions of a young woman. Her marriage was in tatters, dissolution unthinkable. She would have to endure. But when the rains let up, and it could not be soon enough, she would take the train—or dare to drive the Packard—to New Orleans. Aunt Margaret would take her in. Of that she was certain.

Chapter Forty

Old man Norris had mixed feelings. He was inordinately fond of his favorite employee. His own wife was long dead, his two sons and a daughter married and moved away. His business—the river itself—were his only joy in life. So what if the young man wasn't exactly white? Unlike most of the riff-raff on his payroll, Curtis was educated and more attuned to the rhythms of the river than anyone Norris had come across in his line of work. When Curtis sheepishly told him, hat in hand, his weight shifting from foot to foot, that he hadn't been accepted by the Corps but that he'd be pleased to continue in his present capacity, indeed, to take on whatever was required if the waters kept rising and more barges ran aground, his boss had to admit he was relieved. Even elated.

"Their loss, Creole," he snorted, chewing on his customary afternoon wad of tobacco. He had taken to calling Curtis by that term, figuring a supposed mixed-race pedigree might prevent unpleasant incidents with other of his employees. Especially if he put Curtis in charge of operations. Expert tugboat masters were going to be needed in the months to come, Norris figured, and few knew the ports to the South as well as the abashed young man in front of him.

"I've got a mind to send you downstream in the *Starfish*. She's a beaut, best in the fleet. You'd be positioned to help with rescues anywhere from Memphis to Nawlins, depending on how out of hand things get."

Curtis jumped at the offer. As little as he liked being referred to as Creole, what the old man was dangling before him was music to his ears. If it could be worked out, he'd have a chance to salvage what he could from his mother's house and look in on the Taylor estate. And stop off in Vicksburg. Didn't he owe Willy and his wife a visit? He tried to blank others there from his mind.

"I'd be glad to take it on, Mr. Norris."

"Good, good. We'll talk terms tomorrow. Get you on your way in a day or so. March at the latest."

With a nominal promotion and extra cash in his pocket, Curtis set out mid-month with two hardened deck hands, Hank and Lester, long in Norris's employ. Both had worked rescue operations in '12, Lester as far south as Greenville, where a breach had indiscriminately washed cattle, trees and homes into the muddy depths. Though neither was given to hyperbole, he knew the two had a healthy respect for what havoc the river could wreak.

"Right roiling this here patch," Hank called out as they plied their way downstream through the heart of the Delta, unsuspecting fields of cotton as far as the eye could see.

"We'd best dock before nightfall, stock up on some grub before going further. Get a sense of what's going on," Curtis replied.

That night, lying for the first time in two weeks in a proper bed, albeit in a decrepit hotel reserved for coloreds, he flipped through the Greenville paper. Planters had been meeting, one of the most prominent, Leroy Percy, arguing for the city fathers to pull their heads out of the sand, as it were. Further inside was an article telling how Vicksburg was—despite conditions on the river—rushing to break ground on their bridge, the mayor proclaiming that material greatness would follow in the wake. When it did come to pass, the ferry would be no more, Curtis reckoned, conjuring for an instant that last time he had stood on the Louisiana landing and stared across at the lights of the vessel receding, ever fainter.

The *Starfish* pressed on. At Vicksburg, Curtis dropped anchor along the canal in front of the strip of downtown. He gave his crew a two-day break while he ferried over to the Louisiana side. In a rusty but still serviceable Model T from Willy's Tallulah shop, he headed to his mother's house. The cane had thickened and advanced closer to the road in the year he'd been away, as if the land had decided to take back what humans had tried to tame. Just as well, he sighed, figuring that soon the entire landscape of his childhood would revert to a primordial swamp.

He entered the musty-smelling house to retrieve the few things that still mattered to him: the watercolor tacked above the bed, a tintype of his grandpa from his desk, a faded flower, the one Aurelia had worn at Cassie's wedding party, pressed in his *McGuffey's Reader*. Placing the items in the carrying case he had shouldered for the purpose, he headed out the door. No need to lock it, as all the decent furnishings had been removed to New Orleans or parceled out to neighbors. He drove on to the Taylor farm to do what Sarah-Lynn had asked of him. If it meant staying overnight, he would oblige. The horses were dear to her, and if she herself couldn't be there to oversee what had to be done, he, she had written, was the person she most trusted with such a grim task.

Together with Slim, Curtis mixed a final meal of oats and apples for Thunder, though the crippled horse ate little.

"We'll do it in the morning," Curtis said, "while we wait for the man to show up for Cassandra."

They spread fresh hay for the stallion to lie on, closed the stall and headed back to the main house. It occurred to Curtis that his companion walked taller now that Mrs. Taylor had designated him as the caretaker.

"That there horse was a good one. A lot of riding out of him," Slim ventured over fixings he had brought over from his place. "Glad it ain't Hiram doing the honors. He'd right enjoy it." He took a swig from a half-full jug of cider left over from some previous repast.

"Strange not having him around. Where'd he go?"

"Ain't you heard? Up Bastrop way. His cousin's place."

"Heard what?"

"Done clean bled out. Thresher backed over his leg, severed the artery, so they say. Only found him the next morning..."

Curtis poured himself a glass of the cider to keep from saying something inopportune—Slim was white and had presumably gotten along well enough with the former boss man—though "good riddance" did occur to him. Still, such an agonizing end he hardly wished on anyone, even a son-of-a-bitch like Hiram. He bowed his head as though in deference to the deceased.

"Anyhow,"—here Slim took a deeper draught of the homemade brew—"he deserved it, if you ask me. All that fiddling."

"Fiddling?"

"You know. With the ladies. To be specific, with the girls." Slim wiped his mouth with the back of his calloused hand. "Even Sarah-Lynn that Christmas. Though she done defended herself right proper." Curtis could see faint color rising in his companion's cheeks.

"So that's why..."

"Yep. The missus threatened him with that old rifle. Didn't keep him from boastin' about others though. Sarah-Lynn's cousin for one."

"What are you saying? What cousin?" Curtis' tone had sharpened.

Slim looked up from his brisket. "Miss Aurelia. The night of the party—your sister's wedding it was—when he drove her to the landing. Went on and on, when he was in his chops anyway, 'bout how he rode her. 'Broke her in,' he kept mouthing. Bastard." That divulged, Slim looked away, his cheeks stained red.

Curtis shot out of his chair, his abrupt movement tipping it over backwards. He bumbled out the screen door and stood, one hand against the side of the house for support, retching in the rain.

That night Curtis did not sleep. If only I had known, he kept repeating, but then caught himself up with what that would have meant: killing Hiram and likely being lynched for his pains. She knew as much and that's why, he whispered to himself as dawn broke. Shortly thereafter he heard the barn door creak open.

Without any more palaver, he and Slim put Thunder down and buried him behind the rose trellis in the far back yard. A man from Slidell showed up in a truck around ten to fetch Cassandra. It took all three men to get the spooked mare loaded into the trailer and on her way to a new life in New Orleans.

As he climbed into the Ford to make the trip back home, Curtis remembered what needed to be said.

"We didn't get to it, Slim, but the levees around these parts—you've seen 'em—won't hold, whatever people say. Get your folks, your stock, yourself included, to higher ground. Tell the Bianchettis, others you know, too."

"You done studied right into it, from what the missus said. You believe God is punishing us?"

"Not rightly," Curtis replied, as he revved the sputtering motor. "Mother Nature doesn't care what we do; we have to figure out how to deal with what she throws at us."

Once back in Vicksburg, Curtis extracted a sozzled Hank and Lester from the Exchange Saloon, instructing them to wire Norris and let him know they'd likely bide their time, the river hourly more unpredictable, rescue operations likely needed along that stretch as anywhere else. On the ferry crossing he had seen the ominous signs—entire tree trunks uprooted and barreling downstream, a few carcasses swirling in the eddies.

On Washington Street he noted intent on the faces of local shoppers. Nobody gave him the time of day. An illustrated catalog of the latest car models tucked in his bag, he headed to Willy's shop on

Jackson Street, forcing himself not to detour down Adams Street. Besides, given what Claudette had told him, Aurelia no longer resided there.

She is married; she will have recovered. And, did he not so urge her that time—that furtive afternoon in New Orleans—to get on with her life? Still, he would write a short note to James, just to say...

Chapter Forty-One

By the time the levees broke at Greenville, rumors were swirling. Several bodies had been fished out of the choppy waters north of Vicksburg, apparently shot rather than drowned. A few of Willy's customers had heard about the troubles. Blacks rounded up, sometimes at gunpoint, to sand bag wherever whitey instructed. Any man who refused or slacked off was pistol-whipped. Or worse.

"You be a lucky son-of-a-bitch, Willy, to be old," one of his customers had told him while he monkeyed around under the hood. "Them bags are the dickens to lift and they ain't no good 'gainst them currents."

Willy nodded in noncommittal assent as he disentangled himself from the innards of the old jalopy. His customer was right. He was old. Curtis would have had this vehicle's valve problem sorted in a jiffy. It had taken Willy more than an hour.

Bodies fished from the river? Better not to speculate. Never argue with a customer nor appear to have any opinions that anyone might object to, or even remember. Yet, he too had gotten wind of several incidents. Muttered in the pews on Sunday during "Go Down, Moses," his wife glaring at him to raise his voice in song, but he with ears pricked, trying to catch what the men behind him were on about. The levee at Mounds Landing had melted away like jelly on Maundy Thursday, but the blacks had nonetheless been ordered to keep bagging.

Rising to the occasion that Easter morning, Pastor Pendleton hastened to impart a lesson on the unfolding calamity. God, as was his privilege, he bellowed, had decided it was time once again to punish the wicked by turning nature topsy-turvy. Bears, panthers, and boar were at that very hour being swept into the raging waters and washed downstream. Alligators prowled the banks of the Yazoo. Snakes slithered on top of the waves. The preacher paused for effect. Then, lowering his voice an octave, he gave his parishioners what they came for: succor and assurance. The innocent, he told them, scanning the congregation to alight on a row of fidgeting young people, would inevitably suffer too, but through their faith—steadfast it must be—they would persevere. And thus, like their Savior, they too would rise again.

Amen, amen, came from the back rows where most of the Bethel widows arrayed themselves. Willy looked around as the sermon wound down, hoping to spot Curtis. His young friend had intimated a few days previous that he had a notion to take the tug upstream to help with rescue efforts. Willy hoped Curtis had changed his mind.

It was not the wisest of plans. Even Hank and Lester, accustomed as they were to the capriciousness of rivers, were wide-eyed at the devastation, not thirty miles upstream from Vicksburg. The currents were so fast and the debris churned up so hazardous that they had to proceed at a snail's pace. Getting back up to Greenville out of the question. Best they could do, Curtis resolved, was chug up and down backwaters, tossing ropes to frantic stragglers on rooftops or huddled on makeshift rafts as the water, thick with mud, spread over the disoriented land.

At one point along the Yazoo, a huge white oak came uprooted and tumbled into the water alongside the *Starfish*, grazing the hull; at another the tug got tangled in a maze of fallen limbs and cow carcasses, it taking the strength of all three men to dislodge the vessel. After three days and nights, the *Starfish* had run low on fuel, the crew on food and rest.

They turned south, scooping up a woman and three children clinging to the sidings from their shack not far from where Eagle Lake should have been. From what Curtis could tease out of her, the husband had gone off in a skiff two days before to help neighbors but had never made it back.

"He done told us to pack up and get to the camp for coloreds, but then the water reached us. Everything's swept away," she revealed in spurts, sobbing in between, her children listless and cold beside her. Lester pulled out a relatively clean bandanna from his overalls and handed it to the woman. Hank ducked below deck for an Army blanket off his own cot. Without a word he draped it round the children. Curtis consulted his maps, figuring they could lodge the tug near a place called Waltersville and make their way by foot to the refugee camp, a mile or two to the east.

His calculations weren't far off. As they trudged through the soaked woodlands bordering the creek where they tied up the tug, buzzards circled in what was, for the first time in weeks, a cerulean sky. From what Curtis could figure, the storms had continued to sweep southward, following the bulging river and carrying their own misery downstream as successive levees gave way like buttons on a too-tight shirt. By now, he also surmised, the Corps of Engineers would be making frantic recommendations to shore up New Orleans, this or that barrier upstream dynamited to take the pressure off the metropolis.

If only they had...

Useless to dwell. There were more practical matters to contend with, like how to get his mother in Gretna to higher ground, to beseech Mrs. Taylor to take her in, if it came to that. Unless the phone lines were down, he would ring from Willy's shop as soon as they got back to Vicksburg. But personal affairs couldn't be tended to until tomorrow; traveling at night in roiling waters would be foolhardy. Like the family they had rescued, the crew would have to make do at the camp. However white his two boat swains, they too would need to sleep. No standing on ceremony during a catastrophe.

"Ouch," cried the smallest of the children, as thorns from a patch of wild blackberries ripped her face. Lester hoisted the little girl onto his shoulders and took the lead, beating back the brambles in their path. Hank took charge of the two boys, helping them avoid puddles and fallen logs. Curtis in the rear lifted the mother clear of the worst stretches, her worn-down shoes barely clinging to her feet. The occasional cottonmouth slinked out from under a rock.

As the afternoon faded to purple and the wind picked up, a stench wafted over the bedraggled party, a mixture of smoke, sweat and urine so pungent as to take the breath away. They halted at the top of the next ridge. A sprawling city of tents lay before them as far as the eye could see. At the front edge a couple of torches flamed. A few men stood sentry. Even from a distance Curtis could tell they were white. And shouldering rifles.

But there was no turning back.

When the group straggled up to the makeshift gate, one of the guards tossed his cigarette, extended his arm and called for them to halt. Curtis let Lester do the talking. Soon, the woman and three children were motioned to a nearby table where they were handed a pass, meal tickets and a tent number. Two white women with Red Cross insignia on their jackets led them inside the encampment.

"He the husband?" the guard asked, jerking the barrel of his rifle toward Curtis.

Lester looked flustered. "No, not at all. He's one of us. In charge of the *Starfish*. Happened on those other folks on our way down river."

The guard was no longer listening. "In charge, you say. Well, I'll be damned." A sneer came over the man's unshaven face as he gave Curtis the once-over. He shifted his rifle from one shoulder to the other. "Get over here, Fletcher. We done got us a captain to help dig latrines tonight."

Another man, heavy-set, a jagged scar above his right eye, moseyed over. He too carried a rifle.

For a moment no one spoke.

It was Hank who broke the silence. "You can leave him be. He's with us, just for the night. Then we're headed out."

"He's a nigger, ain't he?" Fletcher snarled. "It's their camp. They'll shovel their own shit."

The guard directed his gaze straight at Curtis who, calculating the odds of dissuading these two ruffians, let alone the half-dozen others milling about, resigned himself to what they had in store. He was exhausted, but so too were the folks washed up here in the flood's wake. Lend a hand, his mother would have said.

"Don't worry about it, Hank. I can handle a shovel. Meet you here in the morning, and we'll head back to the tug."

Aurelia awoke early that Easter morning, elated to have something purposeful to do even if her father, had he known the details, would have frowned upon such an excursion. Motoring along back roads to a camp for black refugees could be tricky, not to mention unorthodox on the part of two young white women. She regretted not joining him in the family pew at Trinity but, with Charles in New Orleans, this was an ideal time to help out. Blacks were taking the hardest hit, their shacks washed away, chickens and pigs scattered or drowned. With little but the clothes on their backs, many had fled to higher ground—and help. Bethel had taken the lead in supplying them with food, medicine and blankets. As occasional volunteers, Aurelia and Henrietta were now in demand.

They had access to a car. It took only a little doing to persuade James to accompany them in his roomy Briscoe, and to keep the plan to himself.

The threesome left town early, having the night before loaded the car with blankets from Aurelia's own linen closets, salt, sugar, flour and rice from Henrietta's pantry, and an assortment of clothes and tools donated and boxed up by the Bethel congregation. The sun had nosed up as if wary that more clouds would roll in to spoil its ascent. James stepped on the pedal, trying to get them close enough to their destination before another downpour but potholes and a washed-out bridge hampered their progress. The three chatted intermittently—wondering aloud if Aristide would be in the official party to greet Coolidge and whether the president, or anyone else, would find a way to salvage what could be salvaged from the watery world all about them. On the final leg, James had to swerve to avoid a disoriented deer. Aurelia shuddered; the image of Hiram's blood-streaked car had surfaced.

As they pulled alongside the parked cars and vans near the camp's entrance, a foul odor nearly overpowered them. None spoke of it; rather, they stretched their legs and headed toward a noisy knot at the gate. Several white men, including one wearing a faded U.S. Army jacket, were brandishing weapons as they shouted at a dozen sullen Negroes. One of the corralled blacks, it sounded to Aurelia, had the audacity to be talking back.

It was Curtis. Taller than the other men, and the only one without his head lowered. The side of his face was bruised. He was staring down two grizzled white men with guns.

"You cannot expect these men—who've been digging through slime all night—to pile sandbags all day," he was arguing in as even a tone as he could. "Especially since you're ordering them to do so where it will be absolutely no good."

"Get a load of him, Mike. A know-it-all," Fletcher said to the guard closest to him, the one holding what seemed to be a horse whip. "What do you know about it anyway?" he snarled at the troublemaker.

"We've been up and down these backwaters," Curtis continued, a note of exasperation now slipping in. "Nothing along any of them is going to hold, not on the Big Black, not on the Yazoo, not on any of your creeks. Best to salvage goods and livestock, what's left of them, rather than send these men on a fool's errand."

"Son-of-a-bitch. Are you calling us fools?" the man called Mike screeched. He raised his arm, the one with the whip. Another guard pointed his rifle in the direction of Curtis. He turned his bruised cheek away but otherwise did not flinch.

"You can't do that. You have no right."

All eyes turned toward a woman who had broken into the circle of men. James put his hand on his sister's shoulder but more to back her up than to dissuade her.

"You might want to mind your own business, miss. Plenty for you women to fuss about inside the camp," Fletcher advised acidly.

With the commotion, the crowd began to swell but no one stepped forward to remove the newcomers. Mike lowered his arm, the whip dragging in the mud.

When Curtis turned to see who had spoken up on his behalf, Aurelia saw his jaw drop.

"This man—Mr. Jefferson," she went on undeterred, "is a friend of ours, and he happens to be an engineer. So I would hazard that he does know of what he speaks."

The elaborateness of Aurelia's retort had its desired effect.

Fletcher and Mike darted their eyes about as if hoping for some diversionary tactic. A couple of the other guards studied their boots. The black men began to mutter among themselves.

"You would do well to let these men unload our vehicle," James interjected in a tone so forceful, he stunned Aurelia. "We've brought supplies from town. So, you might better get on with it."

This last volley was fired off at Fletcher, who seemingly was the guard most convinced he was in charge. James straightened his Branham & Hughes-trained shoulders and paused. Fletcher jerked his head as a signal for a couple of the blacks to move toward the parking area. "In the meantime—Fletcher, is it? —we'll help Mr. Jefferson locate his fellow shipmates," James added, and again Aurelia was amazed at the conviction in his voice. "Then we'll all be out of your way."

Out of nowhere Hank and Lester broke through the throng and followed James back to his vehicle, where they waited silently for the boxes from the trunk to be unloaded. Aurelia glanced at Curtis from under her lashes, twisting the diamond ring on her finger. She saw him flinch when he noticed her gesture and then he stepped away until James called him to get in the car.

"You three men take the back seat. Henrietta, Aurelia, you two up front with me," James ordered. "We'll take you as far as the road will allow, which should get you a mile or so closer. Better go fill a couple of canteens though."

The trip back toward the *Starfish* passed in vague disquiet. As the driver, James had to concentrate on avoiding flooded terrain and sticking to whatever passed for a road. Curtis—relieved somehow during the long night of his map, he told them—tried to figure the best direction at each unmarked junction. At one point the Briscoe stalled. It took Curtis fifteen minutes to get it going again. Later, the men jumped out to remove an uprooted elm in their path. The delays made Aurelia fidget.

"I can see how admirable he is," Henrietta finally declared while the men worked to drag the trunk off the road. Aurelia did not respond. "And, like him, you were brave back there, at the camp." Aurelia ignored Henrietta's sidelong glance, but that did nothing to dissuade the other woman from her conjecture. "Whatever might have once been between you two, as children practically, you will have put aside, I trust. Even if you weren't married to someone else…"

"Ah, married," Aurelia fumed under her breath, shaking her head as if to cast off the recollection of it.

"None of them is perfect, Aurelia. Even mine, short-lived as it was." Rarely did Henrietta refer out loud to her marriage to Eric. Her tone was wistful, but to Aurelia's ear it smacked of condescension. She bridled; Henrietta persevered. "Whatever our differences though, there was love between us. I was blessed with Emily and that is great solace. So too will you be—"

"Don't, Henrietta! Have you not listened? Not seen?" Aurelia cried out. She flung open the car door and stepped down into the mud, oblivious to the splatter. Henrietta remained in the car, silent after Aurelia's outburst. The men looked up briefly from their labors to see Aurelia sidestep her way toward a stand of pines.

For several minutes she stood with her eyes closed. The wind sifted through the needles, smoothing the brittle air. Less agitated, she breathed in the resinous odor. As the men finished hauling the limbs off the road, they one by one ambled into the underbrush to relieve themselves. A car door slammed. Without turning around, Aurelia felt a warm breath on her neck.

"Odd, how beautiful such devastation can appear. At least until one gets up close," Curtis murmured. "I can assist you back to the car if you like."

A flock of discombobulated wood ducks, flashing iridescent in the intermittent sunlight, flew in erratic loops overhead. Aurelia ignored his offer.

"I was wondering about the deer. Will they all drown?"

"Depends," he responded, and Aurelia knew he was thinking of the clearing, those many years ago where they had stood in almost the same arrangement, she slightly in front. "Most will survive—the strong, the lucky."

"And the ghosts?"

"They'll always be with us. Rarely visible but ever present," he replied, thick-voiced.

She shifted from foot to foot and eyed her mud-caked hem.

He changed course, momentarily sparing them both of their own regrets. "It's people that will be ruined. All the way downstream. Even New Orleans is at risk. It'll be years before—"

"But things will get back to normal once the waters recede, won't they?"

"In time."

"You two coming?" James called out from the car. The sound of howling, of wild dogs or wolves, hurried Aurelia and Curtis back toward the vehicle's relative safety.

Ten minutes later as they rounded a curve they spotted vultures clustered over a ravine, cawing to one another. James stepped on the gas to get around the likely carrion but Hank, at the back window on the right, called out: "Stop the car. Something's off here."

He and Curtis scrambled out, took one look in the ditch, and motioned to the other men. Aurelia gawked out of the front seat window in time to see Lester gag.

"We'll have to get it—him—into the trunk. If you've got a blanket, anything, bring it over," Curtis said. "And, James, make the ladies stay in the car."

The dead man was gray and bloated, having apparently drowned, but the teeth marks on his limbs suggested animals had gotten to him. His clothes were ripped but his boots, encrusted though they were with thick Delta loam, were of excellent make. As best they could, they enfolded him in a tarp James retrieved from the trunk. It took all four men to carry the body to the back of the car. Once deposited inside, they sprinkled the remains of James' canteen over their arms to remove the stench.

The vultures wheeled overhead, their raucous cries sounding to Aurelia like a protest over their missed meal.

"Once you take the ladies home, you'll want to alert the authorities or take him yourself to the coroner's office," Curtis said to James. "Someone might be able to identify him. We'll be docked at the riverfront by nightfall, if all goes well, and you need us."

"But we can take you further. Obviously, it's not safe out here anymore," James objected.

"Road's turned to ruts. No need to ruin your car," Curtis objected. "Close enough?" he asked, turning to his two mates. Both shrugged.

"Shouldn't be more than half a mile, give or take." Hank said. "I remember those shacks." He pointed to rubble in the distance, the only object still upright a brick chimney.

Lester tapped on the window. Aurelia rolled the glass down. "We're off, ladies. Much obliged to you all. Be careful going home."

For the first time since at the camp, Curtis looked straight into

Aurelia's eyes.

"How long will—?"

"A few days, at Willy's shop."

James started the engine, which, to everyone's relief, turned over instantly. He shifted into reverse, alternating the clutch and the accelerator, to maneuver the car around in the muddy road. The three men were soon out of sight.

Chapter Forty-Two

Feet on the desk, Aristide puffed on a cigar, the first he had indulged in since the party at Henrietta's. Despite the catastrophe that engulfed the town, he had his own small victory to celebrate. Horace Hilliard had been proven wrong.

"Bet against Mother Nature and lost. Our money as well as his own," as Paxton, another of the bank's board members, had groused that Monday morning. Not only had Hilliard been blind to the need to prepare for the flood waters, but he had bullied, if not bamboozled, the bank into making loans for bridge construction and road extensions that at this point would never get repaid. His own investments were heavily weighted toward the insurance companies, which given the dimensions of the disaster, would be hard hit by claimants up and down the river basin. To cap it off, and this Aristide only learned when Alfred took him into his confidence the night before, Hilliard had months earlier become a financial partner in one of the outfits which won a key contract for the laying of pylons.

"Surely he would have run such a move by his lawyers, right, Son?' Aristide had asked.

"Not so. Greene only found out last week. Must have engaged another firm to handle the paper work." Alfred took another sip of bourbon. Father and son were alone at the Adams Street dinner table, Caroline occupied at home with the baby, and James and Aurelia tied up with "relief efforts." Aristide twirled the tawny liquid in his glass, considering the implications of Alfred's revelation.

"I know what you're thinking, Father. My own father-in-law sat on the city council and lobbied on behalf of that bid. I'd reckon it's all in the minutes."

Aristide could visualize Mayor Hayes' no-nonsense secretary, one Miss Simpson, in her resolutely ankle-length skirts and wool jackets whatever the season, madly scribbling on that yellow-lined tablet. Never changing expression even when the councilmen argued or turned coarse. All was logged. All would in due course come out.

"Highly improper the non-disclosure but perhaps, strictly speaking, not illegal," Aristide tossed out, realizing that any suspicion of a conflict of interest, let alone a court hearing, would in such a small town inevitably sully the Hilliard name. Plausibly, by extension, Alfred's.

"We shall see," Alfred responded. He downed the last of the alcohol and picked up a soda cracker. "Shouldn't affect us greatly at the firm, if that's what you're worried about. Still, it hasn't made things any more pleasant at home, I can tell you that."

Discreet when it came to personal matters, Aristide did not inquire further into the state of his son's marriage. Despite his distaste for Horace Hilliard, he had considered Caroline a fine catch, her jewelry notwithstanding. No marriage is perfect, he thought to say but decided such an empty cliché would irritate his son as much as bromides did him. Better something positive, to get his son's mind off his domestic travails.

"I've been meaning to bring up something else, a development that I think you'll find interesting. I have asked Henrietta to marry me, and she has kindly agreed to consider it."

Alfred's jaw dropped. He reached for the decanter. Aristide cupped his hand over his half-empty glass; his son refilled his own. Almost to the brim.

"I'm sure Henrietta would make you, or any man, very happy," he finally responded.

For the rest of the evening they talked of the ongoing salvage operations and of what Coolidge and his right hand man Hoover might do. Fortunately, Vicksburg proper escaped the worst of the damage, thanks largely to its hills. True, the low-lying warehouses, liquor stores and brothels on Levee Street were swamped, rail lines and saw mills underwater and the bridge project, without anyone having to say so, scrapped indefinitely. The main commercial shops up along Washington Street and most of the residential areas, the white ones at least, were high and dry. Further afield was another story. Barges had collided in the channel proper or capsized in the canal, fields of cotton and corn were lost upstream and down, cattle scattered, countless homes, be they plantations or shanties, overwhelmed by the rushing water. In an instant people were made destitute—or worse.

"Don't forget, Father, you'll be needed tomorrow at City Hall and then at the morgue. A body of a white man was found several miles east of Waltersville, brought in late this afternoon, from what I understand. Several Negroes on the slab too, one with a bullet in his back."

Aristide extinguished his cigar in the ash tray and rose to look out his office window. Washington Street was practically deserted, most able-bodied men having been enlisted to help save what could be saved down near the water's edge. Most shops were shuttered across the street, though the Gem Café had as usual its lopsided "open" sign in the window. He would stop in for beef stew before heading to the mayor's office at two for an emergency session and thereafter the morgue.

As Aristide suspected, Hilliard was subdued during the discussion about what needed to be delivered in writing to Hoover, since, it was still unclear if the Secretary of the Interior would actually deplane to meet with the city fathers. From what the papers had reported, his focus on the trip was New Orleans and which levees should be blown in order to spare that city. Still, "if we citizens want to have our voices heard, they need to be officially raised," Greene, who as a lawyer believed everything should be put to paper, advised. Mayor Hayes himself hastened through the agenda, calling for appropriations for a Jackson-based clean-up crew, several additional tugs to help with obstructions on the river, and hardship pay for police to keep law and order.

"I guess you all heard about bodies washing up, identifications to be made, foul play to be investigated," Judge Thigpen interposed. Hands went up. Double overtime for sheriff deputies and police sergeants. Miss Simpson scribbled nonstop. The mayor waited until her pencil was once again poised in mid-air.

"Take down these names," the mayor instructed, indicating to the assembled that the meeting was adjourned but making sure they heard this final order. "If there is to be a colloquy with the powers-that-be from Washington, I want Greene, Bloom, Paxton, Chief Barrett, Major Lee, Judge Thigpen, the sheriff—don't know where he is—and Ackermann here. That's it."

Hilliard looked peeved but didn't object. The others avoided him as they shuffled out. Word must have gotten out.

At the morgue Aristide was instructed to wait in the dank vestibule. He studied the framed diplomas on the drab wall. Holloway was the coroner's name, same one who had handled the flu victims right after the war. Acid rose in his throat. Must be the stew, he thought, vowing yet again to take Henrietta's advice to eat less during the day, and at night, for that matter.

"Sorry to keep you waiting, sir," a harried-looking man in a gray smock said, approaching from behind a swinging door. His hand felt clammy, oddly appropriate for the job, Aristide thought.

"I'm the coroner. Had to finish paperwork with the men who brought in the latest casualty. Some folks thought you might be able to identify the white gentleman. Come on back," he said, motioning.

It took a few seconds for Aristide to realize he somehow was acquainted with the tall, good-looking man standing a few yards away from the corpse laid out under the unforgiving lights. Incongruous though it was, he thought of that brothel, the creole girls he had long ago cavorted with.

"Are you all right, sir? I know this isn't a pleasant task," Holloway said.

"Yes, yes. Do proceed."

"These are the two men, the tugboat skipper—Lester, right? —and his man who retrieved the Negro, over there. (The black cadaver lay uncovered not far from the door.) "Up a ways, on some back water, late yesterday, correct?"

"Yes, sir," Curtis and Lester both said.

"I remember you now," Aristide said to the taller man. "Curtis. The loan for the repair shop. I thought that's where you worked."

"I do. I mean I did, sir. Then I went to Chicago to study."

Holloway looked impatient, Lester amused.

"That out of the way, I'd like you, sir, to take a look at the body here, Mr., Mr.—I do apologize." The coroner ushered Aristide closer to the gurney and drew back the sheet. The sight of the distended hulk made his stomach turn.

Aristide shook his head. "I'm sorry but I don't know this poor creature. Never saw him before."

Holloway sighed in apparent frustration, and Aristide wondered if it was because he couldn't, without an identification, complete his paperwork.

"I guess we're done here. Appreciate your coming in, sir." The coroner walked to the door and called for his assistant to help slide the two bodies into vaults.

On his way out, Aristide glanced sideways at the other corpse. He stopped in his tracks.

"Wait. I know this one. That's Grover, Cleveland's nephew." He stared at the smooth face of a twenty-year-old, who not a month ago was out in the garage helping his uncle repair the Ackermann carriage. "A strapping young man, 'could lift Bessie if he had to,' Cleveland used to say. 'Headstrong though.'"

"Are you sure? They tend to look alike," Holloway said, but Aristide would not be put off.

"What happened to him?" he asked, looking at the two riverboat men.

"Seems, sir, like a bullet to the back," Lester said. "Fished him out not two miles upstream, near some earthworks. Place where they must have been sandbagging."

Aristide took this in, turning back to the otherwise unscathed body lying before him.

"Useless that sandbagging. River washed right over the bank. We was tired of dodging debris out in the shipping lanes or we wouldn't have spotted him. Clothes caught in the thicket, kept him from being swept out." Lester took a deep breath, as if he rarely put more than two or three words together.

"Thank you, captain," Aristide said. "What did the sheriff have to say about it?" he then queried, turning back to the coroner.

"Why, not much," Holloway replied, clearly annoyed. "Said he had a lot on his plate."

"Too bad. I'll be adding this back on it. And notifying next of kin. They will want to see the body."

"I'll need to write down your name, proper-like, as making the identification." Holloway fumbled in the pocket of his smock for his notebook.

"Ackermann, Aristide Ackermann. 1202 Adams Street. The deceased's name is Grover, something or other. Anyway, his uncle is my longtime handyman, Cleveland Ellis."

Holloway took down the names.

Back out on the street a light rain had slicked the pavement, but

Aristide again eyed the young man who had so impressed him at the bank—and given Hilliard his first excuse to go after him for supposedly ill-advised loans. He turned then to the one named Lester.

"It occurred to me," Aristide began, "the city is looking to hire a few tugs, week or two anyway, to help with the clean-up. If you're interested, Captain—?"

"Actually, Curtis here is the captain. Me and Hank are the mates."

Aristide shifted his gaze in acknowledgement.

"Yes, we would be interested, Mr. Ackermann," Curtis said.

"Good. Go by City Hall tomorrow. Tell them I sent you if need be."

Aristide pulled down his felt hat and set off toward home, leaving the two men on the wet sidewalk. Quite a coincidence, he thought, as he crossed Cherry Street. Here I am helping out this fellow for a second time—and didn't he say, or didn't Alfred say, he knew Margaret? Really must find out more. He quickened his pace and tried to prepare for breaking the bad news to Cleveland.

Chapter Forty-Three

Aurelia arrived on Adams St. promptly a few nights later.

Her father had whispered that morning at the graveside that he wished to speak to her, and to James, before the others arrived to hear the president's remarks on the radio. She arranged herself across from her father's empty armchair, wondering what exactly he had pieced together of his children's Easter escapade. She looked over at the Timby. It had turned six, and she hoped James would get there before any discussion began. Susanna was bustling about in the kitchen, humming one of the hymns from the morning's service at Beulah Cemetery. Several had been sung, all led vigorously by Pastor Pendleton, who had, also vigorously, eulogized young Grover.

The Ackermanns were the only whites in attendance, other than Chief Barrett and two cops who, since an investigation had been ordered, were advised, again by Aristide, to make a show of interest in the case. But they remained on the perimeter, unaware of the mumblings from some of the blacks how Grover was, among others, corralled at gunpoint to buttress the levees, one heavy sandbag at a time. And how he had balked at the task and stormed off. "Shot in the back like it was nothing," she had heard one of them mutter.

"Would you like a cup of tea, Miss Aurelia?" Susanna asked as she passed through the parlor to retrieve a vase of flowers for the dining room table.

"I'm fine. Father and James should be along soon. We're listening to the president before dinner. So take your time." A key turned in the front door lock.

As it turned out, Coolidge demurred, delegating the government's official response to the emergency to his right hand man. When Herbert Hoover did take to the airwaves, Aurelia took nothing in, except his surprise reference to their town.

"At Vicksburg the flood is 6000 feet wide and 50 feet deep. Behind this crest the ruin of 200,000 people..."

Aid for the stricken, emergency teams, Americans pulling together—all government promises which washed over Aurelia. The others, Evelyn, Henrietta and Caroline included, strained forward on their chairs to catch every phrase. She was still parsing her father's words, wincing at her own lame responses, thankful that her brother had chimed in in her defense. But, even so, she, not he, was the object of paternal displeasure, a woman who had overstepped her proper bounds, even though, as her father admitted—and said he supported—that those bounds had been loosened since the war.

"Even your dresses," he had said, eyeing her exposed ankles.

The lighter note did not last.

Not enough, he had gone on, that it was Easter Day, that she had made a spectacle of herself (that's how it had been reported to Alfred) at the refugee camp, and that she had been defenseless in a car, with a black man as a passenger, in the middle of nowhere. Having dragged Henrietta along as well only made matters worse. So dangerous an area that they had stumbled upon a cadaver, and, once again, though it was their civic responsibility to transport the body to the proper authorities, creating an occasion for people to talk.

All of this Aurelia bore without a defense other than to say she had not thought through the consequences since she, and James as well, were bent solely on helping out the unfortunate. Much of what happened had been unforeseen, including (and here James shook his head in support) their *fortuitous*, that was the word she chose, encounter with Curtis and his crew.

Her father paused to clear his throat.

"Ah, this Curtis. I am ever so aware of his merits. I spoke with Margaret—and yes, she and Sarah-Lynn are weathering the storm so far, Sybil and Philip too—and she vouched, more than vouched, for him. Said you were all friends, from that time toward the end of the war..."

"A good friend to us both. He went n-n-north and became an engineer. Been working on the river e-e-ever since," James rushed to interpose.

Aristide looked impatient.

"Not the point I'm trying to make," he snapped. James slumped back into his chair. "Boundaries," Aristide declared. "They exist and however much they may have shifted, you are obligated to recognize where they are. That's how the world works. Curtis Jefferson is black and that's all there is to it."

James glanced at Aurelia, his look saying she should not try to counter this pronouncement.

"Actually, Father, he's of mixed race, on both his mother's and his father's sides, I believe. If I'm not mistaken..." Aurelia trailed off, her tone less confident than she might have wished, thinner at the edges.

"Be that as it may. If it pleases you to know, I have once again assisted the young man. His tug is contracted to assist with salvaging. I'm simply submitting that there's a distance to be observed between the races, which they appreciate as well—consider, for example, where we respectfully stood this morning at the cemetery."

Boundaries. Because she could not bear to hurt her father, Aurelia would not blurt out that already, long ago in fact, (and wishing to again if ever it were feasible), she had crashed through the strongest barrier that divided the races. And in so doing shattered whatever tangential hold on the truth she had hoped to preserve. In her wordless shame, she hung her head.

Mercifully the doorbell rang. Aristide gestured for James to attend to their guests.

"I would think, Aurelia—and this is the last I will pronounce on the matter," her father concluded, rising from his armchair, "that you would remember that you are married, and that Charles will have a view as to what is appropriate for you to do, as a wife, and, it is hoped, as a mother."

I am living two lies. Aurelia sighed with bitter resignation. Loving someone off-limits and living with another in a mockery of a marriage. She felt constricted, unable to breath. What was it Claudette had said when they threw off their corsets—when was it, their second year of college? —"Your body will feel looser but don't be fooled. Takes more than that to set you free."

"Are you all right, Aurelia? You look distraught. Our guests are waiting."

"Yes, Father, I'll be along, right behind you." Familial bonds, she thought as she watched her father cross the room, his weight heavy on the cane, were tighter whalebone than she had reckoned.

Chapter Forty-Four

Charles had forgotten how much he relished the anonymity of New Orleans. To his dismay, Vicksburg was proving altogether too constrained a place. Not that he was proud of his proclivities—he had tried to tamp them, even submitting to a round of injections, in his case toxic to the body—but that was long ago and those efforts had failed. He had hoped that his marriage to Aurelia would somehow stimulate his desire to enter into and sustain a physical union with the opposite sex. Why, he had asked himself at the time, was that so far-fetched? At the outset he found her loose and straitlaced at the same time, an arresting combination in a young lady. Still, he had to admit—this as the streetcar rattled down St. Charles Avenue on the way to a rendezvous with a few of his chums—that what had cinched the deal was money. Not hers, though the Ackermanns were prosperous and she was the only daughter, but his, or rather what would be his, if he adhered to certain stipulations. They had been read out to him by the family lawyer when he was twenty-five, a year or so after his father had ceased speaking to him. Other than a monthly allowance from his mother that was deposited directly into the Hibernia, he would not come into his portion of the Truard fortune until he married—a proper union, Mr. Broussard had emphasized in his fusty office on Tchoupitoulas Street. One-half once the nuptials took place, the remainder if he managed to hold onto a position in a reputable firm for three years, or if his wife gave birth. Whichever came first.

Charles needed an Aurelia. After three local law firms in New Orleans had, for reasons that remained obscure, dismissed him in turn, he still dressed in the latest style and dined out though penniless, borrowing off one or another in his nocturnal entourage. Or taking his chance at cards. Even after the wedding, the considerable sum transferred to his account at the First National dwindled more than he had anticipated. Being married was expensive, even if he had finagled a good deal on the rented Wilkerson house and Aurelia could hardly be counted as profligate.

What he hadn't bargained on was the flood. Worse than anyone had expected, certainly, but that it could upend his family's shipping business, Truard Transport being a household word in the Crescent City, was unfathomable to him, because he had never paid the least attention to it. He had assumed there would always be a need for barges to transport goods up and down the river. As long as they floated and were manned properly, what could go wrong? Especially with his exacting father at the helm of the company. But as soon as he walked into the parlor, his mother staring out the window at the water-logged garden, he knew something was amiss.

"I thought I'd find you here," Charles said in a voice as neutral as possible.

Lucille Truard released the edge of the drapes and twisted to face her son. He thought she looked bleached out. "I wasn't aware you were coming. Is that Aurelia person with you?"

"No, no. I wanted to check that you and Father were all right. Quite something this flood. Upriver anyway. What are they saying down here?"

She sighed and returned to her settee, adjusting a crocheted shawl around her shoulders. Her long thin hand swept upward to indicate the armchair across from her.

"They're doing what they can to spare the city. Dynamiting the Atchafalaya. But, even so, your father's losing sleep. One of our barges ran aground. A pilot fell overboard and drowned. I haven't asked for details but—are you staying long? If so, you can talk to him yourself."

C.T. nodded, accustomed as he was to humoring his mother. She had never acknowledged the rift between father and son, holding staunchly to the belief that families, to survive intact, needed to pretend relations, however frayed, were excellent.

"Business leaders are meeting in the Quarter, so I doubt he'll be home until late. Herbert Hoover is in town, if the *Picayune* can be trusted."

"Perhaps the government can do something of use," he replied, his mind already calculating how he could broach the subject of money with his father in such circumstances. Highly inconvenient, this flood thing.

Mrs. Truard scrutinized her son.

"I'm surprised your wife didn't bother to come. She has family here after all." She paused. "Or is she...?"

C.T. was annoyed. "She's busy—volunteering. Refugees and the like. The flood has displaced all the riff-raff. Besides, work at my firm has slowed. Seemed like a good moment to get away for a spell."

Mrs. Truard blinked in tacit agreement.

"Well, since you're here, you should enjoy yourself. I'm sure your old friends—no doubt they will be glad to see you." She extended her blue-veined arm for the bell on the table beside her couch. Out the window, Charles could make out a fine sheet of rain falling on the banana leaves.

"Carson, do help Mr. Charles with his luggage. His old room, please." It was the signal that the *tête-à-tête* between mother and son, such as it was, was over. C.T. rose to assist his mother to her feet. It was three o'clock, time for her customary afternoon nap.

"As I was intimating," she wound up, her tone suggesting she well knew the reason her son had come home. "If you approach him with care, I'm sure your father will advance you what he can, even if a baby is not yet on the way."

"With care, Mother? What would to your mind that entail?" he asked.

She shrugged. "That you will have to discover yourself."

When father and son did cross paths several days later, Lucille could hear from across the house the sharp words that flew between them. Something about her son being a mollycoddled mother's boy who needed to buck up and—this shouted—be a man, be a man. Her hands unsteady, she hastened out into the garden and across the wet grass to the rose bushes along the back fence. Clippers. She would get the clippers from the shed and cut a bouquet. Thus engaged, she didn't altogether catch her son's angry tirade.

"I wouldn't be what I've become if you weren't a bully. And a whoremonger to boot. I suspect that's where your precious money goes, right?" C.T. had become red in the face as he paced in front of his father, rather enjoying his own dramatic outburst. "And don't for one minute think Mother doesn't know."

C.T. eventually ran out of material.

Richard Truard twirled his drink and took a long swig. "As I was trying to get across," he resumed, sucking in his breath and raising his head for the first time to face his son, "the family fortune that you persist in referencing is largely a myth. What you haven't already frittered away is floating away. If you'll forgive the metaphor, Truard Transport may soon be drowning in debt."

The color drained from C.T.'s face. It was one thing to imagine that his father's business would suffer a downturn, another thing altogether to imagine that the company was going under. He was at a loss for words, unsure whether he was sorrier for his father, whose entire life had centered on those barges, or for himself, who had taken for granted the business while blithely relying on its profits. He stared out the window, his mother doing something to the bushes against the far fence. Then again, for all C.T. knew, his father could be lying.

"In case you don't believe me," Truard Sr. added, "think about what havoc awaits in the heartland. Without cotton or corn or lumber or oil, what will the company have to ship? Owning a barge will be well-nigh nugatory."

His son said nothing.

"If I were you," he went on, "I'd cleave to that wife of yours. She seems to have a head on her shoulders so it may be she can talk sense into you. Lead a decent, hard-working life up there." This advice was the last thing C.T. wanted to hear. He felt queasy, as when someone called his bluff at poker and he held only a deuce.

"Privileges," his father added, almost as an afterthought. "What the war didn't end for us, Mother Nature will have. We may as well get used to it." Truard Sr. quaffed the last of the bourbon, set the glass on the mantel and left the room. C.T. wilted onto his mother's settee and buried his face in his hands.

Chapter Forty-Five

The women of Bethel redoubled their efforts in the weeks following the flood, canvassing for more blankets, cough syrups and foodstuffs for the displaced. Despite her father's implicit displeasure, Aurelia continued to show up at the church, including the first Sunday afternoon in May. She knew better than to volunteer to return to the refugee camp but she could stuff boxes and organize pick-ups. A few other white women made sporadic appearances at the black church, including Henrietta, though the latter kept her distance. Things between them had not yet thawed.

Whether she marries my father or not, it's clear, Aurelia mused. I have in their eyes transgressed, and they have dissociated themselves. Deceived my father. Deceived my friend. In the offing deceived even myself?

As for Charles, she shuddered to think what he might say or do when he reappeared, whenever that might be. She folded the last of the Army blankets piled on the table and looked around for string to tie the flaps of the boxes she had readied.

"Why, Miss Aurelia, you look like you be running the place. All these boxes. Mighty kind of you."

Startled, Aurelia looked up into the pleasant face of Willy Mayfield's wife, who since their transfer from Tallulah to Vicksburg had become a regular community volunteer. Not three feet behind her was Curtis. He held a skipper's cap in his hand and looked less ravaged than when last she saw him at the camp.

"Our Curtis been on the river day and night. Needs a hot meal as well as some church-going."

He nodded self-consciously, acquiescing to his former teacher's strong arm and stronger will. She dragged him back to the makeshift kitchen from which he reappeared a minute or so later with two bowls of soup.

"She told me to give one to you," he said to Aurelia.

The two erstwhile lovers sat among the boxes, sipping broth in silence. Several boys—Aurelia recognized them as regular members of the congregation—filed past, looked around and one by one carried the tied-up supplies outside for loading.

Several minutes passed. They could hear the choir rehearsing in a room off the apse. Eventually Curtis put his spoon down. He had relaxed, perhaps because he was in the one place where blacks were in charge. Their church. Here, Aurelia was the ostensible outsider.

"Your mother's house? Aunt Margaret's?" she asked, to break the silence.

"From what I can tell, ground floor soaked through but still standing. Most of the folks will have left. Slim and I, a couple of months ago, tended to the horses. Cassandra is down in New Orleans with Sarah-Lynn."

More questions raced through Aurelia's mind, but Mrs. Mayfield was approaching with Reverend Pendleton in tow. Before she could stop herself, she whispered, "Come tonight. After dark." Curtis looked stunned. "To the carriage house. A lamp will be lit."

His cap pulled down over his forehead, Curtis arrived by foot at the darkened house on Baum Street around 8:30, having berated himself all afternoon about the dangers implicit in such a meeting. But there was something so inviting in her voice. He had been smitten anew.

The spring air was thick, though not as rancid as out on the water. His heart raced. Scanning the street, he filled his lungs and took the creaky stairs of the carriage house two at a time. Before he could knock Aurelia had cracked the door.

"Don't worry," she murmured. "My husband is away. The maid is asleep in the back of the house. I know this is folly, but I had to see you. There's so much to say."

Gently, he took her hands in his and raised them to his cheek. He thought suddenly of Chicago: the arch of her back, her moans, his own gasps. A double bed was feet in front of him, but instead, Aurelia led him toward the couch against the wall, and away from the lamp in the front window.

For a long while they held each other, listening to their hearts beat. Then a torrent of words overtook them—what had raced through their minds when they saw each other at the camp, and everything that had changed since New Orleans. Aurelia wanted to know more about Loretta, but he insisted their uses for each other had ceased. What stung him more, the rejection by the Corps of Engineers.

"And you? You haven't said a word about your marriage." Aurelia released her hold on Curtis' arm and looked away.

"I'm sorry," Curtis said. "You don't have to say anything if it upsets you."

"That's not it, Curtis. I have tried, I have so tried," she blurted out.

He reached out for her hand, hoping to help her regain her

composure.

"Unlike what you said about things between you and Loretta, Charles has no interest in me."

Curtis was flummoxed. "I don't follow."

Aurelia glanced toward the bed. "We have never—in all this time, in the same house, under the same roof…" She spoke the words as if the revelation was as incredible to her as it undoubtedly was to him.

"Are you saying he is in love with someone else, and never told you before, or since…?"

She shook her head sideways. "It's not that. It's worse, for him and for me. I could sympathize if he would allow or admit, but he can't or won't." She paused, took a deep breath. "At times he is contrite, even kind; but at others, he spurns me, loathes me." She stared at the far wall.

Curtis placed her hand back in her lap. The diamond on her ring finger sparkled in the light. He rose. He paced the floor. Of all the scenarios he had conjured of Aurelia's life without him, such a disconcerting version of her marriage had never crossed his mind. He eyed the bed again...he was too unsettled. Several books lay on the night table, Oscar Wilde, somebody Forster. On the wall a couple of prints, a modernist school, somebody Beardsley. He wondered who slept in such a room.

"Have you confided in anyone about this, Aurelia? Your brother?"

"James is aware that I am unhappy but I can't imagine he will have figured out why."

"It's unnatural, Aurelia—what he has become." He couldn't bring himself to pronounce her husband's name. "You do recognize that, don't you?"

"Don't be harsh, Curtis. Strange as it sounds, I pity him. His heart is elsewhere but so is mine. I cannot hate someone for what he cannot help." She looked across the room to see how this registered.

"Cannot help? If I understand rightly, he married you well knowing...In any case, for ulterior motives, whatever they might be."

(Money was near the top of his list of possible reasons but it seemed to him mean-spirited to say so.)

"Enough about all this, Curtis. I shall manage."

He shook his head in disgust, the idea of this other man more distasteful than if...

"Come sit with me, darling." She patted the space beside her. "We have so little time."

For the next hour they spoke of other people—the Taylors, his mother, Claudette and Rufus—and of his plan to build up the tugboat business as far south as New Orleans, and thus, the possibility that they might see each other again.

Round midnight, Curtis disengaged himself from her embrace. "Only this, Aurelia, you must promise. If this man—Charles—is cruel to you, you must get away. Go home to your father or to James. It's not the Ackermann name you must protect; it is yourself."

As she opened the door, they kissed one final time. Over her shoulder, he glimpsed a curtain twitch in the alcove of the main house. Strange.

Curtis took the stairs two at a time and lit out for Cherry Street. In the distance he could hear dogs howling. A gibbous moon floated high in the cloudless sky. He reached to pull his cap down, only to realize he had forgotten it in the carriage house. Too dangerous to go back. He headed to Willy's shop as fast as he could without breaking into a run.

Chapter Forty-Six

"Smooth as a looking glass," Aurelia exclaimed one day toward the end of June as she surveyed the glistening river from the top of the bluff at Fort Nogales. It had been James' idea to make the jaunt—and to get away from the mosquitoes that had amassed in town in the wake of the flood. Along with Evelyn and Henrietta they had spread a checkered tablecloth and feasted on the fried chicken and potato salad Susanna had prepared that Saturday morning. Afterwards, as was the local custom, they climbed the spiral staircase of the nearby observation tower.

"We were the lucky ones," James pointed out, indicating the far distance where the water met the western horizon. "Most everything was inundated on the other side—it's so flat, and the levees were utterly inadequate." Their hands shading their eyes, the women squinted to see what James was alluding to. He removed the binoculars from around his neck and handed them to Henrietta.

"At least that's what Curtis told me—about the levees," he added, making sure he did not turn his gaze toward his sister. And yet he wondered. She seemed so serene of late, a new hair-do, a hint of rouge. Their mutual friend had spent more than a month on the river near Vicksburg on contract to the city, sleeping sometimes aboard the *Starfish* with his crew, other times at Willy's Motor Works. The two friends had run into each other a week ago when James went late one afternoon to pick up his Briscoe. The suspension had never been the same since the excursion to the refugee camp.

"Look, look, a huge flock. You can hear them too," Henrietta exclaimed, pointing out over the vast expanse of water. *Ha-ronk, ka-lunk, ha-ronk*. She passed the binoculars to Aurelia.

"Geese, from the sound of them," Aurelia guessed, handing the glasses off to Evelyn. "At least the buzzards have disappeared. Things will soon be back to normal, don't you think, James?"

"Can't happen soon enough," he said. When Evelyn walked over to the other side of the tower to take a look at the woods below, James followed. He had often thought such a weekend outing—Evelyn had never been to the park, something James had found unfathomable—might be the perfect time to propose. But that was before. Before the flood, before mounting claims would surely pull Mr. Cartwright's insurance business under, his own meager job with it, before whatever blow the Ackermann family might sustain. Better to wait, see what develops, and savor the day laid before them.

He touched Evelyn's bare arm as she leaned over the balustrade. She drew away.

"Funny no one ever said a word about this place."

James felt sorry for them both. Evelyn had lacked advantages; he was doing his best to supply a few, but of late she seemed either bored or distracted.

Eventually they piled into the car and motored through the

bister-tinged hills of the park, encountering only a smattering of other sightseers. Cows fortunate to have survived the flood grazed in the gullies.

"This you have to do," he instructed Evelyn when they pulled up in front of the Illinois Monument. She looked unenthused. "We call it the 'holler' house, both because the dome is hollow and, because when you holler, you can hear your echo." She acquiesced.

Once inside, Aurelia and James raised their voices until they bounced off the chamber walls. Then, as they had done as children, he ran his fingers over the names of Civil War soldiers long dead, listening only intermittently to his sister and Henrietta.

"They're talking about a monument in town to commemorate the fallen in the war. Did you read about that?"

"Yes, it's a good thing. Your father's involved."

James looked up from his perusal of the names engraved on the bronze wall to locate Evelyn.

"Let's hope they don't get sidetracked by everything else going on," Henrietta added. "No one seems to want to remember anymore."

"I think no one wants another war. Still, no one who lost his life, your Earl included, should be forgotten."

Aurelia held out her arm and the two headed out of the monument and into the sunlight. With sadness James realized Evelyn had already left the dome.

Chapter Forty-Seven

In the darkness Charles did not immediately spot the battered cap on the hat rack. He had returned from New Orleans exhausted and chary. Having avoided his father after their altercation, he had spent his final evenings in the Quarter. He did not mention to his mother the card games he had returned to, nor the losses he racked up. Eventually, though, the renewed pleasures of Rampart Street wore thin; besides, he suspected he was being tailed. He left in his Essex roadster (another extravagance he could ill-afford) on a muggy June afternoon, pulling over only once to relieve himself, since swarms of mosquitoes instantly targeted him. The Wilkerson home itself dark, he climbed the steps of the carriage house, dropped his suitcase and sprawled across the bed. He slept. Only the next morning did the cap catch his eye. Meticulous in his habits, he couldn't imagine how it had been left there, nor by whom.

He would ask Rose for an explanation.

More immediately, he would surprise his wife at breakfast, a bag of beignets and a can of chicory coffee in hand in a rare show of spousal appreciation. He had made a few such gestures during their marriage, but each time something had gone awry. Now more than ever he needed Aurelia on his side. If he were to keep pesky creditors at bay, he would need ready cash. Assuming he had eluded the most insistent of these sharks in New Orleans, Vicksburg, he had found, was a harder place to hide. He wouldn't be able to put them off for long, riverboat scum that they were.

None of this he planned to tell Aurelia. Rather, he would talk about a down payment on some plot of land where they could eventually build. Old Mrs. Wilkerson's house was not likely available to them for much longer and his own assets were tied up in investments, he would explain. Not to mention that the flood had opened up opportunities to those who had the wherewithal to seize them.

To his relief the next morning, Aurelia greeted him cheerily, seeming pleased by his thoughtfulness. She set about making coffee and warming the stale beignets in the oven. Rather than pepper him with questions, she regaled him with a description of a recent party at the B.B. Club.

"Very impromptu, everyone eager to toast Lindbergh. Nobody talked about the flood. Several asked after you, including a few I wasn't acquainted with."

Nothing accusatory in her tone. Charles felt encouraged. "Likewise. You were missed in New Orleans," he lied. "Mother sends regards as does Father." He didn't elaborate. She smiled. "Oh yes. You might be amused to know the latest craze—everyone's playing Mah Jong. We should set up some tables and have folks over."

Aurelia laughed. "It might be wise to learn first, don't you think?"

"It's hardly bridge. But yes, I'll ask around. I imagine Caroline is already an expert, self-declared anyway." He caught Aurelia eying her watch. "Are you going out? Surely classes are over for the year."

"They missed so much they're extending the term through July. I'm teaching an advanced French seminar at 8:30 and an English class at 10:00. So far I've resisted entreaties to handle basic German, since Mrs. Kreisler is sick."

Aurelia sensed that Charles was no longer listening. She nibbled at the beignet—never edible these confections on the second day, but she knew better than to criticize. Her husband had made an effort.

"Oh, I did want to let you know. The roof. Leaks have sprung over the parlor as well as the library. Rose and I have done what we could but with so much rain..."

He looked cross.

"So where is that ninny? She should have made breakfast."

"I've given her a few days off, here and there. So little to do, with you away." Aurelia stuttered over the lie, the real reason being so the snoopy maid wouldn't suspect anything if her mistress came and went at odd hours. Like the night at the B.B. Club. She had sipped champagne, danced a foxtrot of sorts with Mr. Greene, and still managed to slip away early. A few blocks away at Mayfield's Motor Works, she lodged the car between others that needed repairs and tapped on the back window of the building. Almost an entire night with Curtis. The danger of their trysts had become intoxicating.

"Since you mention the roof, I did want to bring something important up."

Aurelia looked across the table, not wanting to be late but not daring to aggravate her husband further. "And that is?"

"We should think about a house of our own. Buy the land now while it's relatively cheap. Pool our resources of course."

Dismay clouded her face. Tethered. How would she bear being further tied down to this man—or he to her—in a house of their own? If Charles were apprised of the account her father had set up a decade ago, her own savings would be purposed for it. Surely the lease didn't run out for months and months, a year or so. Enough time...

"I'm running late, Charles. I suspect you are too. Why don't we discuss it tonight?"

"If we must," he said icily. The old Charles had re-emerged. "Do make sure Rose returns by this evening. The carriage house needs dusting."

Aurelia nodded and left the breakfast nook. She grabbed her straw hat off the rack and hurried out, trying to focus on her French lesson. *Madame Bovary*, she had thought of introducing until she was overruled. "Too risqué for sixteen-year-old girls," the principal, a spinster named Miss Williams, had ruled, eyeing her askance. And yet, she would have been able to convey the feel of the novel like no other. The claustrophobia Emma strove against.

"Je le sais, je le sens, moi aussi," she whispered.

Rose reappeared late that afternoon. As soon as the kitchen was tidied, she headed for the carriage house, feather duster in hand. When Charles got home, he went straight outside and up the stairs. For a few minutes he watched as the maid went through the motions.

"I say, Rose, how do you explain the cap I found here on the hat rack? You know this place is off-limits when I'm away."

"Ain't nothing to do with me, Mr. Charles. I is only ever up here to clean." She turned to straighten the half-dozen books lying on the plantation table in the corner.

"So, it's a mystery. Is that it?" he persisted, enjoying the idea of making the girl wriggle.

"No mystery to me, sir. That's a fact."

"Is that so?" He eyed her harder, hoping to make her squirm.

"Two weeks ago 'twas. Man comes down the stairs round midnight. Quick like a fox but I seen him from the parlor window. And he ain't got no hat on his head."

"Now how could that be, Rose? A man all alone in the carriage house. Dreaming, were you?" He was having fun picking her account apart.

"Not ten minutes later, more creaking. Miss Aurelia, she tiptoes down them same steps."

"Are you sure what you're saying? Doesn't make any sense."

"Strange is right, Mr. Charles. He being black and all..." She continued to rearrange the books in no particular order.

"Black?" He searched the far corners of his mind for what that could mean. For a moment neither spoke. "Ah, likely as not Cleveland, over to fix something."

"Not that I seen. Real young, this one. Good-lookin'." She dusted the table top with gusto.

Charles took a long draw on his Camel and flicked the ashes on the bare floor.

"That will do, Rose. You can go now. Mrs. Truard will likely need your help with dinner."

For an instant Rose eyed him with a smirk on her face, then squatted to dab at the ashes. Charles crossed the room and swung open the door, motioning for her to leave.

A conundrum, to be filed away, he told himself. As long as this nitwit keeps things to herself.

PART FIVE

And the brute crowd, whose envious zeal
Huzzas each turn of fortune's wheel,
And loudest shouts when lowest lie
Exalted worth and station high

Sir Walter Scott

Chapter Forty - Eight

When he came into the First National that first Monday in October of ’27, Aristide should have felt vindicated. Not only had he been re-elected president of the board but he was now ensconced in a redecorated head office. Mr. Gauge was hanging the last of the newly acquired paintings, still nattering on about the Dempsey-Tunney bout the week before. A new secretary had been designated for him, the first female employee at the bank whose tight skirts barely brushed her kneecaps.

He didn’t mind. What bothered him was less overt but more insidious. The uncontrollable rise of the market and people’s uncontrollable urge to get in on it. Even local citizens, whom he had always thought of as conservative folks, had caught the fever, cornering him to ask what he thought about Studebaker at 110 or Westinghouse at 83 ¾. Close friends, ones who should have known better, were ploughing their savings into this or that stock, most of which they knew next to nothing about, and paying a pretty penny to unscrupulous brokers for the privilege.

Caroline's mother for one, bangles accentuating her jarring tone, chided her husband at an Elks Club party for being "slow off the mark when everyone else..." For an instant he empathized with the hen-pecked Hilliard, who had other things to worry about, like staying out of jail for his misdeeds. The poor man managed and made a point of trumpeting over the roast beef that he had not a week before bought a hundred shares of American Linseed and they had since shot up.

Not that Aristide held himself up as an expert in money matters. His knowledge of economics was rudimentary—Delta-raised, he believed in the worth of what lay under his feet, especially if that soil was rich loam—but he had lived through a couple of so-called bubbles and seen what havoc they could wreak. Despite the euphoria around Lindbergh's flight and Ruth's batting arm, the country, he reckoned, was headed for trouble. Why couldn't people read the tea leaves? Sophie used to inquire rhetorically. The flood had disrupted trade throughout the river basin and created a refugee problem not seen since the war. And now this.

"Before I tell anyone to gamble with their hard-earned cash, anyone I know personally, I'm going to walk them down to Levee Street to see the damage—and that's just one street in one small town." So he had boasted to Henrietta one evening when she remarked that her own parents seemed to be talking of nothing else but Wall Street. Aristide wondered if she knew how precarious the finances of her own father's insurance company were or about the loan the First National had extended him back in August. Out of delicacy, he did not inquire.

When the pert Miss Paxton read off Aristide's appointments for the day, Mr. Cartwright was once again on the list. Worse than precarious it turned out. What with claims mounting for properties up and down the river that were literally underwater, he was forced to scale back. That meant letting poor James go, one reason for Cartwright's visit to the bank. The other was to ask for an extension on the loan. "Your son, Aristide, is very conscientious. Nary a problem other than those spells of his. Hate to do this, but we've got little Emily to think about. Henrietta too for that matter."

Looking at his friend's scrumbled forehead, Aristide felt obliged to extend what credit he could, and at the same time to warn Cartwright not to overplay his hand in the market. A couple of Cuban cigars sealed the deal. A little bourbon washed it down. Even so, it didn't seem the appropriate moment to divulge that he planned to press his suit with Henrietta that very evening. To his own surprise, Aristide had grown sensitive about the age difference between them and did not want to be reproved, especially by one of his peers, and most especially by the father of the young woman in question. On the other hand, he calculated, his proposal might now be looked upon with favor, perhaps even with enthusiasm, since his own financial health would make up for any limits to his physical prowess.

"Now, remember, Cartwright, don't go whole-hog with Woolworth. And don't fret about letting James go. I appreciate what you've done for him."

Walking home that evening, Aristide breathed in the autumnal air, the pungent odor from the river no longer detectable. The hill though took extra effort, especially after liquor. He paused to allow the ache in his chest to pass. He had almost forgotten. Something would need to be done for James.

"I'll make him a clerk. Get Gauge on it in the morning," he vowed aloud. But what that girl from Valley Dry Goods sees in him....

Chapter Forty-Nine

As the Twenties ticked toward an end, what counted was being scrappy. Those that could take advantage of the chaos thrived; those wedded to the old ways succumbed. Truard Transport, for one, lost its ballast in the aftermath of the flood, its proud owner unable, or unwilling, to adapt.

Black though he was and thus by definition disadvantaged, Curtis rose to the occasion. He commanded a tug and it was versatile enough to do anything required. Up and down the river, from St. Louis to New Orleans he found work, on behalf of Norris & Co. or off the books on his own. After eight months, Hank and Lester returned to Memphis, having pocketed more cash under their captain than in the five years previous. "Ain't a bad sort, the Creole," was Lester's final pronouncement on the matter.

From then on Curtis hired river rats on an ad hoc basis, or when he had to (because some rednecks refused to work for him), took on jobs singlehanded. None was too menial, few too ambitious or dangerous, such that by the end of 1928 he had amassed a tidy sum, most of which he stuffed in a leather bag and hid under the new floorboards in his mother's house; the rest he deposited at the Hibernia Bank. When not out on contract, he docked the *Starfish* along the edge of the warehouse district. Rarely did he amuse himself, other than to read himself to sleep or listen to Bix Beiderbecke on the radio. The knot of desire inside him was so tangled as to be best left alone.

Out of filial duty he now and then accompanied Wilena to the Saenger Theatre to see—and hear! —the latest talkies, chafing each time they were consigned to the balcony. Afterwards they licked ice cream cones as they meandered along Canal Street.

"I know you be sad, Son. But you need to be prepared. Miz Taylor is planning a get-together for Sarah-Lynn, come September. Back at the farm," Wilena said out of the blue. She paused, leaning on the cane he had carved for her. "Miss Aurelia is coming. Miss Margaret done told me yesterday. Wants you to be there too."

Curtis fixed on the brass instruments displayed in the window of Werlein's, their price tags turned discreetly face down. He swallowed hard, aware of his heart pounding, an ache further down. After what? Two years on the water where all men were equaled out, their cares easily drowned; yet here on land he was undone. Not only relegated to balconies and back streets but made helpless by a woman's name. It might be 1929, but little had changed.

Still, he did not respond.

"Just because Miss Margaret is civilized—she don't distinguish between the races—don't mean they ain't there. You be smart, Curtis, so feelings got to be put aside. Miss Aurelia, like that friend of hers up north, be married ladies now, married white ladies. I don't need to remind you."

"No, Mama. You don't need to remind me."

On the crowded trolley to Uptown, Wilena and Curtis stood in the back as custom dictated. Only when they approached the Taylor residence on foot did Wilena let out what Curtis could tell had been building in her mind. "I seen how they look at you, Curtis, at that movie house. You could pass if you had a mind to. Lord knows it would make things easier for you. I 'spect your pappy did so, when it suited him."

Rarely had Wilena invoked her long dead husband and never had she dared suggest to her son that his color could be fungible. Taken aback, Curtis hesitated. He didn't want to admit that he had more than once, deep in the night, toyed with such a notion. Rufus had argued he should so scheme—"reinvent yourself," had been his unsolicited advice. But, unlike his Chicago friend, Curtis had neither the suppleness of mind nor a flair for pretense. Besides, he didn't want to be white: he wanted the world to be color-blind.

"You know better, Mama. I am what I am."

"You be stubborn, ain't no denying. But to see you pine away is some terrible sight. And not getting that job to save the river—you a bonafide engineer. The best that college ever turn out."

Curtis hugged his mother. "Don't worry so about me. I'm fine. And I will come by next week before going back upriver. Sarah-Lynn wants to go riding, over in Gretna. I've got to put new shoes on Cassandra beforehand." He turned and headed back toward St. Charles Avenue before Margaret or Sarah-Lynn came to the door.

Time to celebrate. So Margaret had declared as Sarah-Lynn's graduation from Sophie Newcomb approached. The land had largely dried out since the flood, the stock market was on a tear, and her homestead upriver had, thanks to Slim's oversight, been put back to rights.

She missed the place. Further, as little as she wished to dwell on it, the move to New Orleans hadn't been all she had hoped. Before the war, she was young, pretty and married; now she was middle-aged, widowed and, as one of her few new friends put it, "not a flower native to the Garden District."

Sophie's sister Sybil Durrell had been less kind. "Too countrified, too opinionated and, for all we know, a Bolshevik," Margaret had overheard her say to her husband Philip after the one dinner to which they invited her and "the too exuberant daughter." Margaret had not ventured to call upon Aurelia's even snootier in-laws, having heard, again from the same new friend, a Tulane biology professor named Dr. Ballard, that the Truards, Francophiles in the extreme, had never gotten over the Louisiana Purchase.

More distressing to Margaret than social snubs was her reflection in the mirror. To obscure the lines that had begun to etch themselves on her forehead, she over-applied expensive face powder from Maison Blanche; to comb under the unruly gray in her hair she layered on expensive pomade. Until she couldn't bear returning for more jars from the contemptuous clerk behind the cosmetics counter. Thus, she concentrated her energies on Sarah-Lynn, and to her delight, her daughter ranked top of her class.

Whatever her own disappointments, she now had something to be enthusiastic about. They would throw a summer party before Sarah-Lynn was to head off to L.S.U.'s School of Veterinary Medicine in the fall.

"But back home, Mother, and only for the people we really care about. Like old times," Sarah-Lynn, ebullient as ever, had insisted. "Don't forget Aurelia and James. Cassie and Lawrence too. I'll tell Curtis. Wherever he is, I know he'll come."

Margaret suspected so too.

Chapter Fifty

Brother and sister boarded the ferry on a bright September day, geese coursing in V formation overhead. At first the vessel glided as if through oil, creating barely a ripple. But in the distance a barge bulging with cotton bales chugged its way upstream. In its wake, they grasped the iron railing, higher and sturdier than before since the ferry now accommodated cars as well as passengers. James spotted a large purple bruise on Aurelia's exposed arm. Oblivious, she stared at the dock on the far side.

"I assume Charles didn't want you to go, let alone deign to accompany you," James ventured, hoping to draw his sister out. So taciturn had she become in the last few months that she rarely mentioned her husband at all. Which in James' mind made whatever the situation on Baum Street that much more untenable.

Aurelia saw it differently. Too beautiful an outing to spoil it by disabusing her brother. She and Charles communicated only when something displeased him. As far as she knew, he was still employed though where his money—indeed, where a goodly portion of her own teacher's salary—had gone, she had no clue. Buying land, building a house was another ruse, she had concluded. And was relieved. She looked north where another barge, this one laden with coal, was skirting the first, headed downstream.

Charles and I, like ships passing each other, indifferent. Except when we collide, she mused. The arm-twisting, the back of the hand across the face, that was new. Like when she mentioned the jaunt to her aunt's old home across the river. "Don't you see? I'm under scrutiny. If the firm looks askance, it's over, over, over," he fairly screamed, blood rushing to his head. Her wrist still ached from his grasp.

Aurelia changed the subject with her brother.

"Evelyn might have enjoyed a weekend away from the Valley. Did she not wish to come?"

James wrinkled his forehead. "She's been distracted."

"Oh?"

"Some friends on the steamer. Coming through town again, right about n-n-now."

Aurelia sensed that her brother did not know any of these friends. Exotic though, the idea, of meeting someone off the *Belle of the Bends*. A surprising young woman, Evelyn.

Once the ropes were knotted, one of the dock workers helped hand Aurelia to the pier while James lugged the two leather bags. Slim wasn't due to pick them up until eleven, so they went straight into MacGregor's rebuilt store, complete with a professionally painted bright green sign. A young man bustled about inside, arranging jars of preserves and measuring out cups of rice to a smattering of other customers. Aurelia and James each picked out a Nu-grape from the iced container and plopped down two nickels on the counter. The clerk eyed them but said nothing. It was Mrs. MacGregor's grandson, only less scrawny and more sallow-skinned.

Shaking off a memory of the last time she was in the store, Aurelia took James' arm and hurried outside to wait. Eventually Slim, with his wide grin and buck teeth, pulled up in his old Templar, the car reborn, he kept assuring them on the trip, Curtis having toyed with the engine.

"Now these roads here are another story," he chuckled as they bounced around over the ruts left by the retreating waters.

"How are things, Slim, with the house, and the horses?"

"Not bad, ma'am, considering. Being as the house commands the highest rise in three counties, only the ground floor was ruined. Fixed up good as new. Other folks not so lucky. Animals, neither..."

The car being noisy and Slim's conversational abilities limited, the three traveled the rest of the way to the Taylor place in silence.

The first person they saw as they came up the winding driveway was Curtis, heading toward the barn with what looked like a new saddle draped over his arm. Before the car came to a complete halt, James leapt out and hurried over to his friend.

"Let me hang this in the stall—it's a surprise gift for Sarah-Lynn—and then we'll help your sister into the house," Curtis said, beaming.

No one felt anything uncomfortable that evening about having Curtis in their midst, eating, singing, playing charades. For once he did not have to look over his shoulder, nor Aurelia to fear suspicious stares. Their hands touched only when he ventured to turn the page of the songbook she was playing from. Her fingers and her heart missed a beat.

The only new guest, Dr. Ballard, couldn't help but notice. The next morning after the young people set off on horseback for the day, the professor queried his hostess.

"Should I presume that more is going on between those two than meets the eye?" he asked over coffee. Margaret put her finger to her lips, nodding toward the pantry where Wilena was arranging the supplies Slim had brought back from MacGregor's.

"We've all tried to dissuade them, or trusted time would dim their ardor," she whispered. "They too have no doubt tried. My niece is lovely, and loving; and he is honorable..."

"But?"

"No need to spell it out. It's immoral, or rather, it's considered immoral. And it's illegal."

"Down here it is. Clearly, they need either a remote place"—Dr. Ballard looked around as if to suggest the very house he was in—"or a big city where they would be largely ignored."

"Even so…it's hard to countenance. My brother, for one, as open-minded as he purports to be, would disown her." Margaret shook her head.

"And her husband? I saw the ring."

Margaret shrugged. "Off-putting. Doesn't strike me as, well—she doesn't talk about him, in any case."

Dr. Ballard sipped his coffee, sensing that Margaret had thought long and hard about the two lovers and their predicament without ever coming up with an adequate solution. Nor could he.

"Strange world," he mused. "Everyone desperate to be so modern, and yet so superstitious, or bigoted. And you ask why I focus my expertise on animals!"

Margaret smiled and passed her guest another piece of toast thick with her homemade plum preserves.

"Against my better judgment," he said, reaching for the slice. He looked closer at Margaret.

"You seem preoccupied. Something wrong?"

"No, no. Just praying somehow those two manage to be happy—Sarah-Lynn, too. Everyone, actually."

He looked at her in sympathy but didn't respond.

Wilena cleared her throat in the doorway. "If that be all, Miss Margaret, the pantry's stocked. I'll be making the beds and tidying upstairs."

"Oh, yes. That would be fine, Wilena."

Dust cloth in hand, she turned to go, then paused. "Oh, I meant to say. Curtis too done got some news. He's quitting the river to work as an engineer, like he studied for. In Chicago it is, but that's where the jobs are. Lots of our folk headed that way, he says."

"Why, that's wonderful. He can tell us more tonight."

Margaret and Dr. Ballard exchanged glances.

James and Sarah-Lynn, Curtis and Aurelia rode through the early morning mist and into meadows matted with clover. Some fences were still in disrepair but several fields, probably the Bianchettis' spread, Aurelia surmised, had been replanted. Eventually they circled back to the lake and let the horses graze while they fished from the bank. The occasional mallard floated past, unconcerned. After a swim and lunch, Sarah-Lynn and James stretched out on the moss under one of the white oaks and napped. Curtis and Aurelia walked over to the clearing at the far end of the lake. For a few minutes they stood gazing at the woods beyond, the treetops jutting taller than before the flood.

"Not that much has changed here," Aurelia observed.

"In magical places time stands still," he replied, reaching for her hand. Her fingers entwined his.

"And yet for us...."

"Feelings haven't changed, Aurelia. Circumstances have. The only thing for me to do is to take this job. Believe it or not, I have money. I'll have more, enough for..." Curtis shook his head. "What I'm trying to say is that life would be easier—for us—if ever. All you would have to do is let me know. Write to Claudette. The world is changing, Aurelia. Not here, as yet. But I can sense it's coming."

Aurelia closed her eyes to imagine how she could disentangle herself. From everything. From everyone. The effort made her weak-kneed. She lodged her back into her lover's ample chest, his near arm automatically encircling her waist. They stood motionless, relishing the reciprocal heat of their bodies.

Eventually Aurelia readied a reply, but Curtis stiffened. He gestured toward cottonwoods. "Do you see it?"

Her eyes shifted. She blinked in the dazzling sunshine. A lone doe, deathly pale, threaded her way through the trees. The two held their breaths; the deer paused, sniffed the air, and slipped back into the shadows.

Curtis relaxed his grip on her arm. "The ghosts have come back," he said. "To see one—and not disturb it—is good luck."

"Our encounters are not that different, wouldn't you say? But you give me too much credit. I haven't your courage—"

He hushed her by pulling her closer. "Something to ponder, Aurelia. If ever you are able to follow your heart, then I will be in the clearing, as it were, waiting for you."

Chapter Fifty-One

Puzzled, Charles scratched his days-old stubble. He had of late lingered on Levee Street long after the swift dark or, when no one accosted him out of the shadows, ambled down to the waterfront. Ill-advised as such loitering might be, gamblers from the steamboats could not be circumvented indefinitely. Lenders expected to collect—no excuses, the roiling stock market or anything else. The last thing he wanted was for some irate card sharp from the *Belle of the Bends* to come pounding on his front door. Better to make what payments he could under cover of darkness.

Always alert, he had noticed the same tugboat bobbing at anchor in the canal for several days, *Starfish* painted in bright green on its bow, *Norris & Co.* in smaller letters underneath. There was something suspicious about that vessel, though he couldn't put his finger on it. Besides, he had more pressing problems. Through the summer, he had frittered away what sums Aurelia had handed over to buy land; and now his more reputable bets, stocks that this or that acquaintance had recommended, had plummeted. Making matters worse, his brother-in-law had gotten wind of a card game which had gone long into the night aboard the *Belle*. It had ended in a scuffle, the local police got called in, and the papers were right behind. Thanks to some pressure from the firm on the *Herald*, Charles had been referred to as "an innocent bystander." Still, his occasional pastime, as he described it to his bosses, did not sit well with Jeffries, Greene. To come into whatever remained of his inheritance, he needed to stick it out another year.

He resolved to pay off what debts he could, stay clear of the boats, and remain civil to his wife. He even considered apologizing for having so lost his temper—he couldn't recall precisely why—that he wrenched her arm. But Aurelia had locked herself in the bedroom, then left to visit her aunt. The bruise would have faded. As long as she didn't in coming months do anything else—what would be the word? erratic or improper—all would work out.

Chapter Fifty-Two

When Aurelia, James and Curtis stepped off the ferry that late September afternoon, Curtis striding separately toward Willy's repair shop for his last night in Vicksburg, James and Aurelia heading up to Adams Street to check on their father, all were unaware of anything amiss. The bell in the Trinity Church tower pealed the six o'clock hour. Shoppers and sales people scurried home, cars clanked their way up and down Washington Street. Intermittent showers had cleansed the air, leaving a crisp hint of fall. It was, Aurelia thought, Vicksburg the way she relished it—pristine, expectant. As much as she dreaded going home to Charles, she had the long weekend with Curtis to savor and cherish. As did James, who had confided to them both that he was determined to act on his plan to propose to Evelyn, however meager his own means, however negligible hers.

Aurelia and James climbed Clay Street both convinced that time would clarify things, strengthen their resolve to be braver, provide prospects they could not but seize upon.

No stuttering, no stumbling.

To their surprise, they found their father hunched over a pile of papers on his desk, the phone in one hand, a grim-faced Alfred leaning over his shoulder. Aristide was practically shouting into the mouthpiece, apparently to the hapless Mr. Gauge. Something about bolting the front door of the bank from the inside, and exiting out the back.

Even hemlines had plunged, Aurelia noticed six months after what everyone referred to as the Crash, as if in some contorted tandem with the stock market. She was flipping through the latest *Ladies Home Journal* in Henrietta's parlor while her friend coaxed Emily through her math assignment. Afterwards, the two friends would take the car and head downtown for a fitting at the Valley, Henrietta having insisted to Aristide that a fancier wedding gown from Maison Blanche in New Orleans would be inappropriate for a widow. Aurelia thought nothing could have pleased her father more, as it would also be frivolous to overspend on an outfit given the losses—still difficult to calculate—that both families will have sustained.

Aristide had acquiesced, secretly pleased that his betrothed was possessed of such probative instincts. To be sure, six months after the market bottomed out in November of '29, it was unclear how much the value of land or property or even money itself would be worth.

"We see prosperity returning in no time," President Hoover kept pronouncing deep into March, into April, into May. Fewer and fewer citizens believed him. Aristide himself reckoned that having settled considerable sums on his children years before had been a wise move, and that his cotton, and of late soybean, fields would continue to turn a profit. Further, he had withdrawn the entirety of Aurelia's and James' savings accounts back in September, entrusting them to the safe in the jewelry store across the street, most locals in the know reckoning it the most secure vault in town. Especially now.

Others had less foresight or took greater risks. Henrietta's father for one had suffered heavy losses, betting that Anaconda and Alcoa stock were as solid as the minerals they mined. How could Jasper Cartwright not then be gracious, nay grateful, when Aristide sought his company to announce that Henrietta, however much his junior, had accepted his hand?

Aurelia too found it hard not to be pleased seeing her father, despite the troubles at the bank, with a lilt in his step and Henrietta with a glow in her cheeks. They would marry mid-June, six weeks before James would tie the knot with Evelyn.

Sharply at 3:30, Henrietta sent her eleven-year-old upstairs to study on her own. Aurelia put down her magazine and drove her friend downtown.

Oddly, the ground floor of the Valley was empty of customers. A few of the younger sales clerks, all women, were chattering over near the shoe department. Evelyn was nowhere in sight. They headed to the rear of the store for the elevator to the dress department.

"Funny not to see her. Doesn't she work Saturdays as well? Always seems so dedicated to her job," Henrietta said as they got off.

"Stores do funny things. Perhaps she's been assigned to another floor," Aurelia replied, trying to recall what James had told her the last time they spoke. Something about Evelyn having applied for yet another promotion but having been rebuffed, the management passing her over for a man, a less experienced one at that. Surely she wouldn't have resigned over such a rejection, given the times they were in.

For the next hour the two friends shelved that mystery, as the matronly Mrs. Cornwell, who ran the bridal department like a private fiefdom, brought a half-dozen gowns into the dressing room.

"Everything we have in for the season that isn't white," she had announced, in a tone that hinted she didn't altogether approve of women who remarried.

Eventually, with Aurelia's encouragement, Henrietta settled on a pale apricot affair, which set off her still youthful figure and her charcoal hair. Aurelia envied her friend's happiness as keenly as she regretted her own nuptials. However, shopping was fun no matter the occasion, even in a Depression. They returned to the ground floor to buy matching shoes.

While waiting for the head clerk, a Mr. Tanner, to return from the depository, they overheard the gossip.

"You saw him. Wednesday it was. Well-dressed, a little flashy, out-of-towner of course."

"And the way they made eyes at each over. Over diamond tie pins, of all things."

"The next day too. I knew something was up."

More tittering.

Boxes in hand, Mr. Tanner glowered at the gigglers. Henrietta and Aurelia exchanged flummoxed glances. They both settled on beige satin heels, the store not carrying anything to match precisely the color of the wedding gown.

Days later Aurelia got the full story from a distraught James, waving the note Evelyn had left behind.

"One of the gamblers from the boats—one Ashley, if even that about him can be believed—stopped off to buy jewelry, flashing his ru-ru-rubied finger. Evelyn waited on him. The next day he came back; took her to dinner at the Carroll." Red-faced and riled up, James paced the floor. "A friend of mine spotted them—holding hands across the table—and she and I en-en-engaged."

Aurelia had rarely seen her brother so overwrought. She was relieved Charles had gone out and that so far her brother had not apprised their father. In a weird way, Mr. Ackermann liked Evelyn—and likely would blame his son for the fiasco.

"By Saturday morning she had decided. Didn't even show up at the Valley," he added, still waving the fateful note in his hand.

"So, how did she explain—"

“Not even addressed to me.” He flung the single sheet of paper in Aurelia’s lap. Men, she thought, are generally more enraged about public shaming than distressed by private sorrow. Or perhaps she was uncharitable. James was not like others.

She looked down at the sloppily composed missive. Suddenly she was glad her brother had not actually hitched his star to this hard-boiled shop girl’s.

Mother,

In case you wonder where I’ve disappeared to, I left town. For good. Because of Ashley, who travels by steamer, making his living, real good to, with cards. (He wears rubys. Promised to buy one for me.) The Valley is a dead end. All the pawing. Tell James I’m sorry. Not my cup of tea.

Evelyn

Aurelia read it over twice, not knowing quite how to respond, her main impression one of the shallowness of the young woman who had spurned her own—deeply sensitive—brother. Words failed her.

Chapter Fifty-Three

Out of the blue Aurelia announced she was taking the train to Chicago to visit Claudette, the heat of August in Vicksburg too oppressive. Moreover, James would accompany her, a respite, she had suggested to Henrietta, from the snickering he had endured since Evelyn had thrown him over. She didn't mention what had wounded her brother even more—Aristide's unconcealed exasperation, which made James babble inchoately at the Sunday dinner table. And reeling as it was, the bank had let him go shortly after Aristide and Henrietta's marriage. From what Aurelia pieced together, their father (he was, after all, back in charge) had not lifted a finger to save his son's job. Her doubly-jilted brother took it hard. Walking home that afternoon, a box of pencils and a ledger in his arms, James had suffered another of his episodes, severe enough to cause a stranger to rush across Clay Street and assist him home.

When she found out about the seizure, Aurelia feared James was coming apart. Likely, he needs a friend like Curtis more than I do, she told herself.

She was not wrong. The two men took in all the major sights, sometimes with Claudette and Aurelia alongside.

"Does them both good, your brother being so sad, Curtis so lonely after Rufus was rounded up in that police sting," Claudette observed. "Naturally," she went on, "they nabbed him. A lowly cork in the wheel. Not that Caproni crook who runs it all."

"You mean Capone, Al Capone." Aurelia corrected her. "And, it's *cog*, not *cork* in the wheel, in case you care."

Claudette looked amused. "Were you living here, Aurelia, my English would be impeccable. Your French too might improve." Now they both smiled. They were sitting in the coffee shop at the Art Institute, Curtis and James still wandering separately through the exhibits upstairs. They sipped in silence for a few minutes, enjoying the comings-and-goings of other visitors.

"Still, have you noticed? Everyone's got the jitters. People losing their jobs, lining up for soup. *Comme après la guerre*. My husband, too. Always traveling—Detroit, Buffalo (which she still mispronounced), Cincinnati...Not that I mind, but *tu sais*..."

Aurelia nodded, not knowing what it was she was supposed to know, other than that Claudette still finagled "in midst of other woe" (was that not how Shakespeare put it?) to live her life much as she pleased. She was outrageous but unfailingly endearing.

"'Falling to pieces, the country.' That's what Stan says. Anyway, the only one who hasn't lost his balance, that I know of, is Curtis. Though, *ça va sans dire*, he pines for you."

Back in Vicksburg, the late-summer heat of 1930 was stifling.

Often Charles awoke drenched in sweat. Drinking didn't help. But he had largely stayed clear of old haunts; his debts had dwindled. If he could hold on through October, the third anniversary of his hiring at the firm, he would have his reward. Money. So what if the stock market had rattled nerves? Truard Transport was still trundling along. His mother was ever upbeat when they spoke.

"Don't worry, C.T. Your father remains at the helm," she had constantly reassured him.

As for the coincidence of the tugboat and the skipper's cap in his carriage house, the mystery still nagged at him. Ninny though she was, Rose had little reason to make up something so preposterous. The occasional rumor about Aurelia, vague, unsubstantiated, reached his ear.

Black.

He could go no further in his speculation. Until an otherwise innocuous card game, with Caroline, more acid-tongued than ever, as his bridge partner.

Her dislike for her sister-in-law had grown exponentially since marriage to Alfred. How was it that her erstwhile friend (and now a relative) continued to live by her own rules, unhampered by conventions that other women—weren't they all thirty or older? — duly wrapped themselves in? That's how Caroline parsed it, and that's why she seized upon any hint of transgression on Aurelia's part. In so doing, she sought to strengthen her own hand with her husband, either massaging his own ego by comparison or putting him on the defensive by criticizing his sibling.

Caroline looked out over her hand—an eighteen count; she would easily make game—at her partner. Whatever his weaknesses as a male (Alfred had let slip that those faults were barely tolerable, his colleague barely employable), Charles was, well, no dummy. She smiled at her own *double entendre*.

"Gone to Chicago, you say. To visit that French floosy? You'd have thought Aurelia would grow out of such companions."

Charles might have squirmed at the aspersion cast on his wife but Alfred was playing at another table, way across the room. Intent on his bidding.

"She took her pathetic brother. That was her rationale for the trip," Charles replied tersely.

"Humph. If I'm not deceived, your wife has other reasons for wanting to go up north."

His expression puzzled, Charles stared at the cards laid out in front of him; their opponents looked annoyed by the chit-chat.

Reaching across the table, Caroline picked up the ace of spades, waving it under Charles' nose. "Think about this," she said, taunting him. She took the trick and the game.

Within days Charles pieced the puzzle together, amazed that it had taken him so long to realize that the so-called "friend of the Ackermann family" was one Curtis Jefferson, who worked on the river, and who also, somehow, was connected to one of the law firm's clients, Mayfield's Motor Works. Where Aurelia so often took that Packard, where...

Repulsed though he was by the idea of a relationship between the two, even more was Charles incensed by Aurelia's ability to thumb her nose at him. He'd been duped, deceived, inveigled.

"Even the help knew," he seethed.

Still, as August wore on and rain finally took the edge off, Charles' anger abated. Without being aware of it, he had become like his father: coldly calculating rather than flailing. Along with his own inheritance he would, through threat of exposure, compel Aurelia to turn over whatever other cash reserves she might have on hand. And be gone.

Chapter Fifty-Four

By tacit agreement, none of the foursome spoke of the nights Curtis and Aurelia snatched to be alone together in the small house he had bought north of Chicago proper. The furnishings, she noted, mirrored his personality: sturdy, durable, without ostentation. She sat down on the barely used couch in the living room and let him wait on her. He made tea, noisily, as men did, and, more adeptly, he arranged jazz recordings on the Victrola. When he sat down beside her, the tense lines around her mouth relaxed. He took her in his arms, their delight in each other tangible.

And to be shared, even if Claudette and James were the only

two with whom they could do so openly. On the weekends, they bought tickets to watch the White Sox take on the Yankees, took a pleasure cruise on Lake Michigan and rode the El to the end of the line and back to the Loop.

"He has found his *raison d'être*," Claudette said to Aurelia in describing Curtis' newfound confidence.

The two women had paid a visit to the Nowitskis' high-rise apartment overlooking the lake and were washing the dishes after dinner, the elders having gone to bed early. "We are doing *sans* a maid, you see, no? Too expensive," Mrs. Nowitski had explained to their guest in her rudimentary English.

"From what Rufus tells me, the money is good—for an engineer anyway."

"Yes, finally, a job that takes advantage of his skills, the things he trained for," Aurelia added, unsure what Claudette was getting at.

"One thing about you Americans," her friend further reflected, drying the china and stacking the damp plates one atop the other in, what she called the European style. "Despite the prejudices that everyone walks around with, money melts them away. Rufus, for example. He can afford a fancy lawyer. A few months and he'll be out."

Aurelia let the warm soapy water run over her arms as she rinsed the last of Mrs. Nowitski's dessert saucers. She nodded in tacit agreement, not wanting her friend to delve any further into what she and Curtis may have decided to do.

In truth, no promises had been made, no plans spelled out, no pressures applied. By either of the lovers. Aurelia had seen Curtis in what was arguably the best of circumstances that he could attain. She only knew she did not want the visit to end. Ever.

But on a blustery afternoon in early September the four said their goodbyes on a crowded platform, and the Panama Limited clanked out of Union Station. Aurelia and James buried themselves in books Claudette had presented them with: hers, the latest Hemingway, *A Farewell to Arms*, and his, Lewis' *Main Street*. So concentrated, brother and sister hardly spoke until the train lurched in the middle of the night. It had broken down not far outside St. Louis. Another six hours for repairs. By the time the train finally arrived at the station in Jackson, they were exhausted and short-tempered. To make matters worse, they had to drive the fifty miles home to Vicksburg in a rainstorm.

"You should come in, James, wash up and dry off. I'm sure there's more in our pantry than in yours," Aurelia said, as they stood on the porch of the house on Baum Street. He started to demur but she put her hand on his arm. "Please just stay until—"

As she wrestled with the key in the lock, a light went on in the vestibule. The door was pushed open from inside. It was Rose.

"I've never been adept with keys," Aurelia said, as the maid scowled at the disheveled pair as though they were unwanted guests.

"You been out of practice, Miz Truard."

James glanced at his sister's face. Rose made no move to help. He picked up the two suitcases, skirted the two women, and walked into the foyer.

"Don't trouble with us, Rose. My brother and I will fumble around in the kitchen on our own."

Rose closed the door behind them but leaned back against it as though hoping to deter any other interlopers.

"And Mr. Truard. Did he indicate when he'd likely be home?"

"Not specific, he didn't. He left me in charge," Rose retorted with the emphasis on the *me*.

Was she being impudent? Aurelia wasn't sure, but her brother interposed, his stammer resurfacing as it did when he was out of sorts or on the defensive. "As your mistress was s-s-saying, Rose, we'll manage on our own. You can go back to whatever you were doing."

At first, Rose opened her mouth to object, but then flounced out of the room. The two siblings shrugged as if to indicate par for the course.

Aurelia soon set about to slice roast beef from the icebox and to cut up tomatoes for a salad. A bowl of over-ripe apricots sat on the table, a pesky fly flitting from one piece of fruit to another. She could hear James as he cleaned up in the downstairs bathroom. He was humming "Take Me Out to the Ballgame."

Of a sudden a shadow fell across the table. She glanced up. Charles stood in the doorway. In the light his eyes looked red-hot. In one hand he was holding a pouch. His other held the door frame, something unsteady in his stance.

"Why Charles, we this instant returned. Would you like to join us for cold cuts?"

He glared at her, nostrils flared.

"Or, if you prefer, I could make you something hot?"

Silence, except for the in and out of her husband's breath.

Flustered, she began to chop the lettuce in front of her, accidentally slicing deep into her left index finger. Blood spurted, staining her hand bright red. She made a fist to stanch the flow.

"You lied to me, Aurelia. I never would have known. Except by chance."

She felt the blood rush from her face, her cheeks turn cold. How could he know about Chicago? Impossible. She winced from the sting of her cut but did not move.

Charles staggered into the kitchen, one hand grasping the countertop, the other brandishing the packet. An unmistakable odor of alcohol accompanied him. "To hide this from me, when you knew—"

"Whatever are you talking about, Charles?" She looked up and into his blood-shot eyes and saw only loathing. "You're not making sense, and I am tired."

He flung the pouch onto the stone table. It landed next to the bowl of fruit, startling the fly.

"About twenty-five thousand dollars' worth of lies, Aurelia, which, had I not entered that jewelry store—innocently, to purchase a watch for my mother's birthday. Had they not mentioned it...thought I, as the husband—" He was breathing fire.

"I have no idea what you are going on about. Do sit down and don't make a scene." Her voice was shrill, pitched an octave higher than she intended.

She plunged the knife into a tomato, meticulously coring out a brown spot and stalling for time. Could it be that the money was from that savings account, that somehow her father had moved it before the run on the bank? This is not about Curtis. Charles wouldn't even care, except for the scandal. He's a money grabber. Her lips curled in contempt.

"I will not be made a fool. By you or anyone else," he snarled, teetering back and forth.

She raised her eyebrows. Chop, chop, chop.

Suddenly he lunged at her, grabbing her wrist. She tried to wrench free. He tightened his grip, twisting her arm.

"You're hurting me."

He let go and put both hands around her neck. Automatically she raised the knife.

From the doorway, James saw blood streaming down his sister's arm. Without a second thought, he flung himself upon her assailant from behind, knocking him sideways, pommeling his shoulders with his fists. Charles lost his footing. His head crashed into the corner of the stone table, gashing it open. Blood gushed.

From the far side of the kitchen Rose stood in the pantry entrance. Motionless.

Brother and sister both knelt, Aurelia cradling her husband's battered head in her arms, James trying to expose the wound and stop the bleeding.

"Lawd, Lawd, Mr. James. What did you do, Mr. James?" Rose wailed.

"Get to the telephone. Call an ambulance. Now, Rose," Aurelia shouted.

The maid rocked back and forth, emitting a strange whimper. She did not budge.

"Then bring some towels. Clean water. I'll call the ambulance."

Aurelia scrambled to her feet, bloodied and flushed. She raced to the parlor.

In her absence, James fumbled for a pulse. He ripped his own shirt off and as adroitly as he could, secured it around the gaping hole behind his brother-in-law's left temple. Within seconds the blood soaked through the silk.

"You and her done an awful thing. Poor Mr. Charles, poor Mr. Charles."

By the time medics arrived thirty minutes later, it was too late.

Chapter Fifty-Five

Fancy lawyers. Like Claudette said.

Only in this case Charles' mother did the hiring. On behalf of the prosecution. That she doted on her son—and turned a blind eye to his failings—spurred her to action. That and the fact that she had her own money to spend, and nothing else of consequence to live for. Two months after the incident in Vicksburg, her own husband blew his brains out.

Not everything came out in the trial. In their different spheres, Aristide and Alfred still had influence around town and old Mr. Greene, leaning ever more heavily on his cane (and other lawyers' notes), did his best to exonerate the two Ackermann siblings. An unfortunate accident, pure and simple.

But the prosecution painted a different picture. Aurelia was spiteful and uncaring, James conniving and uncontrolled. Lucille Truard had urged the prosecutors to harp on her daughter-in-law's willful neglect of her husband, in matters both private and public. Her ostentatious preference for "consorting with others"—those were the words she insisted the lawyers use—including members of the town's colored community. To the extent that they dug, the investigators came up with nothing more damning than Aurelia's charitable activities at Bethel and her occasional sojourns (*sans* husband) across the river to visit relatives.

Compensating for the lack of hard evidence, Charles' mother made the most of her own appearance on the stand, testifying (wrongly) that her husband was so stricken by the loss of his only son he took his own life. Then she sobbed expertly in describing her son's last act.

"Always so selfless, he had that very day purchased an expensive birthday present for me." She raised her trembling arm to reveal the *Gübelin* on her bony wrist.

The jury shrugged at learning that Charles overplayed his hand, as it were, at the card tables. A few members actually found the idea of his gambling habit romantic, or at least in keeping with the vices associated with young gentlemen, especially those from big cities whose morals were notably looser. About his sexual predilections, not a word was uttered in front of the jury. Out of her own sense of guilt, Aurelia did not wish further to sully her deceased husband's name nor further to pain his mother. Besides, any such insinuation, if believed or not, would reflect badly on the law firm and on Alfred, however far it might go to explain the estrangement between husband and wife. Nor did Charles' temper tantrums come to light or that he had, on previous occasions, laid hands on his wife.

In the end though it was Rose's testimony that clenched the verdict.

"A scuffle, them two—here she pointed at the defendants—waving a knife at Mr. Charles—him who never hurt a flea. Such a gentleman. They set upon my master, they did. Pushed him right into that table. That Mr. James not quite right in the head."

More eloquent English Rose had never spoken. Aurelia was sure she had been coached.

The jury bought it. Voluntary manslaughter. But due to James' "mental defect," he got off with diminished responsibility and was consigned to the state psychiatric facility. For not less than five years. Aurelia was acquitted, though Judge Thigpen couldn't resist a parting shot.

"A sorry excuse for a spouse," he muttered loud enough to be heard in the back row after the verdicts were read.

It was Evelyn who, having been ditched by her ruby-fingered lover and found her way back to town in time to catch the closing arguments, summed up what many in Vicksburg were thinking.

"I never in a million years imagined an Ackermann would end up in the looney bin. Especially not James."

Small towns can be unforgiving, as Aurelia found out within weeks of the trial. Many erstwhile acquaintances gave her wide berth. Invitations dropped off. No more card games at Caroline's and Alfred's, no more dances at the B.B. Club. No more lunches at the Carroll. A month later, she returned to Main Street School to resume her teaching duties, but as soon as she crossed the threshold Miss Williams rushed to corner her.

"In your absence, Mrs. Truard, the decision was made to dispense with language classes for the remainder of the term. Funds, as you know, are running low. We're concentrating solely on Latin. Mrs. Larsen will oversee those."

"But French is so useful. For young ladies," Aurelia objected. Miss Williams looked as though she doubted Aurelia could know what a young lady might require.

"Perhaps next year," she said, her voice cold.

A few people around town saw things in a different light.

Mr. Gauge, for one, showed up unannounced one day at the Wilkerson house to help Aurelia box up belongings. Madame André bumped into her on the streetcar and made a point of chatting, animatedly, about an art exhibit (of her own paintings of course). The minister at Bethel prayed for Aurelia, indeed for all the Ackermanns, during his Sunday sermon, Susanna told her one evening.

For her part, Henrietta defended Aurelia publicly whenever the scandal came up, but more to the point, she did her best to persuade Aristide that none of this tragedy could have been foreseen or prevented. That his daughter had been as much a victim of the unfortunate marriage as had Charles.

"But I should have seen it coming. Intervened. Helped her extricate herself, Henrietta."

"Perhaps you did, unconsciously, by moving her savings to that jewelry store, to make it easier for her. Had she gone there first, before Charles happened to..."

"You mean, so that she could follow her heart. Return to Chicago and live with—with this Curtis?"

Henrietta nodded her head in the affirmative. Aristide rubbed his ring.

They both knew what had to be. They would not try to stop her.

The guards fidgeted. James' paperwork was still being processed and he had a female visitor in his cell at the county jail. According to the circuit court's instructions, he was to be transported to the facility at Whitfield by sunset. They eyed the clock on the wall.

Brother and sister were oblivious to the flurry around them. They spoke in near whispers, his hand on hers. She was crying; he was trying to console her.

"I ask only one thing, Aurelia. Go to him. Curtis loves you and somehow, there, you and he will figure out how to live. If it must be among strangers, so be it."

The warden, an older man whom the Ackermann family had known for decades, approached the cell door. His keys rattled.

"When you're ready, sir." He then walked down the corridor

back to his office.

"When all this is done, and everyone's forgotten and I get out, I will visit you two. And, you can come back home to see us. Besides—"

Aurelia nodded, smiling as her eyes filled yet again.

None of this would be easy.

Epilogue

Red, white and blue balloons. All the way from Jackson.

The word went around Whitfield early in the morning, after the usual breakfast of lumpy grits and greasy scrambled eggs, just as James was headed over to the laundry. He had agreed to take another patient's things as well, without noting, let alone commenting on, the frayed night gowns that this Nell gathered up and stuffed into her institution-labeled duffel bag.

He had been distracted, not only by the rumors about the war winding down but by the latest letter from his brother, in that punctilious tone that over the years Alfred had adopted toward his younger, and, to his mind, still troublesome sibling. So unlike the missives from his sister, James mused as he skirted the lake—not much more than a muddy pond but for an insane asylum not an unpleasant amenity. The residents could wade in the shallow water. An occasional mallard might paddle past. For James the place had long ago become familiar. And yet, he might not be consigned for much longer.

Cured? Well, he didn't know precisely of what he suffered, nor had the doctors ever come up with a specific diagnosis. But that wasn't the point, James was convinced, as he paused to watch a half-dozen turtles stick out their necks and slip from their soggy log into the water. It was *what* he had done that evening in 1930, not the *why*, that had mattered. He knew that, and that however woebegone he had felt cut off from home, better institutionalized at Whitfield than incarcerated at Parchman prison.

"Whatever are you up to, Mr. James?" a voice from behind him prodded. It was one of the more pleasant aides, Addie May, who, being black, was assigned to the West building where Negro patients were housed.

"I guess you folks in East done heard the news. The war be ended and them soldiers is all coming home. Gwine be a party tonight. Balloons, Roman candles too if the doctors give the OK. Whatcha think about that, Mr. James?"

"Ain't nobody that wouldn't be happy about that," James responded diplomatically, turning from the turtles to give Addie May a broad smile.

Not losing a beat, she dug into a paper bag and brought out a loaf of freshly baked bread, breaking off a slab and handing it to James. "Ain't never as tasty as right out them ovens. You enjoy, Mr. James." With that pronouncement, Addie May gave him a toothy grin and toddled off toward the West building.

James bit into the warm dough, savoring the salty taste. If little else, he would miss Whitfield's bakery, those smells that emanated every morning around ten, just as doctors began their rounds. His own fits had subsided for good in '42, his stutter too—so much so that the doctors began calling upon James to assist with the more intractable cases. He exuded "empathy," they had told him, the lead physician, a Dr. Emerson, commending his ability to calm what he poetically referred to as "the teeming brains" of the most recalcitrant.

The wailings of female patients like Nell, however, still unnerved him, shock therapy having done little but make such designated "hysterics" less responsive.

"My husband said I was 'getting in the way of his social life,'" Nell had revealed early on in their acquaintance. Though James didn't say so, it was, in such cases, almost always a spouse...as it would have been for Aurelia if he hadn't done what he did. He shook off the memory. As he had many times before.

Thus, partially to help the other patients and partly to keep his own mind occupied, James had, in the late '30s, instituted a book club at Whitfield, utilizing the volumes Aurelia regularly shipped from Chicago. Mostly, he read aloud, the literacy among the inmates being scant, their ability to focus for long stretches limited. Nevertheless, they flocked to the monthly sessions, which in the spring and fall he held on the banks of the lake. That he invited black as well as white patients to join the club caused an initial stir though eventually everyone shrugged it off. It was the enlightened Dr. Emerson whom James overheard suggest to the staff that *Oliver Twist* was doing more for the patients than any of their therapies.

Years came and went. The club tackled all of Dickens.

While the clothes spun around, James combed through Alfred's letter again, trying to extract what hidden meanings or lingering accusations might be embedded therein.

As you might suspect, I've huddled once again with your counsel here at Jeffries, Ackermann, and he informs me that prospects for your imminent release are propitious. What with a positive report from that Dr. Emerson and the winding down of the war, we have every hope that a legal end can be put to this tiresome affair.

So like Alfred, James thought. Charles, inert in his late summer seersucker on the tiled floor, a stunned expression on his face; Aurelia, freed and bound for Chicago; he himself consigned to a mental institution. Only his brother, whose reputation was barely bruised by the scandal, could have re-defined what transpired all those years ago as nothing more than tiresome.

Still, it could be argued Alfred had done the decent thing, assiduous through the years in his pressing of the pertinent legal levers and solicitous with respect to the medical personnel in charge of James' treatment.

As for visitors, his father and Henrietta drove over for James' birthday for an entire decade—until, that is, that awful December day in '41, when, upon hurrying home from the bank to catch Roosevelt on the radio, Aristide suffered a heart attack at the top of the hill. The loss of his father triggered the return of James' seizures, his then pending release postponed.

For her part, Aurelia took the train home every winter, in the last few years bringing along the child, little Jimmy. Too dangerous to make the trip in their company, Curtis showed up at Whitfield alone whenever he could arrange it.

James read on.

The court handling the petition and the probationary officers concur that your release should be no later than December 31. And given what's going on abroad, perhaps sooner. You'll remember what happened after the last war: an immediate influx of returning soldiers, some unfit to function in the outside world.

Heading back past the bakery to his tiny room in the East building, James marveled at his brother's unremitting efforts to reinforce the scaffolding of southern respectability. Now, in reconstructing such an image of the Ackermann family, Alfred had contrived for his younger brother to return to his modest job at the First National. Likely, James surmised as he tried to feel grateful, he'd be calculating interest payments in a cubbyhole no larger than his quarters at Whitfield.

Nor had Alfred overlooked Aurelia. She had been asked to travel home (alone) to celebrate the reunion with her brothers, at least for as long as it took to sit for a family portrait at the Unglaub Studio, which, knowing Alfred (and Caroline), would promptly be featured in the *Post*. Ironic in so many ways.

And yet, he would be home, and happy so to be. The soft hills and the summer breezes, the rowdy riverfront and the clatter of commerce, the picnics in the park, the ferry to what he and his sister referred to as "the other side." In his memory the steeple that soared above Trinity Church seemed to pierce the very canopy of heaven. How was it that, growing up, he had never stopped to admire these, had so taken for granted the morning scent of sweet olive or the sun setting over the river?

For the rest of the day he trundled about, eyeing the few possessions to be boxed up for Adams Street. And he slept, dreaming fitfully about that first war and its aftermath.

James was mouthing Aurelia's name when the commotion broke out. Raising the shade on his barred window, he surveyed the scene. Most all the patients, black and white, had gathered in front of the lake. Nurses were blowing up balloons, twisting and tying their ends. A couple of champagne bottles, for the medical staff only, were uncorked. Popsicles were parceled out. Somebody had turned up a radio full-blast, a few of the less inhibited patients cavorting to John Philip Sousa. Even Nell appeared to be enjoying herself, waving her arms in concentric circles, a sparkler alight in each, a rare smile on her lips. He joined the festivities.

About the author

Elizabeth Guider is a longtime entertainment journalist who has worked in Rome, Paris and London as well as in New York and Los Angeles. Born in the South, she holds a doctorate in Renaissance Studies from New York University. During the late 1970's she was based in Rome where she taught English and American literature and where much of the action of her first novel, The Passionate Palazzo, takes place. While in Europe she worked as an entertainment reporter for the showbiz newspaper Variety, focusing on the film business, television and theater.

She also traveled widely, reporting on the politics affecting media from Eastern Europe to Hong Kong as well as covering various festivals and trade shows in Cannes, Monte Carlo, Venice and Berlin. Back in the States since the early 1990's, she specialized on the burgeoning TV industry and eventually held top editor positions at Variety and latterly at The Hollywood Reporter. Most recently she has freelanced for World Screen News as senior contributing editor.

She mostly divides her time between Los Angeles and Vicksburg, MS where she grew up and which is the setting for Milk and Honey on the Other Side.

MORE TITLES AVAILABLE THROUGH FOUNDATIONS, LLC

Easy Peasey, Learning is Easy!
By: Alissa B. Gregory

Easy Peasey, Learning is Easy' is written and illustrated by Alissa B. Gregory and is the first of several children's books meant to teach, inspire and help your little one grow and learn. With pretty colors, rhyming words, and simple learning, this fun and playful book is just right for babies and curious toddlers!

Circles of Trust

By: Christine Hart

That day started like any other.

It ended - on the beach, at sunset - in the most disheartening way possible.

What happens when a dominant is unable to dominate his own world?

Davis believed he had found perfection, until he realized how many imperfections life held.

Imanya. Kaena. Two very different women. Dark and blonde. Joy and sorrow. Hurt and healing. If he's the dominant, why are they in control of his mind, his thoughts...and his heart?
Intended for adult readers who don't mind a little BDSM and like to smile at happy endings.

Water Dreams

By: Kathering Eddinger Smits

Nik—an outwardly normal, young woman terrified by water, living in the Greek-American town of Tarpon Springs, Florida.

Bas—a shapeshifter merman tasked with obtaining Nik's help to gain what his species most deSires.

The Nerei—a race of beings who want humans to continue to believe they are mythological. What happens when Nik refuses to help Bas and the Nerei?

Suncatcher

By: Robin Leigh Anderson

A miner crash lands on an unknown planet and discovers the last inhabitant, a stunning silicon-based lifeform who has the appearance of a stained glass ornament. Her telepathy helps her to learn him as they both struggle to survive the particle storm that wrecked his craft and ruined her world.

They survive more than either can believe to form a new colony on this rich mining world, and he takes a startling step in the evolution of mankind.

Farm House

By: Steve Soderquist

10 years ago a little girl was supposedly murdered. 10 years ago that little girl got away.

Now after eight years of living on her own, feeding from garbage cans and doing what she must to survive and still remain anonymous, the lies that had been told to her have led her; her sense of vengeance and retribution back to the door-step of whom she considers to blame.

Those who stand in her way receive nothing of mercy, as her relentless pursuit to extract revenge on those who robbed her of her life come to a
chilling close as nothing will stop her...and no one is to be spared.